PENGUIN BOOKS

12-21

Dustin Thomason graduated from Harvard College and received his MD from Columbia University. He is the co-author of the international bestseller *The Rule of Four* and has written and produced several television series, including *Lie to Me*. He lives in Venice Beach, California.

Re
D1322124
3412601083248 6

12-21

DUSTIN THOMASON

PENGUIN BOOKS

PENGUIN BOOKS

Published by the Penguin Group
Penguin Books Ltd, 80 Strand, London WC2R 0RL, England
Penguin Group (USA) Inc., 375 Hudson Street, New York, New York 10014, USA
Penguin Group (Canada), 90 Eglinton Avenue East, Suite 700, Toronto, Ontario, Canada M4P 2Y3
(a division of Pearson Penguin Canada Inc.)
Penguin Ireland, 25 St Stephen's Green, Dublin 2, Ireland (a division of Penguin Books Ltd)
Penguin Group (Australia), 250 Camberwell Road,
Camberwell, Victoria 3124, Australia (a division of Pearson Australia Group Pty Ltd)
Penguin Books India Pvt Ltd, 11 Community Centre, Panchsheel Park,
New Delhi – 110 017, India
Penguin Group (NZ), 67 Apollo Drive, Rosedale, Auckland 0632, New Zealand
(a division of Pearson New Zealand Ltd)
Penguin Books (South Africa) (Pty) Ltd, Block D, Rosebank Office Park,
181 Jan Smuts Avenue, Parktown North, Gauteng 2193, South Africa

Penguin Books Ltd, Registered Offices: 80 Strand, London WC2R 0RL, England

www.penguin.com

First published in the United States of America by The Dial Press, an imprint of
The Random House Publishing Group, a division of Random House, Inc, New York 2012
First published in Great Britain in Penguin Books 2012
001

Text copyright © Dustin Thomason, 2012
Maps copyright © David Lindroth, Inc. 2012
All rights reserved

The moral right of the author has been asserted
Printed in Great Britain by Clays Ltd, St Ives plc

This is a work of fiction. Names, characters, places and incidents are the products of the author's imagination or are used fictitiously. Any resemblance to actual events, locales or persons, living or dead, is entirely coincidental.

Except in the United States of America, this book is sold subject to the condition that it shall not, by way of trade or otherwise, be lent, re-sold, hired out, or otherwise circulated without the publisher's prior consent in any form of binding or cover other than that in which it is published and without a similar condition including this condition being imposed on the subsequent purchaser

ISBN: 978–0–718–19395–9

www.greenpenguin.co.uk

Penguin Books is committed to a sustainable future for our business, our readers and our planet. This book is made from Forest Stewardship Council™ certified paper.

ALWAYS LEARNING PEARSON

12-21

Prologue

He stands silently in the moonlight against the wall of the temple, the small bundle held tightly under his arm. The sisal wrapping chafes against his skin, but he welcomes the feeling. It reassures him. In this drought-stricken city, he would not trade this package, even for water. The ground beneath his sandals is cracked and dry. The green world of his childhood is gone, and he is beginning to wonder if soon he will be too.

Satisfied that the temple guards haven't detected his presence, he hurries toward the central square, where artisans and tattoo-painters once thrived. Now it is populated only by beggars, and beggars, when hungry, can be dangerous. But tonight he is lucky. There are only two men standing by the east temple. They have seen him before, and they know he gives to them what he can. Still, he holds the bundle close as he goes.

At the boundary between the central square and the maize silos, there is a guard posted. No more than a boy. For a moment, he considers burying the bundle and returning for it later, but the earth is dust, and the winds drive through fields where trees once stood. Nothing in this parched city remains buried for long.

He takes a breath and continues walking forward.

'Royal and Holy One,' calls the boy. 'Where are you

going?' The boy's eyes are tired, hungry, but spark when they take in the bundle under the man's arm.

'To my fasting cave.'

'What are you carrying?'

'Incense for my dedications.'

The man tightens his arm around the parcel and prays silently to Itzamnaaj.

'But there has been no incense at the market for days, Royal and Holy One.' The guard's voice is jaded. As if all men lie now to survive. As if all innocence has fled with the rains. 'Give it to me.'

'Warrior, you are right. It is not incense but a gift for the king.' He has no choice but to invoke the king's name, though the king would have his heart ripped out if he knew what he was carrying.

'Give it to me,' the boy says again.

The man reluctantly obeys.

The boy's fingers unwrap the bundle roughly, but when the sisal falls away, he sees disappointment in the young guard's eyes. What had he been hoping for? Maize? Cacao? He does not understand what he has seen. Like most boys in these times, he understands only hunger.

Rewrapping it quickly, the man hurries away from the guard, offering thanks to the gods for his good fortune. His small cave lies at the eastern edge of the city, and he slips through the opening undetected.

There are cloths spread across the floor, placed here in preparation for this moment. He lights his candle, sets the bundle at a careful distance from the wax, then carefully wipes his hands. He drops to his knees and reaches for the sisal. Inside is a folded stack of pages made from the bark of a fig tree, hardened with a glaze of limestone paste.

With the great but seemingly effortless care of a man who has trained for this act his entire life, he unfolds the paper. Twenty-five times it has been doubled back on itself, and when it is completely unfurled, the blank pages stretch across the width of the cave.

From behind his hearth, he gathers three small bowls of paint. He has scraped cooking pots to make black ink, shaved rust from the rocks to make red, and searched fields and riverbeds for anil and clay to make indigo. Finally, he makes a puncture in the skin of his arm. He watches the crimson rivulets run over his wrist and into the bowls of paint before him, sanctifying the ink with his blood.

Then he begins to write.

12.19.19.17.10
December 11, 2012

I

Dr Gabriel Stanton's condo sat at the end of the Boardwalk, before the Venice Beach footpath morphed into lush lawns where the tai chi lovers gathered. The modest duplex wasn't entirely to Stanton's taste. He would have preferred something with more history. But on this odd stretch of the California coastline, the only options to choose between were run-down shacks and contemporary stone and glass. Stanton left his home just after seven a.m. on his old Gary Fisher bike and headed south with Dogma, his yellow Labrador, running beside him. Groundwork, the best coffee in LA, was only six blocks away, and there Jillian would have a triple shot of Black Gold ready for him the minute he walked in.

Dogma loved the mornings as much as his owner did. But the dog wasn't allowed into Groundwork, so after Stanton tied him up, he made his way inside alone, waved at Jillian, collected his cup, and checked out the scene. A lot of the early clientele were surfers, their wetsuits still dripping. Stanton was usually up by six, but these guys had been up for hours.

Sitting at his usual table was one of the boardwalk's best-known and strangest-looking residents. His entire face and shaved head were covered with intricate designs, as well as rings, studs, and small chains protruding from his earlobes, nose, and lips. Stanton often wondered where a man like Monster came from. What had happened to him in early life that led to the decision to cover his body entirely with art? For some reason, whenever Stanton imagined Monster's origins, he saw a split-level home near a military base – exactly the type of houses in which he himself had spent his childhood.

'How's the world out there doing?' Stanton asked.

Monster looked up from his computer. He was an obsessive news junkie, and when he wasn't working at his tattoo shop or entertaining tourists as part of the Venice Beach Freak Show, he was here posting comments on political blogs.

'Other than there being only two weeks before the galactic alignment makes the magnetic poles reverse and we all die?' he asked.

'Other than that.'

'Hell of a nice day out there.'

'How's your lady?'

'Electrifying, thanks.'

Stanton headed for the door. 'If we're still here, I'll see you tomorrow, Monster.'

After Stanton downed his Black Gold outside, he and Dogma continued south. A century ago, miles of canals snaked through the streets of Venice, tobacco magnate Abbot Kinney's re-creation of the famed Italian city. Now virtually all of the waterways where gondoliers once ferried residents were paved over and covered with steroid-fueled gyms, greasy-food stands, and novelty T-shirt shops.

Stanton had ruefully watched a rash of 'Mayan apocalypse' graffiti and trinkets pop up all over Venice in recent weeks, vendors taking advantage of all the hype. He'd been raised Catholic but hadn't been in a church in years. If people wanted to seek their destiny or believe in some ancient clock, they could go right ahead; he'd stick to testable hypotheses and the scientific method.

Fortunately, it seemed not everyone in Venice believed December 21 would bring the end of the world; red and green lights also decorated the boardwalk, just in case the crackpots had it wrong. Yuletide was a strange time in LA. Few transplants understood how to celebrate the holidays at seventy degrees, but Stanton loved the contrast – Santa hats on rollerbladers, suntan lotion in stockings, surfboards festooned with antlers. A ride along the beach on Christmas was as spiritual as he got these days.

Ten minutes later, he and the dog reached the northern tip of Marina del Rey. They made their way past the old lighthouse and the sailboats and souped-up fishing vessels bobbing quietly in the harbor. Stanton let Dogma off his leash, and the dog bounded ahead while Stanton trotted behind, listening for music. The woman they were here to see surrounded herself with jazz at all times, and when you heard Bill Evans's piano or Miles's trumpet over the other noises of the waterfront, she wasn't far. For most of the last decade, Nina Countner had been the woman in Stanton's life. While there had been a few others in the three years since they'd split, none had been more than a substitute for her.

Stanton trailed Dogma onto the dock of the marina and caught the mournful sound of a saxophone in the distance. The dog had arrived at the tip of the south jetty above Nina's massive dual-engine McGray, twenty-two pristine feet of metal and wood, squeezed into the last slip at the end of the dock.

Nina crouched beside Dogma, already rubbing his belly. 'You guys found me.'

'In an actual marina for a change,' said Stanton.

He kissed her on the cheek and breathed her in. Despite spending most of her time at sea, Nina always managed to smell like rose-water. Stanton stepped back to look at her. She had a dimpled chin and striking green eyes, but her nose was a little crooked, and her mouth was small. To Stanton, it was all just right.

'You ever going to let me get you a real slip?' he asked.

Nina gave him a look. He'd offered to rent her a permanent boat slip so many times, hoping it would lure her back to shore more often, but she'd never accepted, and he knew she probably never would. Her freelance magazine assignments hardly provided a steady income, so she'd mastered the art of finding open slips, out-of-sight beaches, and off-the-radar docks that few others knew about.

'How's the experiment coming?' Nina asked as Stanton followed her onto the boat. *Plan A*'s deck was simply appointed, just two folding seats, a collection of loose CDs strewn around the skipper's chair, and bowls for Dogma's water and food.

'More results this morning,' he told her. 'Should be interesting.'

She took the captain's seat. 'You look tired.'

He wondered if it was the encroaching tide of age she was seeing on his face, crow's-feet beneath his rimless glasses. But Stanton had slept a full seven hours last night. Rare for him. 'I feel fine.'

'The lawsuit's all over? For good?'

'It's been over for weeks. Let's celebrate. Got some champagne in my fridge.'

'Skipper and I are headed to Catalina,' Nina said. She flipped the gauges and switches that Stanton had never bothered to really master, firing up the boat's GPS and electrical system.

The faint outline of Catalina Island was just visible through the marine layer. 'What if I came with you?' he asked.

'While you waited patiently for results from the center? Please, Gabe.'

'Don't patronize me.'

Nina walked up, cupped his chin in her hand. 'I'm not your *ex*-wife for nothing.'

The decision had been hers, but Stanton blamed himself, and part of him had never given up on a future for them together. During the three years they were married, his work took him out of the country for months at a time, while she escaped to the ocean, where her heart had always been. He'd let her drift away, and it seemed like she was happiest that way – sailing solo.

A container ship sounded its horn in the distance, sending Dogma into a frenzy. He barked repeatedly at the noise before proceeding to chase his own tail.

'I'll bring him back tomorrow night,' Nina said.

'Stay for dinner,' Stanton told her. 'I'll cook whatever you want.'

Nina eyed him. 'How will your girlfriend feel about us having dinner?'

'I don't have a girlfriend.'

'What happened to what's-her-name? The mathematician.'

'We went on four dates.'

'And?'

'I had to go see a man about a horse.'

'Come on.'

'Seriously. I had to check out a horse in England they thought might have scrapie, and she told me I wasn't fully committed to her.'

'Was she right?'

'We went on four dates. So, are we on for dinner tomorrow?'

Nina fired up *Plan A*'s engine as Stanton hopped onto the dock to collect his bike. 'Get a decent bottle of wine,' she called back as she un-moored, leaving him once again in her wake. 'Then we'll see. . . .'

The Centers for Disease Control's Prion Center in Boyle Heights had been Stanton's professional home for nearly ten years. When he moved west to become its first director, the center had occupied only one small lab in a mobile trailer at Los Angeles County & USC Medical Center. Now it spanned the entire sixth floor of the LAC & USC main hospital building, the same building that for more than three decades had served as the exterior for the soap opera *General Hospital.*

Stanton headed through the double doors into what his postdocs often referred to as his 'lair'. One of them had strung Christmas lights around the main area, and Stanton flipped them on along with the halogens, casting green and red across the microscope benches stretching across the lab. After dropping his bag in his office, Stanton threw on a mask and gloves and headed for the back. This was the first morning they'd be able to collect results in an experiment his team had been working on for weeks, and he was very eager for them.

The center's 'Animal Room' was nearly the length of a basketball court and contained computerized inventory stalls, touch-screen data-recording centers, and electronic vivisection and autopsy stations. Stanton made his way toward the first of twelve cages shelved on the south wall and peered inside. The cage contained two animals: a two-foot-long black-and-orange coral snake and a small gray mouse. At first glance it looked like the most natural thing in the world: a snake waiting for the right moment to feed on its prey. But in reality something unnatural was happening inside this cage.

The mouse was nonchalantly poking the snake's head with its nose. Even when the snake hissed, the mouse continued to nudge it carelessly – it didn't run to the corner of the cage or try to escape. The mouse was as unafraid of the snake as it would have been of another mouse. The first time Stanton saw this behavior, he and his team at the Prion Center erupted in cheers. Using genetic engineering, they'd removed a set of tiny proteins called 'prions' from the surface membrane of the mouse's brain cells. They'd succeded in their strange experiment, disrupting the natural order in the mouse's brain and eradicating its innate fear of the snake. It was a crucial step toward understanding the deadly proteins that had been Stanton's life's work.

Prions occur in all normal animal brains, including those of humans, yet after decades of research, neither he nor anyone else understood why they existed. Some of Stanton's colleagues believed prion proteins were involved in memory or were important in the formation of bone marrow. No one knew for sure.

Most of the time, these prions sat benignly on neuron cells in the brain. But in rare cases, these proteins could become 'sick' and multiply. Like Alzheimer's and Parkinson's, prion diseases destroyed healthy tissue and replaced it with useless plaques, squeezing out the normal function of the brain. But there was one key, terrifying difference: While Alzheimer's and Parkinson's were strictly genetic diseases, certain prion diseases could be passed through contaminated meat. In the mid-1980s, mutated prions from sick cows in England got into the local food supply through tainted beef, and the entire world became familiar with a prion infection. Mad cow disease killed two hundred thousand cattle in Europe and then spread to humans. First patients had difficulty walking and shook uncontrollably, then they lost their memories and the ability to identify friends and family. Brain death soon followed.

Early in his career, Stanton had become one of the world's experts on mad cow, and when the CDC founded the National Prion Center, he was the natural choice to head it. Back then it had seemed like the opportunity of a lifetime, and he was thrilled to make the move to California; never before had there been a dedicated research center for the study of prions and prion diseases in the United States. With Stanton's leadership, the center was created to diagnose, study, and eventually fight the most mysterious infectious agents on earth.

Only it never happened. By the end of the decade, the beef industry had launched a successful campaign to show that just one person living in the United States had ever been diagnosed with mad cow. Grants for Stanton's lab became smaller, and, with fewer cases in England as well, the public quickly lost interest. The worst part was they still couldn't cure a single prion disease; years of testing various drugs and other therapies had produced one false hope after the next. Yet Stanton had always been as stubborn as he was optimistic and had never given up on the possibility that answers were just one experiment away.

Moving on to the next animal cage, he found another snake and another tiny mouse merely bored by its predator. Through this experiment, Stanton and his team were exploring a role for prions in controlling 'innate instincts', including fear. Mice didn't have to be taught to be afraid of the rustling of the grass signaling a predator's approach – terror was programmed into their genes. But after their prions were genetically 'knocked out' in an earlier experiment, the mice began acting aggressively and irrationally. So Stanton and his staff started directly testing the effects of deleting prions on the animals' most fundamental fears.

Stanton's cellphone vibrated in the pocket of his white coat. 'Hello?'

'Is this Dr Stanton?' It was a female voice he didn't recognize, but it had to be a doctor or a nurse; only a health professional wouldn't apologize first for calling before eight in the morning.

'What can I do for you?'

'My name's Michaela Thane,' she said. 'Third-year resident at East LA Presbyterian Hospital. CDC gave me your number. We believe we have a case of prion disease here.'

Stanton smiled, pushed his glasses up the bridge of his nose, and said, '*Okay*,' as he moved on to the third animal cage. Inside, another mouse pawed its predator's tail. The snake seemed almost befuddled by this reversal of nature.

'"Okay?"' Thane asked. 'That's it?'

'Send over the samples to my office and my team will look at them,' he said. 'A Dr Davies will call you back with the results.'

'Which will be when? A week? Maybe I wasn't being clear, Doctor. Sometimes I talk too fast for people. We think we have a case of *prion* disease here.'

'I understand that's what you believe,' Stanton said. 'What about the genetic tests? Have they come back?'

'No, but –'

'Listen, Dr . . . Thane? We get thousands of calls a

year,' Stanton interrupted, 'and only a handful turn out to be prion disease. If the genetic tests are positive, call us back.'

'Doctor, the symptoms are highly consistent with a diagnosis of –'

'Let me guess. Your patient is having trouble walking.'

'No.'

'Memory loss?'

'We don't know.'

Stanton tapped on the glass of one of the cages, curious to see if either of the animals would react. Neither acknowledged him. 'Then what's your presumptive symptom, Doctor?' he asked Thane.

'Dementia and hallucinations, erratic behavior, tremor, and sweating. And a terrible case of insomnia.'

'Insomnia?'

'We thought it was alcohol withdrawal when he was admitted,' Thane said. 'But there was no folate deficiency to indicate alcoholism, so I ran more tests, and I believe it could be fatal familial insomnia.'

Now she had Stanton's attention.

'When was he admitted?'

'Three days ago.'

FFI was a strange and rapidly progressing condition that arose because of a mutated gene. Passed down from parent to child, it was one of the few prion diseases that was strictly genetic. Stanton had seen half a dozen cases in his career. Most FFI patients first came in for medical attention because they were sweating constantly and having trouble falling asleep at night. Within months, their insomnia was total. Patients became impotent, experienced panic attacks, had difficulty walking. Caught between a hallucinatory waking state and panic-inducing alertness, nearly all FFI patients died after a few weeks of total sleeplessness, and there was nothing Stanton or any other doctor could do to help them.

'Don't get ahead of yourself,' he told Thane. 'Worldwide incidence of FFI is one in thirty-three million.'

'What else could cause complete insomnia?' Thane asked.

'A misdiagnosed methamphetamine addiction.'

'This is East L.A. I get the pleasure of smelling meth-breath every day. This guy's tox screen was negative.'

'FFI affects fewer than forty families in the world,' Stanton said, moving down the line of cages. 'And if there was a family history, you would've told me already.'

'Actually, we haven't been able to talk to him, because we can't understand him. He looks Latino or possibly indigenous. Central or South American maybe. We're working on it with the translator service. 'Course, most days here, that's one guy with a GED and a stack of remaindered dictionaries.'

Stanton peered through the glass of the next cage. This snake was still, and there was a tiny gray tail hanging out of its mouth. In the next twenty-four hours, when the other snakes got hungry, it would happen in every cage in the room. Even after years in the lab, Stanton didn't enjoy dwelling on his role in the death of these mice.

'Who brought the patient in?' he asked.

'Ambulance, according to the admission report, but I can't find a record of what service it was.'

This was consistent with everything Stanton knew about Presbyterian Hospital, one of the most overcrowded and debt-ridden facilities in East LA. 'How old is the patient?' Stanton asked.

'Early thirties probably. I know that's unusual, but I read your paper on age aberrations in prion diseases, and I thought maybe this could be one.'

Thane was doing her job right, but her diligence didn't change the facts. 'I'm sure when genetics comes back, it will clear all this up quickly,' he told her. 'Feel free to call Dr Davies later with any further questions.'

'*Wait, Doctor.* Hold on. Don't hang up.'

Stanton had to admire her insistence; he was a pain in the ass when he was a resident too. 'Yes?'

'There was a study last year on amylase levels, how they're markers for sleep debt.'

'I'm aware of the study. And?'

'With my patient it was three hundred units per milliliter, which suggests he hasn't slept in more than a week.'

Stanton stood up from the cage. A week without sleep? 'Have there been seizures?'

'There's some evidence on his brain scan,' Thane said.

'And what do the patient's pupils look like?'

'Pinpricks.'

'What happens in reaction to light?'

'Unresponsive.'

A week of insomnia. Sweating. Seizures.

Pinprick pupils.

Of the few conditions that could cause that combination of symptoms, the others were even rarer than FFI. Stanton peeled off his gloves, his mice forgotten. 'Don't let anyone in the room until I get there.'

2

As usual, Chel Manu arrived at Our Lady of the Angels – mother church for Los Angeles's four million Catholics – just as services were ending. The journey from her office at the Getty Museum to the cathedral downtown took almost an hour during rush hour, but she relished making it every week. Most of the time she was cooped up at her research lab at the Getty or in lecture halls at UCLA, and this was her chance to leave the west side, get on the freeway, and drive. Even the traffic, bane of LA, didn't bother her. The trip to the church was a kind of meditative break, the one time she could turn off all the noise: her research, her budget, her colleagues, her faculty committees, her mother. She'd have a smoke (or two), turn up the alt-rock of KCRW, and zone out a little. She always pulled off the exit ramp wishing she could just keep driving.

Outside the enormous cathedral, she dashed out the end of her second cigarette, flicking it into a trash can beneath the strange, androgynous statue of the Virgin guarding the entrance. Then she pushed open the heavy bronze doors. Inside, Chel took in the familiar sights and sensations: sweet incense in the air, chanting from the sanctuary, and the largest collection of alabaster windows in the world, casting earth-toned light across the faces of the community of Maya immigrants gathered in the pews. These men and women were directly descended from the ancient people who ruled Central America for nearly a thousand years, who built the most advanced pre-Columbian civilization in the New World. They were also Chel's friends.

At the pulpit, beneath five golden frames representing the phases of Jesus's life, stood Maraka, the elderly bearded 'daykeeper'. He waved a censer back and forth.

'Tewichim,' he chanted in Qu'iche, the branch of the Mayan language spoken by more than a million *indígenas* in Guatemala. *'Tewchuninaq ub'antajik q'ukumatz, ajyo'l k'aslemal.'*

Blessed is the plumed serpent, giver of life.

Maraka turned to face eastward, then took a long drink of *baalché*, the milky-white sacred combination of tree bark, cinnamon and honey. When he finished, he motioned to the crowd, and the church filled with chants again, one of the many ancient traditions that the archbishop let them practice here once or twice a week, as long as some of the *indígenas* continued to attend regular Catholic Mass as well.

Chel made her way down the side of the nave, trying not to draw attention, though at least one man saw her and waved enthusiastically. He'd asked her out half a dozen times since she'd helped him with an immigration form last month. She had lied and told him she was seeing someone. At five-foot-two, she might not look like most women in Los Angeles, but many here thought she was beautiful.

Beside the incense altar, Chel waited for the service to

end. She looked out at the mix of congregants, including more than two dozen white faces. Until recently, there were only sixty members of *Fraternidad*. The group met here on Tuesday mornings to honor the gods and traditions of their ancestors in a steady stream of immigrants from all over the Maya region, including Chel's own Guatemala.

But then the apocalypse groupies had started to show up. The press called them '2012ers,' and some seemed to believe that attending Maya ceremonies would exempt them from the end of the world, which they believed was less than two weeks away. Many other 2012ers didn't bother to come here at all – they just preached ideas about the end of the 'Long Count' calendar cycle from their own pulpits. Some argued that the oceans would flood, earthquakes would rip open fault lines, and the magnetic poles would switch. Some claimed it would bring a return to a more basic existence, banishing the excesses of technology. Still others believed that it would usher in a 'fifth age' of man and wipe away the entire 'fourth race', all the humans who now walked the earth.

Serious Maya experts, including Chel, found the idea of an apocalypse on December 21 ridiculous. It was true that one of her ancestors' signal achievements was a complex calendar system, and 2012ers were right when they claimed that according to the more than five-thousand-year-old Long Count, human history has consisted of four ages. But there was no credible reason to believe that the end of the thirteenth cycle of the Long Count would be different from any other calendar turn. Just a few months before, archaeologists had uncovered a new tomb in Xultun, Guatemala, with wall paintings that again indicated the calendar was meant to continue long past December 21. Of course, that hadn't stopped 2012ers from using ancient Maya wisdom to sell T-shirts and conference tickets or from making Chel's people the butt of jokes on late-night TV.

'Chel?'

She turned to find Maraka behind her. She hadn't even noticed that the ceremony had ended and people were filing out of their seats.

The daykeeper put a hand on her shoulder. He was almost eighty now, and his once-black hair had gone entirely white. 'Welcome,' he said. 'The office is ready. Of course, we'd all love to see you at an actual service again one of these weeks.'

Chel shrugged. 'I'll try to make it to one soon, I promise. I've just been very busy, Daykeeper.'

Maraka smiled. 'Of course you are, Chel. *In Lak'ech.*'

I am you, and you are me.

Chel bowed her head toward him. It was a tradition that had fallen into disuse even in Guatemala, but many of the elders still appreciated it, and it felt like the least she could do given her own dwindling interest in prayer.

'In Lak'ech,' she repeated quietly before begging off to the back of the church.

Outside the priest's office Chel used every week, the Larakams were first in line. She had heard that Vicente, the husband, was taken in by a bottom feeder in the moneylending business who preyed on people like them: newly arrived, unable to believe that what might be ahead could be worse than what they'd left behind in Guatemala. Chel wondered if his wife, Ina, who impressed her as an intelligent woman, had known better. Ina wore a floor-length skirt and a cotton *huipil* with intricate zigzag patterns. She still dressed in the traditional way, and the traditional role of wife in their culture would be to support her husband no matter how bad his judgment.

'Thank you for seeing us,' she said quietly.

Vicente slowly explained that he had signed a contract at exorbitant interest in order to rent a one-room apartment in Echo Park, and now he had to pay out more than he earned working as a landscaper. He had the haggard look of someone with the weight of the world on him. Ina stood quietly by his side, but her eyes implored Chel. An unspoken message passed between the two women, and now Chel understood what it had cost Vicente to come to her and ask for help.

Silently, he gave Chel the papers he'd signed, and as she read the fine print she felt the familiar anger blooming inside her. Vicentc and Ina were only two in a vast sea of immigrants from Guatemala trying to navigate this overwhelming new country, and there were many willing to take advantage. Still, on the whole, it was the Maya way to be too trusting. Five hundred years of oppression hadn't managed to instill even survival-level cynicism in most of Chel's people, and it cost them.

Fortunately for the Larakams, her contacts were extensive, particularly in the areas of legal aid. She wrote down the name of a lawyer and was about to call in the next person when Ina reached into her bag and handed Chel a plastic container.

'Pepian,' she said. 'My daughter and I made it for you.'

Chel's freezer was already full of the sweet-tasting chicken dish she was always gifted by *Fraternidad* members, but she took it anyway. It made her happy to think about Ina and her young daughter cooking it together and to know that this community had a future in L.A. Chel's own mother, who'd grown up in a small village in Guatemala, was probably spending the morning in communion with *Good Morning America* over a bowl of Special K.

'Let me know what happens,' Chel said as she handed Vicente back their papers, 'and next time don't get involved with anyone whose face you see on bus-stop benches. That doesn't make them famous. Not good famous, anyway. Come to me instead.'

Vicente took his wife's hand and smiled tightly as they departed.

So it went for the next hour. Chel explained a vaccination program to a pregnant woman, weighed in on a credit-card dispute for the junior daykeeper, and dealt with a landlord complaint against an old friend of her mother's.

Once her last visitor left, Chel leaned back in her chair and closed her eyes, thinking about a ceramic vase she'd been working on at the Getty, the inside of which contained some of the first physical residues of ancient tobacco ever discovered. No wonder it was proving so damn hard for her to quit smoking. People had been doing it for millennia.

A persistent knocking pulled her back to reality.

Chel stood up, surprised by the man she saw standing in the doorway. She hadn't seen him in over a year, and he belonged to such a different world from the *indígenas* who worshipped at *Fraternidad* services that it startled her to see him.

'What are you doing here?' she asked as Hector Gutierrez stepped inside.

'I need to talk to you.'

The few times she'd met him, Gutierrez had seemed reasonably well put together. Now there were shadows under his eyes and a tired pinch in his stare. His head was covered with sweat, and he dabbed anxiously at it with a handkerchief. Chel had never seen him unshaven before. His beard crept up toward the port-wine stain beneath his left temple. In his hand, she noticed, was a black duffel bag.

'How did you know I was here?'

'I called your office.'

Chel reminded herself to make sure no one in her lab ever gave out that information again.

'I have something you need to see,' he continued.

She glanced down at the duffel bag, wary. 'You shouldn't be here.'

'I need your help. They found the old storage unit where I kept my inventory.'

Chel looked to the doorway to make sure no one was listening. *They* could mean only one thing: He'd been busted by Immigration and Customs Enforcement, the agency responsible for policing illegal antiquities smuggling.

'I'd already emptied the unit,' Gutierrez said. 'But they

raided it. It's only a matter of time before they come to my house.'

Chel's throat tightened as she thought of the turtle-shell vessel she'd bought from him more than a year ago. 'And your records? Did they get those too?'

'Don't worry. You're protected for now. But there's something I need you to keep for me, Dr Manu. Just till it's safe.'

He held out the bag.

Chel looked at the door again and said, 'You know I can't do that.'

'You have vaults at the Getty. Put it there for a few days. No one will notice.'

Chel knew she should just tell him to get rid of whatever the hell it was. She also knew that whatever was in that bag had to be of great value or he wouldn't risk bringing it to her. Gutierrez was not a man to be trusted, but he was a nimble purveyor of antiquities, and he knew her weakness for the artifacts of her people.

Chel quickly ushered him out. 'Come with me.'

A few stray worshippers glanced at them as she led him down to the church's lower level. They pushed through the glass doors engraved with angels at the entrance and into the mausoleum, where niches in the walls contained the ashes of thousands of the city's Catholics. Chel chose one of the sitting rooms, where stone benches lined gleaming white walls engraved with names and dates, a tidy bibliography of death.

Finally Chel sealed them inside. 'Show me.'

From inside his bag, Gutierrez pulled a one-foot-square

wooden box wrapped in a sheath of plastic. When he began to unwrap it, the room filled with the sharp, unmistakable odor of bat guano – the smell of something that recently came from an ancient tomb. 'It needs proper preservation before it deteriorates any more,' Gutierrez said as he removed the cover of the box.

At first, Chel assumed she was staring at some kind of paper packing material, but then she leaned in and realized the paper was actually broken yellowed bark pages, floating loosely inside the box. The pages were covered with writing – words and even entire sentences in the language of her ancestors. The ancient Maya script used hieroglyphic-like symbols called 'glyphs', and here were hundreds of them inscribed on the fragments, along with detailed pictures of gods in ornate costumes.

'A codex?' Chel said. 'Come on. Don't be absurd.'

Maya codices were the written histories of her ancestors, painted by a royal scribe working for a king. Chel had heard people use the word *rare* to describe blue diamonds or Gutenberg Bibles, but this was what *rare* really meant: Only four ancient Maya books had survived into modernity. So how could Gutierrez think for a minute she would believe he had come into possession of a new one?

'There hasn't been a new codex discovered in thirty years,' Chel told him.

The man peeled off his jacket. 'Until now.'

She stared into the small box once more. As a graduate student, Chel had had the rare opportunity to see an original codex, so she knew exactly what it was supposed to look and feel like. Deep in a vault in Germany, armed guards had watched her as she turned the pages of the Dresden Codex, its images and words transporting her back a thousand years in a breathtaking flash. It was the defining experience that had inspired her to focus her graduate studies on the language and writing of her ancestors.

'Obviously it's a fake,' she told him, resisting the urge to keep looking. These days, more than half of the artifacts she was offered by even the most legitimate dealers were forged. The bat-guano smell was even forgeable. 'And, for the record, when you sold me that turtle-shell vessel, I didn't know it was looted. You misled me with the paperwork. So don't try to tell the police otherwise.'

The truth was more complex. In her work as the curator of Maya antiquities for the Getty Museum, every item Chel purchased had to be officially documented and traced back to its origin. All of which she'd done properly for the turtle-shell vessel Gutierrez had sold her, but, unfortunately, weeks after the purchase, she'd found a problem in the chain of possession. Chel knew the risks of not revealing her discovery to the museum but couldn't bring herself to part with the incredible piece of history, so she'd kept it and said nothing. To her, the larger scandal was that her people's whole heritage was for sale on the black market, and any artifacts she didn't buy disappeared into the homes of collectors forever.

'Please,' Gutierrez said, ignoring her claim about the pottery he'd sold her. 'Just keep it for me for a few days.'

Chel decided to settle this. She reached into her purse and pulled out a pair of white cotton gloves and tweezers.

'What are you doing?' he asked.

'Finding something that'll prove to you that this thing was forged.'

The plastic covering was still damp from his palms, and Chel tensed at the feeling of his sweat. Gutierrez pinched the bridge of his nose, rubbing two fingers deep into his eyes. Above the bat guano she could smell his body odor. But when Chel's fingers dipped inside the box and started handling the chipped pages of tree bark, everything else in the room fell away. Her first thought was that the glyphs were too old. Ancient Maya history was divided into two periods: the 'classic', encompassing the rise and efflorescence of the civilization, from around A.D. 200 to 900; and the 'post-classic', spanning its decline until the arrival of the Spanish around 1500. The style and content of written Mayan language had evolved over time as a result of external influences, and writing from each period looked distinct.

Chel continued searching the box. There had never been so much as a single piece of bark paper with writing discovered from the classic; all four of the known Maya codices were from hundreds of years later. They only knew what classic writing looked like from inscriptions at the ruins. But the language on these pages appeared to Chel to have been written somewhere between the time of A.D. 800 to 900, making the book an utter impossibility: If it were real, it would be the most valuable artifact in the history of Mesoamerican studies.

Her eyes scanned the lines, searching for a mistake – a glyph improperly drawn, a picture of a god without the right headdress, a date out of sequence. She couldn't find any. The black and red ink was correctly faded. The blue ink held its color, just as real Maya blue did. The paper was weathered as if it had been inside a cave for a thousand years. The bark was brittle.

Even more impressive, the writing felt fluent. The glyph combinations made intuitive sense, as did the pictograms. The glyphs appeared to have been written in an early version of 'classic Ch'olan', as expected in a codex like this. But what Chel couldn't take her eyes off of were the phonetic 'complements' on the glyphs that helped a reader identify their meaning. They were written in Qu'iche.

The known post-classic codices with their Mexican influences were written in Yucatec and Ch'olan Mayan. But Chel had long imagined that a classic book from Guatemala might well have been written with complements in the dialect her mother and father had grown up speaking. The presence of those here represented a deep and nuanced understanding of the history and language on the part of the forger.

Chel couldn't believe the sophistication, and she suspected that many of even her smartest colleagues would have been fooled.

Then a sequence of glyphs stopped her cold.

On one of the largest bark-paper pieces Chel had seen in the box, three pictograms were written in sequence to form a sentence fragment: *Water, made to shoot from stone.*

Chel blinked, confused. The writer could only be describing a *fountain*. Yet no forger in the world could have written about a fountain, because until recently no scholar knew the classic Maya used them in their cities. It had been less than a month since an archaeologist from Penn State figured out that, contrary to popular belief, the Spanish hadn't introduced pressurized aqueducts to the New World; the Maya built them centuries before Europeans arrived.

A codex like this could never have been forged in less than a month. So it couldn't have been forged at all.

Chel looked up at Gutierrez in disbelief. 'Where did you get this?'

'You know I can't tell you that.'

The obvious answer was that it had been looted from a tomb in the Maya ruins, stolen like so much else from her ancestors' graves.

'Who else knows about it?' Chel pressed.

'Only my source,' Gutierrez said. 'But now you understand its value?'

If she was right, there could be more information about Maya history on these pages than in all the known ruins combined. The Dresden Codex, the most complete of the four ancient Maya books, would fetch ten million dollars at auction – and the pages in front of her would put the Dresden to shame.

'Are you going to sell it?' she asked Gutierrez.

'When the time is right.'

Even if she'd had the kind of money he would demand, the time would probably never be right for Chel. She couldn't buy it legally, because it had obviously been stolen, and the work it would take to properly reconstruct and decipher a codex would make it impossible to hide for long. If a looted codex were ever discovered in her possession, she'd lose her job and could face criminal charges.

'Why should I hold it for you?' Chel asked.

Gutierrez said, 'To give me time to figure out how to make papers so it can be sold to an American museum – I hope yours. And because if ICE finds this now, neither of us will ever see it again.'

Chel knew he was right about ICE: If they confiscated the book, they'd repatriate it to the Guatemalan government, which didn't have the expertise or infrastructure to properly display and study a codex. The Grolier Fragment, found in Mexico, had been rotting in a vault there since the eighties.

Gutierrez packed the book back in its box. Chel already felt impatient to touch it again. The bark paper was disintegrating and needed preservation. More than that, the world needed to know what these pages said, because they testified to the history of her people. And the history of her people was disappearing.

3

East LA Presbyterian Hospital: bars guarded the windows, and the typical crowd of smokers always seen around run-down hospitals stood outside puffing away. The front entrance was closed due to a leak in the lobby ceiling, so security shuffled visitors and patients alike into the hospital through the ER.

Inside, Stanton was hit by overlapping smells: alcohol, dirt, blood, urine, vomit, solvent, air freshener and tobacco. On chairs around the waiting room sat dozens of suffering people waiting their turn. Stanton rarely spent time in facilities like this one: when a hospital deals with gang violence on a daily basis, there's not much demand for a prion specialist to give academic lectures.

A clearly stressed-out nurse, sitting behind a bulletproof-glass window, agreed to page Thane as Stanton joined a group of visitors gathered around a TV mounted on the wall. An airplane was being pulled from the ocean by a Coast Guard salvage vessel. Rescue boats and helicopters circled the remains of Aero Globale flight 126, which had crashed off the coast of Baja California on its way from LA to Mexico City. Seventy-two passengers and eight crew members had died.

This is the way things can end, Stanton thought. No matter how many times life forced him to realize it, the thought still took him by surprise. You exercised and ate well, got yearly physicals, worked hard 24/7 and never complained about it, and then one day you just got on the wrong plane.

'Dr Stanton?'

The first thing he noticed about the tall black woman in scrubs standing behind him was how broad her shoulders were. She was in her early thirties, with cropped hair and thick black-rimmed glasses, giving her a kind of rugby-player-turned-hipster look.

'I'm Michaela Thane.'

'Gabriel Stanton,' he said, shaking her hand.

Thane glanced up at the television. 'Terrible, huh?'

'Do they know what happened?'

'They're saying human error,' she said, leading him out of the ER. 'Or as we say here – CTFL. Call the fucking lawyers.'

'Speaking of which, I assume you called County Health?' Stanton asked her as they headed toward the elevators.

Thane repeatedly pressed an elevator button that refused to light up. 'They promised to send someone.'

'Don't hold your breath.'

She mimed taking a huge gasp of air in as they waited. Stanton smiled. She was his type of resident.

Finally the car arrived. Thane hit the button for six. When her scrub sleeve pulled back, Stanton saw a bald eagle with a scroll between the bird's wings tattooed on her triceps.

'You're Army?' he asked her.

'Five Hundred Sixty-fifth Medical Company, at your service.'

'Out of Fort Polk?'

'Yeah,' Thane said. 'You know the battalion?'

'My father was Forty-sixth Engineers. We lived at Fort Polk for three years. You served before residency?'

'Did ROTC for med school and they pulled me over there after internship,' she said. 'Two tours near Kabul doing helicopter retrievals. I was O-Three by the end.'

Stanton was impressed. Airlifting soldiers from the front lines was about the most dangerous army medical assignment there was.

'How many cases of FFI have you seen before?' Thane asked. The elevator finally started to ascend.

'Seven,' Stanton told her.

'All of them died?'

'Yes. All of them. Has genetics come back yet?'

'Should be soon. But I did manage to find out how the patient got here. LAPD arrested him at a Super 8 motel a few blocks away, after he assaulted some other guests. Cops brought him here when they realized he was sick.'

'After a week of insomnia, we're lucky he didn't do a lot worse.'

Even following the loss of a single night of sleep, deterioration of cognitive function was like a blood-alcohol level of 0.1 and could cause hallucinations, delirium, and wild mood swings. After weeks of progressively worse insomnia, FFI drove its victims to suicidal thinking. But most of the victims Stanton had seen simply succumbed from the devastation insomnia wreaked on their bodies.

'Dr Thane, was it you who came up with the idea of testing the amylase levels?' They had arrived on the sixth floor.

'Yeah. Why?'

'Putting FFI on the differential diagnosis list isn't something most residents would've considered.'

Thane shrugged. 'Saw a homeless guy in the ER this morning who'd eaten eight bags of banana chips to make his potassium so high that we'd have to admit him. Spend a little more time in East LA. You'll see we have to consider just about everything.'

Stanton noticed that every staff member smiled or nodded or waved at Thane as they approached the nerve center of the floor. The reception area looked as if it hadn't been updated in decades, complete with ancient computers. Nurses and interns scribbled notes in fading plastic binders. Orderlies finished their rounds, clearing scratched trays from patients' rooms.

A security guard was posted outside room 621. He was middle-aged, with dark skin and a crew cut, and wore a pink mask over his face.

'Everything all right in there?' Thane asked.

'He's not moving too much right now,' the guard said, closing his book of crossword puzzles. 'Couple of short outbursts, but for the most part pretty quiet.'

'This is Mariano,' Thane said. 'Mariano, this is Dr Stanton. He'll be working the John Doe with us.'

Mariano's dark-brown eyes, the only part of his face visible above the mask, were trained on Stanton. 'He's been flailing around for most of the past three days. Gets pretty loud in there. He's still saying *vooge vooge vooge* over and over.'

'Saying *what*?' Stanton asked.

'Sounds like *vooge* to me. Hell if I know what it means.'

'I typed it in on Google and got nothing that made sense in any language,' Thane said.

Mariano pulled the strings of his mask firmly behind his ears. 'Hey, Doc, if you're the expert, can I ask you a question about this?'

Stanton glanced at Thane. 'Of course.'

'What this guy has,' the guard said. 'It's not contagious, is it?'

'No, don't worry,' Stanton said, following Thane into the room.

'He's got like six kids, I think,' Thane whispered once they were out of earshot. 'He's always talking about how he doesn't want to pass on anything from here. I've never seen him without a mask.'

Stanton pulled a fresh mask from a dispenser on the wall and fastened it to his face. 'We should be following his lead,' he said, handing another mask to Thane. 'Insomnia compromises the immune system, so we have to avoid infecting John Doe with a cold or anything else he won't be able to fight off. Everyone needs masks and gloves when they go in. Post a sign on the door.'

Stanton had seen worse patient rooms, but not in the United States. Room 621 contained two metal beds, cracked night tables, two orange chairs, and curtains with worn edges. Dispensers of Purell clung loosely to the wall, and there was water damage on the ceiling. Lying in the bed closest to the window was their John Doe: about five-foot-six, thin, with dark skin and long black hair that draped over his shoulders. His head was covered with tiny stickers, from which wires extended toward an EEG machine, measuring brain waves. The patient's gown clung to him like damp tissue paper, and he was groaning softly.

The doctors watched the patient tossing and turning. Stanton noted John Doe's eye movements, the strange, staccato breathing, and the involuntary tremor in his hands. In Austria, Stanton had treated a woman with FFI who'd had to be chained to her bed because her tremor was so bad. By that time, her children were overcome by grief and helplessness and by the knowledge they might someday die the same way. It had been hard to watch.

Thane bent down to flip the pillow beneath John Doe's head. 'How long can you live without sleeping?' she asked.

'Twenty days max of total insomnia,' Stanton said.

Even most doctors knew virtually nothing about sleep. Medical schools spent less than one day out of four years on it, and Stanton himself had learned what he knew only through his FFI cases. Part of it was that no one knew why humans needed sleep in the first place: its function and importance were as mysterious as the existence of prions. Some experts believed sleep recharged the brain, assisted in the healing of wounds, and aided in metabolism. Some suggested it protected animals against the dangers of night or that sleep was an energy-conservation technique. But no one had ever been able to explain why not sleeping killed Stanton's FFI patients.

Suddenly John Doe's bloodshot eyes went wide. '*Vooge, vooge, vooge!*' he moaned, more loudly than before.

At the monitor, Stanton studied the patient's brain activity like a musician looking at sheet music he'd played a thousand times. The four stages of normal sleep ran in ninety-minute cycles, each with characteristic patterns, and, as expected, there was no evidence of any of them. No stage-one or -two slow-wave sleep, no REM, nothing. The machine confirmed what Stanton already knew from instinct and experience: This was no meth addiction.

'*Vooge, vooge, vooge!*'

'So what do you think?' asked Thane.

Stanton met her eyes. 'This could be the first case of FFI in US history.'

Though she'd been proven right, Thane didn't look satisfied. 'He's going to the hundredth floor, isn't he?'

'Probably.'

'There's nothing we can do for him?'

It was the question Stanton had been asking for a decade. Before prions were discovered, scientists believed that food-borne diseases came from bacteria, viruses, or fungi and replicated themselves with DNA or RNA. Yet prions had neither: they were made of pure protein and they 'replicated' by causing other nearby proteins to mutate their shape as well. All of which meant that none of the conventional cures for bacteria or viruses worked on prions. Not antibiotics or antivirals or anything else.

'I read about pentosan and quinacrine,' Thane said. 'What about those?'

'Quinacrine is toxic to the liver,' Stanton explained. 'And we can't get pentosan into the brain without doing even more damage.' There were some highly experimental treatments, he told her, but none that were ready for human testing and none that were FDA approved.

But there were ways they could make John Doe more comfortable before the inevitable happened. 'Where are the temperature controls?' Stanton asked.

'They're all central, down in the basement,' Thane said.

He scanned the wall, started pulling back curtains and moving furniture. 'Call down there and tell them to turn up the air-conditioning on this floor. We need to get the temperature in this room down as low as it'll go.'

'You'll freeze every other patient on the floor.'

'That's what blankets are for. Let's get fresh sheets and gowns for him too. He'll keep sweating through them, so tell the nurses we need new ones every hour.'

Thane hurried out, and Stanton flipped off all the lights and shut the door. He pulled the curtain over the window, preventing any outside light from spilling in, then picked up a towel and tossed it over the EEG monitor, extinguishing its light.

The thalamus – a tiny collection of neurons in the midsection of the brain – was the body's 'sleep shield'. When it was time for sleep, it shut off 'waking' signals from the outside world, like noise and light. In every FFI patient he'd treated, Stanton had seen the horrific effects of destroying this part of the brain. Nothing could be shut off or even tamped down, making victims painfully sensitive to light and sound. So while working with Clara, his

Austrian patient, Stanton learned to relieve her distress in a small way by turning her room into a kind of cave.

He gently put a hand on John Doe's shoulder. *'Habla español?'*

'Tinimit vooge. Tinimit vooge.'

There would be no getting through to him without a translator, so Stanton began his physical exam. John Doe's pulse was bounding, his nervous system firing on all cylinders. His breathing was coarse through his mouth, his bowels had ground digestion to a halt, and his tongue was swollen. All further confirmation of FFI.

Thane reappeared, fastening a new mask over her mouth and nose. In her gloved hand she held a printout in Stanton's direction. 'Genetics just came back.'

They'd extracted DNA from John Doe's blood and mapped out chromosome 20, where the FFI mutation always occurred. This should be the final proof.

When Stanton scanned the results, he saw a normal DNA sequence staring back at him. 'There must've been a mistake in the lab,' he said, glancing at Thane. He could only imagine what the lab in this place looked like and how frequently there were mix-ups. 'Tell them to run it again.'

'Why?'

He handed it back to her. 'Because there's no mutation here.'

'They ran it twice. They knew how important it was,' Thane said as she studied the results. 'I know the geneticist, and she doesn't screw things up.'

Was it possible Stanton had misjudged the clinical

signs? How was there no mutation? In every case of FFI he had seen, a DNA mutation caused prions in the thalamus to transform and then cause symptoms.

'Could it be something other than FFI?' asked Thane.

John Doe opened his eyes again, and Stanton caught a glimpse of the pinprick pupils. There'd been no doubt in his mind that this was a case of FFI. All the signs were there. Progressing faster than usual, but there.

'*Vooge, vooge, vooge!*' the man yelled again.

'We have to find a way to communicate with him,' Stanton said.

'We've got a team from the translator service coming in that can identify almost every American language, Central and South,' said Thane. 'When we know what he's speaking, we'll bring in someone fluent.'

'Get them in here now.'

Thane said, 'If he doesn't have the genetic mutation, he can't have FFI, right?'

Stanton glanced up at her, his mind racing with new possibilities. 'Right.'

'So it's not prion disease?'

'It is. But if there's no mutation, he must have gotten it another way.'

'What other way?'

For decades, doctors knew of a rare genetic prion affliction called CJD – Creutzfeldt-Jakob disease. Then, suddenly, dozens of people who'd all eaten from the same meat supply in Britain came down with symptoms identical to CJD, giving mad cow its proper name – *variant* CJD. The only difference was that one came from a genetic mutation and the other from contaminated meat. And that one destroyed entire economies and food-supply standards forever. It stood to reason that something similar was happening here with FFI.

'He must have eaten tainted meat,' Stanton said.

John Doe thrashed around, rattling the handrails. Stanton had so many questions: What was the patient saying? Where had he come from? What work did he do?

'Jesus,' Thane said. 'You mean a new prion strain that mimics the symptoms of FFI? How do you know it's from meat?'

'Vooge, vooge, vooge . . .'

'Because it's the only other way to get prion disease.'

And if Stanton was right – if this new cousin of FFI was being carried through meat – they had to trace it back to wherever it came from and figure out how it got into the food supply. Most of all, they had to make sure there weren't other people out there who were already sick.

John Doe was full-on yelling now. *'Vooge, vooge, vooge!'*

'What do we do?' Thane called out over him.

Stanton pulled out his phone and dialed a number in Atlanta known to fewer than fifty people in the world. The operator picked up on the first ring. 'Centers for Disease Control. This is the secure emergency line.'

4

The worn leather couch in Chel's study was piled high with old academic articles and back issues of *Journal of Mayan Linguistics.* Her drafting table and desk chair were covered with a broken PC, immigration forms, mortgage applications, and other paperwork for members of *Fraternidad.* The only space not hidden by books overflowing from the shelves was a small patch on the Oriental rug. That's where Chel had been for the last hour, on the floor, staring at the box in front of her.

She'd gotten a glimpse of the marvels inside – the glyphs that would tell some incredible story of the ancients, the artistry used in representing the gods. Chel had devoted her career to Mayan epigraphy – the study of ancient inscriptions – and she wanted so badly to remove the plastic casing once more and to look at the glyphs again, to photograph them, to dig beyond what she'd already seen. But the image of a former colleague languishing in an Italian courtroom under the scrutiny of news cameras had been in Chel's mind since she'd watched Gutierrez drive away from the church. The Getty's previous curator of antiquities, who used to work just down the hall from Chel, had become embroiled in a legal battle when she was accused by Italian officials of acquiring illegally excavated artifacts for her collection.

Chel knew that both the Getty and ICE would make an even bigger example of her if they discovered what she'd done. To forge paperwork after the fact, as she'd done with Gutierrez's turtle shell, was one thing. A codex was different. There wasn't a museum board in the world that would believe she hadn't known what she was doing when she accepted it at the church.

Chel gently picked up the box again. It weighed no more than five pounds. How had it even survived? In the mid-sixteenth century, inquisitors for the Catholic Church tried to rid the Maya of pagan influences and presided over an *auto-da-fé*, a massive bonfire where thousands of sacred Maya books, artworks and inscriptions were destroyed. Until today, Chel and everyone else in her field believed only four codices had been saved. The Grolier Fragment marked the cycles of Venus; the Madrid Codex referred to omens about crops; and the Paris Codex was a guide to rituals and New Year ceremonies. Chel's revered Dresden Codex – oldest of the known Maya books, dating to sometime around A.D. 1200 – contained astrology, histories of kings and predictions of the harvest. Yet even the Dresden didn't come from the classic era of Maya civilization. How could this volume have been preserved for so long?

The doorbell rang.

It was after eight. Could it be Gutierrez already, back to collect his treasure? Why had she not opened the box? Then again, what if it was ICE? What if the dealer had already been arrested? Had ICE been watching when he came to the church?

Chel picked up the box and hurried to the study closet. No one knew about the cubbyhole she'd discovered there, full of stacks of some previous tenant's 1920s LA memorabilia. She buried the codex beneath a collection of black-and-white photographs of Wolfskill Farm – what Westwood was called before the First World War.

The doorbell rang again as she went to answer it.

Chel breathed a sigh of relief when she peeked through the window to see her mother standing in the entryway.

'Want me to stand here all night?' Ha'ana asked as Chel opened the door. She stood just over five feet tall and wore a knee-length navy cotton dress, one of many acquired from the company at which she'd been a seamstress since they'd been in America. Even with her silver hair and several extra pounds, Ha'ana still had a radiance about her.

'Mom, what are you doing here?'

Ha'ana held canvas bags up in the air. 'Cooking you dinner, remember? Now, will you make me stand out here in the cold or will you invite an old woman in?'

In the day's turmoil, Chel had forgotten all about their dinner plans.

'This place used to be a lot cleaner,' Ha'ana said as she stepped inside and saw the state of the house. 'When Patrick was here.'

Patrick. Chel had dated him for almost a year and Ha'ana wouldn't let it go. The reasons they'd broken up were more complicated than Chel ever felt like getting into with Ha'ana. But her mother was right: since he moved out four months ago, Chel's house near the UCLA campus had come to feel like little more than a stopover between her offices at the university and the Getty. After exhausting days, she often came home, undressed and fell asleep watching the Discovery Channel.

'Are you going to help me?' Ha'ana called from the kitchen.

Chel joined her and helped unload the groceries. Difficulties with her back had made physical activity more challenging for Ha'ana recently, and even though the last thing Chel wanted was to sit for a meal, she'd never been good at saying no to her mother.

Dinner was a four-cheese and spinach lasagna concoction with an excess of garlic. Growing up, Chel usually couldn't get Ha'ana to cook Maya food – she'd been stuffed with macaroni and sandwiches on white bread. These days her mother watched the Food Network non-stop, and her continental cooking had improved. As they ate, Chel stared at her and listened to her chat about her day at the factory. But Chel's mind was always in the other room with the codex. Ordinarily she would've been attentive to her mother. But not tonight.

'Are you all right?'

Chel looked up from her plate to see Ha'ana studying her. 'I'm fine, Mom.' She doused her lasagna with red pepper. 'So . . . I'm excited you're coming to class next week.'

'Oh, I forgot to tell you. I'm not going to be able to next week. Sorry.'

'Why not?'

'I have a job too, Chel.'

Ha'ana had hardly missed a day's work in thirty years. 'If you told your boss what you were doing, they'd want you to go. I can talk to her if you want.'

'I'm working a double shift that day.'

'Look, I've been telling the class all about the village's oral history, and I think it would be fascinating for them to hear from someone who actually lived in Kiaqix.'

'Yes,' Ha'ana said. 'Someone must tell them all about our incredible Original Trio.' The irony in her voice was hard to miss.

Beya Kiaqix, the tiny hamlet where both women were born, was rife with myth, particularly the legend of its origins. The story went that a noble man and his two wives had fled their ancient city, under the rule of a despotic king, and had founded the village. More than fifty generations of Chel's ancestors had since lived in the Valley of the Scarlet Macaw, in the El Petén region of Guatemala.

Chel and her mother were among the very few who'd left. By the time Chel was two years old, Guatemala was at the height of *La Revolución*, the longest and bloodiest civil war in Central American history. Afraid for her daughter's life and for her own, Ha'ana had taken them out of Kiaqix – as the villagers called it – and never looked back. Thirty-three years ago they arrived in America, and she found a job and quickly taught herself English. By the time Chel was four, Ha'ana had her green card; soon they were both citizens.

'You lived in Kiaqix too,' Ha'ana went on as she took another bite. 'You know the myths. You don't need me.'

Since she was a child, Chel had watched her mother do everything she could to avoid talking about her past. Even if it could have been proven that every word of the oral history of their village was true, Ha'ana would find a way to ridicule it. Long ago, Chel had realized that it was her mother's only way to escape the trauma of what had happened.

Suddenly she wanted nothing so much as to run to the closet, retrieve the codex and drop it in her mother's lap. Even Ha'ana wouldn't be able to resist its pull.

'When was the last time you read a book written in Mayan?' Chel asked.

'Why read a Mayan book when I spent all that time learning English? Besides, I haven't heard of any good mysteries in Qu'iche lately.'

'Mom, you know I'm not talking about a modern book. I'm talking about something written during the ancient era. Like the *Popol Vuh*.'

Ha'ana rolled her eyes. 'I actually saw a copy of the *Popol Vuh* at the bookstore the other day. They're putting it with all that 12-21 nonsense. Loudmouth monkeys and flowery gods – that's what you get in Mayan.'

Chel shook her head. 'Father wrote his letters in Qu'iche, Mom.'

In 1979, two years after Chel was born, the Guatemalan army imprisoned her father for helping lead Kiaqix into rebellion. From jail, Alvar Manu secretly wrote a series of letters encouraging his village never to surrender. Ha'ana herself had smuggled out more than thirty entreaties into the hands of village leaders across El Petén, resulting in a doubling of the volunteer army in weeks. But the letters were also Chel's father's death warrant: when his jailers discovered him writing in his cell, he was executed without a trial.

'Why do we always talk about this?' Ha'ana asked, standing to clear the plates.

Chel felt frustrations toward her mother bubbling up. She loved her, and she would always be grateful for the opportunities Ha'ana had given her. But deep down, Chel also felt that her mother had abandoned their people, which was why Ha'ana hated to be reminded of it, and why showing her the codex in its current condition would be useless. Until Chel could figure out what it said, her mother would see the book as little more than disintegrating fragments of history she wanted to forget.

'Leave the dishes,' Chel said, standing up.

'They will only take a minute,' Ha'ana said. 'Otherwise they'll pile up like everything else in the house.'

Chel took a breath. 'I have to go.'

'Go where?'

'To the museum.'

'It's nine o'clock, Chel. What kind of job is this?'

'Thank you for dinner, Mom. But I really have to go.'

'This would be an insult in Kiaqix,' Ha'ana said. 'When a woman cooks for you, you don't invite her to leave.'

Ha'ana used their customs as a religion of convenience, invoking them to her advantage when she could, ridiculing them when they got in her way.

'Well, then,' Chel said, 'it's a good thing we're not in Kiaqix anymore.'

Over the past eight years, Chel had built a state-of-the-art Mesoamerican research facility at what was once California's most traditional museum. When she had the time after hours, she liked to stroll through the empty galleries, set spectacularly high above Los Angeles. Walking past van Gogh's *Irises* or Pontormo's *Portrait of a Halberdier*, she had fun imagining how John Paul Getty, the billionaire oilman who founded the museum, would have felt about exhibiting ceramic statues of kneeling Maya worshippers and Mesoamerican gods beside his beloved European artifacts.

Not tonight, though. Just after two a.m., Chel stood in Getty research lab 214A with Dr Rolando Chacon, her most experienced antiquities-restoration expert, surrounded by high-def cameras, mass spectrometers, and conservation tools. Normally, every one of the long wooden tables set up in rows throughout the room was covered with lumps of jade, pottery and ancient head masks, but now they'd cleared several in the back to make room for the codex. On the walls hung photographs from ruins, which Chel had taken during fieldwork, quiet reminders of the emotional ride that returning to her people's ancient home always was.

She and Rolando had delicately removed the contents of Gutierrez's box piece by piece, lifting and separating each fragment using sets of long tweezers and metal specula, then spreading them out onto glass plates sitting atop illuminated light tables. Some were as small as a postage stamp, but even these were heavy, dense fig-bark paper weighed down even more by the dust and moisture of a tomb.

They'd been at it four hours and had gotten through only the top of page one, but, staring down at the assembled fragments, Chel was pulled back to the former glory of her ancestors. The first words, already coming together, seemed to be an invocation of rain and the stars – a prayer – a magic carpet to another world.

'So I assume we'll have to work on this at night?' Rolando asked. Chel's restorer was a six-foot-two, hundred-fifty-pound sliver of a man with a week's worth of stubble.

'Sleep during the day,' she told him. 'With apologies to your girlfriend.'

'I just hope she notices I'm gone. Maybe it'll inject a little mystery into our relationship. And you? When will you sleep?'

'Whenever. There's no one who'll notice I'm gone.'

Rolando placed another fragment carefully onto the glass. Chel knew no one with a greater knack for handling delicate objects or with better instincts when it came to reconstructing fragile antiquities. She trusted him implicitly; he'd been a loyal member of her team longer than anyone else. She didn't like putting him at risk, but she needed his help.

'You wish I'd called someone else?' Chel asked him.

'Hell no,' Rolando said. 'I'm your one and only *ladino*,

and I'm not going to let you squeeze me out of this bombshell.'

Ladino was slang for all seven million non-indigenous descendants of the Spanish living in Guatemala. All her life Chel had listened to her mother talking about how *ladinos* supported the army-sponsored genocide of the Maya and how they used the *indígenas* as scapegoats for their economic woes. But despite the tensions that still existed between the two groups, working so closely and for so long with Rolando had shifted her perspective. During the revolution, his family protested on behalf of the indigenous people. His father had even been arrested for it once before moving the family to America.

'I don't see how this could be from any of the major ruins,' he said, tinkering with the edges until he'd jigsawed a match.

Chel agreed. The more than sixty known sites of classic-era Maya ruins in Guatemala, Honduras, Mexico, Belize and El Salvador were packed with archaeologists, tourists and locals year-round. Not even the most sophisticated looters could operate in those conditions, so Chel believed the book had to have been taken from a newly discovered site. Every year, satellites, helicopter tourists and loggers stumbled across long-hidden architectural features in the jungle, and she guessed that the looter – likely a professional scout – had stumbled on the site and then returned with a crew.

'You think the looter could have discovered a lost city?' Rolando asked.

Chel shrugged. 'If they did, every *indígena* in Guatemala will claim it as their own.'

So many Maya villages had oral histories that told of an incredible lost city where their ancestors had once lived. During the revolution, a cousin of Chel's father even claimed to have found Kiaqix's lost city, from which the Original Trio had supposedly fled. The reality was less sexy: Many Maya had always lived in small villages in the forest, and, for Chel's people, claiming a connection to a lost city was like white Americans saying they had an ancestor on the *Mayflower* – easy (and desirable) to say, harder to prove.

'So I'm not asking again where the hell you got this . . .' Rolando said as he matched another fragment, 'but, based on the iconography, this does look like it's from the end of the classic. Maybe 800 to 925? It's unbelievable.'

Chel said, 'Hope the carbon dating agrees.'

Rolando put down his tweezers. 'And I know we can't tell anyone, but . . . there's a lot of complicated syntax here. We could really use Victor on this. No one knows classic syntax better than he does.'

From the moment she saw the codex, Chel had wanted to call Victor Granning, but she was too afraid of how he might react. They hadn't spoken in months; she had good reasons for avoiding him. 'We'll be just fine on our own,' she told Rolando.

'Okay,' he said. He knew better than to press. Granning was a sore spot. Chel loved her old mentor, but he was too much of a diehard. And a little nuts.

Trying to put Granning out of her mind, Chel studied

the puzzle of 'stacked' glyphs Rolando had started to assemble from the first page:

Mayan glyphs came in two basic varieties. They could be combinations of syllables strung together to approximate the sound of words (just like English or other alphabetical systems). But often they were more like Chinese, with each glyph or glyph combination symbolizing an object or idea. Once Chel had broken the blocks down and deciphered each component, using the established catalogs of one hundred fifty de-coded syllables and the catalog of the eight hundred-plus known 'picture' glyphs, she strung them into sentences.

Words like *jäb* were entirely familiar; it was the same word the modern Qu'iche used for *rain*. Some, like *wulij*, could only be loosely translated, because there was no corresponding word in English: to *take down* was the closest she could get, carrying none of the religious implications the word had in Mayan. Researchers had identified about a hundred fifty glyphs that still hadn't been deciphered, and not only did a few of these appear on the very first page of the codex, there were others Chel had never seen before. When the entire text was reconstructed, she suspected there would be dozens of new glyphs to analyze.

Three hours later, Chel's legs had cramped, and her eyes were so dry and irritated that she had to replace her contacts with the glasses she hated. But finally they had a rough translation of the first glyph block:

> Come rain is none, ____ of nourishment, ____ star's half cycle. Harvest, take down fields of Kanuataba, raze ___ and trees, push out deer, birds, jaguar, land guardians. Rededication ____ tracts. Destroy hillsides, swarm insects, fed leaves soils are not. Have none, shelter, animals, butterflies, plants given by Holy Bearer for spirit lives. Bear no flesh, animals, cook us.

Yet for Chel, these literal words weren't enough – a completed translation had to capture the essence of what the scribe was trying to convey. Codices were written from the perspective of an omniscient narrator, and they were often very formal in tone. So she did her best to insert missing words from context and typical word pairings seen in the other books until they had a better rendering of the first paragraph:

> No rain has come to give nourishment in a half cycle of the great star. The fields of Kanuataba have been harvested and destroyed, the trees and plants razed, and the deer and birds and jaguar guardians of the land have been pushed out. Farming tracts cannot be rededicated.

> Hillsides have been ruined, insects swarm, and soils are no longer fed by falling leaves. The animals and butterflies and plants given by the Holy Bearer have nowhere to go to continue their spirit lives. The animals bear no flesh for cooking.

'It's talking about a drought,' Rolando said. 'Who would've been allowed to write something like this?'

Chel had never seen anything like it. Written Maya records were generally ancient press releases for kings. The royal 'scribes' who wrote them – half press secretaries, half religious leaders – didn't dare mention anything that undermined their rulers.

Never before had Chel seen a scribe writing about the difficulties of daily life. Predictions of rain were inscribed on stone columns at the ruins and in the Madrid and Dresden Codices, but for a scribe to report an ongoing drought was unheard of. It was a king's job to bring the rains, and such a discussion would embarrass any king who couldn't deliver.

'Only a scribe could have this kind of skill,' Rolando said, gesturing at a perfectly executed picture of the maize god.

Chel studied the words again. The penalty for writing this could well have been death. *No rain has come to give nourishment in a half cycle of the great star.* The great star was Venus, and a half cycle was almost fifteen months. What the scribe was describing would be by far the longest drought in the known Mayan record.

'What is it?' asked Rolando.

'It's not just the drought. He's talking about the depletion of the maize stores,' Chel said. 'He's talking about endangered animals and diminishing amounts of arable land. No one would have been permitted to write something like this. It's basically a description of the end of the civilization.'

Rolando flashed another grin. 'You think . . .'

'He's writing about the collapse.'

Over the course of Chel's career, the question that had bedeviled her more than any other was the 'collapse' of her ancestors' civilization at the end of the first millennium. For seven centuries, the Maya had built cities and innovated in art, architecture, agriculture, mathematics, astronomy and commerce. But then, six hundred years before the Spanish conquistadores arrived, city-states stopped expanding, construction halted, and scribes in the lowlands of Guatemala and Honduras stopped writing. Within a span of only half a century, urban centers were abandoned, the institution of kingship disappeared, and the classic era of Maya civilization came to an end.

Colleagues of Chel's had a variety of theories about what caused the collapse. Some suggested eco-recklessness: aggressive farming practices and disregard for deforestation. Others claimed that, through continuous warfare, hyper-religiosity and sacrificial bloodlust, the ancients brought on their own demise.

Chel had a skeptical view of all these ideas. She believed they were rooted in a European inclination to belittle *indígenas*. Exaggerations of human sacrifice had plagued the Maya since the Spanish landed, and the collapse had been used for centuries as proof that the conquistadores were more evolved than the savages they'd conquered. Proof the Maya couldn't be trusted to rule themselves.

Chel believed that the collapse was caused by natural mega-droughts that spanned decades and made large-scale agriculture impossible for her ancestors. Studies done on riverbeds in the area suggested that the end of the classic era was the driest in seven millennia. When these extended dry periods made cities uninhabitable, the Maya simply adapted. They reverted to subsistence farming and migrated to small villages like Kiaqix.

'If we could prove this is an actual description of the collapse,' Rolando said giddily, 'it would be a landmark.'

Chel imagined what else they might find on these pages. Imagined how far the codex would go toward answering what had, to date, been unanswerable. Imagined how she could one day show it to the world.

'And if we could prove the collapse was the result of mega-droughts,' Rolando continued, 'it would cut the balls right off those generals too.'

This possibility gave Chel yet another surge of adrenaline. In the last three years, tensions had flared again between *ladinos* and the *indígenas*. Civil-rights activists had been killed, crimes perpetrated by the same ex-generals who'd murdered Chel's father. Politicians had actually invoked the collapse on the floor of Parliament: the Maya were savages who'd destroyed their environment once, they'd claimed, and would do it again if they were allowed to keep their valuable land.

Could the book prove otherwise once and for all?

The phone rang in Chel's office at the back of the lab. She checked the clock. It was just after eight a.m. They needed to pack up the codex and put it in the vault. People would start filtering into the museum soon, and they couldn't risk questions.

'I'll get it,' Rolando said.

'I'm not here,' she called after him. 'You have no idea when I will be back.'

A minute later, Rolando returned with a curious look on his face. 'It's a translator service from a hospital,' he said.

'What do they want?'

'They have a sick man who was brought in three days ago, and no one's been able to talk to him. Now somehow they've concluded he's speaking Qu'iche.'

'Tell them to call the church in the morning,' she told him. 'Someone over there can translate for them.'

'They told me the patient keeps saying one word over and over again, repeating it like some kind of mantra.'

'What word?'

'Wuj.'

12.19.19.17.11
December 12, 2012

5

They repeated the genetic testing at the Prion Center. John Doe's chart, lab tests and MRI scans were scrutinized at CDC headquarters in Atlanta. By the following morning, after all-night meetings and emergency conference calls, the doctors all agreed with Stanton: the patient had a new strain of prion disease, and it came from tainted meat.

After dawn, Stanton reviewed the case with his deputy, Alan Davies, a brilliant English doctor who'd spent years studying mad cow across the Atlantic.

'Just got off with USDA,' said Davies. They were in Stanton's office at the Prion Center. 'No positive tests for prion at any of the major meat packagers. Nothing suspicious in the herd records or feed logs.'

Davies wore the vest and pants from a pin-striped three-piece suit, and his long brown hair was so perfectly set on his head, it looked like a toupee. He was the only lab rat Stanton had known who wore a suit, his way of showing Americans how much more civilized their British cousins were.

'I want to see the tests myself,' Stanton said, rubbing his eyes. He was having trouble fighting his exhaustion.

'That's just the big farms,' Davies replied, smirking. 'USDA couldn't cover all the small farms if they had a year. Never mind the sheep and pigs. Somewhere out there, some careless bugger is probably still grinding up contaminated brains or whatever the hell else and shipping them to God-knows-where.'

Tracking the original source was crucial in any food-borne illness. Vegetables with *E. coli* had to be traced back to the farms where they were grown, so the farms could be shut down and their wares pulled from the shelves. Salmonella had to be traced back to the chicken coop, so every egg could be recalled. It could be the difference between one victim and thousands.

Stanton and his team didn't even know what animal source to concentrate on. Cows' prions could obviously cross the species barrier, so beef was the first suspect. But pigs had prions remarkably similar to those of cows. And a prion disease called scrapie had killed hundreds of thousands of sheep throughout Europe; Stanton had long feared lamb might one day carry mutated prions to humans too.

Once they figured out *what* got John Doe sick, the real work of containment would begin. The unnatural way meat was processed and packaged meant flesh from a single animal could be distributed across thousands of different products and end up all over the world. Stanton had traced meat from a single cow to jerky in Columbus and hamburgers in Düsseldorf.

'I want people on the ground checking all the local hospitals,' he told Davies. John Doe was the only case so far, but prion disease was difficult to diagnose, and Stanton was convinced there could be more out there. 'See if they've had any unusual cases of insomnia. Or any other unusual admissions. And check the psych ERs for anyone coming in with delusions or strange behavior.'

Davies smiled. 'That would be everyone in LA.' After matters sartorial, making fun of the Southland was his primary amusement.

'What else?' Stanton asked.

'Cavanagh called.'

As head of prion investigations for the CDC, Stanton reported to the deputy director. Emily Cavanagh was known for her preternatural calm, but she also understood how serious prion disease was and took nothing lightly. After butting countless heads over money and treatment protocols, Stanton had enemies in Atlanta; Cavanagh was one of the few who remained an ally.

'What are we calling this thing anyway?' Davies asked.

'VFI for now,' Stanton said. '*Variant* fatal insomnia. But you find me where it came from and we'll call it Davies's disease.'

Stanton listened to a dozen new investigation-related voice mails before he heard Nina's voice.

'Got your messages,' she said, 'and I assume this is another one of your ploys to get me to go vegan or whatever. Don't worry. Most of the meat in the fridge was ancient and needed to be thrown out anyway. Guess your furry friend and I'll survive on fish out here for a while. Call me back when you can. And be careful.'

Stanton glanced at his team, seated at their microscopes. Per orders from CDC headquarters in Atlanta, they weren't supposed to tell anyone about the possibility of meat-borne illness yet. Every time there was even a hint of a possibility of mad cow, the public panicked, beef futures collapsed, and billions of dollars were lost. So Stanton hadn't told Nina about John Doe. He'd just hinted that it would be a very good idea to listen to what he'd been saying all these years about not eating meat.

'Dr Stanton, I've got slides.'

One of his postdocs waved him over. Stanton hung up the phone and hurried to a protective hood on the opposite side of the lab. Jiao Chen was sitting next to Michaela Thane. Stanton had invited Thane to the lab after her shift at Presbyterian ended so she could stay in on the ground floor of the investigation. If and when a case of meat-borne FFI broke, he wanted to make sure credit was given where it was due.

'The shape is identical to FFI,' Jiao said, surrendering her seat. 'But you won't believe the progression. It's moving so much faster.'

Stanton looked through the sights of the powerful electron microscope. Normal prion proteins were shaped like helices, like DNA, but here the helices had unwound and refolded into what looked like accordion fans.

'How long's it been since the baseline was taken?' Stanton asked.

Jiao answered, 'Only two hours.'

The prions he was used to progressed over a course of months or longer. In investigating mad cow victims, he often had to go back three or four years to find the contaminated meat. But these proteins were changing faster than anything Stanton had ever seen. With the speed of a virus.

'At this rate,' Jiao said, 'it'll take over the entire thalamus within a matter of days. And then only a few more days before brain death.'

'The infection must have been recent,' Stanton said.

Jiao nodded. 'If it weren't, he'd be dead already.'

Stanton looked up at Davies. 'We have to try the antibodies.'

'Gabe . . .'

'What antibodies?' Thane asked.

It was their most recent attempt at a cure, Stanton explained. Humans couldn't mount an 'antibody' defense against foreign prions because the immune system confused them with the normal prion proteins in the brain. So the Prion Center team had 'knocked out' these normal prions in mice (one of the side effects was making them unafraid of snakes) and then injected them with *abnormal* prions. The mice produced antibodies to the foreign prion, which could be harvested and theoretically used as a treatment. Stanton and his team hadn't gotten it to work in a human yet, but it had shown considerable potential in a petri dish.

Davies said, 'Believe me, no one wants to tell the FDA to go screw themselves more than I do. But, Gabe, you don't need another lawsuit.'

Thane asked, 'What lawsuit?'

'We don't need to go into this,' Stanton said.

'It's quite relevant,' Davies said. He turned to Thane.

'He gave a victim of genetic prion disease an unapproved treatment.'

'The family asked for antibody therapy,' Jiao interjected, 'and then after he gave it, and the patient didn't make it, they changed their minds.'

Thane shook her head. 'Gotta love patient families. The old *hypocritic* oath.'

They were interrupted by another of the postdocs. Christian wasn't wearing the earbuds through which he usually played hardcore rap at all hours – an undeniable sign of the heightened tension in the lab. 'The cops called again,' he said. 'They searched the Super 8 motel room where they picked up our John Doe, and they found a receipt from a Mexican restaurant. It's right by the hotel.'

'Where do they source their meat from?' Stanton asked.

'Industrial farm in the San Joaquin. They put out about a million pounds of beef a year. They haven't had any breaches, but they also do their own rendering.'

Stanton glanced at his partner.

'It's possible,' Davies said.

'Rendering?' Thane asked.

'You know the toothpaste you use?' Davies said, all too delighted to discuss the nastier side of the meat business. 'And the mouthwash you gargle with? How about the toys little children play with? They're all made with the byproducts of rendered meat after animals have been slaughtered.'

'Rendering was probably the original source of the mad cow outbreak,' Stanton explained. 'Cows were fed remains of other cow brains.'

'Cannibalism by force,' Thane said.

Stanton turned back to his postdoc. 'Which industrial supplier is it?'

'Havermore Farms,' said Christian.

Stanton sat up in his chair. 'The Mexican restaurant sources from Havermore?'

'Why? Do you know that name?' Thane asked.

He reached for his phone. 'They supply all the meat for the Los Angeles Unified School District.'

Havermore Farms nestled in the valley of the San Emigdio Mountains, where the wind couldn't carry its smell anywhere near civilization. It took Stanton and Davies an hour to get there in morning traffic, which left them two hours to prove that the mutated prion had come from here, before the LA public schools served Havermore Farms lunch meat to a million students.

The doctors sped past the cow pens, where thousands of cattle were crowded together. These were the slaughter animals Stanton was worried about; they were being force-fed corn, and their diets were likely being supplemented with protein cakes from the other side of the facility, a potential source of the new strain of prion.

They'd arranged to go directly to the rendering floor, where the protein cakes were made, the likeliest place for contamination. Stanton and Davies followed Mastras, the floor manager, past conveyor belts on which sat heads and hooves that once belonged to pigs, cattle and horses, and euthanized cats and dogs. Men wearing bandannas, goggles and masks yelled to one another in Spanish while bulldozing skinned and defleshed carcasses into a large pit where cow limbs were mixed with pig jaws, hair and bone. Only the traces of Vicks VapoRub they'd placed beneath their noses upon arrival kept the smell tolerable.

'We've been open with the inspectors,' Mastras said. 'They poke around, we give them feed logs, the whole thing. We've always come up clean.'

'You mean the tiny fraction of samples the USDA tests has come up clean,' Davies said.

'You know we'll be screwed as soon as word gets out you guys are investigating us,' Mastras yelled over the bulldozers. He had red hair and pasty skin, and Stanton had taken an instant dislike to him. 'It won't even matter if it's true or not.'

'We're not making anything public until we find the source,' said Davies. 'CDC is keeping this all under wraps.'

Stanton ran a quick calculation of the animal remains he could see scattered throughout the room. 'This is a lot more than what you're slaughtering here,' he said. 'Are you rendering material from other farms?'

'Some,' Mastras said. 'But we don't take any meat that's still in the plastic from supermarkets, and we don't grind up any flea collars with those insecticides either. The pound takes off the collars before dropping their animals off, or we don't take them. Bosses insist, because they want the highest standards.'

Davies said, 'Or, as we call it, the law.'

They arrived in front of a series of conveyor belts, on which carcasses of different animals came in off the trucks once they were skinned. All the belts were covered with indistinguishable organs, bloody skin, masses of mixed bones, and broken sets of teeth.

Davies started with the belt on which the pig remains were carried inside. Using forceps and an X-Acto knife, he cut samples from the belt and dropped them into a specimen retrieval cup for the ELISA – enzyme-linked immunosorbent assay – a test they'd developed years ago for finding traces of mad cow. Stanton focused on the cattle remains, placing pieces of flesh on a plastic plate with twenty different holes, each of which contained a clear protein-infused liquid. If there was any mutated prion, the solution would turn dark green.

Ten minutes later, after checking a dozen samples coming in on the conveyor belt, there was no change in any of the solutions. When Stanton repeated the process, the result was the same.

'No reaction,' Davies said as he came back across the floor.

Stanton turned to the floor manager. 'Where are your trucks?'

Out on the loading docks, they worked over every inch of the vehicles used to cart the remains in from the slaughterhouse. They swabbed and tested the bloodstained walls and floors of all twenty-two trucks.

But swab after swab was negative, and when they got through all of them, the ELISA solutions stayed clear.

Mastras was smiling now. He hopped out of the last truck and called upstairs to report that they could begin serving to LAUSD immediately.

'I told you,' Mastras said. 'We've always been clean.'

Stanton prayed they hadn't missed anything and chided himself for believing they'd find the answer so quickly. Rendering was only one of the dangerous ways man manipulated meat. They'd just have to widen their search for what made John Doe sick. With every passing hour, others could be infected.

When Stanton stepped out of the truck, he saw that Mastras had left the loading dock and walked off down the road. He was staring at something in the distance. Stanton followed the manager until he had a clear look. Dust rose up in clouds beneath the tires of vans with antennas pointed in all directions.

'Motherfucker,' Mastras said, looking back at Stanton.

News crews were speeding toward them.

6

The mass of press congregated outside Presbyterian Hospital made Chel even more nervous than she already was. The doctor she'd spoken to on the phone told her the case was highly confidential, which suited her perfectly. Her motives here were complicated, and the less attention drawn to them the better. Still, it was clear some big news story had broken; in the parking lot there were news crews and cameras and reporters everywhere.

She sat in her car, considering the odds that the press presence had anything to do with why she was here. If she went inside and there was a connection between the sick man and the book, she could end up in serious trouble. But if she didn't, she might never know how it was possible that a sick indigenous man was repeating the Mayan word for *codex* a day after Gutierrez showed up with possibly the most important document in her people's history. Her curiosity trumped her fear.

Ten minutes later, Chel stood in the patient's room on the sixth floor of the hospital with Dr Thane, her curiosity forgotten. They hovered over the patient's bed, watching a man who was suffering terribly, sweating and in obvious pain. How he had ended up here, Chel didn't know, but to die in an unfamiliar place, far from home, was the worst of all fates.

'We need to find out his name, how long he's been in the States, and when he got sick,' Thane said. 'And anything else you can tell us. Any detail could be important.'

Chel looked back at John Doe. *'Rajawxik chew . . .'* he mumbled in Qu'iche.

'Can we get him some water?' Chel asked Thane.

Thane motioned at his IV. 'He's more hydrated than I am right now.'

'He says he's thirsty.'

The doctor picked up the pitcher on John Doe's tray table, filled it in the sink, and then poured water into his cup. He grabbed it in both hands and gulped it down.

'It's safe to get close to him?' Chel asked.

'It's not contagious that way,' Thane told her. 'The disease spreads through tainted meat. The masks are so we don't give him another infection while his defenses are down.'

Chel adjusted the straps on her face mask and moved closer. It was unlikely the man worked in commerce; Maya who peddled their wares to tourists along the roads of Guatemala picked up some Spanish. He had no tattoos or piercings, so he wasn't a shaman or a daykeeper. But his palms were callused, hardened across the base of each finger, with strips of cracked skin extending from the knuckle to the butt of the thumb. It was the sign of the machete, the hand tool *indígenas* used to clear land for farming. It was also what looters used to search the jungles for ruins.

Was it possible she was looking at the man who discovered the codex?

Thane said, 'Okay, let's start with his name.'

'What is your family's name, brother?' Chel asked him. 'I am a Manu,' she said. 'My given name is Chel. What do they call you?'

'Rapapem Volcy,' he whispered hoarsely.

Rapapem, meaning *flight*. Volcy was a common surname. From the inflection of his vowels, Chel believed he was from somewhere in the south Petén.

'My family comes from El Petén,' she said. 'Does yours?'

Volcy said nothing. Chel tried asking a few different ways, but he'd gone silent.

'What about when he came to the United States?' Thane asked.

Chel translated and got a clearer answer. 'Five suns ago.'

Thane looked surprised. 'Only five days ago?'

Chel looked back at Volcy. 'You came across the border through Mexico?'

The man squirmed in his bed and didn't answer. Instead, he closed his eyes. '*Vooge,*' he repeated again.

'What about that?' Thane asked. '*Vooge*, is it? What does it mean? I looked it up with every spelling I could imagine and couldn't find anything.'

'It's *w-u-j*,' Chel explained. '*W* is pronounced like a *v*.'

'What does it mean?'

'It's the Qu'iche word we use to refer to the *Popol Vuh,* the holy creation epic of our people,' Chel said. 'He knows he's sick, and he probably wants the comfort the book gives him.'

'So he wants us to bring one to him?'

Chel reached into her bag, pulled out a tattered copy of the holy book, and set it on the nightstand. 'Like a Christian might want a Bible.'

No *indígena* would use only the word *wuj* – what the Maya called their ancient books – for the proper name of the *Popol Vuh*. But no one would question her here.

'See if he can tell us anything about when he got sick,' Thane said. 'Ask him if he remembers when he first had trouble sleeping.'

As Chel translated the doctor's questions into Qu'iche, Volcy opened his eyes a little. 'In the jungle,' he said.

Chel blinked, confused. 'You were sick in the jungle?'

He nodded.

'You were sick when you came here, Volcy?'

'For three suns before I came here, I had not slept.'

'He was sick in Guatemala?' Thane asked. 'You're sure that's what he said?'

Chel nodded. 'Why? What does that mean?'

'It means I need to make some calls.'

Chel put a hand on the crease between Volcy's neck and shoulder. It was a technique her mother had used when Chel was a little girl, to calm her after a nightmare or a bad scrape; her grandmother had done the same for her mother. As Chel rubbed her hand back and forth, she felt the tension in Volcy's body loosening. She didn't know how long the doctor would be gone. This was her chance.

'Tell me, brother,' she whispered. 'Why did you come from El Petén?'

Volcy spoke. *'Che'qriqa' ali Janotha.'*

Help me find Janotha.

'Please,' he continued. 'I have to get back to my wife and my daughter.'

She leaned in. 'You have a daughter?'

'A newborn,' he said. 'Sama. Now Janotha must care for her alone.'

Chel knew that, but for a twist of fate, she could easily have been Janotha, waiting with a newborn in a palm-thatched house for a man to come home, watching his empty hammock hanging from the roof. Somewhere in Guatemala, Janotha was pressing corn into tortillas over a hearth and promising her infant daughter that her father would return to them soon.

Volcy seemed to fade in and out, but Chel decided to press her advantage. 'Do you know the ancient book, brother?'

His eyes suddenly focused on her in a way they hadn't before.

'I have seen the *wuj*, brother,' Chel continued. 'Can you tell me about it?'

Volcy stared at her. 'I did what any man does to help his family.'

'What did you do to help your family?' she asked. 'Sell the book?'

'It was broken into pieces,' he whispered. 'On the floor of the temple . . . dried up by a hundred thousand days.'

So Chel had been right: The man lying here in front of her was the looter. Tensions in Guatemala had left *indígenas* like Volcy – manual laborers – with little option. Yet somehow, against all odds, he'd found a temple with a book that he understood would command a fortune in America. The amazing thing was that he had managed to bring it here himself.

'Brother, you brought the book to America to sell?'

'Je', Volcy said. Yes.

Chel glanced back over her shoulder to make sure she was still alone before asking, 'Did you sell it to someone? Did you sell it to Hector Gutierrez?'

Volcy said nothing.

'Tell me this,' Chel said, trying a different tack. She put a finger to her cheek. 'Did you sell it to a man with red ink on his cheek? Just above his beard?'

He nodded.

'Did you meet him here or in the Petén?'

He pointed down at the floor, at this foreign land he would no doubt die in. Volcy found the tomb, looted the book, made his way here, and somehow hooked up with Guticrrcz. Within a week, the book was sitting in Chel's lab at the Getty.

'Brother, where is this temple?' she asked. 'There is so much good that could come to our people if you will tell me where the temple is.'

Instead of answering, Volcy whipped his body toward his side table, his arms flailing at the pitcher of water. The phone and alarm clock crashed to the ground. He grabbed the top off the pitcher and poured the rest of the water into his mouth. Chel stumbled back and her chair fell to the floor.

When Volcy finished drinking, Chel reached for the end of his blanket and dried his face. She knew she had little time to get the answers she needed. He was calm again, so she pressed on. 'Can you tell me where Janotha lives?' she asked. 'What village are you and Janotha from? We can send word to your family and let them know you are here.' The temple couldn't be far from his own home.

Volcy looked confused. 'Who will you send there?'

'We have many from all over Guatemala in *Fraternidad Maya.* Someone will know the way to your village, I promise.'

'Fraternidad?'

'This is our *church,*' Chel said. 'Where Maya here in Los Angeles worship.'

Volcy's eyes filled with distrust. 'That is Spanish. You worship with *ladinos*?'

'No,' Chel said. '*Fraternidad* is a safe place of worship for the *indígenas.*'

'I will tell *ladinos* nothing!'

Chel had made a mistake. *Fraternidad* meant *brotherhood* in Spanish. Living here in Los Angeles, commingling of Spanish, Mayan and English was common. But where Volcy had come from, it was reasonable to doubt a Maya church with such a word in its name.

'*Fraternidad* cannot know,' Volcy continued. 'I will never lead the *ladinos* to Janotha and Sama. . . . *You are ajwaral!'*

There was no single English word for it. It meant literally, *You are a native of here.* But Volcy intended it as an indigenous slur. Even though Chel had been born in a village like his, even though she devoted her life to studying the ancients – to men like him, she would always be an outsider.

'Dr Manu?' said a voice from behind her.

She turned and found a white-coated figure standing in the doorway.

'I'm Gabriel Stanton.'

Chel trailed the new doctor past the masked security guard and out into the hallway. His voice was full of purpose, and his height gave him a commanding presence. How long had he been watching? Had he sensed the uncomfortable direction her conversation with Volcy had taken?

Stanton turned. 'So Mr Volcy says he was sick before he got to the States?'

'That's what he told me.'

'We have to know for sure,' Stanton told her. 'We've been looking for a source here in LA. If what he says is true, we need to be looking in Guatemala instead. Did he say where in the country he was from?'

'Based on his accent, I have to assume he's from the Petén,' she told him. 'It's the largest department – the equivalent of states. But I haven't gotten anything more about the village he's from. And he won't say how he got into America.'

'Either way,' Stanton said, 'we could be talking about Guatemalan meat as our vector. And if he's from some small indigenous village, then it has to be something he would have had access to. Far as I understand, thousands of acres of tropical forest have been cut to make way for cattle farms down there. That right?'

Chel nodded. His knowledge was impressive, and he was clearly a smart guy, if intimidating.

'Volcy could've been exposed to tainted meat from any

of those cattle farms,' Stanton said. 'We need to know all the meat he ate before his symptoms began. Far back as he can remember. Beef especially, but also chicken, pork – anything.'

'Villagers can eat meat from half a dozen different animals at a single meal.'

Dr Stanton appeared to be studying her. She noticed that the doctor's glasses were crooked and felt an unaccountable urge to fix them. He was at least a foot taller than she was, and she had to crane her neck to gaze at him.

'I need you to get him to dig as deep as he can,' Stanton said.

'I'll do my best.'

'Did he say what he's doing here? Did he come looking for work?'

'No,' she lied. 'He didn't say. He was fading in and out by the end and not really answering my questions.'

'People with this kind of insomnia can wax and wane by the minute. Let's try it another way.'

Inside the room, Volcy now lay with his eyes closed, his breathing hard and labored. Chel was afraid of how he would react when he saw her, and for a split second she considered telling Stanton the truth – coming clean about the codex and Volcy's connection to it.

But she didn't. She was too worried about ICE or the Getty finding out. She was too afraid of losing everything she'd worked for *and* the codex at the same time.

'We've learned from Alzheimer's that patients with this kind of brain damage sometimes respond better to questions if there are triggers,' Stanton said. 'The key is to go one step at a time and lead them from question to question.'

Volcy opened his eyes and looked at Stanton before turning his gaze to Chel. When they locked stares, she waited for his hostility to surface.

Nothing.

'Start with his name,' Stanton said.

'We know his name.'

'Exactly. Tell him: Your name is Volcy.'

Chel turned to the patient. *'At, Volcy ri' ab'i'.'*

When Volcy said nothing, she repeated it again. *'At, Volcy ri' ab'i'.'*

*'In, Volcy ri nub'i',' * he said finally. *My name is Volcy.* There was no hostility in his voice. It was as if he'd forgotten about their *Fraternidad* exchange.

'He understood,' Chel whispered.

'Now ask him: Did your parents call you Volcy?'

'My parents called me Daring One.'

'Keep going,' Stanton said. 'Ask him why.'

So she went on, and with each back-and-forth, Chel was amazed at how Volcy's eyes became clearer, more focused.

'Why did they call you Daring One?'

'Because I always dared to do what no boy would.'

'What was it no other boy would dare to do?'

'Go into the jungle as fearlessly as I did.'

'When you fearlessly went into the jungle as a boy, how did you survive?'

'I survived by the will of the gods.'

'The gods protected you in the jungle when you were a boy?'

'Until I offended them as a man, they protected me.'

'What happened when they stopped protecting you as a man?'

'In the jungle they would not let me pass to the other side.'

'The other side, into the dream state?'

'They would not let my soul rest or gather strength in the spirit world.'

Chel stopped the back-and-forth. She wanted to make sure she'd heard right, and she leaned in closer. 'Volcy. You were unable to pass into the dream state since you were in the jungle? Since you got the ancient book?'

He nodded.

'What's going on?' Stanton asked.

Chel ignored him. She had to know the answer. 'Where was the temple in the jungle?' she asked Volcy.

But he had gone silent again.

Stanton sounded impatient. 'Why'd he stop talking? What'd you say?'

'He said he first got sick in the jungle,' Chel said.

'Why was he in the jungle? Is that where he's from?'

'No.' Chel paused only a beat. 'He was there to do a kind of meditation. He says that during this ritual was when he first had insomnia.'

'You're sure about that?'

'I'm sure.'

What did it matter if she lied about why he was in the

jungle? Whether he was there to get the book or to meditate, either way he'd gotten sick.

'Then he left the jungle and came north?' Stanton asked.

'That's what it sounds like.'

'Why did he come across the border?'

'He didn't say.'

'Would there be cattle ranches near the jungle where he was . . . meditating?'

'I don't know what part of the Petén we're talking about,' Chel said truthfully. 'But there are cattle ranches everywhere in the highlands.'

'What would he have been eating during this jungle ritual?' Stanton asked.

'Whatever he could trap or find.'

'So he's camping, living in the jungle or on the outskirts of one of these cattle ranches. He's there for weeks, and he has to eat something. So maybe he decides to kill one of the cows.'

'I guess that's possible.'

Stanton told her to keep pursuing this line of inquiry, continuing with his word-linking technique. Which she did, steering clear of any discussion of why Volcy was in the jungle in the first place.

'Did you eat the meat of a cow in the jungle?'

'There was no cow meat to eat.'

'Did you eat the meat of a chicken in the jungle?'

'What chickens are found in the wild?'

'Wild deer are found in the jungle. Did you eat the meat of a deer?'

'I have never cooked the meat of a deer on my hearth.'

'When you were in the wild, did you bring a stone hearth to cook on?'

'We cooked only tortillas on the hearth.'

'Was this hearth used to prepare meat back in your village?'

'*Chuyum-thul* would not allow meat on the hearth. I am *Chuyum-thul,* who presides over the jungle from the sky, who has guided my human form since birth.'

Chuyum-thul was a hawk and must be Volcy's spirit animal, which Chel knew he would have been assigned by the village shaman. A man's *wayob* was a symbol of who he was: The brave man, like a king, was a jaguar; the funny man, a howler monkey; the slow man, a turtle. For both their ancerstors and the modern Maya, a man's name and his *wayob* could be used interchangeably, exactly as Volcy was now doing.

'I am *Pape,* the tiger-stripe butterfly,' Chel said. 'My human form honors my *wayob* form daily. *Chuyum-thul* knows you have shown him reverence, if you have followed his guidance about what to prepare on your hearth.'

'I have followed his guidance for twelve moons,' Volcy said, his eyes softening again when he saw she understood. 'He has shown me the souls of the animals of the jungle and how he watches over them. He told me how no human shall destroy them.'

Stanton cut in. 'What is he saying?'

Again Chel ignored him. She had earned back Volcy's trust, and she needed answers of her own before he faded away again.

'Was it the hawk who led you to the great temple, to the place where you could provide for your family?' she asked. 'For Janotha and Sama?'

Slowly he nodded.

'How far from the village was this temple *Chuyum-thul* led you to?'

'Three days' walk.'

'In which direction?'

He didn't answer.

'Please, you must tell me in which direction you went three days' walk.'

But Volcy had shut down again.

Frustrated, Chel shifted gears. 'You followed the guidance of *Chuyum-thul* for twelve moons? What was his guidance?'

'He commanded I subsist for twelve moons, that he would give me guidance to bring splendor to the village,' Volcy said. 'Then he led me to the temple.'

When she heard the words, Chel was confused. *Subsist for twelve moons?*

How could that be?

Subsistence was a practice that went back to the ancients, in which shamans would retreat to their caves to commune with the gods and survive on only water and a few fruits for months at a time.

'You have subsisted for twelve moons, brother?' Chel asked Volcy slowly. 'And have you kept that oath?'

He nodded.

'What the hell is he saying?' Stanton demanded.

Chel turned to him. 'You said this disease came from meat, right?'

'All non-genetic prion disease comes from meat. That's why I need to know what kind of meat he's eaten. As far back as he can remember.'

'He hasn't been eating any meat.'

'What are you saying?'

'He's been on a subsistence diet. For our people that means no meat.'

'That's not possible.'

'I'm telling you,' Chel said. 'He says he's been a vegetarian for the past year.'

7

Volcy's mouth, his throat, and even his stomach were as dry as if he'd sowed plots for two days straight. Like the thirst Janotha said she had felt when she delivered Sama, a thirst that couldn't be quenched. The lights flickered in and out as he opened and closed his eyes, trying to grasp how he'd gotten into the bed in the first place.

I'll never see Sama again. I'll die here, and she won't know I took the book from the ancients for her, only for her.

When the drought came, the shaman chanted and made offerings to Chaak every day, but still no rain came. Families broke up, children got shipped off to relatives in the cities, elders died from the heat. Janotha worried her milk would dry.

But you – the hawk – would never let that happen – never.

When Volcy was a boy, and his mother would go hungry to feed the children, he would creep across the floor of their hut while his parents slept, sneak out of their house, and steal maize from a family with more than they needed.

The hawk, never afraid.

Years later, Volcy had heeded the call of his *wayob* when his family was in need again. While he fasted, the hawk heard the call that would lead him to the ruins. He and his partner, Malcin, traveled three days into the forest, searching. Only Ix Chel, goddess of the moon, gave light. Malcin was afraid they might anger the gods. But slivers of pottery were being sold for thousands to white men because of the coming end of the Long Count cycle.

The gods had led them to the ruins, and, between towering trees, they found the building with walls wrecked by wind and rain. Inside the tomb was glory: obsidian blades; stucco-painted gourds and crystals; beads and pottery. A head mask and jade teeth on skulls. And the book. The cursed book. They had had no idea what the designs or words on the bark paper meant, but they were mesmerized.

Now Volcy was alone in the darkness – but where? The man and the Qu'iche woman were gone. Volcy reached for his water glass again. But the glass was empty.

He threw his legs onto the floor and lurched away unsteadily. His limbs were failing him like his vision. But he had to drink. He dragged the pole he was attached to into the bathroom, got to the sink, threw the handles wide, and shoved his head under the stream, forcing gulps. But it wasn't enough. Water doused his nostrils and mouth and ran down his face, but he needed more. The curse of the book was sucking him dry, parching every inch of his skin. He had let the white man's obsession with the Long Count compel him to sacrifice the honor of his ancestors.

The hawk lifted up from beneath the faucet and saw his face in the mirror. His head was soaked, but his thirst was still there.

Stanton, on the phone with Davies, paced in the courtyard in front of the hospital. Red and blue lights flashed everywhere; LAPD had been called in to hold back the metastasizing press. The leak about John Doe and his mysterious medical condition had apparently come from an orderly, who'd overheard Thane talking to an attending physician and posted something in a mad cow chat room. Now every major news organization in the country had dispatched reporters here as well.

'What if John Doe is lying?' Davies asked.

'Why would he lie?'

'I don't know – maybe his wife's some kind of rabid vegan, and he doesn't want her to know he's been chowing down on Big Macs.'

'Come on.'

'Okay then, maybe he got sick before he stopped eating meat?'

'You saw the slides. He got sick much more recently than a year ago.'

Davies sighed. 'Your translator said it's possible he could have had cheese or milk, right? It's time to start talking about dairy.'

They had only the testimony of one patient up against decades of research, and Stanton was still skeptical of a vector other than meat. But they had to explore the possibility. *E. coli*, Listeria, and salmonella had all been found in cow's milk, and Stanton had long feared that prion could get into the dairy supply. Per capita beef consumption in the United States was forty pounds a year; dairy was over three hundred. And milk from a single cow was often used in thousands of different products over its life-span, making finding the source that much more complicated.

'I'll see what infrastructure the Guatemalans have for tracking their dairy,' Davies said. 'But we're talking about a Third World health service investigating a disease they won't want anyone to know came from inside their borders. Not a recipe for good epidemiology.'

'How's the hospital search here going?'

'Still nothing,' Davies said. 'Team called every ER in LA, and I sent Jiao down to look at a couple of suspicious patients, but they were false alarms.'

'Have them check again,' Stanton said. 'Every twenty-four hours.'

They hung up, and Stanton hurried around the edge of the building. The press weren't the only ones crowding the parking lot; a cavalcade of ambulances was outside the ER, lights blazing. Paramedics swarmed, and doctors and nurses barked orders as patients were unloaded on stretchers. There'd been a major car accident on the 101 freeway, and dozens of critical patients had been transported here.

Stanton made another quick call as he headed back for the front door of the building. 'It's me,' he said quietly when he got Nina's voice mail again. He glanced around to make sure no one was listening. 'Do me a favor and throw your milk and cheese overboard too.'

Inside the ER, Stanton squeezed himself against the wall to make room for gurneys from the car accident flying by.

An elderly man, with his arm wrapped in gauze and a tourniquet, screamed in pain. Surgeons were operating in the non-sterile ER on patients too critical to get to the ORs. He gave silent thanks that triage wasn't his area of expertise.

Back on the sixth floor, Stanton found Chel Manu in the waiting area. Even in her heels she was tiny, and he again found his eyes drifting down to the nape of her neck, where her black hair fell. It wasn't just that she was attractive – she was clearly sharp too. She'd already managed to get key information from Volcy, so he'd asked her to stay.

'You want coffee while we wait for the nurses to finish?' he asked, motioning toward the vending machine.

'No, but I could use a cigarette,' Chel said.

Stanton dropped quarters into the slot, filling a Styrofoam cup. It was hardly groundwork, but it would have to do. 'Probably won't find many of those in here.'

She shrugged. 'Promised myself I'd quit by the end of the year anyway.'

Stanton sipped the weak coffee. 'Guess that means you don't believe the Mayan apocalypse is coming.'

'No, I don't.'

'Me neither.' He smiled, thinking they were just making easy banter, but didn't get one in return. Maybe it wasn't something she wanted to joke about.

'So what now?' she asked, deadpan.

'Soon as the nurses are done in there,' Stanton said, 'we should try to get Volcy to tell us all the dairy items he might have had in the last month or so.'

'I'll do my best,' she said, 'but I'm not sure he completely trusts me.'

'Just keep doing what you're doing.'

Stanton was surprised to find no one standing outside Volcy's room. Mariano, the security guard, was nowhere to be seen, and no replacement had arrived. Every guard in the building must have been called down to control the crowd from the freeway accident.

Inside, Stanton and Chel found nothing but an empty bed.

'Did they move him?' Chel asked.

Stanton flipped on the lights and scanned the room. Seconds later they heard a hissing coming from behind the bathroom door. He put his ear to it. 'Volcy?' The hissing was high-pitched and sounded like a leak, but there was no answer.

Turning the doorknob, Stanton found it unlocked. Then he saw Volcy. He was facedown on the ground in a pool of water. The sink was still running.

'Masam . . . ahrana . . . Janotha . . .' Volcy mumbled.

Stanton dropped to the ground and touched the patient's shoulder. 'Are you okay? Can you hear me?'

No answer.

He pulled the man's arm around his neck to lift him up. Stanton could feel how distended Volcy's body was; the man's arms, legs and torso all looked like they had been pumped too full of air. Like they were desperate to be punctured. The skin was cold.

'Get the care team!' Stanton yelled to Chel.

She seemed paralyzed.

'Go!'

Chel darted, and Stanton turned back to the patient. 'I need you to hold on to me, Volcy.' Stanton tried to get him back to the bed, where they could put him on a ventilator. '*Come on*,' he grunted, 'stay with me.'

By the time the rest of the medical team got there, Volcy was barely breathing. He had ingested so much water that it was overloading his heart, and he was close to cardiac arrest. Two nurses and an anesthesiologist joined Stanton at the bedside, and they began to inject drugs. They covered Volcy's face with an oxygen mask, but it was a losing battle. Three minutes later, Volcy's heart stopped.

The anesthesiologist applied a series of electric pulses, each stronger than the last. The defibrillator paddles left scorch marks as the patient's body arched up. Stanton began chest compressions, something he hadn't done since his residency. He threw his weight down from his shoulders and delivered a series of rapid pulses to Volcy's chest, just above the sternum. The body rose and fell with each, *one*, *two*, *three*, *four* . . .

Finally the anesthesiologist grabbed Stanton's arm and urged him back from the bed. She said the words: 'Time of death twelve twenty-six p.m.'

More ambulances screamed from the 101 freeway toward the ER. Stanton tried to block out the sounds while he and Thane watched the orderly team lifting Volcy's corpse into the body bag.

'He's been sweating for a week straight, right?' Thane said. 'He must have been dehydrated.'

Stanton looked down at the blue, bloated corpse. 'This didn't come from his kidneys. It came from his brain.'

Thane looked confused. 'You mean like a polydipsia?'

Stanton nodded. Patients with psychogenic polydipsia were driven to drink excessively: sinks had to be disabled, toilets drained. In the worst cases, like this one, the heart failed due to fluid overload. Stanton had never seen an FFI patient do it before, but he was angry at himself for not considering the possibility.

'I thought that was a symptom of schizophrenia.' Thane was rummaging through the man's chart, trying to grasp what had happened.

'After a week without sleep, he might as well have had schizophrenia.'

As the orderlies zipped the body bag, Stanton imagined Volcy's horrific last minutes. Schizophrenia caused abnormalities in the perception of reality; FFI patients exhibited many of the same symptoms. Stanton had often wondered if sleep was all that kept healthy people out of insane asylums.

'What happened to Dr Manu?' Thane asked.

'She was here a minute ago.'

'Guess you can't blame her for freaking when she saw this.'

'She was the last person to talk to him,' Stanton said. 'We need her to write down everything he said as precisely as possible. Track her down.'

The orderlies lifted Volcy's body onto the gurney and

wheeled it out. After the corpse was prepared, Stanton would meet the pathologists down in the morgue for the autopsy.

'I should've been here,' Thane said. 'I got pulled down to the ER. They're sending way too many critical patients here from that accident. It looks like an Afghan fucking field clinic down there now.'

'Nothing you could've done,' Stanton said, pulling off his glasses.

'Some asshole falls asleep in his SUV on the freeway, and the rest of our patients suffer,' Thane said.

He walked to the window, moved the curtain aside, and gazed down below. A siren blared as yet another ambulance pulled into the ER bay. 'The driver that caused the crash fell asleep at the wheel?' he asked.

Thane shrugged. 'That's what the cops said.'

Stanton focused on the flashing lights below.

8

It was painful for Hector Gutierrez to lie to his wife about the trouble he was in and even more painful to think that, if he got caught, their little boy probably wouldn't even recognize him by the time his father got out of prison. Hector thanked God he'd already emptied the storage unit before the cops had raided it. But he was sure his house was next. His source at ICE who'd tipped him off (and been paid handsomely for doing so) said they'd been gathering evidence against him for months. If they found everything, Hector could face up to ten years.

Maria wasn't working on Monday, so he couldn't move the goods out of the house until the next day. Instead, he took Ernesto to Six Flags, where the two of them hurtled around on old roller coasters. It made Hector happy that his son had a blast, but he was convinced someone was following them, tracking them through the park. There were shadows in the funnel-cake lines and lingering faces at the arcade. He sweated anxiously all day, despite the fact that winter had finally come to LA. By the time they got back home, he'd soaked through his shirt and socks.

That night, he cranked up the air-conditioning and watched an hour of sitcoms with Maria, desperately trying to figure out how to tell her what was going on. By two a.m., she'd already been asleep for hours, blissfully unaware, while Hector was still wide awake in front of the TV and covered in sweat. Not since his teenage love affair with cocaine had he felt so on edge. His ears stung with every noise: the hum of the cable box, the teeth-clenching sound Ernesto made when he slept, the cars out on 94th Street, each of which sounded like it was coming for him.

Past three, Hector climbed into bed. His mouth was dry, and he could barely keep his eyes open. But still he couldn't sleep, and every turn of the clock was another reminder of how little night was left – he had a huge day of moving everything out of the house ahead of him. Finally he woke his wife in a last-ditch effort to tire himself out.

Even after the most electric sex they'd had in months, he couldn't sleep. Hector lay naked next to Maria for almost two hours, soaking through the sheets, flesh and fabric glued together by sweat. He rapped his head against the mattress. Then he got up and surfed the Internet, where he found pills from Canada that promised sleep within ten minutes. But of course you had to call during regular business hours.

Soon came the chirping of birds, and behind the shades Hector saw the first rays of a new day. He lay awake for another hour. When he got up, he cut himself shaving. His hands were shaking from exhaustion. Fortunately, after downing oatmeal and coffee in the kitchen, he experienced a surge of energy. When he stepped outside to catch the bus, the breeze was a balm.

By seven a.m., he was at a garage near LAX, where he picked up the green Ford Explorer with fake plates he used when he needed to covertly transport antiquities. When he was sure Maria and Ernesto had left, he returned to the house to cart the rest of the items he had hidden in his home to the new facility he'd rented in West Hollywood that nobody knew about.

The sweating was bad again by the time he reached Our Lady of the Angels, where he had found Chel Manu. But he'd managed to hide his suffering and to convince her to take the codex. Either she'd find a way to pay, or she was the perfect solution to his problem. If he got pulled in, she was a far bigger fish for ICE. There was no one they'd rather make an example of than a curator. He'd get full immunity if he testified against her.

Following his visit to the church, Hector tried to focus on the traffic speeding by. The neon billboards on the 101 appeared dull to him, as if someone had bled the colors out. The regular noises of the car and its engine were hammers on his eardrums. He spent the rest of the day checking places he frequently did business with buyers and sellers. Paying bribes to motel clerks and body shop mechanics and strip club bouncers. Trying to get rid of any evidence ICE could use against him.

Halfway home that night, Hector panicked when he saw a black Lincoln in his rearview. By the time he got back to Inglewood and parked several blocks from the house, he'd gone back and forth a dozen times in his mind on whether the car had been following him.

Maria was watching him from the window when he walked up the driveway. She started yammering and wouldn't let him get a word in. It'd been almost thirty-six hours since Hector had last slept, and she could see it in his eyes. She immediately gave him a glass of red wine, turned the stereo to classical music, and lit candles. Her mother was an insomniac, and she'd learned all the tricks.

Yet at two a.m., Hector lay awake next to her in their bed, reflecting on his life. Each hour became a referendum: at three, he judged himself a good father; at four, a bad husband.

Finally he nestled against Maria again, stroking her breasts. But when she put her hand between his legs, Hector couldn't get an erection. Even when she straddled him, nothing happened. Every part of Hector's body was betraying him, all the things he never thought to doubt. He apologized to Maria, then, with his hands shaking, his eyes blurry, and his breathing labored, he went out to the stoop and sat alone in the chilly night. When he saw the first planes swooping in from overhead, signaling another dawn without sleep, Hector felt something else he hadn't in years: the urge to cry.

He heard a voice coming from somewhere behind him. Who the hell was in his house at five o'clock in the morning? Hector stormed back into the kitchen. It took him a second to process who in the hell the man standing there was.

It was *the birdman*. The birdman was at Hector's dinner table.

'What are you doing in my house?' Hector demanded. '*Get out!*'

The birdman stood up, and before the man could respond, Hector threw a quick blow across his chin, knocking him onto the floor.

Maria ran into the room. *'What did you do?'* she screamed. 'Why did you hit him?'

When Hector pointed at the birdman to try to explain, nothing made sense. The crumpled person on the floor was Ernesto, looking back at him in shock.

'Papa,' the boy cried.

Hector felt as if he might vomit. Long ago he'd sworn to Maria he'd never take his anger out on her or their son the way his father had on him. She started flailing at him. He wasn't even thinking as he threw his wife to the floor.

The last time Maria Gutierrez saw her husband, he was running down the street toward the Ford Explorer.

9

Every corner of the Presbyterian ER was filled with trauma patients. Stanton hurried through the aftermath of the highway accident. Bumping into techs. Knocking over crash carts. Frantically searching for the man who caused this. Car accidents were common in FFI case reports; in one German case, it was the first sign that the insomnia had become complete. From a witness's perspective it appeared the driver had fallen asleep on the autobahn.

Stanton ripped back curtain after curtain in the overwhelmed ER, behind which he saw unsupervised surgical residents performing operations they had no business attempting and nurses making medical decisions alone because there weren't enough doctors. The one thing he didn't see was anyone who could tell him who caused the accident and whether the person had been brought here.

Stanton stopped and scanned the room. Two paramedics stood across the bay, conscripted into service because the hospital was so understaffed.

He ran over. They were squeezing oxygen through a patient's mask. 'Were you guys on the scene? Who caused the accident?'

'Latino guy,' one of them said.

'Where is he? Here?'

'Look for a John Doe.'

Stanton studied the patient board. Another John Doe? Even if there was no ID on the driver, they should've tracked his car already.

Near the bottom of the board, he found an unnamed patient. He darted back toward curtain 14. Tore it open. There was a flurry of motion inside – doctors yelling orders and moaning coming from the bloody, writhing man.

'I have to talk to him.' Stanton flashed his CDC ID.

They looked confused but gave him room to approach.

He leaned close to the man's ear. 'Sir, have you had trouble sleeping?'

No answer.

'Have you been sick, sir?'

The monitors beeped loudly. 'His pressure's falling,' warned one of the nurses.

An ER doc pushed Stanton out of the way. Injected the man's IV with more drugs. They all watched the monitor. Pressure continued to drop as the man's heart slowed.

'Crash cart!' yelled the other doctor.

'Sir!' Stanton called out from behind them. 'What is your name?'

'Ernesto had his face,' the driver groaned finally. 'I didn't mean to hit him. . . .'

'Please,' Stanton said, 'your name!'

The driver's eyes flickered. 'I thought Ernesto was the birdman. The birdman did this to me.'

These words sent a shiver through Stanton that he couldn't explain. 'The birdman,' he pressed. 'Who is the birdman?'

A long sigh came from the driver's throat, then the familiar sequence followed: flatline, yelling, crash cart, paddles, injections, more yelling. Then silence. And time of death.

Chel sat in her office at the Getty, smoking her pack's last cigarette. She'd never watched a man die before. After seeing Volcy expire on the table, she'd fled without a word to the doctors. For hours, she'd ignored phone calls from the hospital, including two from Stanton. She just stared numbly at her computer screen, refreshing the relevant sites again and again.

The CDC knew Volcy was a vegetarian, but the press was still focusing their coverage on how his disease probably came from tainted meat. The blogosphere was on fire with headlines about the Long Count and nutty theories about how it couldn't be a coincidence that some new strain similar to mad cow had appeared only a week before 12-21.

There was a quiet knock on her office door, followed by Rolando Chacon popping his head inside. 'Got a minute?'

She waved him in. He'd listened without judgment as she told him about the hospital, including how she'd lied to the doctors about Volcy's reasons for coming to the States.

'You okay?' Rolando asked, taking the seat in front of her.

She shrugged.

'Maybe you should go home and get some sleep.'

'I'm fine,' she said. 'What is it?'

'The C-14 dating came back: 930 plus or minus 150. Exactly what we thought. Middle of the terminal classic.'

Chel should have been ecstatic. This was the proof they'd been waiting for. Everything she'd learned and understood about her work had come together, and the codex could be a portal to immense understanding. Still, she felt nothing.

'Great,' she told Ronaldo without emotion.

'I'm also moving forward with the reconstruction,' he said. 'But there's a problem.' He passed Chel a piece of paper, on which he'd drawn two symbols:

In ancient Mayan, they were pronounced *chit* and *unen*. 'A father, and a male child of the father,' Chel said absently. 'A father and his son.'

'But that's not how the scribe is using it.' Rolando handed her another page. 'That's a rough translation of the second paragraph.'

The father and his son is not noble by birth, and so there is much the father and his son will never fathom about the ways of the gods that watch over us, there is much

> the father and his son does not hear that the gods would whisper in the ears of a king.

'So it has to be one thing he's referring to,' Rolando said. 'One noble. One king. Something like that. Whatever it is, the pair of symbols appears all over the manuscript.'

Chel studied the glyphs again. Scribes commonly used word pairings in new ways for stylistic flourish, so it was likely this one was using the pair to signify something other than the literal translation.

'Could it have something to do with noble titles being passed down from fathers to their sons?' Rolando asked. 'Patrilinearity?'

Chel doubted it but was having trouble focusing. 'Let me think about it.'

Rolando tapped on her desk. 'I know you don't want to hear this, and I understand your concerns, really. But this is really a syntax question, and Victor's the best there is. He could be very helpful with this, and I think you have to put your personal issues aside.'

'You and I can figure it out,' Chel said.

'Until we know what this is, it'll be difficult to make much more progress. On the first page alone the combination appears ten times after the first paragraph. On some of the later pages it shows up two dozen times.'

'*I'll* work on it,' Chel told him. 'Thanks,' she added.

Rolando retreated into the lab, and Chel went back to her laptop. Checking the *Los Angeles Times* site, she found newly posted articles about Volcy and Presbyterian. But something else caught her attention: photographs of cars piled up atop one another on the 101 freeway, and people being pulled from the wreckage.

In the middle of it all was a green SUV.

Stanton stood with Davies in the morgue, deep in the basement of the hospital. The driver's body lay on one metal table; beside them, on a second table, lay Volcy's.

Davies made an incision from ear to ear on the driver's skull, then draped the flap of skin and removed the skull-cap to expose the brain.

'Ready,' he said.

Stanton stepped forward, cut the central cortex away from the cranial nerves, and disconnected it from the spinal cord. Reaching inside, he removed the brain from its skull. Hidden in the folds of this organ was his best hope for figuring out VFI. He placed the brain on a sterile table, trying to ignore the fact that it was still warm.

Stanton and Davies began to slice. During his gross exam of the thalamus, Stanton saw clusters of tiny holes; under the microscope he saw a wasteland of craters and deformed tissue. Textbook FFI. Only much, much more aggressive.

'Anything?' Davies asked.

'Give me a second.' Stanton rubbed his eyes.

'You look knackered,' Davies said.

'I have no idea what that means.'

'You look like shit. You need to sleep, Gabe.'

'We all do.'

Davies snickered. 'I'll sleep when I'm like these blokes.'

'Come on.'

'Too soon?'

Once they finished with the driver's brain, they performed the same operation on Volcy's distended body. When they had sections from both brains ready, Stanton put his eye to the microscope again, upping the background light. The craters in Volcy's brain ran deeper and the cortex looked more deformed. He had definitely been infected first.

Stanton had suspected as much, but until now he hadn't realized what he could do with the information. 'Make images of all these sections,' he told Davies. 'And I want you to find the MRIs we took of Volcy when he was still alive. Figure out how fast the disease was spreading in his brain, then model everything backward. If we can figure out the rate of progression, then we can estimate when they both got sick.'

Davies nodded. 'A timeline.'

If they could determine when Volcy took ill, they might be able to figure out *where* he'd gotten sick. With luck, they could do the same for the driver. The driver was the key: Someone in this city knew him. Once the driver was identified, there'd be bank statements and credit-card receipts showing where he bought his groceries, where he ate. A paper trail leading straight to the source.

'Cavanagh's on the line,' Davies said, holding out his cellphone.

Stanton peeled off his second layer of gloves. Into the phone he said one word: 'Confirmed.'

Cavanagh took a deep breath. 'You're sure?'

'Same disease, different stages.'

'I'm getting on a plane right now. Tell me what you need to keep this under control.'

'An ID on the driver. We have two patients, and they were both John Does when they came in.' The Explorer was unregistered, and its driver, like Volcy, carried nothing to identify him. The worry was that this somehow wasn't a coincidence. But what would that mean?

'The police are working on it,' Cavanagh said. 'What else?'

'The public needs to know we found a second case. And they need to know it from us. Not from some blogger who makes half of it up.'

'If you're asking for a press conference, the answer is no. Not yet. Everyone in the city will think they're sick.'

'Then at least get the grocery stores to put a hold on dairy, and meat too, just to be safe. Get USDA to investigate all possible imports from Guatemala. And tell people they need to throw away the milk and all the rest in their refrigerators.'

'Not until we confirm the source of the disease.'

'If you want confirmation, get all of our agents here checking the pupil size of every patient in every hospital,' he said. 'And I'm not just talking about LA. I'm talking about the valley, Long Beach, Anaheim. I need more than two data points.'

'I'm supervising agents on the ground there already. Let them do their jobs.'

Stanton pictured Cavanagh's unflappable stare. She'd become the brightest star at CDC in 2007, when an airplane passenger was suspected of carrying drug-resistant

TB. She was one of the few at the center to remain levelheaded until the scare passed and had been a favorite in Washington ever since. But now wasn't the time to be levelheaded.

'How can you be so calm?' Stanton asked Cavanagh.

'Because I have you to not be,' she said. 'Now tell me something. How much sleep have *you* gotten? I'll be on the ground in six hours, and I'm going to need you sharp and rested. If you haven't slept, do it now.'

'Emily, I don't –'

'I wasn't making a suggestion, Gabe. That was an order.'

Back in Venice, Stanton was surprised to see that nothing had changed. The evening crowds were in the beer gardens. Homeless drifters sat beneath the retail-shop awnings. Out on the boardwalk, men were still hawking charms to ward off the Maya apocalypse. For a moment, all this life made Stanton feel a bit better.

Just after eleven p.m., he stood in his kitchen, on the phone with the chief medical officer for the Guatemalan Health Service, Dr Fernando Sandoval.

'Mr Volcy told us that he came across the border *after* he was already sick,' Stanton said. 'He was clear about that. You need to search clinics, facilities on the Pan-American Highway, and every local doctor's office that serves indigenous people.'

'We have teams searching the area where he says he got sick,' Sandoval told him. 'Despite the fact that it will cost us millions of dollars we don't have, we've got people visiting every farm in the entire Petén and sampling cattle. So far they've come up with nothing, of course. Not a single trace of prion of any kind.'

'Not yet. But you understand how urgent this is, don't you? From what we're seeing here, you could have an epidemic soon.'

'There's zero evidence that your second patient was ever here, Dr Stanton.'

They'd broadcast the second victim's photograph everywhere on the evening news, but no family or friends of the driver had come forward. 'We haven't ID'd him yet, but –'

'We have no other cases, and it is irresponsible of you to suggest anything of the kind. Neither of your patients got sick here. Though of course we will do everything we can to aid you in your investigation.'

The call ended abruptly, leaving Stanton frustrated. With no reported cases, the Guatemalans weren't scared enough yet to take real action. Until they had a confirmed case of their own, Stanton knew it would be hard to get much at all from them, and, even then, their public-health capabilities were poor.

Stanton heard a key going into the lock and animal feet scurrying across the floor. He hurried to the living room, where he found Nina in worn jeans, a windbreaker, and still-glistening galoshes. Dogma ran toward him, and Nina followed, looping her arms around Stanton's neck.

'Guess you found a place to dock, Captain,' he said, kissing her on the cheek.

'Should be fine until sunrise. You look like shit.'

'So everyone keeps telling me.'

Dogma started to whine, and Stanton rubbed the dog's ears in circles.

Nina peeled off her coat. 'When was the last time you ate something?'

'No idea.'

Nina beckoned him into the kitchen. 'Don't make me use force.'

There was a half-eaten container of Chinese delivery in the fridge, and she made Stanton eat it but let him listen to NPR updates while he did. The news program's host was interviewing a CDC communications specialist Stanton had never heard of. They were talking about VFI in a way that made it obvious neither one of them had any real knowledge of prion science. A tightness grew in Stanton's chest.

'What's wrong?' Nina asked.

He fiddled with his fork, pressing liquid from the microwaved cubes of tofu. 'This is going to get worse.'

'Good thing they've got you, then.'

'Soon people'll realize we don't know how to control a disease like this.'

'You've been warning them about this day forever.'

'I don't mean CDC. I mean everyone else who'll ask why we have no vaccine. Congress will go crazy. They'll want to know what we've been doing since mad cow.'

'You did everything you could. Always have.'

Her voice was comforting. He reached out and took her hand. There was so much he wanted to say.

Nina kissed the back of his hand, led him into the living room, and turned on the TV. She leaned her head on his shoulder. Wolf Blitzer reported from the Situation Room, explaining that the identity of the second patient was still unknown.

'Do you have enough supplies on the boat?' Stanton asked her.

'For what?' she said. 'Don't get glass-half-empty on me. It depresses the dog.'

Looking at her, Stanton felt something he'd never expected before tonight. After a decade in the lab, a decade of fighting for funding to improve prion-disease readiness, a decade of warning that an outbreak was always just one accident away, now the unavoidable had come, and all Stanton wanted was to follow Nina back to the dock, get on *Plan A* with her and Dogma, and forget prion disease forever.

'What if we left?' Stanton asked.

Nina lifted her head. 'And went where?'

'Who knows? Hawaii?'

'Don't do this, Gabe.'

'I'm serious,' he said, staring into her eyes. 'All I want is to be with you right now. I don't care about anything else. I love you.'

She smiled, but there was something sad in it. 'I love you too.'

Stanton leaned forward to kiss her, but before he could plant his lips on hers, Nina turned away.

'What?' he asked, pulling back.

'You're under a lot of pressure, Gabe. You'll get through this.'

'I want to get through it with you. Tell me what you want.'

'Please, Gabe.'

'Tell me.'

She didn't look away as she spoke. 'I want someone who doesn't care if he shows up late to work because we spent too long in bed. Someone who'd actually get on that boat and leave all this behind. You're the most driven man I've ever known, and I love that about you. But even if you came with me, in two days you'd be swimming back to the lab. You wouldn't really walk away. Especially now.'

Stanton wanted to prove to her that the man she was describing didn't exist, that it was a made-up version of him she'd concocted long ago. But at some level he knew she was right. He wasn't getting on any boat right now.

Nina laid her head on his shoulder again. They sat in silence, and soon Stanton heard the slow breathing he knew so well. He wasn't surprised; Nina could sleep anywhere, anytime – on park benches, in theaters, on crowded beaches. Stanton closed his eyes too. The tenseness in his jaw lessened. He thought of calling Davies, to ask how the timeline was going. But the notion floated away in a wave of exhaustion and sadness. He wanted to hide in the comfort of unconsciousness.

Still, sleep wouldn't come. As he watched the minutes tick by, he found himself reiterating all the reasons he couldn't be sick. He hadn't consumed dairy in months. He hadn't had meat in years. Yet he found himself appreciating Cavanagh's concerns about how easy it might be for people to believe they had VFI.

Stanton picked up Nina and carried her into the bedroom, putting her on her old side of the bed. Dogma wandered in, and although he rarely allowed the dog on the bed, Stanton patted the mattress several times, and Dogma came bounding up and lay next to Nina.

Stanton was heading to his study to check email again when his cellphone buzzed with a number he didn't recognize.

'Dr Stanton? It's Chel Manu. Sorry to disturb you so late.'

'Dr Manu. Where did you go? We've been calling you.'

'I'm sorry it's taken me so long to get back to you.'

Stanton heard something in her voice. 'Are you all right?'

'I need to talk to you.'

10

The street vendors who'd won a lottery spot on the seaward side of the boardwalk were gone, their African reeds and birdhouses and octopus bongs packed in crates until morning. It was just after midnight, and the police were sweeping the beaches for partyers and the homeless. Stanton opened his front door to find Chel standing on his stoop.

He motioned her toward two weathered wicker chairs on the porch of his condo. Barefoot men and women poured toward them like newly hatched amphibians crawling onto the land, searching for a place to curl up until the beach reopened at five.

As Stanton and Chel sat, a hulking Asian man wearing a heavy overcoat and camouflage pants stepped onto the boardwalk, carrying a sign: PARTY LIKE IT'S 2012. He plopped down in the middle of Ocean Front Walk, directly across from them. 'It will be completed the thirteenth *b'ak'tun*,' he chanted.

Stanton shook his head and turned to Chel, who stared at the man with a look he couldn't categorize.

'What can I do for you?' Stanton asked her.

He listened in disbelief as she told him her story, beginning with the codex, through the real reason for her trip to the hospital. Once she finished, he had trouble resisting the urge to shake her. 'Why the hell did you lie to us?'

'Because the manuscript was looted, so it's illegal for me to have it,' she said. 'But there's something else you should know too.'

'What?'

'I think the man who caused the accident on the 101 is the man who gave me the codex in the first place. His name's Hector Gutierrez. He's an antiquities dealer.'

'How do you know it was him?'

'I watched him drive away from my church in that same car.'

'Jesus. Was Gutierrez sick when you saw him?'

'He just seemed anxious to me. I'm not sure.'

Stanton processed this. 'Did Gutierrez ever travel to Guatemala?'

'I don't know. He may well have.'

'Wait a second. Were you lying about Volcy being sick before he came here?'

'No, that was what he told me. The only thing I didn't tell you was that he started having trouble sleeping near the temple he looted the book from. He wasn't out there meditating. But he really hadn't been eating meat for a year.'

Stanton was furious. 'The Guatemalans have teams on the ground searching every dairy farm in the Petén because of the information you gave us. And they already think we're wasting their time and money. Now we have to tell them our translator lied, and they should be searching for ruins in the jungle?'

A skateboarder rolled down the boardwalk and called out, 'Chill, bro.'

'I'll tell immigration everything,' Chel whispered after the kid had passed.

'You think I give a shit about immigration? This is about public safety. If you hadn't lied, we could have asked him more questions, and we could already be searching the jungle for the real source.'

Chel ran a shaky hand through her hair. 'I know that now.'

'What else did he tell you?'

'He said the temple where he got the book was three days' walk from his village in the Petén,' she said. 'Less than a hundred miles, probably.'

'Where's his village?'

Hair strands blew across Chel's face in the ocean wind. 'He wouldn't say.'

'So somewhere in the vicinity of those ruins,' Stanton said, 'could be VFI's original source. Some sick cow putting off milk that's being shipped all over the world. Hell, for all we know, the runoff could be going into the water supply down there. Did he tell you anything that could point us toward it? Anything at all?'

Chel shook her head. 'The only other things he told me were that his spirit animal was a hawk and that he had a wife and daughter.'

'What's a spirit animal?'

'It's an animal every Maya gets paired with at birth. He said his was *Chuyum-thul*. The hawk.'

Stanton was pulled back to the ER, where he'd watched

the other victim die. 'Gutierrez said, *The birdman did this to me*,' he told Chel. 'He was blaming Volcy for getting him sick.'

'Why would he do that?'

'Maybe Volcy brought some kind of food across the border with him, not realizing it was what got him sick in the first place.'

'And what could that be?'

'You tell me,' Stanton said. 'What would a Maya man give to someone he does business with? Something Gutierrez could've eaten or drunk with dairy in it?'

'There are a lot of possibilities,' Chel said.

Suddenly Stanton turned for his door. 'Meet me at my car,' he told her, his voice full of purpose. 'Around back.'

'Why?'

'Because before you turn yourself in to the police, we're going to find out.'

11

What did it say about her, Chel wondered, that even now she was fixated on the codex and the fact that she'd probably never be allowed to see it again? That she might never get a chance to find out who the writer was and why he risked his life to go against his king? What did it say about her that even now, as she and the doctor drove toward Gutierrez's house, she was still focused on all the wrong things? To Stanton, sitting silently in the driver's seat, Chel knew she was beneath contempt. He'd spent his life trying to stop disease from spreading, and her little academic exercise had put the whole city at risk.

Strangely, it was Patrick's voice she now heard in her head. They were in Charlottesville, Virginia, for a meeting about the Mayan Epigraphic Database Project, and they were planning to hike the Appalachian Trail after it was over. When Chel told him she'd agreed to head another committee and couldn't go, Patrick gave it to her. 'Someday you'll realize you've sacrificed too much for your work, and you can't get it back,' he'd said. Chel thought he was speaking out of spite, and that it would blow over like all the other times. He'd moved out a month later.

She shifted in her seat and felt something catch on the heel of her shoe: a dog's leash. From the size of the collar, it looked like the dog wasn't a small one.

'Throw it in the back,' Stanton said, no warmth discernible in his voice. It was the first he'd spoken on their journey south. Chel watched him as he drove, both hands on the wheel like a driving-school student. Probably he was the type who never broke any rule. Stanton seemed to her to be a stern man, and Chel wondered if he was as lonely as he appeared. At least he had a dog. Chel stared out the windshield at the billboard-dotted Pacific Coast Highway. Maybe she'd get a pet once they fired her from the Getty and she had more time on her hands.

'Give it to me,' Stanton said.

Chel glanced over. 'What?' Then she realized she was still clutching the dog's leash, ridiculously. Stanton reached for it and tossed it into the backseat as he accelerated.

Chel had remembered that Hector Gutierrez lived in Inglewood, north of the airport. As they pulled up in front of the two-story Californian, she didn't know what to expect. It was still possible the man's family had no idea what had happened; no one had come forward yet to ID him.

'Let's go,' Stanton said, turning off the car engine.

At the front door, he knocked, and a minute later a light went on inside. A raven-haired Latina woman came to the door in a long navy robe. Her puffy eyes suggested she'd been crying. It was clear to Chel that she already knew. And Chel also realized why she hadn't gotten in touch with the authorities: not only had the woman lost her husband, she was in danger of losing everything else. ICE and the FBI were unrelenting in their seizures of black-market profits.

'Mrs Gutierrez?'

'Yes?'

'I'm Dr Stanton from the Centers for Disease Control. This is Chel Manu, who has done business with your husband. We're here with some very difficult news. Did you know your husband was involved in an accident today?'

Maria nodded slowly.

'May we come in?' Stanton asked.

'Outside is fine,' she said. 'My son is trying to sleep.'

'We're very sorry for your loss, Mrs Gutierrez,' Stanton said. 'I can only imagine what you and your son must be going through right now, but I have to ask you some questions.' He paused, and when she finally nodded, he continued. 'Your husband was very sick, wasn't he?'

'Yes.'

'Have *you* been having any trouble sleeping?' Stanton asked.

'My husband was awake the entire night for the last two nights. Now I have to explain to my son that he's dead. So, yes, I have had a little trouble sleeping.'

'Any unusual sweating?' Stanton pressed.

'No.'

'Have you heard what's happening at Presbyterian Hospital?'

Maria pulled the robe tighter around her. 'I've seen the news.'

Stanton said, 'Well, another man was very sick and died this morning, and we now know that he and your husband had the same disease. We believe the disease is spreading through some food item that could have been given to your husband by the first patient when he came up from Guatemala. Do you have any idea when or where your husband might've done business with a man named Volcy?'

Maria shook her head. 'I didn't know any of Hector's business.'

'We need to search your house, Mrs Gutierrez, to see if we can find out anything more. And we need to sample everything in your refrigerator.'

Maria covered her face with her hand, rubbing her eyes, as if she couldn't bear to look at them anymore.

'This is an emergency,' Stanton said. 'You have to help us.'

'No,' Maria said, resisting weakly. 'Please leave.'

'Mrs Gutierrez,' Chel said. 'Yesterday morning your husband came to me with a stolen object and asked me to hold it for him. And I did it. I did it, and then I lied about it, and it turns out my lie might mean more people are sick now. I'll have to live with that. But you won't if you listen to us. Please let us come in.'

Stanton turned back to Chel, surprised by the commitment in her voice.

Maria opened the door.

They followed her down a narrow hallway lined with photographs of soccer games and backyard birthday parties. In the kitchen, Stanton pulled everything out of the refrigerator and had Chel do the same with the pantries. They soon had more than sixty items on the countertop, including many with dairy in them, but none came from

Guatemala, and none was unusual or imported. Stanton quickly searched through the trash and found nothing of interest there either.

'Is there anywhere your husband worked when he was home?' Stanton asked.

Maria led them to a study on the far end of the house. A stained white couch, a metal desk, and a few low bookshelves sat on top of an imitation Oriental rug. The small room reeked of cigarette smoke. The rest of the house was a shrine to the family, but there were no pictures inside the office. Whatever he did in here, Gutierrez didn't want his son or his wife watching him do it.

Stanton started with the desk drawers. Tearing each one open, he found office supplies, a mess of bills, and other household paperwork: mortgage documents, payroll forms, electronics manuals.

Chel pulled her glasses out and focused on the computer. 'There isn't a dealer in the world who doesn't sell online now,' she told Stanton.

She went on eBay. Log-in HGD*ealer* popped up, asking for a pass-word.

'Try *Ernesto*,' Maria said from the doorway.

A list of items appeared on the screen.

1. Authentic Pre-Columbian flint $1,472.00 sale completed
2. Mayan sarcophagus section $1,200.00 auction expired
3. Authentic Mayan stone planter $904.00 sale completed
4. Jade Mayan necklace $1,895.00 sale completed
5. Honduran clay jar artifact $280.00 auction expired
6. Classic Mayan jaguar bowl $1,400.00 sale completed

'It stores sold items for sixty days,' Chel said. 'This is what he's unloaded or tried to unload over the last two months.'

'This is what Gutierrez was selling, right?' Stanton asked. 'But he *bought* the book. Do we have to get into Volcy's account for that?' Scanning the interface, he asked, 'How would Volcy have even known how to use a site like this? Where would he have gotten access?'

'Everyone down there knows how it works,' Chel said. 'People will travel for days to get to a computer if they have items to sell. But he wouldn't have sold a codex on eBay anyway. It would draw too much attention. The most expensive item here costs less than fifteen hundred dollars; there's a limit to what people are willing to pay for something online. So sellers with high-end items find a way to make contact on eBay, then do their business in person.'

She clicked on a tab at the top and up popped an eBay email window, with an in-box full of nearly a thousand messages. Many of them were exchanges about items Gutierrez had listed here. But there were also messages with places and dates and times he was planning to meet people looking to sell items to him.

'They all use screen names,' Chel said.

'How can we find out which one could be Volcy?'

Stanton looked for Maria, but she had left the room.

'Look,' Chel said. She moved the cursor over a message that had been sent a week ago from screen name *Chuyum-thul*.

The hawk.

From: Chuyum-thul
Sent: Dec. 5, 2012 10:25 a.m.

Something very valuable I possess, definitely you will want.

Reach Phone +52 553 77038

'It looks like it was translated for him by the computer,' said Chel. 'The way he's writing is basically Mayan syntax.'

'Where is country code fifty-two?'

'Mexico,' Chel said. 'And the area code is Mexico City. It's an antiquities hotbed, and probably Volcy's best chance south of the border at getting a decent price for the book. If he couldn't get what he wanted there, then he'd have turned to the States.'

The sound of a child crying came from upstairs. Stanton and Chel exchanged a look of pity, but continued searching. When Chel found an email addressed to *Chuyum-thul*, the circle started to close:

From: HGDealer
Sent: Dec. 6, 2012 2:47 p.m.

Friday, December 7, 2012
AG Flight 224
Depart Mexico City, Mexico (MEX) 6:05 a.m.
Arrive Los Angeles, CA (LAX) 9:12 a.m.

Tuesday, December 11, 2012
AG Flight 126
Depart Los Angeles, CA (LAX) 7:20 a.m.
Arrive Mexico City, Mexico (MEX) 12:05 p.m.

Chel said, 'Gutierrez must have bought Volcy this ticket.'

Stanton pieced together the chronology. Volcy got on a plane from Mexico, sold Gutierrez the codex, then holed up in a Super 8, waiting for his flight back. Only that night the cops were called, and they took him to the hospital. He never got on AG 126 back to Mexico City.

'What happened to the money Gutierrez paid him? The cops didn't find any money in the hotel room.'

Chel said, 'He would have known better than to try to fly across the border with that much cash. Probably deposited it into an account of a bank here that has branches in Central America.'

But then Stanton glanced back at Volcy's itinerary, and suddenly something else struck him: AG flight 126. It was strangely familiar.

Then he realized why. 'The return flight *crashed* yesterday morning.'

Chel looked up. 'What are you talking about?'

Stanton pulled out his smartphone and showed her proof of the impossible: Aero Globale 126 was the flight that ended up in the Pacific Ocean.

'Is that some kind of coincidence?' Chel asked.

'They have to be linked somehow.'

'Volcy didn't even get on that plane.'

'Maybe not,' Stanton said. 'But what if he still brought it down?'

'How?'

His mind raced as the logic came into focus. Human error was the suggested cause, they'd said again and again on the news.

'Volcy got on the *first* flight,' Stanton said. 'Pilots fly regular routes back and forth. What if the pilot who crashed also flew the Mexico City-to-LA plane Volcy was on? Volcy could have come in contact with him or her on that leg.'

'You think Volcy gave the pilot whatever was contaminated?' Chel asked.

Only now Stanton was already considering another possibility – a vastly more terrifying one. These were the kinds of connections seen in clusters of TB. Or Ebola. If two men Volcy came in casual contact with both became infected in two different places, there was only one epidemiological possibility.

Stanton had a vertiginous feeling. 'Volcy gets infected in Guatemala, flies from Mexico City, and crosses paths with the pilot. Maybe they shake hands on his way off the plane and the prion passes. Volcy meets up with Gutierrez. They make a deal, go their separate ways. A day later, the pilot gets sick. Then Gutierrez does too. A few days later, the pilot crashes the plane, then the next day Gutierrez crashes his car.'

'But what got them sick?' Chel asked.

'*Volcy* did,' Stanton said, darting for the door. 'Volcy himself.'

The boy was crying again, and now Stanton hurried for the stairs, yelling to Maria not to touch anything in her home.

12.19.19.17.12
December 13, 2012

12

Everyone who came in proximity with any of the victims had to be contacted and quarantined. The CDC needed to make an announcement alerting the public, encouraging everyone in Los Angeles to wear masks. Flights had to be grounded, public events shut down. Almost no measure would be too extreme, Stanton believed, if they could prove that this disease with a one hundred percent fatality rate had become infectious.

Within minutes, the FAA had confirmed that Joseph Zarrow, the pilot who brought down the Aero Globale flight, flew the Mexico City-to-LA leg four days earlier. *Human error* suddenly had new meaning. But the connections were still circumstantial, and before any real action would be taken, before they would cause the public to panic, Stanton needed scientific evidence that VFI spread from person to person through casual contact.

Shortly after five a.m., he stood gloved, gowned, and masked, working with his researchers beneath a protective hood in the lab. Stanton had woken his entire Prion Center team and summoned them in the middle of the night. He had just finished preparing the solution that he hoped would react with the prion, wherever it was hiding.

There were only a few ways an infectious agent could spread between humans via casual contact. Stanton suspected the vector was a fluid from the nose or mouth. He had to discover if it was transmitted by saliva, nasal mucus, or sputum from the lungs – and how VFI migrated from the brain into one of these organs.

With the test solution ready to go, he pipetted drops of secretion samples onto glass slides and added the reactant. Then, beginning with samples of Volcy's and Gutierrez's saliva, Stanton searched. He examined every slide, shifting them across left to right, up one half field of view, and finally right to left.

'Negative,' he told Davies.

They repeated the process with sputum. Coughed up from the throat and lungs, sputum transmitted a variety of illnesses, including life-threatening fungi like tuberculosis. But just like the saliva, the samples were completely negative.

'Like a common cold, then,' Davies said.

But as Stanton triple-checked every one of the slides he'd prepared from the nasal secretions, his anxiety grew. When he got to the last slide, he closed his eyes, confused. Like the others, the nasal secretions were all clear.

'How the hell is it spreading?' Davies said.

'It doesn't make sense,' Jiao Chen said. 'Our casual contact theory can't be wrong.'

Stanton stood. 'Neither can the slides.'

If they couldn't prove how the prion spread, he wouldn't be able to convince Atlanta that serious action must be taken to contain it. Was there a flaw in his logic connecting the men? If the prion was spreading through casual contact, it had to pass through a secretion. But the lab findings were unequivocal: none of the three they tested contained the protein.

The phone rang.

'It's Cavanagh,' said Davies. 'What do I tell her?'

The lab was tense as Stanton's team of researchers waited for him to respond. They all wore masks over the lower half of their faces, but their eyes conveyed a mix of anxiety and exhaustion. They'd been working on little sleep since the day Volcy was diagnosed.

Jiao Chen removed her glasses and started to rub her eyes. 'Maybe we're doing something wrong with the preparations,' she said.

Besides Stanton, Jiao had slept the least of everyone here. And as she rubbed her eyes with her fingertips, something gnawed at him. Exhaustion subsumed his postdoc's face as she slid her palms down her cheeks.

Stanton grabbed the phone. 'Emily, it's in the *eyes*.'

Diseases that spread through the eyes were so rare that even surgeons sometimes didn't wear goggles when they operated. But when Stanton and his team sampled the lacrimal fluid – the fluid coating Volcy's and Gutierrez's eyes – they found prion concentrated almost as densely there as it was in the brain.

Contagion began when people with VFI touched their eyes. The prion got on their hands, then they shook someone else's hand or touched a nearby surface. Humans naturally touched their faces more than a hundred times a day, and insomnia was sure to make things even worse: The more tired victims became, the more they yawned and rubbed their eyes. With victims awake around the clock, their eyes were almost never closed, and the disease had eight extra hours a day to spread. In the same way that common colds caused runny noses and then spread through mucus, and malaria caused drowsiness so more mosquitoes could feed on sleeping victims, VFI had built itself the perfect vector.

The CDC called everyone who could've come in contact with Volcy, Gutierrez, or Zarrow, and the results were harrowing. A stewardess, two copilots and two passengers associated with Aero Globale, plus the proprietor of the Super 8 and three guests, were the first of the second wave.

By midday, they were using the word: *epidemic*.

The worst news came out of Presbyterian Hospital. Six nurses, two ER docs and three orderlies had all been suffering from insomnia for the last two nights. A test for detecting prion in sheep's blood, developed years before, turned out to be effective as a rough indicator for VFI before the onset of symptoms. Already they were getting multiple positive results.

Stanton was angry at himself for how long it'd taken him to realize the prion was infectious, and fearful that he might soon be counted among the victims as well. His own test results were pending, and he hadn't had an opportunity to even try to sleep. He had permission to continue working until he knew for sure, as long as he wore a biohazard suit at all times.

Throngs of desperate people stood at the ER entrance when he returned to Presbyterian, fighting through the heat, discomfort and bulkiness of his pressurized yellow suit. More than a hundred possible victims had already been identified by symptoms, and the panic Cavanagh had predicted was unleashed after the CDC's press conference. In normal times, one in three adults in America had insomnia. Thousands of panicked Angelenos were now flooding every hospital in the city, convinced they were sick.

'Sorry for the wait,' a CDC officer was telling eighty primary contacts in the emergency room. 'The doctors are working as fast as they can, and you will all have your blood tests completed soon. In the meantime, please keep your eye shields and masks fastened, and be careful not to touch your eyes or your faces.'

Stanton made his way through the ER, trying not to obsess over the idea that he, Thane, and Chel Manu had all been exposed more directly to the disease than anyone waiting here.

'I don't ever sleep,' an elderly man called out. 'How will they know if I got it?'

'Make sure to tell the doctors everything you can about your normal sleeping patterns,' the CDC officer told the man. 'And anything else they should know.'

'This place is festering,' a Latino woman carrying a baby said. 'If we weren't sick before, we'll get sick here.'

'Keep your eye shields fastened,' the CDC man told her, 'and don't touch your eyes or anything else, and you'll be safe.'

Eye shields were a crucial part of the containment effort. The CDC was encouraging people to wear masks as well. But Stanton believed eye shields and masks and education weren't nearly enough. He'd sent a CDC-wide email recommending complete transparency with the public, as well as a home-isolation period of forty-eight hours, and making eye shields mandatory in LA schools until they could slow the spread.

He made his way to the makeshift CDC command center in the rear of the hospital. Health-department regulations were taped to every wall, covering peeling paint. More than thirty Epidemic Intelligence Service officers, administrators and CDC nurses were packed into the conference room, and everyone wore masks and eye shields. Stanton was the only one in a biohazard suit, and everyone eyed him, knowing what possibility it suggested.

The highest-ranking doctors sat around a table in the middle of the room. Deputy CDC Director Cavanagh ran the meeting. Her long white hair was pulled back, and her blue eyes flashed brightly from behind her eye shield. Despite more than thirty years of service to CDC, the skin on her forehead was still smooth. Stanton sometimes imagined she'd simply ordered it not to wrinkle.

'We've got two hundred thousand more eye shields coming by morning,' Cavanagh said. Stanton squeezed into the seat next to her, an almost comical challenge in his bulky suit. 'Trucked and flown in from all over.'

'And we can get another fifty thousand by the day after tomorrow,' someone behind them chimed in.

'We need four million,' Stanton said into the small microphone inside his helmet, wasting no time.

'Well, two hundred fifty thousand are available,' Cavanagh

said. 'That's going to have to be enough. First priority will be to supply health-care workers, obviously. Next will be anyone with a connection to any of the infected, and the rest will go to the distribution centers and get doled out first-come-first-served. The last thing we need is to create a panic and cause people to leave en masse. Or this thing could burn across the country.'

Stanton piped up again. 'We have to consider a quarantine.'

'What do you think we're doing here?' Katherine Leeds from the viral division said. Leeds was a tiny woman, but she was tough. Over the years, she and Stanton had clashed many times. 'We have a quarantine, and we're coordinating them in other hospitals too.'

'I'm not talking about the hospitals,' Stanton said. He looked at the group. 'I'm talking about the entire city.'

There was a low murmur throughout the room.

'Do you have any idea what ten million people will do when they find out the government is telling them they can't leave?' Leeds said. 'There's a reason it's never been done before.'

'There could be a thousand cases tomorrow,' Stanton said, unflinching. 'And five thousand the day after. People'll start to flee the city, and some will be sick. If we don't stop the flow out of LA, VFI will be in every city in the country by week's end.'

'Even if it were feasible,' Leeds said, 'it's probably not constitutional.'

'We're talking about a disease that spreads like a cold,' Stanton said, 'but that's as deadly as Ebola and that's impossible to get rid of on fomites. It doesn't die like a bacteria, and it can't be destroyed like a virus.'

Whereas most pathogens were no longer contagious after twenty-four hours or less on 'fomites' – hard and soft surfaces – prion could stay infectious indefinitely, and there was no known way to disinfect the surfaces. Earlier in the day, the same ELISA test with which Stanton and Davies found no prion at Havermore Farms yielded a very different result from the planes at LAX, Volcy's hospital room, and Gutierrez's house. Doorknobs, furniture, cockpit switches, seat cushions and seat-belt buckles on the planes Zarrow had flown in the last week were all covered with prion.

'Every plane leaving LA could have passengers about to spread it around the world,' Stanton said.

'What about the highways out of town?' one of the other doctors said. 'You want to shut those down too?'

Beneath the weight of Stanton's suit, everyone in the room sounded far away. He had to imagine that his voice through the helmet didn't exactly have a commanding effect. 'We have to cut off the flow. We call in the California Guard and the army if we have to. I'm not saying it will be easy, but if we don't act fast and decisively, we'll pay the price.'

'There'll be riots and hoarding and all the rest,' Leeds said. 'It'll be like Port-au-Prince in a couple of days.'

'We have to explain to people that it's a precautionary measure and that they'll be allowed to leave when we know how to stop the disease from spreading –'

'We need to be extremely careful with what we tell

people,' Cavanagh cut in, 'or there will be mass panic. It's got huge liabilities, but so does allowing clusters of cases to develop in every city in America.' She stood up. 'Quarantine is a last option, but we certainly must consider it.'

The entire command center was stunned to hear her agree with Stanton. He was as surprised as anyone – despite the fact that she'd long been his champion at CDC, Cavanagh wasn't usually one to consider drastic measures so quickly. She clearly understood what they were up against.

Once the meeting was adjourned, Stanton waited for her to finish giving division directors their assignments. He stood in front of a massive whiteboard depicting the spiderweb of connections between the patients showing symptoms, with Volcy in the middle. Volcy, Gutierrez, and Zarrow had red circles around their names, indicating they were deceased. The other hundred and twenty-four names were arranged in four concentric rings.

Cavanagh approached him, and Stanton resumed his plea. 'We have to do it *now,* Emily. Or it'll spread.'

'I heard you, Gabe.'

'Good,' he said. 'Then if that's settled, how are we going to pursue a treatment? Once we have the quarantine in place, that must be our priority.'

They left the room and paused in the corridor outside the shuttered gift shop. Through the glass, Stanton could see boxes of candy bars, gum and granola bars lining the counters and helium balloons losing gas.

'You've been looking for a cure for prion disease for how long?' Cavanagh asked.

‘We’re making progress.’

‘And how many patients have you cured?’

‘People upstairs are dying, Emily.’

‘Gabe, you’re already trying to sell me on the idea of quarantining a whole damn city. Don’t get sanctimonious on me too.’

‘Containment’s essential,’ he said. ‘But we need to explore possibilities for a cure, and we need the FDA to suspend its normal experimental protocols. We need to be able to test patients right away.’

‘Are you talking about quinacrine and pentosan? You know the problems with them better than anyone.’

Quinacrine was an old treatment for prion disease that had now been shown to have little use. Pentosan was different: derived from the wood of beech trees, it was once Stanton’s best hope. Unfortunately, the drug couldn’t pass the human blood–brain barrier, which protected neurons from dangerous chemicals. Stanton and his team had tried everything, from changing the drug’s physical structure to giving it through a shunt, but they had found no way to get pentosan into the brain without causing even more harm.

‘Quinacrine won’t work,’ Stanton said. ‘And the old problems with pentosan still exist.’

‘So then what are we even talking about?’ Cavanagh asked.

‘We could start purifying antibodies.’

‘After your lawsuit, Director Kanuth won’t hear anything about antibodies. Besides, you have absolutely no idea if they work *in vivo*, and we’re not using VFI victims as stage-one guinea pigs.’

‘So that’s it for the people already sick?’ Stanton asked. ‘That’s what we tell them and their families?’

‘Don’t lecture me,’ Cavanagh said. ‘I was there at the beginning of HIV when we were trying to shut down the bathhouses. From the first moment, there were researchers screaming about diverting money and resources to explore a cure, which is how we ended up razor-thin on containment, and more were infected. And how long did it take before they found something that could treat HIV? Fifteen years.’

Stanton was silent.

‘Our priority right now is containment,’ Cavanagh continued. ‘Yours is educating the public about how to prevent the spread and figuring out how to destroy the prions once they’re outside the body. Once the number of cases stabilizes, we’ll talk more about a cure. Understand?’

From the look on her face, Stanton sensed that for now there would be no convincing his boss otherwise. ‘I understand,’ he said.

When she spoke again, Cavanagh’s voice was calm. ‘Anything else on your mind I need to know, Gabe?’

‘We need to get a team down to Guatemala now. With Ebola and hantavirus, we had teams in Africa in days to cut it off. Even if we get a quarantine here, it’ll be no use if we don’t shut it down at the original source. It’ll keep spreading around the world from there.’

‘The Guatemalans don’t want any Americans who could have the disease entering their country. They won’t let us across the border. And I can hardly blame them, given that we still have no substantive proof it came from there.’

'We don't even know what this thing is, Emily. Think about Marburg. We didn't have any idea how to stop the virus until we found the original source. What if we could pinpoint where Volcy came from? If we can find these ruins where he was camped out? Then would they allow a team in there?'

'I have no idea.'

A voice came from behind them. 'Deputy Cavanagh?' They turned to find a baby-faced administrator holding a folder labeled CONFIDENTIAL.

They were the results of the blood for the patients in the original contact group.

Cavanagh grabbed the folder. 'How many positives?' she asked.

'Nearly two hundred,' the administrator said.

Two hundred patients with VFI. More than had ever been diagnosed with mad cow, and they'd only known about VFI for forty-eight hours.

Cavanagh glanced up at Stanton, and flipped quickly to the final pages, toward the end of the alphabet. He realized she was searching for his name.

13

At the north end of the Getty campus, Chel and her attorney sat in the main administrative office. They were across the table from senior members of the board, the museum's head curator, and an agent from ICE. Everyone wore eye shields, per the latest CDC recommendations, and everyone had a copy of Chel's official statement in front of them.

Dana McLean, head of one of the largest venture-capital funds in the country and chairman of the board of trustees, leaned back in her chair as she spoke. 'Dr Manu, we have to issue a formal suspension without pay pending further review. You'll have to stop all museum-related activities until a final decision is made.'

'What about my staff?'

'They'll be supervised by the curator, but if it's found there was anyone else involved in the illegal activities, they'll be put under review as well.'

'Dr Manu,' one board member chimed in. 'You claim Dr Chacon had no idea what you were doing, but then why was he here with you on the night of the eleventh?'

Chel looked at her defense lawyer, Erin Billings. When Billings nodded for her to answer the question, Chel tried to maintain an even tone. 'I never told Rolando what I was working on. I asked him to come in and answer some restoration questions for me. But he never saw the codex.'

With everything she'd confessed to in her statement, the group had no reason not to believe her. This was the one lie she felt good about.

'You should know that we'll be looking back at all of your records for any other evidence of professional misconduct,' the ICE agent, Grayson Kisker, told her.

'She understands,' her attorney said.

'What will happen to the codex?' Chel asked.

'It'll be returned to the Guatemalans,' McLean told her.

Kisker said, 'But because the illegal transaction happened on American soil, we'll be the ones filing criminal charges against you.'

Even after the CDC called to inform her that she'd tested negative for any prion in her blood, Chel had felt numb. The last day had been the most overwhelming mix of guilt and confusion and shock in her life. She knew she'd eventually be fired outright and that she'd lose her teaching position at UCLA as well.

But after everything she'd seen, she couldn't bring herself to care.

Chel and Billings stood from the table. Chel tried to prepare herself to gather her things from her lab for the last time.

Then Kisker's cell rang. He listened to someone on the other end of the line, a strange look creeping across his face.

'Yes,' he said, glancing at Chel. 'I'm here with her now.' Slowly, he held his cellphone in her direction. His voice was almost shy. 'My boss wants to talk to you.'

*

The afternoon sun beat down on Chel as she descended the Getty garden walkway into the flowery jungle that sat at the lowest point of the museum grounds, below all the buildings, but still high above LA. Visitors said the views from the museum-on-the-mountain were better than the art itself, but Chel loved the gardens here most of all. Finding herself alone among the pink and red bougainvillea, she reached out to one of the papery flowers, rubbing it between her fingers. She needed a touchstone now.

She was listening to Dr Stanton on her cellphone. 'They haven't found cases in Guatemala yet,' he said. 'But if we can give them a more exact location for where Volcy came from, maybe we could send a team in.'

After talking to the director of ICE, Chel was told to call Stanton for further instructions. She was relieved to learn that he hadn't been infected either. The glasses they each wore probably had given them some small amount of protection, he'd told her quickly, as if it weren't important, before launching in.

'What do you know now about where it might be?'

'It has to be somewhere in the southern highlands,' Chel said. She reached out, ripped one of the pink bougainvillea flowers off its stem, and tossed it into the stream. She surprised herself with how roughly she did it.

'Which is how big an area?' Stanton asked.

'Several thousand square miles. But if the disease is already here, why does it matter where it started?'

'It's like a cancer. Even if it's metastasized, you remove the tumor at the original site so it doesn't spread farther.

We need to know what it is and how it started to have any chance of fighting it.'

'Something in the codex could tell us more,' she said. 'We could find a glyph specific to a smaller area, or some geographic description. But we can't know until the reconstruction is finished.'

'How long will that take?'

'The early pages are in poor condition, and the later ones are worse. Plus there are linguistic obstacles. Difficult glyphs and strange combinations – we've been doing everything we can to decipher them.'

'You better find a way to do it faster.'

Chel dropped onto a metal bench. It was dripping with dew or water from the sprinklers and she could feel it soaking through her pants, but she didn't care. 'I don't understand,' she said. 'Why do you trust me with the codex after I lied to you?'

'I don't,' Stanton said. 'But ICE called in a team of experts who told them the best shot at quickly figuring out where the book came from was you.'

Less than an hour later, Chel was on the 405, headed for Culver City. It was the last place she wanted to go after everything that had happened, but she no longer had a choice. For now there'd be no criminal investigation, and the most important artifact in Maya history would stay in her lab. Whatever hesitations she'd had about involving Victor Granning, all that mattered now was doing whatever she could to help the doctors. She couldn't let her personal issues get in the way.

The Museum of Jurassic Technology on Venice Boulevard was one of the strangest institutions in LA. Maybe in the world. Chel had been there once before, and after she'd oriented to the labyrinthine layout and its dark rooms, she was able to relax and let the museum work its wonders on her imagination. There were tiny sculptures that fit into the eye of a needle, a gallery of cosmonaut dogs sent into space by the Russians in the 1950s, an exhibit about cat's cradles. Each one stranger than the last.

Just past the In-N-Out Burger on Venice Boulevard, Chel spotted the nondescript taupe building and pulled into a spot in front of the deceptively small storefront façade. The other time she'd come here, she was with her ex. Patrick had been obsessed with an exhibit on letters written to Mount Wilson Observatory about the existence of extraterrestrial life. He said the letters reminded him that there were ways to see the skies other than through the eyepiece of a telescope. As they read them together in the darkened space, Patrick's voice never far from her ear, one letter drew Chel in too. The exact words the woman wrote about her experiences in another world had always stayed with Chel: *I have seen all sorts of moons and stars and openings . . .*

At the door to the MJT, Chel pressed a buzzer above a sign that read: RING ONLY ONCE. The door swung open and before her stood an auburn-haired man in his forties, wearing a black cardigan and rumpled khakis. Chel had met Andrew Fisher, the museum's eccentric manager, when she came here the first time. Even the plastic shield he wore over his face couldn't disguise the gentle intelligence in his eyes.

'Welcome back, Dr Manu,' he said.

He remembered her?

'Thank you. I'm looking for Dr Granning. Is he here?'

'Yes,' Fisher said as she stepped inside. 'Chel, isn't it? I've been working on some of Ebbinghaus's memory techniques, which have proven useful. Let's see. You work at the Getty, you're too serious for your own good, and . . . you smoke too much.'

'Victor told you that?'

'He also told me you were the smartest woman he knows.'

'He doesn't know many women.'

Fisher smiled. 'He's in back, working on his exhibit. Fascinating stuff.'

The MJT's small, strange lobby smelled of turpentine and was lit with dark-red and black bulbs. The effect was disorienting after being in the bright light of day. There were bookshelves lining the walls, carrying obscure titles: Sonnabend's *Obliscence,* magician Ricky Jay's *Journal of Anomalies*, and a strange Renaissance volume entitled *Hypnerotomachia Poliphili.* The museum intentionally obscured the lines between fact and fiction. Part of the fun was trying to figure out which exhibits were real. Still, Chel was philosophically ambivalent about a place that inspired confusion and defied logic. Not to mention how uncomfortable she was with the exhibit her old mentor was putting up here.

Fisher led her down a maze of hallways, where a

cacophony of animal sounds and human voices could be heard through scratchy speakers. Chel peered at the weird displays: glass cases mounted on pedestals contained a diorama showing the life cycle of a stink ant. A tiny sculpture of Pope John Paul II stood in the eye of a needle, made visible by a huge magnifying glass.

Next they came around a corner and the maze opened up into a small room with a glass case containing some of the work of a seventeenth-century German scholar named Athanasius Kircher. Hanging from the ceiling in the center of the room was a bell wheel, which made an eerie chime as it turned. In the case were black-and-white drawings of subjects ranging from a sunflower with a cork stuck into the middle, to the Great Wall of China, to the Tower of Babel.

Fisher pointed at a sketch of Kircher. 'He was the last of the great polymaths. He decoded Egyptian hieroglyphics. He invented the megaphone. He found worms in the blood of plague victims.' Fisher touched his plastic shield. 'And these? Did you know he even suggested the public wear masks to protect themselves from disease?' He shook his head. 'In our current obsession with overspecialization, everyone finds smaller and smaller niches, no one ever seeing beyond their own tiny corner of the intellectual spectrum. What a shame it is. How can true genius thrive when there's so little opportunity for our minds to breathe?'

Chel said, 'Sounds like a question only a genius could answer, Mr Fisher.'

He smiled again, and ushered her down another warren

of dark hallways. Finally they arrived at the back of the museum – a well-lit work area, where the exhibits were in varying stages of completion. Fisher led Chel through a narrow doorway, which led to the rearmost room in the building.

'You're very popular today, Victor,' he said as they walked inside.

Chel was surprised to find that Victor wasn't alone. He stood in the square work area with another man, who towered over him. The room was filled with hardware tools, panels of glass, unfinished pieces of shelving, and several wood display pedestals splayed out on the ground.

'Well,' Victor said, stepping around the mess on the floor, 'if it isn't my favorite *indígena.* Save her mother, of course.'

Chel studied her mentor as he walked toward her. He had once been very handsome, and even behind his eye shield she could see his brilliant blue eyes that hadn't dimmed in seventy-five years. He wore a red short-sleeve polo buttoned to the top and tucked into a pair of slacks – the uniform he'd been sporting since his days at UCLA. His silver beard was neatly trimmed.

'Hi,' Chel said.

'Thank you, Andrew,' Victor said, glancing at the museum's manager, who disappeared back into the hall without a word.

There was clear emotion on her mentor's face when he returned his attention to Chel. She felt it too. She always would.

'Chel,' Victor said, 'may I introduce Mr Colton Shetter. Colton, this is Dr Chel Manu, one of the world's leading experts on the script, who, if I say so myself, learned everything she knows from me.'

Shetter had shoulder-length brown hair and several days of unkempt beard growth creeping up his cheeks toward the bottom of his eye shield. He wore a starched white shirt, a tie, black jeans and shiny boots. With how tall he was, it added up to a strangely attractive combination. He had to be six-foot-six at least.

'Nice to meet you,' Chel said.

'What's your specialty, Dr Manu?' Shetter asked. He had a deep voice with a light southern accent. Florida, Chel guessed.

'Epigraphy,' she told him. 'Do you work in the discipline?'

'I dabble a bit, I guess.'

'Is that how you two know each other?'

'I worked for ten years in the Petén,' he said.

'Doing what?'

He glanced at Victor. 'Training the Guatemalan army.'

Those were words no *indígena* wanted to hear. Whatever appeal he had a moment before was gone. 'Training them for what?' she asked.

'Urban combat and counterterrorism, mostly.'

'You're with the CIA?'

'No, ma'am, nothing like that. Army Rangers showing the Guatemalans how to modernize their operation.'

Any help the US government gave to the Guatemalan army was too much for Chel. In the fifties, the CIA had been responsible for bringing down the democratically elected government in order to install a puppet dictatorship.

Many *indígenas* blamed them for instigating the civil war that had taken her father's life.

'Colton is a great admirer of the *indígenas*,' Victor said.

'I spent my leave time in Chajul and Nebaj with the villagers,' Shetter said. 'Amazing people. They took me to the ruins at Tikal, and that's where I met Victor.'

'But you live in Los Angeles now?'

'Sort of. Got a little cottage way up in the Verdugo Mountains.'

Chel had hiked up in the Verdugos a few times but remembered it mostly as a wildlife preserve. 'People live up there?' she asked.

'A lucky few of us do,' said Shetter. 'Reminds me of your highlands, actually. Speaking of which, I should be getting home.' He turned to Victor and pointed at his eye shield. 'Keep that on. Please.'

'Thanks for coming by, Colton.'

Seconds later, the giant man was gone.

'What's his deal?' Chel asked when she was alone with Victor.

Victor shrugged. 'Oh, Colton simply has a lot of experience in dangerous situations. He's out trying to make sure his friends are protecting themselves in these perilous times.'

'He's right. This is serious.'

Chel studied Victor, searching for clues to his mental state. But if there was any sign of tension or pain, she didn't see it.

'Yes, I know,' Victor said. 'So . . . how's Patrick doing in all this?'

'We're not seeing each other anymore.'

'That's too bad,' Victor said. 'I liked him. And I suppose that means I am further and further away from godchildren.'

Victor's old affection for her felt good, even after all they'd been through. 'You should write your next book on the virtues of a one-track mind,' she told him.

He smiled. 'Never mind that, then,' he said. He motioned for her to follow him. 'I'm glad you're here. You can finally see my exhibit.'

They doubled back into a dark gallery where the exhibit was being staged. It was still under construction, but a glass case covering the back wall was illuminated, and Chel walked toward the light, fearful of what she might find. Inside the case were four statues of men, each two feet tall, each constructed from a different material connected to Maya history: the first from chicken bones, the second out of dirt, the third from wood, and the last from kernels of corn. According to the Maya creation myth, there were three unsuccessful attempts by the gods to create mankind. The first race of men was made from the animals themselves, but they could not speak. The second was made from mud but could not walk, and the third race of men, made from wood, could not keep a proper calendar or worship their makers by name. It wasn't until the fourth race of men, fashioned out of corn, that the gods were satisfied.

Studying the glass case, Chel noticed something. What was perhaps most interesting, and to her encouraging about Victor's exhibit, was what he had chosen *not* to represent here: the *fifth* race of man.

'So,' her mentor asked. 'To what do I owe this great pleasure?'

Chel couldn't help feeling that Victor Granning's life had come to mirror the civilization to which he'd devoted his career: rise, fluorescence, collapse. By the time he was finished with graduate school at Harvard, he'd made breakthroughs on the use of syntax and grammar in ancient Maya writing. His academic books were celebrated and eventually made their way into the mainstream when *The New York Times* lauded him as the preeminent Mayanist in the world. After conquering the Ivy League, Victor migrated west to take the chair of UCLA's department of Maya studies, where he helped launch the careers of many of the field's next generation of scholars.

Including Chel. When she began her program at UCLA, Victor became her tutor. Chel could decipher glyphs faster than anyone in the department, even as a first-year. Victor taught her everything he knew about the ancient script. Soon she was more than just another of his mentees. Chel and her mother often spent holidays with Victor and his wife, Rose, at their clapboard house in Cheviot Hills. Chel's first calls when she made tenure, and when she was appointed to the Getty, were to Victor. In the fifteen years since they'd met, he had been a constant source of encouragement, amusement, and, most recently, heartache.

Victor's own collapse began in 2008, when Rose was diagnosed with stomach cancer. Spending every possible moment by her side, Victor began to search for answers.

He couldn't imagine life without Rose, and he became obsessed with Judaism in a way he hadn't before: going to temple every day, keeping kosher and the Sabbath, wearing a yarmulke. But when Rose succumbed a year later, Victor turned against the religion; a God that had allowed her to suffer, he felt, couldn't exist. If there was a higher power, it had to be something else entirely.

It was over the next nine months of mourning that Victor began to theorize about December 21, 2012. Undergraduates began buzzing about some offhand comments he'd made in class about the significance of the end of the Long Count cycle. At first, his students were fascinated, but they grew increasingly less attentive when Victor began using questionable sources that made unsubstantiated claims about Maya beliefs. Lecture time in linguistics classes was spent on the end of the thirteenth cycle and how some believed it would usher in a new era of mankind and a return to a simpler, more ascetic way of life. This was when a few students began to casually mention Victor's classroom eccentricities to Chel. But at the time she didn't yet realize how far off track he'd gone.

Soon his lectures became diatribes about how cancer was caused by processed foods and how it was proof that humans needed to return to a more basic mode of living. Increasingly fearful of technology, he stopped using email for class-related information, forcing his students to come to him in office hours instead. Then he told them not to go on the Internet or drive cars and about how the Long Count would bring what the 2012ers called *synchronicity* – a consciousness of how all things in the world connected – leading to a spiritual renaissance. Chel tried to talk to him about other things, but every conversation veered quickly back to the absurd, and eventually she was at a loss for how to deal with it.

When Victor's name showed up as the keynote speaker at the largest New Age convention in the country, and the press materials touted his UCLA connection, the administration reprimanded him. Then, in mid 2010, as June gloom shrouded the UCLA campus in mist, Victor called Chel at the Getty and asked her to come in to his office. There, he handed her a manually typed manuscript he'd been working on secretly for months. In large block letters, the title page read: *Timewave* 2012.

Chel had turned to the introduction:

> We live in a time of unparalleled technological change. We turn stem cells into any tissue we desire and our vaccines and panaceas will allow the average child born today to live longer than a century. But we also live in a time in which faceless drone operators fire missiles, and in which nuclear secrets steadily leak to oppressive regimes. Superhuman intelligences exist that we may soon be unable to control. The world financial crisis was accelerated by computer algorithms. We destroy our ecosystem with fossil fuels, and invisible carcinogens poison us.
>
> In the late 1970s, philosopher Terence McKenna suggested that the most important points in scientific innovation could be graphed from the beginning of recorded history: the invention of the printing press;

Galileo's discovery that the sun was the center of the solar system; the harnessing of electricity; the discovery of DNA; the atom bomb; computers; the Internet. McKenna found that the rate of innovation was increasing and calculated the exact point when the slope of the line would become vertical. He believed that on that day – which he called Timewave Zero – technological progress would become infinite, and it would be impossible to control or to know what came next for civilization.

That day is December 21, 2012, the end of the thirteenth cycle of the five-thousand-year-old Maya Long Count, the day they predicted the earth would undergo a titanic transformation and the fourth race of man would be replaced. We do not yet know what the fifth race of man will be. But the upheavals we are seeing all over our world prove that a major transformation is coming. In the time left before 12-21, we must prepare ourselves for the change upon us.

'You can't publish this,' Chel had told him.

'I've already shown it to a number of people, and they're excited by it,' he said.

'What people – 2012ers?'

Victor took a breath. 'Smart people, Chel. Some have doctorates, and many have written books themselves.'

Chel could only imagine how revered he was in the 2012 community, especially when he stoked the fire of their misbegotten notions. Victor hadn't done serious scholarship since his wife got sick – and this was his bid to be a star again.

But however much his newfound acolytes might have praised him for it, when he self-published *Timewave* 2012, the book was ridiculed, including in a scathing profile in the *Times*. Among true scholars, it was worse: no one in the academy would ever take Victor seriously again. His grant money dried up, he was quietly forced from the university, and he lost his subsidized house.

Chel couldn't abandon the man who'd given her so much. She let him stay with her in Westwood, and she gave him a research job at the Getty – albeit with conditions: no lectures to Luddites or 2012ers, and no railing against technology to her staff. If he kept those promises, he could use her libraries and be paid a small stipend to get him back on his feet.

For nearly a year, Victor spent his days assisting with whatever decipherment projects arose and his nights watching the History Channel. Someone even saw him using a computer at the Getty. He cobbled together enough money to rent an apartment. After Victor had visited with his grandchildren at the beginning of 2012, his son emailed Chel to say he was greatly relieved to have his father back.

Then, this past July, Victor was supposed to be working on finishing an exhibit on post-classic ruins. Instead, he stole Chel's UCLA ID and used it to get himself into the faculty library. He was caught trying to walk out with several rare books, all of which were related to the Long Count. Chel's trust was fractured, and she'd told Victor he needed to find another job, which was what ultimately led him to the Museum of Jurassic Technology. Since then they'd spoken only a few times, and the conversations had been strained. In the back of her mind, Chel had reassured herself that, sometime after December 22, they would put it behind them for good and try to begin again.

Only now, she couldn't wait for that.

'I need your help,' she said, turning back from the exhibit. She knew how pleased he was to hear these words.

'I seriously doubt that,' Victor said. 'But anything for you.'

'I have a syntax question,' Chel said, reaching into her bag. 'And I need an answer immediately.'

'What's the source?' Victor asked.

She took a breath as she pulled out her laptop. 'A new codex has just been discovered,' she said, filled with a mix of pride and hesitation. 'From the classic.'

Her old mentor laughed. 'You must think I've gone senile.'

Chel pulled up images of the first pages of the codex on the computer screen. In an instant, Victor's face changed. He was one of the few people in the world who would immediately understand the significance of the images in front of him. Staring in awe, he never took his eyes off the computer as Chel explained everything that had happened.

'The Guatemalans don't know about it,' she told him, 'and we can't have anyone else trying to get their hands on it either. I need to be able to trust you.'

Victor looked up at her. 'Then you can, Chel.'

Later that afternoon, they stood together in Chel's lab at the Getty on the same side of the examining table. Victor marveled at the renderings of the gods, the new glyphs he'd never seen before, the old ones in novel combinations and unusual quantities. A part of Chel had been longing to show him the book since she laid eyes on it, and it was a thrill to encounter it again for the first time through his eyes.

Victor had instantly gravitated right toward what she'd brought him back to the Getty to see: the father–son glyph pair she and Rolando had had so much difficulty deciphering.

'I've never seen it as a couplet either,' Victor said. 'And the number of times it appears as both subject and object is unprecedented.'

Together, they examined the paragraph where the pair first appeared:

> The father and his son is not noble by birth, and so there is much the father and his son will never fathom about the ways of the gods that watch over us, there is much the father and his son does not hear that the gods would whisper in the ears of a king.

'It appears more often as a subject,' Victor said. 'So I think we have to focus on nouns that could have been used over and over again.'

'Right,' Chel said. 'Which is why I went back to the other codices and searched for the most frequently used subjects. There are six: *maize, water, underworld, gods, time* and *king*.'

Victor nodded. 'Of those, the only ones that make sense are either *gods* or *king*.'

'There are a dozen references to a drought in the early pages and to the nobles waiting for the deities to bring water,' Chel said.

'But *gods* wouldn't make sense. Not in the context of the father and son waiting for the gods to bring rain. The gods don't wait for the gods to bring rain. The people do.'

'And I tried *king*, but it didn't make sense either. Father and male child. *Chit unen*. Could it be some kind of indication of a ruling family? Maybe *father* is being used metaphorically to mean *king*, and he has a son who will succeed him.'

'There are pairings with husbands and wives to indicate a ruling king and his queen,' Victor said.

'But if we assume the father and son pairing indicates a ruling family, then this sequence would read: *The king and his son are not noble by birth*. That makes no sense either.'

Victor's eyes lit up. 'Mayan syntax is all about context, right?'

'Sure . . .'

'Every subject exists in relation to an object,' Victor said. 'Every date in relation to a god, every king to his polity. We always talk of King K'awiil of Tikal, not simply of King K'awiil. We talk of a ballplayer and his ball as one. Of a man and his spirit animal. Neither word exists without the other. They mean one thing.'

'One idea,' Chel said, 'not two.'

Victor started to pace around the lab. 'Right. So what if these glyphs work the same way? What if the scribe doesn't refer to a father and his son but to a single man with the properties of both?'

It dawned on Chel what he was saying. 'You think the scribe's referring to himself as having the spirit of his father inside him?'

'We use it in English to talk about how similar we are to our parents. You are your mother's child. Or, in your case, your *father*'s child, I suppose. He's referring to himself.'

'It means *I*,' she said, astonished.

'I've never seen it used this exact way,' Victor continued, 'but I have seen grammatical constructions like this used to highlight a noble's connection to a god.'

Chel felt like she was floating. All the other codices were written in the third person – the narrator a distant, detached player in the story he was describing.

This was completely different.

'I am not noble by birth,' Victor read, *'and so there is much I do not fathom about the ways of the gods that watch over us, there is much I do not hear that the gods would whisper in the ears of a king.'*

A *first-person* narrative would be unique in the history of the discipline. There was no telling what could be learned from such an account. It could bridge a thousand-year gap and truly connect Chel's people to the inner lives of their ancestors.

'Well,' Victor said, drawing a pen from his pocket as if it were a weapon. 'I think it's time to find out if this thing is worth all the trouble it's caused.'

14

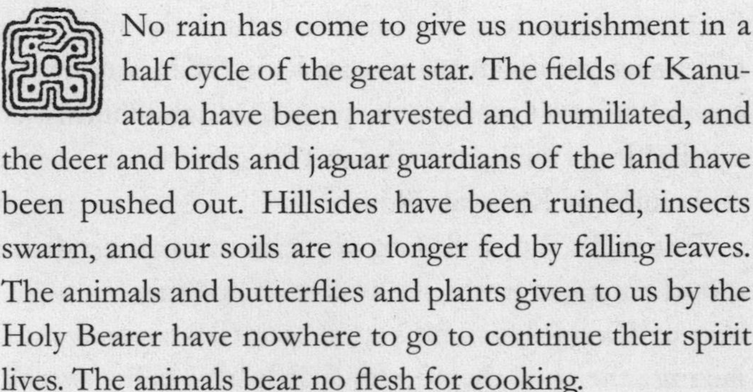

No rain has come to give us nourishment in a half cycle of the great star. The fields of Kanuataba have been harvested and humiliated, and the deer and birds and jaguar guardians of the land have been pushed out. Hillsides have been ruined, insects swarm, and our soils are no longer fed by falling leaves. The animals and butterflies and plants given to us by the Holy Bearer have nowhere to go to continue their spirit lives. The animals bear no flesh for cooking.

I am not noble by birth, and so there is much I do not fathom about the ways of the gods that watch over us, there is much I do not hear that the gods would whisper in the ears of a king. But I do know Kanuataba was once home to the most majestic collection of ceiba trees, the great path to the underworld, in all of the highlands. The ceiba once grew denser than anywhere in the world, blessed by the gods, their trunks nearly touching. Now there are fewer than a dozen still standing in all of Kanuataba! Our holy lake has dried to nothing but dirt. The water made to shoot from stone shoots from the palace and temples no more. In the plazas, untouchables beg us to buy their useless, cracked pots and rotting vegetables, diluted spices for meats that only the nobles can afford. There are no agouti, kinkajou, deer, or tapir to season.

The children of Kanuataba become hungrier with each change of the sun's mighty journey across the sky.

Forgive me then, monkey scribe, whose ring I wear on my hand as the symbol of scribes past! Here in Kanuataba, I commence my record on the virgin bark paper I stole from the king. I have done little worth recording in the books of Kanuataba. I am the tutor to the king's son, and I have painted forty-two books in the service of the court. But now I paint for the people, and the children of our children's children, an honest account of what came in the time of King Jaguar Imix!

Two suns ago, following a night when the quarter moon hung low in the sky, twelve of the thirteen members of King Jaguar Imix's royal council were convened. Jacomo, the royal dwarf, who is as lustful as he is small, was also present. I know dwarfs in the fields who love Kanuataba as much as any man of normal size. But this royal dwarf is something else, something terrible. Jacomo is a glutton, and I watched him chewing on the bark of a great tree and spitting vile liquid from his mouth back into the bowl in his lap. Lately I have seen him seduce women by promising crumbs from his beard, forcing them to pleasure him so that they may feed their hungry babes.

Of the thirteen council members, my friend Auxila, royal overseer of the stores and of zoology and agriculture, was the sole man not in attendance. Five suns ago, at our last meeting, Auxila angered the king, and it seemed most likely he was doing penance. Auxila is a good man, and as trade adviser to the king, he knows much of royal accounting, a burden I would never desire. To count a king's purse is to know the limits of his power.

Galam, bearer of King Jaguar Imix's decrees and daykeeper for ten turns of the Calendar Round, called the council to begin:

– By the word of Jaguar Imix, by the holy word, we commence this meeting in honor of the new sacred god, so named Akabalam. Akabalam is most powerful. Jaguar Imix decrees that we shall worship Akabalam forevermore. –

I am tutor to Prince Smoke Song, next ruler of Kanuataba, and I have memorized all the great books. Nowhere does a god named Akabalam appear in any of them. I asked the daykeeper:

– What form does the god Akabalam take? –

– When Jaguar Imix sees fit to explain more, Paktul, I will share it with the council. I cannot pretend to understand what his holiness knows about the world. –

Without explanation, then, we prayed and burned incense to this new god. I resolved to study the great books of Kanuataba and find the deity Akabalam on my own. To understand what god had revealed itself to his holiness, the king.

Galam the daykeeper spoke:

– I hereby declare the king's intention to begin construction of a great new pyramid in the style of the lost civilization of Teotihuacan, which will someday be the place of his interment. The foundation will be laid in twenty days, less than a thousand paces from the palace. The viewing tower shall be built to face the highest point of the procession of the sun and will create a great holy triangle with the palace and the twin pyramid of red. –

My brothers each clapped twice to signify the glory of Jaguar Imix. But when my turn came to clap twice, I asked of Galam, holy messenger, whether the construction of a pyramid was most prudent when there has been no rain:

– The people of Kanuataba have nothing with which to nourish themselves, and even the mandatory laborers will starve as they carry the stones to the top. A temple in the plaza will require plaster that cannot be made without the burning of our most precious trees and plants to dehydrate the rock. Our flora diminishes by the day. The lake has dried up to nothing, and our reservoirs are dwindling. –

Then Jacomo the wanton dwarf spoke to me with anger:

– Be it understood, Paktul, that King Jaguar Imix has received a prophecy from the god Akabalam telling us to launch a star war, timed to the evening star, against distant kingdoms. We will bring back slaves and all their valuables. Our army has a new way to preserve food, salting its supplies more heavily than before, so that we may launch wars on lands even more distant. These cities are weakened by the great drought, and they cannot defend themselves against our mighty army. So now you understand why you dare not question the king! –

There would be no more argument. Jaguar Imix's power emanates from his ability to communicate with the gods, and each member of the council enjoys rank according to their own abilities to summon the voices of these gods. This we call the hierarchy of divinity. If Jaguar Imix should hear the voice of a god decree that something is most true, and one of his minions should not hear this voice, he shall be considered a man who cannot speak with the gods. His rank in the hierarchy of divinity shall be lowered or stripped from him altogether.

But where will enough water and wood and plumage come from to build a pyramid thirty men high, as it is ordained?

His holiness claims the rain will come in five periods of thirteen days, when the evening star falls nearer to the moon. But will it?

Jaguar Imix would drink the entirety of the water stores if so much water could flow through him and sanctify him, for he believes that his sanctification is the route to our salvation. No royal king of Kanuataba divined by the gods can be evil – I have seen it myself on the stone inscriptions. But his holiness is incapable of admitting to fault. Jaguar Imix believes his power is as strong as the fear he can instill in the hearts of men.

How I wish I could still worship him as I did when I was a boy!

We of the council left the gallery and walked to the great steps atop the royal palace, where I stood and witnessed something to forever change what I believe.

The people outside the palace were chanting, and the blue-painted executioners were standing atop the south twin tower, beginning their rituals. The noise came and went, up and down, high and low. The voices of the royal executioners rose to a near-deafening pitch as the plaza came into my sights.

A small, aristocratic crowd stood at the base of the twin pyramid of white, along the north face, and clapping echoed throughout the plaza. The yellow, red and gold paints that adorn the face of the great pyramid shimmered like the sun on a sea of blue, undulating as if the great beast that lives on the ocean floor had risen. The blue-painted men were at the top of the three hundred sixty-five steps, some holding censers bubbling with smoke.

The grand executioner spoke:

– This soul is commanded to the overworld by the Lord Akabalam! –

Akabalam, once more. The unknown god has demanded sacrifice again, this time in the form of a man's soul!

When the grand executioner plunged his glistening flint knife into the man's chest and ripped open his ribs, the man on the altar let out a wail that will forever ring in my ears. Through the cry that the man exhaled, the grand executioner reached into his body to pull out his heart. And the dying man's words were heard by those of us above the fray, and they were an omen of things to come, as black as the end of the thirteenth cycle:

– Akabalam is falsehood! –

I knew whose voice it was. Auxila, my friend, trusted adviser to the king for three thousand suns, had been sacrificed. Ringing filled my ears. I watched his corpse go lifeless, and everywhere I saw omens in the clouds.

The gods called for such a sacrifice of a high noble

not more than once in fifteen thousand suns. What chance was there the gods had ordained such a sacrifice five days after Auxila spoke out against the plans of the king?

Beyond the reaches of the noisy crowd I saw Auxila's wife, Haniba, standing without tears and watching the executioners encircle the corpse once more, and my heart wept for her and for their children, Flamed Plume and One Butterfly, who stood beside her, weeping.

The bloody priests brought Auxila's corpse back into the recesses of the temple, an unusual handling of a body. It is honorable to throw it down the steps of the great pyramid, but they would not even do Auxila this small justice. They took the body from sight, and I knew they would not emerge again until the blackest of night, as the evening star reached the perfect angle with the temple.

Atop the steps of the royal palace, the perch from which I took in this madness, I felt a hand grasp the back of my knee. I turned and found the dwarf Jacomo, who had crept up beside me, chewing on the same mangled bark piece and smiling.

He spoke:

– Exalted is the name of Jaguar Imix, holy ruler of Kanuataba, whose wisdom guides us through this life. Do you exalt him, Paktul? –

I wanted so much to strike the dwarf right there, but I am not a man of violence. I merely echoed his praise:

– Exalted is the name of Jaguar Imix, holy ruler of Kanuataba, whose wisdom guides us through this life. –

Not until I returned to this cave to begin painting the pages of this secret book did I let go of the scream inside me.

It was a scream for none but the gods to hear.

What am I to understand of a god who'd come with no blessings, who would ordain a temple we cannot build and command the death of a man most loyal to the king! Who is this mighty and mysterious new god called Akabalam?

12.19.19.17.13
December 14, 2012

15

The 10 freeway was shut down near Cloverfield so that the National Guard could transport shipments of supplies and food to the west side. Stanton took the side streets, passing abandoned strip malls, elementary schools and auto-body shops. Traffic moved slowly despite the few cars on the road, with National Guard checkpoints almost every mile. The governor of California had accepted Cavanagh and Stanton's controversial plan and signed an emergency-powers act, enacting the first citywide quarantine in US history.

The boundaries had been secured by the National Guard: from the San Fernando Valley in the north, east into the San Gabriel, south into Orange County, and west to the ocean. No planes were allowed out of the airports, and the coast guard had deployed nearly two hundred boats to secure the port and coastline. So far most Angelenos had reacted to the quarantine with a calm and cooperation that surprised even the most optimistic in Sacramento and Washington.

Beyond the quarantine, the CDC was testing people who'd visited LA or residents who'd traveled out in the last week. They checked manifestos for every plane that left any LA airport recently, hunted down Amtrak travelers through credit-card receipts, and tracked many of those who went by road by toll-booth passes and license-plate snapshots. Thus far they'd found eight cases in New York, four in Chicago, and three in Detroit, in addition to the nearly eleven hundred people now sick with VFI inside the Southland.

Stanton saw devastating patterns as the number of infected grew. All he and the other doctors could do was try to keep patients comfortable. For most victims, partial insomnia and sweating began after a brief latent period, then seizures and fevers and total insomnia followed. Those who'd been awake for three days or more were hardest to watch. They began to have delusions and panic attacks, then the hallucinations and violent outbursts Volcy and Gutierrez had shown. Death was likely within a week. Nearly twenty of the infected had already succumbed.

The sight of camouflage Humvees, and men and women in tan uniforms carrying machine guns on Lincoln Boulevard, was deeply unsettling. Stanton waited to show his ID in a line of cars on his way back to Venice. He glanced down at his phone, to the newest list of names of infected patients. The victims spanned every ethnicity, socioeconomic status, and nearly every age. Glasses had protected some, but plenty who wore them had been infected. The only groups immune to VFI seemed to be blind people, whose optic nerves were severed from their brains, and newborns. The optic nerves were undeveloped in babies, and until the sheath surrounding them matured, the disease couldn't make its way into the brain. That protection wouldn't last beyond six months, so it gave him little solace.

Stanton inched his Audi forward in the security line while scanning the patient list. On it were doctors and nurses he'd met at Presbyterian as well as two CDC officers he knew and liked.

Finally he saw Maria Gutierrez and her son, Ernesto.

He was supposed to be able to deal with mortality. And he had seen some bad cases in his time. But nothing had prepared Stanton for this. He needed grounding, and any other time he would've called Nina. She'd gone back out onto the water again after leaving his condo. He'd called to tell her VFI was airborne. Technically, Stanton should've ordered her to come ashore and get tested. But she had no symptoms of any kind, so he wanted her to stay far, far away. Buses and public bathrooms and almost every hospital in the city showed evidence of prion now, and even hazmat cleaning agents couldn't decontaminate them.

His cellphone rang. 'This is Stanton.'

'It's Chel Manu.'

'Dr Manu. Have you made any progress?'

She described the father–son-glyph revelation and the first section of the codex they'd translated. Though he didn't follow her entirely, Stanton was impressed by her obvious ingenuity, by her command of the complex language, and by the vast amount of history she had at her disposal. He also heard the passion in her voice. He might not be able to trust this woman, but her energy lifted his spirits.

'There's no definite geography in the first section,' Chel went on. 'But it's such a closely written narrative. We're very hopeful the scribe will tell us more about his location in the later pages.'

'How long until you have the rest?' Stanton asked.

'We're working on it. It could be a few days.'

'How long did it take you to do this first section?'

'About twenty hours.'

Stanton glanced at the clock. Like him, she'd been going nonstop. 'Any trouble sleeping?' he asked her.

'I drifted off for a few minutes,' she said. 'I've just been working.'

'Do you have family in the city? Are they okay?'

'Only my mother, and she's fine. What about your family?'

'Don't have much of one,' he said. 'But my dog and ex-wife are okay.' Stanton noticed that the word *ex-wife* rolled off his tongue easier than it had in a while.

Chel sighed, then said, '*Ma k'o ta ne jun ka tere'k.*'

'What does that mean?' he asked.

'It's a prayer *indígenas* say. It means, *Let no one be left behind.*'

After a pause, Stanton said, 'If you have any symptoms, call me first.'

Waves crashing were rarely audible on the Walk, but tonight they were the only sounds Stanton could hear. Gone were the noisy kids usually in front of the marijuana stores, and the whooping from late-night parties in the sand. He parked beneath the massive mural of Abbot Kinney and found the boardwalk empty. The cops had sent everyone home or to one of the local homeless centers.

But when it came to hiding out, the citizens of Ocean Front were some of the craftiest in the city. Stanton pulled the six boxes of eye shields he'd taken from the lab and put them in his bag. There were a thousand things he had to attend to, but the boardwalk freaks were his friends and neighbors. It was hard not to feel powerless right now, and this was one thing he could actually do, no matter how absurd it was.

First he checked the public restrooms, where he found a couple huddled inside. After handing them eye shields, Stanton continued on, and in a nook between tattoo shops he found a guy he knew vaguely, who called himself the 'World's Funniest Wino'. His usual song went 'Jingle Bells, Jingle Bells, let's get drunk.' Tonight, he just laughed boorishly as Stanton laid a shield in front of him.

Behind the Jewish senior center, he found four teenagers hiding in a VW bus, smoking weed. 'You want?' one of them asked, holding the joint toward him.

'Put these eye shields on, guys,' Stanton said, waving it off.

Outside Venice's only plastic-surgery storefront, he stopped to look at the graffiti stenciled across the face of BOTOX ON THE BEACH. Stanton had seen the symbol before around Venice but had never understood what it had to do with 2012:

~~109~~8 DAYS

He continued south, baffled by the strange image. He recalled from somewhere that a snake eating its own tail was a Greek symbol, not, as far as he knew, a Maya one. But people were sure to make all kinds of strange connections now.

The metal gates of Groundwork Coffee were down, and a small sign in the window read: CLOSED UNTIL WE FUCKING SAY SO. The sign reminded Stanton of one person he'd missed. Minutes later Stanton was a few blocks north, climbing the stairs of Monster's Venice Beach Freak Show, just off the boardwalk. He knocked on the yellow question mark painted on the center of the door. The Freak Show was the closest thing his friend had to a home. 'Monster? You in there?'

The entrance cracked open and a porcelain-skinned woman of indeterminate age in striped stockings and a short skirt stood in the entry. The 'Electric Lady' had frizzed black hair, supposedly a result of having been struck by lightning as a child. Stanton once saw her light a gas-covered stick with her tongue while sitting in an electric chair. She was also Monster's girlfriend. *Electrifying.*

'We're not supposed to let anyone in here,' she said.

Stanton held the boxes up. 'These are for you guys.'

The Freak Show had one main room and a small stage, where performers swallowed swords and stapled dollar bills to their skin. The Electric Lady waved Stanton toward the back and then returned to feeding the largest menagerie of bicephalic animals on the planet. There were 'Siamese' turtles, a double-headed albino snake, a two-headed iguana, and a mini-Doberman with five legs. In preserve jars were corpses of a two-headed chicken, a raccoon, and a squirrel.

Stanton found his tattooed friend in the Freak Show's small accounting office. Clothes were strewn across a small cot in the corner. Monster sat at the desk in front of the old laptop he seemed never to be without.

'Your name's everywhere, Gabe,' Monster said. 'Figured you'd be in Atlanta.'

'I'm stuck here like everyone else.'

'Why are you in Venice? Shouldn't you be at a lab somewhere?'

'Don't worry about that.' Stanton held up an eye shield. 'Do me a favor and wear one of these. Take some more and pass them out to anyone who doesn't have one.'

'Thanks,' Monster said. He pulled the straps behind the rings that lined his upper ear and secured the shield. 'You believe this shit from city hall?'

'What shit?'

'You haven't seen it? Broke a few minutes ago. Your name's mentioned a couple of times even.' He turned the laptop so Stanton could see the screen. 'A copy of every internal email from the mayor's office sent in the eight hours before and after the quarantine decision was made popped up on the Internet. One of the secret-leaking websites. Two million hits already.'

Stanton's stomach sank as he scanned the news. There were CDC emails to the mayor's office that described how quickly VFI cases could escalate, offhand questions from within city hall about how many would be dead within the week, and comments about how, given the indestructibility of the prion, public spaces couldn't be decontaminated and parts of LA might never be inhabitable again.

'These are wild guesses at worst-case scenarios,' Stanton said. 'Not facts.'

'This is 2012, brother – there ain't no difference anymore.'

Another article on Monster's computer suggested Volcy could have crossed the border knowing that he was sick, intentionally spreading VFI here for some political purpose. 'That's ridiculous,' said Stanton.

'Won't stop people from believing it. There are a lotta crazies who don't bother with the facts. Not only the 2012ers either. Lots of people are panicked, so be careful out there. Your name's on these pages, dude.'

Stanton wasn't worried about himself, but he was afraid of how the public would react when they saw unfiltered fear from people who were supposed to be in charge. The calm on the streets was fragile, and things could go downhill fast.

'Keep that eye shield on,' Stanton told his friend. 'And if you need anything else, you know I'm just down the Walk.'

Stanton opened the door to his condo to find the entire space upended. The living room sofa and the dining room table were turned on their sides and stuffed into the kitchen. Two rugs, rolled into tubes, stood chest-high on their ends in the corners, and every inch of counter space was stacked with his coffee-table books, lamps, and other bric-a-brac. They needed every available surface.

'Honey, is that you?'

He found Alan Davies sitting at a lab bench in the living room. The furniture had been replaced by storage containers, microscopes and centrifuges. The place reeked of antiseptic solution. They had directly disobeyed orders by setting up this home lab and were only able to sneak out limited equipment. They had to wash and reuse test tubes, beakers and other glass constantly. On top of the TV console, drying racks held glass equipment waiting for their next round.

'Like what I've done with the place?' Davies asked, glancing up from his microscope. Stanton marveled that his partner was still perfectly dressed in a pink tie, white shirt, and blue slacks.

The TV was tuned to CNN: 'Travel restrictions for American citizens in eighty-five countries . . . Bioterrorism explored . . . mayor's office emails leaked . . . YouTube videos show looting at stores in Koreatown and buildings on fire . . .'

'Jesus,' Stanton said. 'There's looting?'

'Rioting in a moment of tension,' Davies said. 'It's practically a way of life in LA.'

Stanton headed into his garage. Behind boxes of research journals, Notre Dame memorabilia and outdated biking equipment was a small safe. Inside he found his self-assembled earthquake/tsunami kit: water-purification tablets, a whistle and signal mirror, a thousand dollars in cash, and a Smith & Wesson 9mm.

Davies stood at the door, peering in. 'I always knew you were a Republican.'

Stanton ignored him and checked to make sure the gun was loaded. Then he put it back in the safe. 'Where are we with the mice?'

'Antibodies should be ready tomorrow if we're lucky,' Davies said.

Despite his orders, Stanton couldn't accept doing nothing to search for a treatment, so they'd set up the secret lab here, away from prying eyes. In the dining room, a dozen cages sat on the wood floor, each containing a knockout mouse.

Only these mice weren't paired with snakes – they were being exposed to VFI. Stanton's hope was that they would soon produce antibodies that could fight the disease. It was the same process they'd had some success with in the lab, and ordinarily it would take weeks. But Davies had come up with an inventive way of creating an ultrahigh concentration of purified VFI prion that they could use to spur a reaction more quickly. Several mice had already begun producing.

A loud knock on the front door pulled Stanton up from the cages.

Michaela Thane looked exhausted. Her hair was tousled and her face gaunt. With Presbyterian quarantined and virtually all patients transferred out, doctors were no longer taking shifts. So Stanton had arranged for her to work full-time with his team.

'Glad to see you made it okay,' he said.

'Had to wait at the checkpoint for about a hundred cop cars and fire trucks heading in the opposite direction. I assume they were on their way down to where those jack-holes are setting buildings on fire.'

She stepped inside, saw all the equipment, and looked at Stanton as if he were stitching together Frankenstein's monster.

'We'll get you an escort on the way back,' Stanton said.

'Tell me you brought my tea,' Davies called. 'Please, God, tell me there is some dignity left in this godforsaken world.'

Thane held up a grocery bag. 'What the hell is going on in here?'

Davies smiled. 'Welcome to the end of our careers.'

Ten minutes later, Thane was still absorbing the makeshift lab – and the fact that Stanton and Davies were having to do it secretly. 'I don't get it. If we can make antibodies, why won't the CDC let us try them?'

'They could prompt an allergic response,' Stanton told her. 'As much as thirty percent of people can react negatively to them.'

Davies seemed to be inhaling his large mug of PG Tips. 'It'll take years before the FDA approves mouse antibodies as therapy in prion disease.'

Thane said, 'But the victims are going to die anyway.'

'It won't be CDC or FDA who kills them, though,' Stanton said.

'We don't make the rules,' Davies said. 'We just break them. Unfortunately, Deputy Cavanagh is monitoring every move we make, and we'll have someone looking over our shoulders every time we're in a patient room.'

'But they won't be watching me,' said Thane, now understanding why she'd been summoned. 'I have patients in the ICU still. I could still get in there.'

Merely setting up this lab could get all of their medical licenses suspended, but a helo-medic knew all about taking chances for her patients. Stanton had watched Thane interact with her patients and with the other staff. He sensed he could trust her.

'You can't tell a soul,' Davies told her. 'Believe me when I tell you I wouldn't fare well in an American prison.'

'The test can be any group of patients we can access, right?' she asked.

'As long as they haven't progressed too far,' Stanton told her. 'Once the disease goes beyond two or three days, nothing will work.'

'Then I have one condition.'

'We all have it,' Davies said. 'I believe the medical term is professional suicide.'

Stanton looked at Thane. 'What's your one condition?'

16

The Getty doubled their security team as looting and arson spread across the city. The Baghdad Museum had lost irreplaceable treasures during its siege in 2003, and no one wanted to see that happen if LA really fell apart. Fortunately, the Getty was perched in the Santa Monica Mountains, almost a thousand feet above the 405 freeway, and the only way up was through the security gates at the bottom of the hill. So the museum where Chel and her team had been holed up for two days was one of the safest places in the city.

Chel was more worried about the safety of the local *indígenas*. According to the news on the TV she'd carted into the lab, 2012 New Agers and Apocalypticists were convening across the city, in violation of the mandate to stay home. Before VFI, 'Believer' gatherings focused on renewed consciousness or apocalypse readiness; CNN now claimed that many meetings had taken a different tone in the shadow of the quarantine. People were desperate, and searching for scapegoats. Maybe it wasn't a coincidence that right before 12-21 a Maya man had brought this disease to America.

In Century City, local *indígenas* had been threatened and their homes had been vandalized with graffiti. In East LA, one man brutally attacked his Maya neighbor following an argument about the end of the Long Count cycle. The elderly Honduran was in a coma from the beating. So now *Fraternidad* leaders had decided that the city's *indígenas* needed a place to congregate for mutual protection. The archbishop had offered them shelter, and there were more than 160 Maya living indefinitely at Our Lady of the Angels.

Chel's mother wasn't among them. 'They say we're supposed to stay home to keep from getting sick,' she'd replied when Chel called to urge her to join the others at the cathedral. Ha'ana's factory had closed, and she hadn't left her bungalow in West Hollywood, declaring she was staying put.

'There's a doctor checking people for VFI before they let anyone through the doors, Mom. The church is the safest place you can be right now.'

'I've lived in this house thirty-three years, and no one has ever bothered me.'

'Then just do it for me,' said Chel.

'And where will you be?'

'At work. I have no choice. There's a project that's extremely time sensitive. It's totally safe here with the museum in lockdown mode.'

'Only you'd be working now, Chel. How long are you going to stay there?'

Chel had gone home and packed a suitcase full of clothes. She'd be here for as long as it took. 'I'd feel a lot better knowing you were at the church, Mom.'

Neither woman was satisfied when they hung up, and Chel allowed herself a frustrated smoke break by the

Getty's reflecting pool. There, her phone alerted her to an incoming email from Stanton. His red exclamation point seemed a little superfluous, under the circumstances. All the message said was:

> anything?

She started typing a long response, explaining where they were in the decipherment, but thought better of it midway through. He didn't need a thousand unnecessary details. He had enough details of his own to worry about.

> Progress on the translation. No location yet. Won't stop till we have it.

Without thinking, she added, *How are you?* and sent it off, then immediately felt absurd. It was a ridiculous question to ask the man in charge of the disease investigation. She knew exactly how he was.

But, to her surprise, she had a response within seconds:

> working hard to keep up. please keep me posted. take care. need you and your team healthy. call if there's anything you need. Gabe

It didn't say much, but something about it was both calming and empowering for Chel. Maybe he was starting to see her as part of the solution to this crisis. Maybe she would be. She stubbed out her cigarette and went back inside.

Rolando was carefully tweezing more tiny fragments of the codex onto the reconstruction table. They'd gotten everything out of the box and taken a complete set of photographs of every piece of the manuscript so they would have it in perpetuity. And once they'd made their breakthrough on the father–son glyph pair, Chel, Rolando and Victor had reconstructed the first eight pages of the codex.

Even with most of the document still left to reconstruct and decipher, they knew that their findings would change Maya scholarship forever. So much more than just the personal thoughts of a scribe, Paktul's codex was a political protest – an indictment of a king's rule and an unprecedented questioning of a god. Chel took comfort in the fact that, no matter what happened to her or her career, the world would eventually see this strange gift of history. It was the work of a moral, learned man willing to risk his own life for what he believed in, which illustrated beyond a doubt the humanity of her ancestors.

But there was still a more pressing issue: finding out where the codex was written, so they could help the CDC identify the source of the disease. Neither Chel nor anyone else in her lab had ever heard the name before, but the scribe called his home *Kanuataba* and referred to it several times as *the terraced city*. Terracing was an agricultural practice whereby the ancients created new patches of farmable land by cutting stairlike plots into the sides of hills. But the practice was used all over the Maya empire, so without more detail, the name gave little evidence of the city's location.

'Anything come up in the databases about Akabalam?' Rolando asked.

Chel shook her head. 'Sent it to Yasee at Berkeley and Francis at Tulane too,' she said. 'But they had no idea.'

Rolando ran a hand through his hair. 'By the end, the glyph appears on almost every one of the fragments. I still don't get what it could be.'

They had never seen such a proliferation of glyphs referring to one god in any of the literature. Understanding its significance would be crucial to completing the translation.

'It's not a question of syntax, like the father–son combination,' Rolando said. 'It's more like Paktul is dedicating the final pages to him.'

Chel nodded. 'Like *adonai* in the Jewish Torah, used to mean both *God* and *Praise God*.'

'But there are fragments where it seems like the scribe is negative about Akabalam,' Rolando said. 'Wouldn't it be heresy for a scribe to openly resent a god?'

'The whole book is heresy. The first glyph block indicts his king. That alone would've been punishable by death.'

'So we'll keep searching. In the meantime, should we talk about page seven?'

'What about it?'

Rolando turned to the section in question and said sheepishly, 'I guess I'm curious what you make of the thirteenth-cycle reference.'

And the dying man's words were heard by those of us above the fray, and they were an omen of things to come, as black as the end of the thirteenth cycle.

Chel sat down. The five-thousand-plus-year Long Count was divided into major periods of about 395 years each, beginning on a mythical creation date of 0.0.0.0.0, the equivalent of August 11th, 3114 B.C. in the Gregorian calendar. In the Long Count, a day was expressed by 0.0.0.0.1, a year by 0.0.1.0.0, and the important 395-year periods by 1.0.0.0.0. 12-21-12 – in the Maya calendar 13.0.0.0.0 – would mark the end of the all-important 'thirteenth cycle', at which point the last Long Count had supposedly come to an end. Just one reference in the *Popal Vuh* and one short inscription at the ruins of Tortuguero, Mexico – IT WILL BE COMPLETED IN THE 13TH CYCLE – had spawned a cottage industry and cultish devotion to the calendar, and the 2012ers, already empowered by VFI, would go out of control if they knew there was now a second reference, from the classical era, let alone one whose appearance was inextricably tied to the epidemic.

Chel glanced over at the door of the lab, next to which an intercom hung on the wall. It could be used to summon the security detail stationed at the bottom of the hill. She hoped never to have to use it.

'He could be talking about a Tzolk'in cycle of thirteen days for all we know,' she told Rolando. 'It might not have anything to do with the Long Count.' Chel wasn't sure if she believed it herself, but she couldn't let 2012 distract her now, nor would she give the Believers anything to hang on to.

One of the Believers she had in mind walked into the lab and caught the tail end of their conversation. Victor's short white hair was combed back and wet, as if he'd just showered, his perpetual polo shirt green this time.

'Please continue,' he said.

Even at Victor's lowest points, Chel had always marveled at his seventy-something energy. When she was in graduate school, he'd do decipherment work for twelve-hour stretches without ever eating or going to the bathroom, and now he'd been instrumental in getting them this far.

Still, as grateful as Chel was, she wasn't eager to bring up 2012 when he was around.

'The thirteenth-cycle reference is up for interpretation,' Victor said, jumping right in.

'I guess it is,' she responded warily.

'I'll check the computers,' Rolando said, taking his cue to leave.

Victor went on, 'But there are many things that will be up for interpretation, depending on people's particular biases. And I believe we have *other* more important things to focus on. Don't you?'

Chel was relieved. 'I do, Victor. Thank you.'

He held up his copy of the translation. 'Good, then,' he said. 'Let us do that.' He put a hand gently on Chel's shoulder, and she reached up to meet it with her own for a moment. 'I think the first things we must discuss are the implications for the collapse, right?'

'What implications?'

'The possibility this book could tell us something about the collapse we aren't prepared for,' he said. 'What do you see in Paktul's discussion of the failing city?'

'I see a community stricken by a mega-drought, trying to survive. Paktul says there are barren markets and starving children. The drought must have been going on for at least eighteen months, based on the likely water stores.'

'We know there were droughts,' Victor said. 'But what about the reference to the food-preservation techniques they're using?'

Our army has a new way to preserve food, salting its supplies more heavily than before, so that we may launch wars on lands even more distant.

'What about it?' Chel asked.

'Heavier salting is a major innovation in warfare,' Victor said. 'You know war between the polities was often hampered by food supply. Figuring out better salting techniques would have let them fight more effectively.'

'What are you implying?'

'I'm just saying, the ability to wage more war ultimately made them more vulnerable.'

'To what?'

'To everything.'

Now she understood. Victor had made this argument

forever, even before his 2012 hysteria: he believed her ancestors were better suited to simpler, more rural lives, and that the cities – for all their glory – fostered the self-destructive excesses of despotic kings. 'The ancients could have ruled for a millennium if it weren't for the droughts,' she said. 'They used their technology to great advantage.'

Victor disagreed. 'Let us not forget that the Maya have endured much longer droughts living in the forests than they ever did in the cities. Once they moved back into the jungle after the classic and stopped building temples and waging more wars and burning all their wood for plaster, they survived the dry periods just fine.'

'So the noble savages could only survive in the jungles? They couldn't handle the pressures of civilization?'

Before Victor could respond, Rolando poked his head back into the lab. 'I'm sorry to interrupt, but there's something you both need to see.'

In the rear of the lab, they had four computers using state-of-the-art 'vision' programs to decipher unknown glyphs and piece together gaps in the text. Due to the unique styles of scribes, even familiar words could be painted in a way that made them unrecognizable. Computer vision used sophisticated algorithms to calculate distances between brushstrokes and then tried to match them to known glyphs with similar shapes, with much greater accuracy than the human eye.

Rolando pointed to a series of faint squiggly lines from the codex. 'You see this glyph? The computer believes it's similar enough to one of the representations of Scorpio seen at Copal to be a match. I think this is a zodiac reference.'

The sun and stars determined every event in ancient life: gods worshipped, names given to children, rituals performed, foods eaten and sacrifices offered. The ancient people studied and worshipped many of the same constellations the ancient Greeks and Chinese did. No one knew whether the Maya zodiac came about independently or was brought across the Bering Land Bridge from Asia into the Americas, but, either way, the parallels were striking.

'So if we substitute that interpretation into the text,' Rolando continued, 'this fragment would read: *When the morning star passed through the reddest part of the great scorpion in the sky once more . . .*'

Chel saw it instantly. 'We could try to recreate Venus's position in the sky at the time when Paktul was writing.'

'I have to assume there are more zodiac references in the text,' said Rolando. 'I've got the computer searching for anything else resembling constellations.'

'We need an expert in archaeoastronomy,' Victor interjected. 'Doesn't Patrick work with the zodiac sometimes?'

Chel's stomach clenched.

'Do we even know if he's around?' Rolando asked.

She knew, of course. Patrick had emailed when the quarantine began to see if she was okay. To let her know he was here if she needed anything. She hadn't even responded.

17

My scarlet feathers are striped blue and yellow. When I came here, I was starving and might have died if he had not saved me. I was on my migration and lost my flock when we passed through Kanuataba and only the scribe gave me life. I ate ground worms he pulled from the dirt. It has been so long since the rains, even the ground worms are shriveled and dry, but we give each other comfort.

I, Paktul, royal scribe of Kanuataba, am buoyed by the presence of a scarlet macaw, who has flown into my cave. My spirit form given to me at birth was a macaw, and the bird has always been a great omen when I have chanced upon one. The night of Auxila's murder, it arrived wounded. I gave it worms because there are no fruit seeds to offer, then let drops of blood out of my tongue to welcome it. Through this, we became one. I embody the spirit of the bird in my dreams. Now I am as grateful for his presence as he is for mine. It is not often a spirit animal finds his man in the flesh, and it is the only happiness I know now.

For there has been no rain but in our dreams, and the people of Kanuataba grow hungrier by the day. Maize and beans and peppers are almost as rare as meat, and the people have taken to feeding on shrubs. I have given my rations to the children of my friends, for I am used to subsistence eating in my communes with the gods, and my appetite has grown small.

The death of Auxila, just twelve suns ago, still haunts me. Auxila was a good man, a holy man, whose father took me in when I was a boy and without parents. I knew only my father, my mother having died when she pushed me from the womb. My father could not handle a boy on his own, but he was not allowed by the king, Jaguar Imix's father, to take another wife from Kanuataba. So he fled alone to the great lake beside the ocean, the land of our ancestors, to rejoin them, as soon the bird will rejoin its flock. He never returned, and Auxila's father took me in as an orphan and made Auxila my brother. Now my brother has been killed by the king I serve.

I headed to the palace with my macaw, on a day when the moon was halved, and the evening star would pass directly through Xibalba. I swallowed my sadness at Auxila's death, for to express discontent at a royal decree is unwise. I had been summoned to the king for reasons I did not know.

The macaw and I passed other nobles standing in the central patio on our way to the palace. Maruva, a member of the council who has never had an idea of his own, leaned against one of the great pillars encircling the patio, dwarfed by the stone that reached seven men high. He spoke to a king's ambassador well known for supplying the black market in the Outskirts with hallucinogens. They both looked at me suspiciously and whispered as I passed.

I reached the palace and was led by one of the guards into the king's quarters. The king and his minions had just finished eating, another secret ritual in which only he and his sycophants are allowed. These men were finishing a royal feast. The smell of incense filled my nostrils and overwhelmed the smell of animal flesh. The incense was distinctive. I have come upon the end of these royal feasts before, and always there is a bitter smell in the air from the fire they burn to sanctify their meal. The secret mix of plants burned is a source of power for kings, the aroma of the incense a great source of pride for Jaguar Imix. When I set the macaw down and kissed the wretched limestone, the aroma had changed, and I could no longer taste it on the back of my tongue as I once had.

Jaguar Imix called me into the recesses of the chamber, ordering me to sit on the floor beneath his royal throne, where the sun shines at solstice and the moon shines when harvest comes. Jaguar Imix's face is sharp, and he has always garnered power from its distinction. His nose is pointed like a bird's, and his flat forehead is offered as evidence of his divine power. He drapes himself in cotton, made on the royal looms and dyed royal green, and he is almost never seen without his jaguar head covering.

Jaguar Imix, the holy ruler, spoke. His voice bellowed for all to hear:

– We will honor the great god Akabalam and the many gifts he has provided my sovereign kingdom. Let us praise him! To you, Akabalam, we shall dedicate a holy feast we prepare, and to you we make this most insignificant offering, that you may bless us with your many gifts. We shall prepare for a feast of meat unlike any the city has ever seen before, for all the inhabitants of Kanuataba. It will be made in honor of Akabalam to sanctify the commencement of the new pyramid. –

I was confused. Of what feast did he speak? And from where would food for such a feast come when our city is starving?

I spoke:

– Pardon, Highness, but there is to be a holy feast? –

– Like none the city has seen in a hundred turns of the Calendar Round. –

– What kind of feast? –

– All will be told in time, scribe. –

Jaguar Imix pointed at a concubine who had come to join us, and she reached into a small bowl beside her and pulled out a length of tree skin. She placed it between her master's teeth and he chewed as he spoke again:

– Paktul, servant, while in a trance I was told by the gods of your disapproval of the new temple. Your questioning of the feast ordained by Akabalam confirms what the gods have told me. You know that I see all, scribe. Is it true what the gods say? That you would dispute that I am their vessel? –

These words were as good as a sentence of death, and I feared as I have never feared before – the eyes of the court were on me, preparing for blood. Even the macaw who sat in his cage beside me could feel it. Auxila had been sacrificed for less. My heart would be ripped out on the altar! I looked over at Jacomo the dwarf, slurping from a cup of chocolate with cinnamon and chili. I knew then there was no god behind this, just a malicious dwarf.

With fear in my heart, I spoke:

– Jaguar Imix, most holy ruler, exalted one, I spoke in the council meeting only to ask if the time to construct the new pyramid was ideal. I wish for the pyramid to stand for ten great cycles, so that your name may be remembered forever as the most holy. I hope to adorn the façade with a thousand glyphs to represent you, but I do not wish to paint on poor limestone because we do not have the men or materials to build it. –

I bowed my head in penitence, and at this, Jaguar Imix spit the skin of the tree from his mouth onto the ground and flashed his teeth. He showed the most beautiful set of jade and pearl inlays ever created in Kanuataba. Jaguar Imix loves to smile and remind everyone below him of his prize. Loyalty is Jaguar Imix's greatest demand of his people, and so many times I have seen him revel in the groveling of a man, only to have him executed before another turn of the great star above.

I closed my eyes and waited for the executioners to come. They would take me to the top of the pyramid and sacrifice me as they did Auxila.

But then the king spoke:

– Paktul, low one, you are forgiven. I pardon your indiscretion and trust that you will redeem yourself in the preparation for the holy feast to honor Akabalam. –

I opened my eyes and could not believe the words. And the king continued:

– My son, the prince, favors you, and so you shall be

forgiven this trespass once, so you may teach Smoke Song to follow in the bloodline of his destiny. You will teach him of the power of Akabalam, most revered god who has revealed himself to me. You will instruct Smoke Song in the virtues of the coming feast. –

Trembling, I choked out words:

– Highness, I have searched the great books, and I have not found this Akabalam. I have searched everywhere, and there are no descriptions of him in the great cycles of time. I wish to teach the prince, but from what shall I teach him? –

– You shall continue in your lessons to the prince as planned, low scribe, from the great books you know so well. And when the feast in honor of Akabalam is prepared, I shall reveal all to you so that you may record it in new holy books, so Smoke Song and the divine kings that shall come after him will know forevermore. –

I departed the royal chambers, dizzy with the new life the king had breathed into me.

The holy prince's lessons are more important than any other charge and had saved my own life from sacrifice. I tried to bury my worries as I went to the palace library to meet the prince, with only the bird in its cage, embodiment of my spirit, to share in my fears.

The royal library, where I teach the prince his lessons, is the most wondrous place in all of our great terraced city. There I have stood beneath the tree of knowledge that the wise men have gathered over ten great turns of the Calendar Round. There are books of every description, read for their holy wisdom. These books give the religious knowledge of the astronomers, who told of the celestial world as the two-headed serpent.

I stepped into the library, a room of stone draped in fabrics dyed with the most royal of blues. The square window in the stone shines white light on the fabric; at dawn on the summer solstice, the sun shines directly in to signify dawn for the passions of learning, which our ancestors brought into the world. There are shelves on which sit the great books, stacks of them, some unfolded, from a time when fig-bark paper was plentiful and no scribe would ever have to steal to paint this book.

Over a thousand suns past, the king entrusted me to teach the royal prince the wisdom of our ancestors, and to help him understand about time, the never-ending loop that bends back on itself. Only by looking to our pasts can we dream of our futures.

Smoke Song, the prince, is a strong boy of twelve turns of the full Calendar Round, with the eyes and nose of the king, his father. But he is not vengeful, and when I came to the library carrying the bird, Smoke Song was concerned.

He spoke:

– I have seen the sacrifice of Auxila, teacher. And in the plaza I saw his daughter, Flamed Plume, whom I favor, mourning her father. Can you tell me where she is now? –

I looked to Kawil, Prince Smoke Song's servant, who always stood waiting for the prince during our lessons. Kawil is a good servant and very tall. He stayed silent and only stared ahead.

It was too painful to explain what would happen to the girls, daughters of Auxila, so I said simply:

– Yes, Prince, she survives, but you must put Flamed Plume out of your mind, for she is untouchable to you. You must focus on your studies. –

The boy seemed sad, but he pointed at the macaw and spoke:

– What is this, teacher? What do you bring me? –

My spirit animal is most sociable, and so I let him out of his cage to show the prince. As we reviewed his knowledge of spirit animals, I explained that mine came to me in the form of this macaw and that I had become one with the bird through the drops of my blood. Then the bird, my animal form, flew about the room, which pleased the boy to see. We flew to the roof and back down; we circled him and landed on his shoulder.

I told the prince my spirit animal had stopped in Kanuataba on the great path of migration every macaw makes with its flock. I told him that in a few weeks we would continue our journey in search of the land that our ancestor birds have returned to every harvest season for thousands of years.

I told the prince:

– Every man must transcend the everyday human world, and the animal self is the embodiment of that ideal. –

Smoke Song's animal self is a jaguar, as befits all future kings. I watched him taking in the bird, considering how the macaw could be my bridge to the overworld. I mourn that Smoke Song might never again see his spirit animal. Few holy jaguars roam the land anymore.

When we finished talking of animal spirits, the boy spoke:

– Wise teacher, my father the king has told me that I may accompany the army on their journey to fight on behalf of the people of Kanuataba. That we may go to Sakamil, Ixtachal, and Laranam and fight them as decreed by the morning star passing into darkness. It will be a great evening-star war. Are you not proud, wise teacher? –

Anger swelled up inside me, and I let go words that could have cost me my life:

– Have you been to the streets and to the barren markets, stricken by drought? It is difficult to witness, Prince, but you see the suffering of the people with your own eyes. Even the army is starving, whatever salting techniques they may have now. We can hardly afford to wage wars in distant lands! –

But the boy snapped back:

– My father has received a divination that we must wage the star war against the distant kingdoms! How can you know better than the stars? We will fight as our gods have commanded! I will fight with the warriors of Kanuataba! –

I looked at the child with a pained heart and spoke:

– Fire ripples through the heart of every man of Kanuataba, Prince. But one day you must lead us, and you must prove your wits. You are in the midst of your studies. I was not brought here to train you as a warrior with a blowgun or length of rope, so that you may die on the warpath! –

The prince ran from the library, hiding the tears that poured from his eyes. I called after him, but he did not return.

I expected the boy's servant, Kawil, to follow the prince quickly, but to my surprise he did not move. Instead, he spoke:

– I will bring him back to you, scribe. –

– Go, then. –

– May I speak first, holy scribe? It concerns Auxila. –

I gave the servant permission.

Kawil told me he was sitting outside the palace walls, several nights after Auxila's sacrifice, and that he had seen Haniba, the wife of Auxila, with her two daughters.

He explained:

– They had come to worship at the altar where Auxila was sacrificed. –

I was shocked to hear this. Every woman knows what she must do when her husband is sacrificed at the altar. Haniba had insulted the gods by failing to do her duty. Kawil explained that he followed her all the way to the Outskirts, where she was living.

Now there was no question in my mind what I had to do.

Someone had to remind Auxila's wife of her duty. It is decreed by Itzamnaaj for all of our history that the wives of sacrificed nobles are to join their husbands in the overworld by an honorable suicide. Auxila was my close friend, my brother, and his wife deserved better than the horrors of the Outskirts.

If she would not heed the call of the gods, I would have to help her.

When the morning star passed through the reddest part of the great scorpion in the sky once more, I dressed in a commoner's loincloth and leather sandals so as not to be recognized.

The Outskirts shelter the dregs of Kanuataba, where men and women have been saved from death by omens but exiled from the city proper for their crimes. Here were thieves and adulterers who had escaped death by an eclipse, errant borrowers who lived only by the grace of the evening star, drug addicts, and even those we are told are the greatest sinners of all, bound to walk the earth for all eternity from the north to the south: those who stupidly worship only those deities who they believe favor them.

No limestone or marble is wasted on the buildings in the Outskirts, and if any of the quarrymen are caught sneaking limestone, they are guaranteed a public death, so the buildings are made of mud and thatch. There are only the illegal trades – the market for dream mushrooms, gambling on ball court games, and whoring.

I had obscured my face with my blotting towel, which I use to prepare the gesso for books. In the palm of my hand I carried several cacao beans and doled out each one as I spoke with women in the streets who might be able to guide me to Haniba. These women all offered me their bodies in exchange for the bean and were utterly confused when I refused them. Instead, I spoke with an old whore. She sent me another two hundred paces down the causeway to a series of stalls, which I had not seen since I was in the Outskirts as a young boy, where I lost my own virginity.

In the back of one of the stalls, I heard a woman moaning. I went around and found a man on top of Haniba, a vile man thrusting himself into her. Haniba was defiling herself! There were four cacao shells laid neatly on the ground beside them, and in the midst of their copulation they could not hear as I leaned down to check the beans. I found no beans inside two of the shells. The man was a cheat.

I picked up a large sitting stone in the corner of the stall and raised it above my head. I bore down with all my might. The man slumped on top of Auxila's wife and she screamed, not understanding. I believe she thought the stone had come down from Iztamnaaj himself to punish her for her trespasses. But when I lifted the man off her and she saw my face, she turned away. Haniba was deeply ashamed. Yet there could be no deeper shame before the gods than that she was still living on this earth.

She spoke:

– They have taken everything from me, Paktul, my house, all of my clothing, and Auxila's goods –

– I know why you are here, and I am come to implore you, Haniba. You must act prudently. Your children starve because no one will take them until you are gone. People will learn you are still alive –

The woman wept, barely able to breathe:

– I cannot heed the order until I know my children are safe. Flamed Plume is turning to the age where she will be taken up by some old man who wishes to have a fresh girl! You have seen the way Prince Smoke Song himself looks at my Flamed Plume – she might have been queen, Paktul! The king was considering their betrothal, and the prince is good, deserving of her. But now that her father has been shamed, we all know they cannot be betrothed. So what good man will take Flamed Plume? Surely you understand, Paktul. Surely this shame is like the shame you felt when your father left you! –

I was tempted to strike her for speaking this way. But when I saw the look of sadness in her eyes, I could not hit this woman I had known since Auxila and I were boys together.

I spoke:

– You must find yourself a length of vine and wrap it around your neck by the turn of the next sun. You must hang yourself proudly, Haniba, to fulfill your duties as wife of a noble sacrificed to the gods –

– But he was not sacrificed to the gods, Paktul! He was murdered by a king! Jaguar Imix ordained his death because Auxila had the courage to speak out against him, and the king sacrificed him in the name of a god that does not exist! This god, Akabalam, surely cannot have called for Auxila's sacrifice, having never revealed his power to us or to any other noble in a dream! –

I said nothing of my own doubts about the new god.

For just as a scribe should not question a divination, it is not for a widow to question a king.

I spoke:

– What can you know of the conversation between a king and a counselor he sacrifices? How can you know the king never revealed Akabalam? –

Haniba buried her head in her hands.

As a nobleman, seeing such a woman make such a transgression against the gods, my duty was to kill her.

But I was powerless in the face of her sadness.

18

The CDC had arranged special dispensation for Chel to be on the roads, and the Getty security team provided an escort who followed her toward Mount Hollywood. From the top of Mulholland Drive, even against the night sky she could see smoke rising from distant corners of the city. Yet as she raced east, Chel felt the first glimmers of hope she had had in days. Patrick had agreed to meet her at the planetarium immediately.

East Mulholland was eerily empty but for the occasional police car and National Guard jeep. Yet there was an acrid smell in the air – maybe the burning was closer than she thought. She started to roll up her window. Just then a woman in exercise clothes ran into the middle of the street, right in front of her car. Chel wouldn't have seen her except for the flash of the woman's reflective running shoes.

Chel swerved, her Volvo's tires skidding across the road, and finally she veered onto the shoulder, heart racing. In her rearview mirror, she saw the jogger keep on going, as if nothing had happened. The woman was on autopilot. Chel had heard stories of VFI victims raiding pharmacies for sleeping pills, drinking to the point of alcohol poisoning, and paying huge prices to drug dealers for illegal sedatives. But the woman now receding behind her was trying to do it naturally, attempting to exhaust herself into oblivion. It looked as if she might collapse in the street at any moment. Yet on and on she went.

The security car following her pulled up alongside the Volvo. Once Chel had insisted she was okay, they wound their way up to the top of the mountain without further incident.

Fifteen minutes later, their caravan reached Griffith Observatory. The massive stone structure had always reminded Chel of a mosque. Patrick had told her that, years ago, before the city lights made most stars too hard to see, this had been the best place in the country to study the night sky. Now it was better suited for city vistas; the entire Southland shone below. From here, the fires burning against the night looked almost beautiful. From here, Chel could almost forget that LA was at risk of its own collapse.

The security detail peeled off, and Chel checked her phone before getting out of the car. No new messages. Nothing from her mom. Or Stanton. She wondered when she could expect another *anything*. The possibility that she'd have something to tell Stanton next time kept her going.

She got out of her car, and a minute later Patrick was greeting her at the observatory entrance. 'Hi there,' he said.

'Hi yourself.'

They held each other for a moment, fitting together perfectly at his very manageable five-foot-six. How strange it was that, after talking to this man every day, living with him, sleeping so many nights next to him, Chel was huddled against him and had no good idea what had been happening in his life for months.

Patrick pulled back from their embrace. 'Glad you got

up here okay.' His blue eyes gleamed beneath his eye shield, and blond hair framed his face. He wore the striped button-down Chel had given him last Christmas, and she wondered if he'd put it on for a reason. He rarely wore it when they were together; it was she who'd used it more, as a nightshirt. He'd liked taking it off her.

'I still can't believe you were in there with patient zero,' he said. 'Jesus.' He stepped back to look at her. 'Pulling all-nighters again?'

'Something like that.'

'Hardly a first for you.'

Chel could hear the note of longing in his voice, his desire to remind her of what they once shared. 'I really appreciate you coming up here,' she said. 'I do.'

'All you had to do was ask,' he said. 'A codex from the classic. Unbelievable.'

Chel looked back over the LA basin behind them. A gray haze of ash filled the sky. 'Let's go inside,' she said. 'It's eerie out here – and the clock is ticking.'

Patrick lingered behind her for a moment, squinting into the darkness. 'Love the stars too fondly to be fearful of the night,' he said, paraphrasing his favorite epitaph.

The three-hundred-seat Oschin Planetarium dome rose seventy-five feet from ground to apex and gave visitors the feeling of standing inside a great unfinished work of art, a basilica ceiling yet to be painted. They stood in the dark, lit only by the glow of the two red EXIT signs and a laptop. While Patrick focused on the images of the codex on the computer, Chel studied the strange contours of the star projector in the middle of the room. It looked like a futuristic monster, a mechanical hydra that projected thousands of stars onto the aluminum ceiling through cratered hemispheres.

'Whoa, I've never seen this before in a codex, a reference to a star war timed to the evening star,' Patrick said. 'It's unbelievable.'

The images of the book had swiftly worked their magic on him too. He dimmed the lights, flipped a switch on the projector, and now the dome filled with stars jetting across the night sky, rotating through hundreds of positions, magically transforming. Chel had been here a dozen times in the year and a half they were together, but every time it felt new.

'There are dozens of astronomical references in what you've already translated,' Patrick said, pointing at the ceiling with a laser. 'Not just the zodiac but positional references and other things we can use to anchor us.'

Chel had never paid enough attention to the details of his work, and now she was embarrassed by how little she knew.

'Come on,' he said. 'You know this stuff. It's a historical–astronomical GPS.'

He was teasing her.

'You'll recall – Dr Manu – that the earth rotates around the sun. And on its own axis. But it's also oscillating back and forth with respect to inertial space, due to the moon's tidal forces. It's like a toy top that wobbles. So the sun's path as we see it across the sky changes a little every year. Which is what 2012ers are all obsessed with, of course.'

'Galactic alignment?'

Patrick nodded. 'The crazies think that because the moon, earth and sun are lined up on the winter solstice, and we're nearing the time when the sun will intersect with some imagined equator of the dark rift of the Milky Way, we'll all be destroyed because of the tidal waves or the sun exploding. Depends who you ask. Never mind that the "equator" they're talking about is totally imagined.'

Projected stars moved in slow concentric circles above their heads. Chel sank down into one of the cloth-covered seats, tired of craning her neck.

'So the earth wobbles back and forth,' Patrick continued. 'And not only does the sun's path across the sky change as a result, but so do the stars'.'

'But even if they shift over time,' Chel asked, 'the stars we see here in Los Angeles aren't very different from the ones they see in Seattle, right? So how are we supposed to get a good location from that? The differences are pretty imperceptible.'

'Imperceptible to our eyes. We have too much light pollution. But the ancients' naked-eye observations were more precise than ours could ever be.'

Patrick's own love affair with the Maya began while he pursued a PhD in archaeoastronomy. He became obsessed with the analyses that the Maya astronomers were able to do from their temples: approximations of planetary cycles, understanding of the concept of galaxies, even a basic grasping of the idea of moons attached to other planets. The modern decline of stargazing was a tragedy, Patrick felt.

They both stared up at the frozen sky. 'So let's start at Tikal,' he said. 'This is what it looked like there on the vernal equinox on the approximate date you got from the carbon dating and the iconography. Let's say: March twentieth, 930 A.D.' He used the laser to highlight a bright object in the western sky. 'According to your scribe, on his vernal equinox, Venus was visible in the dead middle. So we rotate the coordinates of the star projector within the range of the Petén, until we get Venus in the right place.'

The stars spun above them until Venus was at the apex of the planetarium ceiling. 'Looks like about fourteen to sixteen degrees north,' Patrick said finally.

But Chel knew enough to know that from fourteen to sixteen degrees north would span a range of more than two hundred miles wide. 'That's as close as we can get? We have to do better than that.'

Patrick began to shift stars. 'That's only the first constraint. From what you've already translated, we've got dozens more to parse. We'll go as fast as we can.'

They worked side by side, with the projector and Patrick's computerized star charts, the codex providing more inputs. Much of the work was done in silence, with Patrick entirely focused on the sky above.

It was after two a.m., during a long stretch of silence, when Chel found her thoughts drifting uncomfortably to Volcy and his deathbed.

To her relief, Patrick interrupted them. 'So before this all started,' he said, 'did you have a chance to take that trip to the Petén you wanted? Were you writing all the articles you'd hoped to?'

When she'd ended their relationship and he moved out of her house, these were the excuses she gave.

'I guess,' Chel said quietly.

'After this, you'll be a keynote speaker for the rest of your life,' he said.

Patrick already seemed to have forgotten that she might be facing a jail term after this. Yet even now, in the midst of this catastrophe, Chel could hear the tinge of jealousy in his voice. Despite Patrick's cutting-edge scholarship, there were few people who were interested in archaeo-astronomy. He'd spent his career trying to convince the academy that what he did mattered. But he always found himself presenting at the ends of conferences, publishing in obscure journals, and having book proposals rejected.

Chel hadn't really processed how deep his competitive streak ran until the night after she won the American Society of Linguistics' most prestigious award. They'd gotten to the bottom of a second bottle of Sangiovese at their favorite Italian restaurant, and Patrick tilted his glass toward her.

'To you,' he'd said. 'For picking the right specialty.'

'What does that mean?'

'Nothing,' he'd said, downing a long sip of wine. 'I'm just happy epigraphy is well appreciated.'

He did his best to behave every time another of her articles was accepted or she received another award, but it was forced cheer. Eventually, Chel limited what she told him about work to the few frustrations she had with her job: students not doing their work or the politics of the Getty board. She shared every bad thing that happened and none of the good; it was easier. But with each little omission, Chel felt the distance growing between them.

Patrick again shifted the star pattern on the planetarium ceiling. 'I've been seeing someone,' he said.

Chel looked up. 'You have?'

'Yeah. For a couple of months. Her name is Martha.'

'Is it real?'

'I think so. I've been staying at her place. She was anxious about me seeing you tonight, but she understood the urgency. Pretty weird excuse to get together with your ex in the middle of the night.'

'I didn't know anyone under sixty was named Martha.'

'She's plenty south of sixty, if that's what you're asking.'

'So she's a child. Even better.'

'She's thirty-five, and a successful theater director. And she wants to get married.'

Chel was astounded that he was thinking of marriage so soon after their breakup. 'At least you're not in the same field.'

Patrick looked at her. 'What do you mean?'

'Just that you'll never have to worry about . . . work disagreements.'

'You think that was our problem?'

She shrugged. 'I don't know. Maybe.'

'The problem wasn't me competing with you, Chel,' he said slowly. 'Until you realize you've long surpassed whatever expectations your father might have had for you, you'll never be happy. Or be able to make anyone else happy.'

Chel turned back to the codex images. 'We should focus.'

Patrick finally stopped the projector ten minutes later, breaking the silence of the enormous room. 'This matches all of the constraints,' he said, pointing up. 'All eighteen.'

'You're sure?' Chel asked. 'This is it?'

'This is it,' he said. 'Between 15.5 and 16.1 degrees

north and 900 to 970 A.D. We can't know exactly where it falls, but we can apply the mean values. So we're basically talking about fifteen and a half degrees north and 935 A.D. I told you I'd figure it out.'

This was the same sky above Paktul as he had written the codex. The exact same. Chel had plenty of occasion to feel genuine awe in her work, but this feeling of transcending time and space was unique, and she sensed them getting closer to what they needed.

'Near the southern part of the Petén, just like you thought,' Patrick said, rolling up his sleeves. He spread out a map of the Maya region on a desk beside the star projector. The map was positional, with latitude lines marking each half-degree change. 'It's not Tikal or Uaxactun or Piedras Negras; those are in the seventeen-degree range. So we're looking at something farther south.'

He traced an invisible line between the degree markers. The location of each of the known major Maya cities in the southeast Petén was marked, but Patrick's invisible line didn't intersect with any of them, or with any of the minor ones either.

Now something was bothering Chel.

'Is there another computer I can use?' she asked.

Patrick pointed toward a small office in the back of the planetarium.

At the monitor, she found her way to Google Earth and a digital map showing contemporary villages in Guatemala. There were no latitude markings. So Chel pulled up another map online that had detailed latitude lines, then toggled between them until she found what she was searching for.

Fifteen point eight degrees north ran within fifty miles of where she was born.

Chel's only memory from her childhood in Kiaqix was of riding on her father's shoulders. It was early evening in the dry season, and Alvar had finished working for the day, so he took her to settle a claim with a neighbor over a chicken missing from their coop. From her perch, Chel watched as young girls brought pails of cornmeal from the mill back to their mothers, to be used for dinner tortillas and breakfast drinks. Whistle music came from the houses, and a drum was played; Alvar danced to it as he walked, and Chel felt the sandpaper of his beard on her legs.

She'd been back to her homeland several times since her mother took her from Kiaqix, and each time she fell more in love with the communal bonfires where stories of the ancestors were still told, the labor-sharing on the milpas at harvest time, the gifts from the beekeepers, and the villagers' spirited volleyball and soccer games.

Kiaqix was hundreds of miles from any of the big cities, the highways, or the ruins, and reaching it wasn't easy. You could take a small plane to a landing strip five miles east. But there was only one car in the village of two thousand people, so you'd likely be going those last five miles on foot. Factor in the rainy season, which made the one road into town treacherous, and you were dealing with one complicated journey.

More, Chel's mother refused to return to Guatemala and always begged Chel not to either. Ha'ana believed that as long as the *ladinos* controlled the country, the Manu family would never be safe. With tensions high and violence erupting again, Ha'ana's anxiety had only increased.

'What is it?' Patrick asked from the doorway. Behind him, the planetarium was pitch-dark, as if the world ended here, in this tiny office.

She showed him the map she'd pulled up online. He

leaned over her to better see the screen, and instinctively Chel put her hand on the cuff of his shirt, feeling the fabric at her fingertips. Whatever was lost between them, the feel of him was so familiar. 'Are there any major ruins on that latitude?' he asked.

Chel shook her head.

'But Kiaqix is a small village,' Patrick said. 'You said the scribe is talking about a city of tens of thousands.'

He was right: Kiaqix was a no-man's-land for the ancients. No artifacts had been discovered there from the classic era, and the nearest ruins were two hundred miles away.

Then again, Chel thought, staring at the map, the circumstances described in the codex were eerily similar to the stories she knew: the oral history of a king destroying his own city. 'The Original Trio,' she reminded Patrick. 'Kiaqix was supposedly founded when three city-dwellers escaped to the jungle.'

'I thought you didn't believe there was a lost city. That it was a legend.'

'There's no evidence either way,' Chel whispered. 'All we have are the oral history and the people who say they saw the ruins but couldn't prove it.'

Remembering now, Patrick said, 'Your uncle, right?'

'My father's cousin.'

More than three decades ago, Chiam Manu left Kiaqix and went into the jungle for more than a week. When he returned, he claimed to have found Kiaqix's lost city, from which the oral history claimed their ancestors came. But Chiam brought nothing back and would tell no one in which direction the lost city lay. Few believed him; most ridiculed Chiam and called him a liar. When he was murdered by the army weeks later, the truth died with him.

'What about Volcy?' Patrick continued. 'You think it's possible he's from Kiaqix?'

Chel took a breath. 'Everything he said about his village could be said of Kiaqix, I guess. And also about three hundred other villages across the Petén.'

Patrick put his hand on top of hers and leaned closer. Chel smelled traces of the sandalwood soap he always used. 'How does this book land in your lap in the middle of all this? It's one hell of a coincidence, don't you think?'

Chel turned back to the computer screen. There was no word in Qu'iche for *coincidence*, and it wasn't only a problem of translation. When events happened together and pointed in a single direction, her people used a different word. It was the same word Chel's father used in his final letter from prison, when he sensed his death was near: *ch'umilal*.

Fate.

12.19.19.17.14
December 15, 2012

19

Just after six a.m., while Davies and Thane reviewed every detail of their plan for a final time, Stanton stepped out onto the empty boardwalk to join a conference call with government officials in LA, Atlanta, DC, and around the country. The sun was inching toward the coastline and hadn't started cooking the ocean air, so in his thin, long-sleeved shirt and jeans, he was underdressed for the chill lingering on the Walk. The only sound competing with the lapping of the waves was an invisible helicopter churning somewhere in the distance.

Tuning out a procedural roll call, Stanton glimpsed a small circle of men sitting in sun chairs right near the shore, all wearing eye shields. At first he couldn't imagine who was brazen enough to meet right now in violation of the curfew. Then Stanton realized they were sitting in exactly the same spot as the Venice Beach men's AA meeting always did. They often congregated at dawn, and, however surprising, it was a strange comfort to Stanton to know that some appointments couldn't be missed.

'The utilities can't keep up with the demands or the outages,' a FEMA deputy was saying on the phone now. 'No electricity means no potable water.'

Los Angeles had been on the brink of an energy crisis for decades. Now, with half of the city suffering from anxiety-related sleeplessness, lights and televisions and computers ran twenty-four hours a day. Blackouts spread. Water consumption had skyrocketed. Taps could run dry within a week.

'What are we doing about bodies?' Stanton broke in, out of turn. 'Houses across the city could have decaying corpses inside them.'

'We have to take them to a central location,' somebody replied. He didn't recognize the voice – there were so many bureaucrats involved in every decision now.

'We could be talking about thousands in a few days,' Stanton said. There were more than eight thousand known victims of VFI citywide. 'You don't have the equipment for that kind of biohazard, and there'd be no way to ensure the safety of the workers.'

'Well, we have to do something,' Cavanagh cut in, 'and I can't believe I'm saying this, but I'm starting to think that means telling people they have to douse the bodies with acid or lye and let them dissolve in bathtubs.'

Stanton's boss was taking the call from the recession-shuttered post office in East LA that had been turned into a CDC command center. From the tone of Cavanagh's voice, Stanton could feel the toll all this was exacting on her. Already, forty-two CDC investigators and nurses were infected with VFI, and he knew Cavanagh well enough to know that she blamed herself. She'd personally selected many of them to come out from Atlanta to help manage the outbreak.

As the call broke up, Stanton sensed an opening and asked his boss to stay on the line. One way or another, he,

Davies, and Thane were going to test the antibodies in the next twenty-four hours. Their plans were in place. But if he could convince Cavanagh that it was the right thing, they'd have access to a much larger sample group and they'd be acting within the law.

'Emily, the quarantine seal is breaking,' he said. 'Soon they're going to be having this conversation about dead bodies and bathtubs in every city in America. We need to discuss treatment options.'

'Gabe, we talked about this.'

'But I have to tell you again. We could have an experimental antibody therapy available soon if we start immediately. In a day or two.' He glanced back over his shoulder at his condo, not wanting to imagine Cavanagh's reaction if she knew about the antibodies being created inside as they spoke. But he knew that if they could get them to work and could prove it, she'd have no choice but to come around.

The helicopter circled somewhere even closer behind Stanton, getting louder. 'I'll discuss it with the director,' Cavanagh said finally. 'Maybe he can get the White House to issue an executive order and suspend normal FDA protocols.'

'FDA'll drag their feet. They always do.'

'We all want the same thing, Gabe.'

Stanton hung up, frustrated by the resignation in her voice. She'd left him with little choice. Before he got back inside, his phone rang.

He picked up. 'Did you find anything?'

'Dr Stanton? It's Chel Manu.'

'I know. Did you find something more?'

'Sorry. Yes. We did. It could be . . . useful. It's good.'

It was nice to hear someone sounding alive, even hopeful. 'Good is good,' Stanton said. 'What is it?'

Listening to her story – the ancient city's latitude line seemed to intersect with that of the village in which she'd been born? – Stanton didn't know what to think. He had no choice but to trust her at this point: everyone said she knew what she was doing. Yet every revelation of hers seemed more improbable than the last. Everything in her work and her life seemed to constantly circle back on itself.

'You couldn't tell if Volcy was from your village?' Stanton asked.

'We knew he was from the Petén,' she said. 'But not Kiaqix. And he was afraid – he wouldn't say anything specific about where he was from.'

'Is there any way for you to confirm this before we take it further?'

'There are no phones in Kiaqix, but I talked to a cousin of mine. He lives in Guatemala City, but he goes back regularly to visit his father. I had him look at a picture on one of the news sites, and he recognized Volcy from the photo you released.'

Now the helicopter buzzed directly overhead. Stanton glanced up and saw not one but two choppers. They were flying low and seemed to be headed directly for the beach. One was large and looked military. The other was smaller – four seats encased in a glass bubble. Seconds later they both dropped toward the ground in lockstep. It was one of the oddest sights Stanton had ever seen on the boardwalk, and that was saying a hell of a lot.

The men from the AA meeting stood up and shielded their faces from the sand tornadoing up into the air. Finally both helicopters had landed about a hundred yards up the beach, and five men in camouflage carrying machine guns poured from the National Guard helicopter. They ran to the other chopper, pulled out a young pilot, a man in his sixties, and a redhead who couldn't be more than thirty. The older man wore a blazer and slacks, as if headed to a business meeting. The redhead was still wearing her sunglasses and screaming as they were cuffed and arrested. Stanton watched in disbelief: LA's wealthiest were trying to flee the quarantine.

'Dr Stanton?'

He refocused. 'So we need to find out when the last time people in your village saw Volcy and in what direction he might have headed from there to find this . . . lost city,' Stanton told Chel. A jungle Atlantis as the source of VFI was hardly the answer he'd been hoping for. But it was what they had.

'Like I said, no phones. And mail can take weeks to get there. We're really talking about the middle of the jungle.'

'Then we'll send a plane in,' he said.

'I thought the Guatemalans weren't cooperating.'

With thousands now infected here, it would be very difficult to convince anyone in the States, let alone Guatemala, that sending a team into the jungle in search of vanished ruins was the best move. 'Figure out the location and we'll make them do it,' he told her.

'I'll do everything I can,' she said.

'I know you will, Chel.' He spoke her name as she had pronounced it to him when they first met – with a soft syllable, as if he was saying 'shhhell.' It was the first time he'd said it aloud. For a second he worried he'd screwed it up.

All she said was, 'I'll call soon, Gabe.'

Wind rolled in off the ocean, and the marine layer shielded the rising sun. By the time they hung up, the guardsmen had put the quarantine violators into the army helicopter and taken off. Only the small bubble chopper still sat on the sand. Two of the AA guys were peering inside the empty cockpit, probably trying to assess if they could get into the air again.

As one of them reached a heavily inked arm through the window, Stanton was reminded of someone. He turned and hurried down the boardwalk. Metal gates on stores had been pried open and were curled up like old-fashioned sardine cans. Cars had never been allowed on the Walk, but now he had to navigate around abandoned junkers every few feet. A pickup truck had crashed through the brick wall, directly into a store. The lawn area between the pavement and the beach was strewn with dozens of yellow T-shirts with the logo VENICE, WHERE ART MEETS CRIME printed across them.

Approaching the Freak Show, just off the walk, Stanton saw something moving out front. On the steps, a two-headed iguana jerked back and forth. The glass doors to the building had been smashed in by looters, and the animals had gotten out.

The iguana scurried back up into the Freak Show building. Stanton followed.

Inside, everything was destroyed.

The room reeked of formaldehyde spilling out from broken preservation jars. A two-headed garter snake lay dead beneath an overturned pedestal. No trace of the other animals. Stanton ran to the small office in back. Neither Monster nor the Electric Lady was there. The laptop that his friend always had with him was smashed into pieces on the desk, and Monster's windbreaker lay abandoned on the small cot.

Stanton felt hollow as he headed back home. Inside, there was an obstacle course of equipment and power cords hooked up to the portable generator they'd brought in. Drying racks and centrifuges sat on the floor, beside furniture half covered by plastic sheets.

Davies and Thane stood in the kitchen, sipping the last of the coffee from a machine hooked up to the generator. 'Where'd you go?' Davies asked. 'Quick surf? Ice cream cone? I hear the salted caramel is delicious at N'ice Cream.'

Stanton ignored him. 'No one came by at any point when I wasn't here, did they?'

Monster knew where Gabe lived from an Art Walk event Stanton had once invited him to. Maybe, if he'd been in trouble . . .

Davies shook his head. 'Expecting trick-or-treaters? I suppose I must look like I'm dressed for Halloween.'

He was wearing an old button-down and a pair of Stanton's khakis while he washed his own clothes. Seeing Davies dressed down was like the final sign that the world had come undone.

Stanton turned to Thane. 'You all right?'

'Ready to do this thing.'

'Speaking of,' Davies said, 'got a tiny bright spot for you. I think the antibodies are finished sooner than we thought.'

The high-powered microscope in the dining room ran on a second electric generator. Stanton stared into the eyesights. After injecting the knockout mice with VFI, they'd placed antibodies the animals produced into a test tube with more of the diseased human prions, and the results were astounding. Every slide here showed protein transformation that was either slowed or halted entirely.

Davies motioned at Thane. 'Now all she has to do is inject them into her friends' IVs and not get caught.'

Thane's condition for participating was that the test group consist of her sick friends and colleagues from Presbyterian Hospital. She knew she was taking a risk with their lives if the antibody didn't work. She also knew it was the only chance they had.

'How long will it be until we know something?' she asked.

'Don't get ahead of yourself,' Stanton said. 'The preparations won't be ready for another twelve hours.'

Davies smiled. 'Anyone want to go work on their tan?'

'And then?' Thane asked.

'If it works, we should see some results within a day,' Stanton said.

'And if it doesn't?'

'Don't know about you Yanks,' Davies said, 'but if it doesn't, I for one am going to find a way out of this godforsaken country.'

20

He had decided to build their city in the Verdugo Mountains because of its spiritual significance to the Tongva – the people of the earth – who ruled the LA basin for thousands of years before the arrival of the Spanish. On a twenty-acre plot, which he had convinced LA County to sell during the budget crisis, he and his daykeeper and their growing community of followers had quietly built fifteen small stone abodes, each capable of housing up to four members. They had won the necessary permits, befriended the regular hikers, and filed the documents of incorporation for a self-sustaining agrarian community twenty miles outside the city.

'We did this,' he'd told them just a month ago, while his daykeeper looked on with pride. 'All of us. Together.' And he meant it. *They* had done it, even if some of the twenty-six men, women, and now two children born into the community didn't realize their own part in the achievement. That day, a few of them had asked him to speak from the hilltop, rather than from the humble doorstep of his house. But he had just smiled. 'There might be a king among us someday,' he'd told them, 'but not today, and it's certainly not me.'

Once he'd been a soldier. He'd spent most of his life in the deserts: Arizona, Kuwait, Saudi Arabia. The first time they'd sent him to Guatemala, he could barely breathe the wet air. Could barely handle being trapped beneath the teeming tree canopy that sucked up all the light. But then he had fallen in love with the place. Not with Guatemala City and its thieves and beggars; not with the soldiers he was sent to train, with their unearned swagger. He fell in love with the hidden world of the jungle.

At first, the *indígenas* were blurry figures on the sides of the rural roads, hardly looking up from their labor as he hurtled by in a military jeep. But then he explored the ruins of Tikal and Copan on his weekends off base. He read about the culture that survived the conquistadores and then centuries of men like him sent to destroy it. He began to understand the prophecies of their ancestors, how much they'd understood about the secret ways of the world. By the time he met the daykeeper, he knew what he had to do.

Because he had been a soldier, he understood the value of firm command, and he'd used it to bring his followers under his sway. But command could do only so much, he also knew. A soldier learned to follow his leader anywhere, at any cost. That taught men to win battles, but it did not make for enduring cultures. It did not teach habitual followers to become leaders and priests, to set the foundations of a city that would survive longer than he and the daykeeper. Their followers who pleaded with him to climb hilltops and give speeches did it because they *needed* orders. They needed someone to rule from above. They had built a city from scratch with their bare hands, yet they were terrified of building a civilization. They'd sacrificed so much for their beliefs – family, jobs, and more – and now a very frightening thing had happened: they'd been proven right.

He stared out the window of his little house in the mountains, maybe for the last time. After all the preparation, all the planning, these hills had turned out not to be the refuge they'd needed. Remote as it was, it was still in the quarantine zone, among the thousands dying in this city and the tens of thousands more who would be dying soon. He would have to lead his people to a place they knew only from books, and he knew not all of them would survive the journey.

He turned his eyes from the window and composed his expression so that even these senior members – the two men and one woman who now sat around this dining table – would see only inspiring certainty.

'Eighteen months of construction,' Mark Lafferty was saying. 'And now we're going to have to start all over again.'

Lafferty was a middle-aged structural engineer who'd grown up near Three Mile Island, which entitled him to a tragic outlook. He was useful, though. He'd supervised all this construction.

Instead of responding, their leader stood up with a flourish and paced the little room. They watched him appear to gather his thoughts. Sometimes it made him sad how easy it was to play on people's desire for command. If he didn't have the daykeeper to talk to, he'd be bored out of his mind.

'Mark,' he said, 'look at the fantastic job you all did here. Imagine how much better you'll do once you can use the original materials. Clay, wood, proper thatch. And we'll have more room to grow down there too. Much more than we could ever have had here. Besides, look into your heart. You all know as well as I do that these hills were never quite right for us. We always needed to head south.'

He took his seat again. On the table were maps of Los Angeles, the western seaboard, and the path through Mexico into Central America. There were places along the way where Lafferty, if he became a tax on the group morale, could be left behind. Those kinds of decisions lay ahead. First came the escape – and the one task remaining before it.

He knew the next to speak would be David Sarno. Sarno had been one of their earliest recruits. He was an ex-industrial farmer who'd become disgusted with genetically modified organisms. A man who knew soil and crops, he also had an authority that could be cultivated. 'Based on the average temperatures down there, we won't have any trouble growing corn or beans, of course. Wheat may be harder, but we don't need wheat.'

'What does the daykeeper think?' Laura Waller asked. When he had met Laura and recruited her, she was a thirty-two-year-old school-teacher, freshly divorced after four devastating failures at in vitro fertilization. Now she was thirty weeks' pregnant with the child they had conceived naturally.

'He agrees. South is the only way.'

Lafferty spoke up again. 'We need eight trucks to get everything out. How are we going to get that many trucks across the border?'

He shuffled the maps quietly. 'We'll get everything in four trucks at most, prioritizing seeds, medical supplies, and weapons.'

The front door opened. The daykeeper. Relief flooded the room at his safe arrival. The daykeeper meant so much to these people. He was warm. Kind. Compassionate about them and their lives.

'Daykeeper, come, sit. Are you thirsty?'

'I'm fine, Colton. Thank you.'

Victor wiped a bit of sweat from his brow, sat down at the table. 'This might be the only peaceful part of LA County left,' he said.

Lafferty started to dig back into logistics, but Shetter quickly cut him off. 'Thank you all for your counsel. Now would you all give me a few minutes with the daykeeper?'

Shetter kissed Laura on the cheek as she left with the others.

'Are they handling the change of plans?' Victor asked when they were alone.

'They're afraid,' Shetter said.

'We should all be afraid.'

'But they're also stronger than they think they are.'

Even before they'd met, Shetter had known Victor's work. At meetings of his early Internet recruits, Shetter had often read aloud from Victor's writings on the Long Count. Then, eighteen months ago, the two men had found themselves sitting next to each other at the ritual incense ceremony at the ruins of El Mirador. Shetter knew it couldn't be a coincidence. They'd been perfect partners from the start. Victor had an unparalleled command of the ancient history and the capacity to inspire their people, and he left the planning to Shetter.

Victor pulled a sheaf of papers from his satchel. 'Here are the latest pages that have been translated. If anyone's still on the fence, this will put their doubts to rest.'

The codex was the final proof of their collective destiny. It showed not only that the ancients had predicted 2012 but that a prescient few had foreseen the collapse and had survived by escaping the cities.

Shetter read the newest sections of the translation. 'Someday children will know these lines as well as they know the Pledge of Allegiance. Pretty incredible, don't you think?' Around Victor, he allowed himself the excitement that he kept from the others.

Victor nodded but seemed distracted.

'Are you all right?' Shetter asked.

'Fine.'

'Do we have a problem?'

'Not at all.'

Shetter slowly shifted back to business, to the details at hand. 'Did you get the blueprints?'

'We won't need them.'

The diagram Victor handed him was just a simple visitor's map of the Getty Museum. There were no dimensions, no electrical lines, no security schematics. Victor would be invaluable in the new world, but he wasn't prepared in this one.

'Trust me,' Victor said. 'It won't be difficult to get inside.'

Shetter had already decided not to raise the subject of

weapons with the daykeeper. Victor blamed much of the world's decline on the technology of war; he insisted that their new society must not even speak of such things. So Shetter would oblige him for now, by keeping the Luger P08 in his pocket to himself.

21

Chel and Patrick had spent the rest of the night and early morning checking and rechecking the coordinates that suggested a connection between Kiaqix and Paktul's lost city. She left the observatory just after ten a.m. Patrick was headed back to Martha. As they'd said goodbye beneath the central dome, Chel had realized that she had no idea when she'd see him again, or under what circumstances, and she didn't like the feeling. So she tried to do again what had always come easily to her before: putting her work first. She sped west, oblivious to the looting, the fires, and the abandoned vehicles all around her.

'He could've been one of them,' Rolando's voice cut in and out over her Bluetooth. What he was suggesting – that the scribe from the lost city could be one of the Original Trio – was slightly less absurd today than it would have been yesterday.

'We don't even know the city actually exists,' Chel said.

'His spirit animal is a macaw. Wouldn't he be the perfect candidate to consider thousands of macaws in one place a good omen?'

Chel tried to take the leap from myth to history: a nobleman and his two wives wander the forest after fleeing a city in turmoil. On the third day out, they find a glade where hundreds of scarlet macaws are perched in the trees.

Like all the ancient Maya, they believe the birds have great spiritual power. The trio assumes they've found an auspicious place to settle in the jungle, and Kiaqix is founded.

'When we finish translating, maybe we'll see that Paktul married those two little girls, and they became the founders,' Rolando said.

As his voice cut out again, Chel had to swerve around an abandoned Prius in front of the La Brea Tar Pits. Thousands of animals had gotten stuck in the bubbling tar during the last Ice Age, which fossilized everything from mastodons to saber-tooth cats. What would be left of humans here in ten millennia? Chel wondered.

Continuing down Wilshire, she saw graffiti everywhere. The city's street artists had taken advantage of preoccupied police to tag every available surface: Crip signs, Banksy imitators, and the cartoon initials of freelancers. Then, on the side of a building just west of La Brea Avenue, Chel saw scrawled:

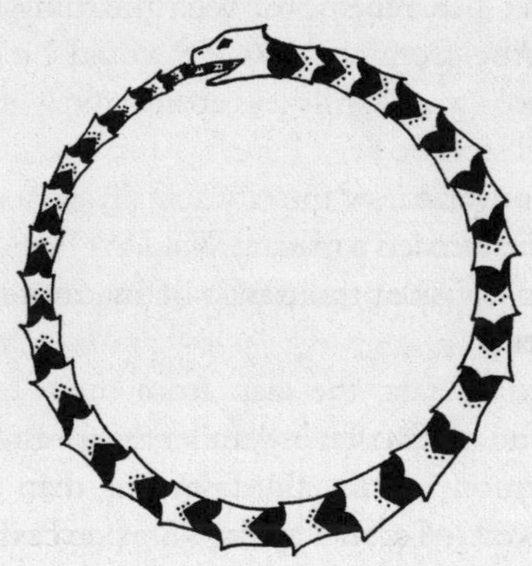

The Maya plumed serpent god – Gukumatz, as the Qu'iche people called it – was sometimes represented by a snake swallowing its own tail. It symbolized the harvest, the cycles of time, and her people's deep connection to their past. The Greeks called it Ouroboros; to them it had represented something similar. But Chel knew that whoever had painted this intended something else. Gukumatz had been appropriated by the 2012ers, not to symbolize renewal but to evoke the destruction they thought would come with the end of the Long Count cycle – as a reminder that every race of man before ours has been destroyed, devoured by the unrelenting serpent of time.

The signal patched itself back together, and Chel heard Rolando's voice in her car again. 'Hello? Chel, you still there?'

'I'm here. Do me a favor. Put Victor on the phone.'

'Try his cell. He went home to get some journal article from the seventies he thought might help with the Akabalam glyph. Apparently he's been hoarding back issues for decades.'

'I'm aware.'

'When will you be back here?'

'As soon as I can.'

'And you're headed to?'

'To talk to the one person who knows more about Kiaqix than I do.'

Chel banged repeatedly on the massive bronze doors of Our Lady of the Angels, which less than a week ago seemed to Chel like the paragon of excess, and now seemed like a godsend. When they finally opened, she was welcomed with a gun pointed at her face.

'Jesus, Jinal, it's me. Chel.'

'Sorry,' he responded in Qu'iche. He holstered his weapon and closed the door behind them. 'There were protestors outside earlier. They wanted to send us all back across the border. Do you know Karana Menchu? She was running low on formula, so she went out – the back way – but they found her and started pushing her around.'

'Is she okay?'

'She's going to be fine, but she was crying when I saw her.'

'Did you call the police?'

'Yes. But we're pretty much at the bottom of the priority list.'

Chel saw tension in his face. Chel had known the young man since 2007, when he came from Honduras after years of work in the tobacco fields. She touched his arm. 'Thanks for watching out for everyone, Jinal,' she said.

'Of course.'

'Have you seen my mother?' Chel had finally convinced Ha'ana to come here with the rest of *Fraternidad.*

Jinal nodded. 'I think she's in the main sanctuary.'

Chel headed past the chaplains' offices and the stairs leading down to the mausoleum, where Gutierrez had shown her the codex. She made her way by the cafeteria, where a handful of *Fraternidad* in eye shields were preparing the large group's next meal, including Vicente and Ina Larakam, who waved at her. Reaching the sanctuary, she inhaled the smell of incense that always greeted her here.

Luis, one of the younger daykeepers, said a prayer at the altar. 'These spirits must be purified, so the people may dream. Save the people from their self-destruction. Deliver them to the earth mother, so they may connect with their spirit animals again.'

The Maya considered sleep a religious experience, a time when people communed with the gods. To them, insomnia was the result of a lack of piety, and Chel knew there were many here who believed that VFI had been sent by the gods as a punishment. In this, they and the picketers were probably more alike than they knew.

Chel tried to calculate how much sleep she'd had in the past four days. She'd stolen catnaps on the love seat in her office, but for all intents and purposes there was little difference between her and someone in the first stages of VFI. She didn't believe in the deities of her ancestors, but she certainly felt like she was being punished.

An elderly man wearing black slacks and a gray button-down shirt headed down the aisle toward her. The entire congregation was wearing eye shields, so it was difficult to differentiate people in the crowd. Only when he got close did Chel recognize his white beard. It was one of the few times she had seen Maraka out of his traditional robes.

'Chel,' he said, embracing her, 'you're safe. Thank God.'

'Daykeeper,' she whispered.

Maraka looked up at the pulpit. 'Luis has been going on and on with prayers all day and night,' he said, not bothering to whisper. 'I think it's excessive. The gods are all-powerful. They hear us, believe me.'

Chel managed a smile.

'But I assume you haven't come here to pray,' Maraka said.

'I need to see my mother.'

Maraka pointed to the far end of the sanctuary, where several *indígenas* women were seated in the pews, far from the altar.

As Chel approached, Ha'ana glanced up from the *People* magazine she was reading. She stood and pulled her daughter close. The magazine was expected, but Chel was surprised by the hug – it had been years since her mother had embraced her in this way. She felt something inside her give, and suddenly a huge wave of fatigue threatened to engulf her.

'You look like you haven't slept,' Ha'ana said.

'I've been working.'

'Still? It's ridiculous, Chel. What could be so important?'

They found a little empty classroom with chairs arranged in a horseshoe, deep in the west arm of the cathedral's cross. Watercolor paintings of Joseph and his famous coat adorned every wall. These circumstances were hardly what Chel had envisioned when she'd imagined showing her mother the codex, but now she had no choice. She talked Ha'ana through the book's connection to the illness and the apparent importance of Kiaqix to finding the source. Chel didn't mention the trouble she faced with ICE and the Getty – the last thing she needed right now was to give Ha'ana cause for disappointment in her.

They scrolled rapidly through pages of the codex on her laptop screen. What it meant to Ha'ana to see something like this and, even more, to learn that the village she'd abandoned years ago was the possible source of VFI, Chel couldn't tell. Her mother's expression revealed nothing.

'So, Mom,' Chel said, 'I need you to try to remember everything that happened when cousin Chiam went to find the lost city.'

Ha'ana put a hand on Chel's arm. 'I've been worried about you. I hope you know that. Now I know I was right to worry. This must be an incredible burden.'

'I'm fine. Now, please, Mom. I need you to remember.'

Ha'ana stood and wandered silently to the window. Chel prepared for her mother's resistance, gathering all the reasons she would give for why Ha'ana had to dig back into a past that she never wanted to revisit.

To Chel's surprise, her mother needed no prompting.

'Your father's cousin was the most skilled tracker in Kiaqix,' she began. 'He could follow a deer for miles through the forest. From the time we were children, he was known as the best hunter in the village. But then the army came to the Petén, and *indígenas* were being murdered in the streets. Hanged from the tops of churches and burned alive. After the army made it to Kiaqix and your father was arrested, Chiam stepped into his place. It was he who read your father's letters from prison aloud in community circle.'

Chel was pleased with the ease of her mother's narration. She hadn't heard Ha'ana volunteer anything about the letters her father wrote from prison for years, and she didn't dare interrupt.

'Chiam was more militant than your father,' she continued. 'He threatened to punish any of us who worked for a *ladino*, swore to kill as many of them as possible. He wanted to kill them as they killed us. Even your father's letters were too soft for Chiam. The two of them had argued, but they were still close. When Alvar was arrested, I knew Chiam would do anything he could to get him out. Prisoners could sometimes be bought for the right price, so Chiam made contact with the guards at Santa Cruz. The price for your father was one hundred thousand quetzals.'

Chel stood up. 'And that's why Chiam tried to find the lost city? Why have you never told me that before?'

'Chiam didn't want anyone to know he'd do business with the *ladinos*, even to get his own cousin out. Plus, if he found anything, he wouldn't be proud of robbing our ancestors to bribe the enemy. Still, he went. And after twenty days he returned and told us what he'd found. He told us there was enough gold and jade to feed Kiaqix for fifty years.'

Chel knew the rest of the story well, but only now did she understand its profound connection to her father's life, and death. His cousin told the villagers that the souls of the ancestors still lived deep in the jungle and that to steal from them would anger the gods. He said the lost city was a spiritual gateway to the other worlds and that it proved the glory of what the Maya once were and could be again. And that once he'd seen the ruins with his own eyes, he couldn't move a single stone or take a single artifact from its resting place. Not for any reason.

The problem was that no one believed him. No one

could accept that he had found treasures and simply left them there. After days of ridicule, Chiam claimed he would lead a team back into the jungle to prove himself. But, before he could, the Guatemalan army hanged him with a dozen other men from across the Petén for their revolutionary activities.

'Chiam gave many details,' Ha'ana continued. 'He said there were twin temples that faced each other, and a great patio with huge columns, where our ancestors would have met to discuss politics. Can you believe it? He thought his stories would remind us we were just as smart as the *ladinos*. But he was not cunning enough, and everyone knew he wasn't telling the truth. He was a good, kind man, but his story was a lie.'

'He said there was a patio?' Chel said. 'With huge columns?'

'Something like that.'

'How tall? Thirty feet?'

'He could have said a thousand feet. No one was listening.'

But Paktul had described a colonnade in Kanuataba's main plaza that circled a small interior court, with pillars that were six or seven men high. And while twin temples existed at dozens of Maya cities, columns built that high existed at only one or two places in Mexico. In Guatemala they were half as tall or less.

'He might have found it,' Chel said. She started to explain the connection she'd made, but her mother wasn't interested in hearing it. 'The lost city is a myth,' Ha'ana said. 'Like all lost cities.'

'We've found lost cities before, Mom. They're out there.'

Ha'ana took a breath. 'I know you want to believe this now, Chel.'

'This isn't about me.'

'Every villager in Kiaqix wants to believe in the lost city,' Ha'ana said. 'They deceive themselves because it gives them hope. But that does not make the oral history any more than what it is: the silly stories of people who cannot know better. I didn't bring you here and raise you to be one of them.'

Chel had been surprised by her mother's willingness to talk about Chiam. But now she knew: no matter what effect these last days had on her, Ha'ana was still the same woman who'd abandoned her family's home, who'd abandoned everything her husband believed in. The same woman who'd spent thirty-three years trying to forget what happened, denying the importance of their culture and tradition.

'Maybe you don't believe in the lost city because of what it would mean for you, Mom.'

'What are you saying?'

It wasn't worth it. 'Forget it. I have to go. I have work to do.'

What time was it?

Chel glanced at her phone. There she found an email from Stanton waiting:

> know you'll send more news when you have it, but wanted to make sure you're okay. – G.

She reread the message. For some reason Chel liked knowing he was keeping tabs on her.

Ha'ana was saying something. 'You're really going to search for these ruins now? In the middle of this?'

Chel stood. 'Mom, we're going to search for them *because* of all this.'

'Search how?'

'With satellites that scan the area for ruins,' Chel said, formulating a plan. 'Or on the ground if we can't find them from the air.'

'Please tell me you won't go into the jungle yourself, Chel.'

'If the doctors need me to, I will.'

'It's not safe. You know it's not safe.'

'Father wasn't afraid to do what he had to.'

'Your father was a tapir,' Ha'ana said. 'And the tapir fights, but he doesn't run into the jaguar's den to be slaughtered.'

'And you were a fox,' Chel said. 'The gray fox that is unafraid of humans, even those who hunt it. But you lost your *wayob*'s spirit when you abandoned Kiaqix.'

Ha'ana turned away. It was a great insult to suggest a Maya wasn't worthy of her *wayob*, and Chel instantly regretted her words. Despite her mother's long, fractured relationship with her origins, her *wayob* was still a part of her.

'You help many people here,' Ha'ana said after a long pause. 'Yet I hear that every time you come, you come only at the end of services. Deep down you don't believe in the gods either. So maybe we are more similar than you think.'

12.19.19.17.15
December 16, 2012

22

Michaela Thane was thirteen when the Rodney King verdict set off looting and burning of thousands of buildings from Korea-town to East LA. Her mother was still alive then, and she had kept Michaela and her brother in the house for nearly four days, where they watched on their nineteen-inch television as rioters set the city ablaze. It was the last time Thane remembered Los Angeles looking as it did now.

On the car radio, she listened to pundits argue about whether it was the email leak from the mayor's office that had started the unrest. One commentator claimed it was the nearly ten thousand estimated sick – agitated and desperate – leading the destruction. Detractors of Stanton's quarantine declared this the inevitable result of trying to contain ten million people. But Thane had spent long enough living and working in this part of LA to know people here didn't need a reason to be angry – they needed a reason *not* to be.

Just before the turn in to Presbyterian, she looked in her rearview mirror to see Davies peel off; he'd trailed her here to ensure her safety. And safe it seemed to be. Floodlights illuminated the night sky, helicopters circled and jeeps swept the perimeter; National Guardsmen with guns patrolled the buildings as if it were a base in Kabul.

Since returning from Afghanistan, Thane had spent nearly every weekday, every third night, and many weekends at Presby. She'd been here on virtually every holiday too, taking the least desirable call nights. Her colleagues thought she did it because she was selfless, but really Thane had nowhere else to go. A hospital operates 365 days a year, twenty-four hours a day, just like a military base. And eating the staff turkey on Thanksgiving and drinking plastic cups of sparkling cider when the clock struck midnight on New Year's was better than being alone.

Working at Presbyterian had never been easy, and sometimes they had to improvise more than medics in the mountains. The hospital was understaffed and overwhelmed. Yet Thane and her colleagues had provided decent care to tens of thousands of patients nonetheless. They helped other services, did favors for critical patients, listened to one another complain, and drank heavily together to try to forget it all. Over the last three years, the Presby staff had been Thane's big, messy, occasionally happy substitute for a platoon.

Now so many of them were dying inside these walls, and Presbyterian itself would soon be a memory too. Even if they could stop or slow the disease, they'd never be able to ensure that all the prion was gone from the floors, the walls, the sinks, the bedrails, and the light switches. The building would be demolished and removed by hazmat, piece by piece.

It was after one a.m., but CDC staff still roamed the halls – tending to patients, trying to calm the victims, barking orders at one another. Thane had difficulty seeing their faces through the helmet of the biohazard suit she'd put on, but that also meant it was difficult for them to see hers. As long as no one recognized her, she could walk the wards unnoticed. The suit was sweltering hot and uncomfortable to move in, but she pressed on past rows of listless patients staring at the walls or restlessly pacing their rooms.

Her first stop was on the fourth floor. Meredith Fentress was a heavy-set woman who just a week ago had manned the lobby. Thane had spent many nights chatting with her about the Dodgers and their never-ending string of disappointments.

Now Fentress was whimpering and tossing, covered in sweat.

'You'll feel better soon,' Thane whispered as she pushed the antibodies from a syringe into the IV, and the yellow-tinged solution dripped into the patient's vein. Thane watched – just as she and Stanton had discussed – to make sure there was no negative reaction that called for an immediate response.

Nothing. When Thane was sure, she made her way from room to room. Occasionally she had to wait for a CDC doctor to finish with the patient and leave, but for the most part, she thought, it was almost like she was invisible.

Amy Singer was a tiny bottle-blond third-year medical student with whom Thane had done a night rotation in the ICU. As she administered the antibodies, Thane remembered a night that they'd both fallen into an uncontrollable fit of laughter after an old man on the floor confused the two of them.

Suddenly a nurse wearing a biohazard suit walked in. She looked at Thane skeptically. 'Can I help you?'

Thane pulled out the CDC ID Stanton had had made for her. 'Just taking some secondary samples,' she said. 'Monitoring how quickly protein loads are growing.'

The nurse seemed satisfied and continued on her rounds. Thane breathed a huge sigh of relief. So far all had gone well. She prayed that the antibodies were doing their work.

Ten patients later, Thane found Bryan Appleton lying quietly in his bed. His eyes were closed, but of course she knew he lingered in a dangerous netherworld. She also took note of the three deep red scratches on the side of his face – when she was done, she'd attach restraints for his own safety. Appleton was one of the kitchen staff, who had practically force-fed Thane meals on her call nights. He'd always seemed to understand that residents survived on the free eats – oatmeal cookies, melon, juice, and coffee – that magically appeared in the call rooms.

Thane watched to make sure the liquid flowed easily through the IV. Then she tried to turn him so she could fasten his arms to the rails.

Appleton's eyes opened.

He grabbed the sleeve of her biohazard suit. 'What are you doing?' he demanded. 'What are you doing to me?'

As gently as she could, Thane maneuvered her arm out of his grip. 'It's Michaela, Bryan. I'm giving you medicine.'

Appleton shot up in bed. 'I don't want any fucking medicine!'

His eyes looked wild. The beeps from the monitor beside his bed came faster. His heart was racing at a hundred eighty beats per minute.

'You have to lie down, Bryan,' Thane said. He was a big man, but she'd dealt with worse. She leaned her weight over the bed, positioning herself. Was he having an allergic reaction to the antibodies? Was it VFI-induced anger and stress causing the tachycardia? Either way, she had to calm him down. 'Please, lie down for a minute and try to relax.'

Appleton threw all his weight and catapulted her over the side table. *'Don't you fucking touch me!'* he screamed as she fell to the ground.

Thane could feel the nasty bruise blooming on her head, but she also knew she had only seconds to get up. Shakily, she got to her feet and glimpsed Appleton's blood pressure: 50/30.

He was having an anaphylactic reaction, and he needed an epinephrine injection. But he was already pulling out his tubes. It would be impossible to get close enough. 'Please, Bryan,' she begged. 'You're having a reaction to the drug. You gotta let me give you something for it.'

'You're poisoning me!' he screamed, throwing his legs over the side of the bed and starting after her. *'I'll kill you, bitch!'*

Thane darted around the bed and headed for the door. Bryan's screams echoed down the hallway, and soon other patients heard him and joined in. Yelling that they were poisoned too. Demanding to be released from the quarantine.

Thane fled to the stairs. Her biohazard suit was suffocating as she descended to the third floor, where she nearly barreled into a man in a hospital gown standing at the top. It was Mariano, the security guard who'd stood outside Volcy's room for days. Thane was hit with a wave of sadness. The man had spent years trying to protect himself from disease with masks. But he hadn't protected his eyes.

'Keep away from my wife,' he shouted. He was sick and obviously hallucinating.

'It's okay, Mariano,' she said. 'It's Michaela Thane.'

Mariano bared his teeth, grabbed the nylon fabric of her biohazard suit, and threw her down the stairs.

Thane's neck broke the moment she hit the landing.

23

I have taken ownership of One Butterfly and Flamed Plume, Auxila's daughters. Haniba did her duty, as is ordained by the gods. The girls visit her grave – marked with a cross signifying the four cardinal directions – every other sun. Her suicide was met with acclaim from the royal council, who believe Auxila was chosen for sacrifice by the gods.

Never knowing me to be carnal, the members of the council were shocked to hear I had taken his daughters as my concubines. Darkened Sun believed me only when I told him I planned to lie with the younger of the two first and that my abstinence was actually a preference for unspoiled youth. I have commanded Flamed Plume to spread word to the other girls of Kanuataba of how her younger sister submits most humbly to my insatiable appetites.

I also told the girls in truth that I would never make them lie with me. At first they seemed terrified I would force myself upon them. One Butterfly, only nine years, was particularly scared at first, but when I bled her gums upon the loss of a tooth, she was grateful and regarded me with softer eyes before confessing her sorrows to her worry dolls. The elder girl was slower to accommodate. Only after weeks did Flamed Plume come to trust me;

for the past four nights we have spent every evening reading the great books of Kanuataba together.

I take no pride in owning these girls, but Haniba had spoken true. I could not let Auxila's daughters be defiled. Their father was a holy man, whose family took me in as an orphan when my father left for the land of our ancestors. And then Auxila set me on the path to nobility, a debt that I can never repay. Still, I do not know what to say to the children when tears pour out of their eyes after visiting their mother's grave. I have never understood the ways of women.

I give them crumbs to feed my bird self, who has taken to perching inside the cave. It gives the smaller girl solace. She is too young to understand that the macaw is my spirit self, but she can muster a smile when he squawks, and it stops her tears, if only for a moment. Despite my efforts, I am a poor substitute for a mother.

Two suns ago, my concubines and I were paid a royal visit by the holy prince, Smoke Song. It is most unusual for the prince's lessons to take place outside the palace, unless we are studying some natural phenomenon. But before the king's recent departure, he agreed to my request to send the prince here. The king is away with his warriors, waging war for three suns against Sakamil. Mercifully, despite his promises, he decided not to take his young son with him.

Upon the prince's arrival, it became clear that Flamed Plume would be a distraction. The prince's eyes lit at the sight of her, and he could focus on nothing else. He had believed he would never see the girl again, this girl of whom he had been most fond for years.

According to custom, when the prince addressed the girl, she went to kiss the ground beneath his feet. Then I listened to them speaking admiringly of the bird, who silently climbed atop Flamed Plume's shoulder, preening. The bird was recovering most rapidly and would be ready to journey in search of his flock in a matter of weeks. Looking at the macaw, the prince postured by pushing his immature braid to the front, still adorned with the white bead indicating servitude to his father.

Then he spoke:

– But this bird is nothing compared to my spirit animal, the mighty jaguar. Have you ever seen one with your own eyes? He is swifter than any animal in the jungle and more capable of attacking his prey than the most skilled archer could ever be. He moves faster than the arrow, and quieter too. I can show you where lie the graves of jaguar bones, which will give you a chill you will not soon forget. Indeed, you might faint upon seeing this, but I will be there to catch you, for my heart and mind are stronger than yours, little girl. –

What happened next between these children surprised me and reminded me in what strange and beautiful ways the gods have fashioned us, the fourth race.

The girl Flamed Plume did not look away from the prince then when he looked into her eyes, as custom dictated. In the royal palace she could be sacrificed for such an indiscretion. But there was no fear on her face, or in her heart. She smiled enough to reveal that she had two front teeth emblazoned with jade but then hid those jade pieces so he could not see more. Since the day I came to her in her parents' home to explain that her mother was dead, there had been no smiles.

Then she spoke as I have never heard a girl speak to a prince:

– But, holy prince, Smoke Song, most revered one, how can the mighty jaguar be faster than a quiver of arrows when I have seen jaguars killed by those very same arrows by our marksmen? Can you explain this contradiction to an intelligence as meek as mine? –

It was not until that moment that I came to understand how strong-willed and noble Flamed Plume is. But how the boy would react to this affront I could not predict. His face indicated puzzlement at her refusal to defer. Yet then Smoke Song smiled and showed Flamed Plume his jade, and I was reminded how little he resembled his father. One day he will make a great leader of Kanuataba, if we can emerge from the calamities that threaten to consume our mighty lands. I was filled with pride for him.

Still, nothing can ever come of the prince and Flamed Plume; her father has been sacrificed to the gods, and she is stuck between worlds, unfit for the company of a king, no better than a bastard. Watching them, and knowing this, took me closer to tears than I have been in many suns.

The prince reached into his satchel. I thought he was pulling from it one of the great books I had instructed him to bring from the royal library, and I swelled with pride, believing he might show his reading skill, which I had taught for so long.

Yet instead he held an ornate ceramic bowl, more than two hands in its depth, as if built for water. The bowl was decorated with colors of death and rebirth, and he held it out toward Flamed Plume at arm's length. Then the prince spoke to her:

– Behold Akabalam, who graces my father with his power and in whose honor we build the new temple. Have you seen Akabalam with your own eyes, girl? –

Flamed Plume went silent, bowed by the invocation of the god who had claimed her father's life. But I was anxious with desire to know: could the king have shown his son what the mysterious god presided over, that I might understand?

Then the prince spoke to the girl again:

– Do not be afraid. I have power over these creatures, this embodiment of Akabalam. Do not be afraid. I will protect you. –

Smoke Song opened the bowl, and I could see inside there stood a count of six insects, long as a finger, color of the leaves of the most vibrant trees that once ruled our forest. The insects climbed atop one another, attempting to scale the walls of the ceramic bowl but without success. Their long, bent legs were entwined beneath their bodies. Their eyes, color of night, protruded from their heads.

The prince spoke:

– I have seen him worshipping these creatures, and I took them from his throne room, where they have their royal feasts, and now I, too, feel their power. –

I studied the insects, those that blend with the forest itself. For what purpose we would worship this creature,

I could not imagine! They made no honey. They could not be roasted for food. Why would the king dedicate a temple and sacrifice his overseer of the stores in the name of a useless insect? Why would a king denigrate us, the gods' holy maize creation, in its name?

I spoke:

– This is what your father calls Akabalam? Only this? –

– Yes. –

– And has he told you the meaning of why we must exalt them? –

– Of course he has. But you, scribe, could never feel what a king would feel in the presence of such power. –

But as I studied the insects more closely and watched them slowly rubbing their tiny front legs together in the air, I believed I understood. Their legs gave them the appearance of a man communing with the gods. No other creature I have seen in the kingdom appears more pious. No other creature is such a model for the way all men must pray to the gods.

Is this why the king so reveres them? Because he believes we have lost our piety in the drought that has lasted nearly two thousand suns, and that they stand as a symbol of commitment to the gods?

The prince turned to the girl and spoke again:

– Only a man ordained by the ancestors can understand Akabalam. –

Beyond his father's influences, Smoke Song is a good child, pure of heart. His is a soul the ancestors of the forest would have loved and respected, as it is written in the great books. While his father might simply have ordered me beheaded if he thought I had defiled a girl he wanted, Smoke Song only intended to impress the girl and win her heart. He stole the insects from the palace, and with them he was showing Flamed Plume how much more powerful he was than I. So I would allow him this pleasure.

The girl watched as I bowed to the boy and kissed his feet.

24

'Two thousand suns,' Rolando said. 'Almost six years. It's a mega-drought.'

He, Chel and Victor stood over five newly reconstructed and deciphered pages of the codex. Chel gazed down again at Paktul's question on the twenty-eighth page: *Because he believes we have lost our piety in the drought that has lasted nearly two thousand suns, and that they stand as a symbol of commitment to the gods?*

'Don't you agree?' Rolando asked Victor, who sat across the Getty lab, studying his copy of the translation and sipping on his tea.

Last night, when Chel returned from seeing her mother at the church, it was Victor she'd wanted to share her frustrations with, certain that he was the only person who'd truly understand. But Victor hadn't come back from his fruitless trip into his obscure stash of academic journals until well after midnight. By then Chel had stolen a quick shower in the Getty Conservation Institute building, washed off the residue of her conversation with Ha'ana completely, and thrown herself back into the work. She hadn't spoken of it since.

'The king wasn't helping matters,' Victor said. 'But, yes, it does seem like there was a major drought and that it must have been the underlying cause.'

In a normal world, it might have been the most important discovery of all of their careers. In landlocked classic cities, the Maya could store water for no longer than eighteen months. Evidence of a six-year drought would convince even Chel's most resistant colleagues that the cause of the collapse was what she had been arguing for years.

But of course the world was no longer normal. What mattered now was the connection between the codex and the lost city, which strengthened with each section they translated. Now that it was clear Paktul had protected the two little girls by taking them in, it seemed nearly inevitable that he would take them as wives. Rolando's theory that they were the Original Trio was more and more plausible.

Groundbreaking as these discoveries were, they still hadn't been able to figure out where exactly the lost city might be located or where Volcy could have gotten sick. Fortunately, they now knew more about the mysterious Akabalam glyph that had impeded their decipherment progress. Based on the scribe's descriptions of insects that looked like they were communing with the gods, Chel, Rolando and Victor all agreed he must have been describing praying mantises. Mantises were common all over the Maya area. And despite the scribe's questions about why they would need to worship them, Chel knew the Maya had occasionally worshipped insects and created gods in their honor.

Yet there was still a missing piece. Thirty-two bark pages were nearly complete, but even with this potential break, the glyph appeared ten or eleven times on a single page in surprising and unusual ways. When Chel inserted *praying mantis* or *praying mantis god* into all the places they saw *Akabalam,* much of the end still didn't make any sense. In the earlier sections, the glyph referred to the name of the new god. But in the final pages, it seemed as if Paktul was using the word to refer to an *action.*

'It has to be something intrinsic to them, right?' Rolando asked. 'The way bees symbolize sweetness.'

'Or how Hunab Ku can be used to indicate transformation,' Victor suggested, referring to the butterfly god.

A boom outside startled all of them, and Chel hurried to the window. Over the last two days, a few cars had made the trek up to the Getty, interlopers in search of easy looting. Each time, they'd seen the security team still patrolling the grounds and turned around.

'Everything all right?' Rolando asked.

It was difficult to see very far into the night. 'I think so,' Chel said.

'So . . . what?' he asked as she turned back. 'Is the king ordaining this new god because the praying mantises appear pious?'

'The droughts probably inspired a lot of doubts among the people,' Chel said. 'Maybe he believed it was inspiration.'

She moved to the glass case containing a fragment they'd partially pieced together from one of the final pages and started substituting in her mind:

Perhaps the king allows [piety] because his call for rain has been thwarted, and he knows no rains will come! But will such wanton [piety] not result in chaos among the people, even among those who fear the gods? There is reason the people of Kanuataba so fear [piety] as I do, the most terrifying transgression of all, even if [piety] is commanded by the king!

'It wouldn't make sense,' she said to the men. 'Why would the scribe be so frightened of piety? And why would it be a transgression?'

Chel studied the pages again, contemplating possibilities.

'Where are we with the satellites?' Rolando asked. As of yesterday, thanks to Stanton, the CDC had arranged for a dozen NASA satellites to be turned toward the area surrounding Kiaqix, to search for any sign of ruins in the jungle rim.

Stanton had been Chel's first call after leaving her mother. It pleased her to be able to tell him that her father's cousin Chiam's account of the lost city matched Paktul's descriptions in the codex. The doctor had listened eagerly, and this time there wasn't any skepticism in his voice. All he'd said was, 'Let's do it.'

She hadn't heard from Stanton since, but Chel checked her phone constantly. Someone from his team would get in touch as soon as there were any images that required her team's expertise, and she hoped it was him.

'The satellites can each take up to a thousand photographs a day,' she said, 'and they've got a team of people searching the images.'

Victor piped up. 'Now we just have to pray that Kanuataba is another Oxpemul.'

In the 1980s, satellites had snapped pictures of the tops of two temples poking out from beneath the leaf canopy very close to a major archaeological site in Mexico, leading to the discovery of an even larger ancient city.

'It's the rainy season, and there's constant cloud cover around Kiaqix right now,' Chel reminded the men. 'The trees could be shielding everything. We're talking about buildings that are more than a thousand years old and are probably crumbling. Not to mention the fact that they've eluded discovery for centuries.'

'Which is why we must focus on the manuscript,' Victor said.

He took no pleasure in how the victims of VFI were suffering or in the fact that so many more were sure to become infected. It horrified him to hear about children falling prey to the disease and about the ways that men had turned on one another in the streets of LA. Yet as Victor had watched the stock market crash and the grocery stores empty, he couldn't help but feel validated. His colleagues had ridiculed him. His family had abandoned him. Until the epidemic began, even he'd begun to wonder if he and the rest of the Believers wouldn't be proven wrong as so many others had, from the Millerites to the Y2K believers to . . . well, every other group who had believed the world was due for a great change.

Just after noon, the team broke up to continue exploring the Akabalam question on their own. Chel had gone into her office that adjoined the lab to think, and Rolando had gone to another building for reconstruction equipment, so Victor was left alone in the room. He stood over the plates, examining the one that contained Paktul's reference to the thirteenth cycle. He lifted the glass off its perch, testing its weight. The case was heavy – fifteen pounds or so – but one man could carry two or three at a time.

Holding part of the codex in his hands, Victor felt its incredible power. In synagogue as a boy, he had learned the story of how rabbis threw themselves over the Torah scrolls when the Romans destroyed the Second Temple of Jerusalem. The rabbis believed the Jewish people couldn't carry on without the written Word and gave their lives to protect it. Victor felt he finally understood what inspired that willingness to sacrifice so much for a book.

'What are you doing?'

He froze at the sound of Rolando's voice. What was he doing back here already? Gently, Victor replaced the page and made a show of adjusting where the case sat on the light table. 'Some of the glass was starting to shift,' he said, 'and I was afraid it might disturb the fragments.'

Rolando joined him in front of the light table. 'Appreciate your help, but it's better if you let me handle the plates, okay?'

Victor moved down the table, pretending to study fragments from the final section. He didn't want to appear too quick to retreat. Rolando, satisfied with whatever he'd come to check on in the first place, headed toward the back of the lab. Then Victor heard a knock on Chel's office and the sound of the door closing.

Did Rolando suspect something? Victor sat down at one of the lab benches as casually as he could. He calculated what he would say if Rolando confronted him.

Minutes later, Victor heard Chel's door creak open

again and her soft footsteps coming into the lab. She stood behind him. He didn't move.

'Can I talk to you?' she asked.

'Of course. What is it?'

She sat down on one of the lab benches. 'I just got off the phone with Patrick. I asked him to come here and help with some of the remaining astronomy glyphs, but he said he wouldn't leave his new girlfriend again. Martha. Who the hell is named Martha in the twenty-first century? I don't know if we can do this without him.'

'First of all,' Victor said, 'he did his part and we don't need him. Second of all . . . you know I never liked him anyway.'

'Liar.'

She smiled, but Victor flinched a little at the word.

'But Patrick was right about one thing,' she said.

'What's that?'

'Volcy. The codex. Kiaqix and the Original Trio. He was the first one to point out that it's all one hell of a coincidence.'

The last thing Victor believed was that any of this was coincidence. 'Anything is possible,' he said carefully.

Chel waited for him to continue, and her expectant look gave Victor a feeling he hadn't had in so long: being needed by someone he truly loved.

'What do you believe?' he asked her.

After a long silence, Chel said, 'The obsession with the Long Count drove up the prices on antiquities, which is probably what sent Volcy into the jungle in the first place. Whatever else is happening right now, this started because of 2012 one way or another.'

Silently, Victor prayed once more that he might be able to convince Chel to come with him and his people. He'd always thought he might be able to get her to the mountains when the end came. Now he hoped that she was beginning to see that the predictions were coming true. Soon, perhaps, she would understand that escape was the only way forward.

'I think if we keep our minds open,' he said gently, 'there's no telling what we may come to understand about the world.'

She took a moment, then said, 'Can I ask you a question?'

'Of course.'

'Do you believe in the Maya gods? The actual gods?'

'You don't have to believe in the pantheon to see the wisdom of the design the ancients saw in the universe. Maybe it's enough to know there's a force that connects us all.'

Chel took a breath. 'Yeah, maybe. Or maybe not. By the way, I wanted to say thank you for staying here with me and for all your help.'

'You're very welcome, Chel.'

Victor watched her go back toward her office. She was the same young woman who'd shown up at his office door on the first day of her graduate program, telling him she'd read all of his work. Who years later gave him a place to go, when no one else would.

And as she disappeared from his sight, he fought back tears.

25

It had been nearly six hours since Davies had dropped Thane outside the hospital, and Stanton was anxious. He stared out the window, watching the sun creep over the horizon, waiting for his phone to break the silence. For anything to break it. The Venice boardwalk was also too quiet for his taste. He wanted to hear one of the vendors yelling at tourists not to take pictures of his 'art', or the bearded guitarist, the Walk's honorary mayor, playing as he roller-skated back and forth. Or hear Monster knocking on his door.

'I'd suggest a nip.'

Davies held a lowball glass of Jack Daniel's in Stanton's direction, but Stanton waved him off. He could use something, though. Why hadn't Thane called? The injections should be done. He'd tried her cell but had been unable to get through. Cell service in LA, always spotty, was basically nonexistent now. Still, Thane should've found a landline.

Finally his phone rang. A local number he didn't know. 'Michaela?'

'It's Emily.'

Cavanagh. Shit. 'What's up?' he asked, trying not to raise suspicion.

'You need to meet me at the command center immediately, Gabe.'

'I've got some denaturing experiments running here,' he lied, glancing over at Davies. 'I could get over there in a few hours.'

'The director's here in LA, and he wants to talk to you,' Cavanagh said. 'I don't care what you're doing. You need to come now.'

CDC Director Adam Kanuth had been in Washington and Atlanta since the outbreak began, and his absence in LA had been noted by nearly everyone, including the press. Advocates said he'd been deftly administrating cases popping up around the country and now the world. Detractors said he'd been avoiding LA because he didn't want to risk infection.

Ash rained down on Stanton as he stepped out of the car at the CDC's command center. Wildfire had erupted in the hills above the HOLLYWOOD sign and consumed a hundred acres, hanging smoke clouds from downtown to the ocean. Stanton did his best to gather himself before going in. He had never liked the CDC director. Kanuth had come from the Big Pharma world, and he talked about science as if it were economics – supply following demand. Rarc diseases got rare grants. Now, Kanuth would want to talk exclusively about containment. He'd want to talk about how quarantines in other cities should be managed. And Stanton would have to do it with still no word from Thane.

Inside the old post office, CDC employees worked behind bulletproof-glass windows that once protected against unhinged postal workers. Aging posters advertising Ronald Reagan *Forever* stamps still hung on the walls. A J-1 officer led Stanton toward the postmaster's office.

Cavanagh sat in a chair in front of the desk. Stanton noticed that she wouldn't look him in the eye. Behind the desk sat Kanuth, a barrel-chested man in his mid-fifties with thinning silver hair and a beard.

'Mr Director. Welcome to Los Angeles.'

There was no chair for Stanton to sit in. Kanuth nodded perfunctorily. 'We have a problem, Gabe.'

'Okay.'

'Did you send a resident from Presbyterian Hospital in to give injections of murine-based antibodies to a group of patients? Despite our orders not to?'

Stanton froze. 'Excuse me?'

Cavanagh stood. 'We found two dozen syringes, and they were full of murine-based antibody solutions.'

Had they caught Thane trying to give the injections?

'Where is Dr Thane now?' Stanton asked carefully.

Kanuth looked at Cavanagh. 'She was found at the bottom of a stairwell with her neck broken. As far as we can tell, she died on impact.'

Stanton was in shock. 'She fell down the stairs?'

Cavanagh stared him down. 'She was killed by a patient.'

'Unless you want to tell me that she was carrying on a secret antibody trial on her own,' said Kanuth, 'I assume that you are responsible for this.'

Stanton closed his eyes and saw Thane's face as he arrived at Presbyterian for the first time, after she'd dragged him in to see a patient he might well have ignored. The look on her face when she saw the lab they'd built inside the condo; her quick willingness to help, with little concern for her own career. He heard the hope in her voice when she left to give the injections to her colleagues.

'I enlisted her to give the antibodies,' he whispered finally.

'You wanted permission to test them on a sample group,' Cavanagh said. 'We'd already brought it to the FDA chief, and we were less than a day away from clearance. We could've done it under controlled conditions. Now a woman is dead because you decided to ignore direct orders.'

Kanuth said, 'Not only that, but when people out there learn what happened – and they will – they'll say we're losing internal control. We have a whole fucking city looking for any reason to burst, and you've given them another one.'

'Turn in your ID, and don't try to go back to the Prion Center or to any other CDC facility,' Cavanagh said. She sounded disgusted.

'You're fired, Dr Stanton,' said Kanuth.

26

Chel sat beneath the apple trees on the Getty's south lawn, smoking and gazing down on the maze of azalea in the courtyard below. She needed a moment to rest, to distract herself, to recharge.

'Chel,' someone called from a distance.

Through the fog she made out Rolando standing at the top of the stairs leading to the central plaza. Behind him was Stanton. Surprised, Chel wondered why he had come. Had the satellites found something? Whatever brought him here, she was pleased to see him.

Rolando waved and peeled off, leaving them alone.

'What's happening?' Chel asked Stanton at the bottom of the stairs. She immediately noticed how exhausted he looked. It was the first time they'd been physically together since the night she'd come clean and they'd visited the Gutierrez house. Whatever she'd been through the past few days didn't compare to what was written on his face.

They moved to one of the chessboard-covered tables on the south-pavilion landing. Stanton told her everything that had led up to Thane's death, then what had happened after.

'I should never have let her take that risk,' he said.

'You were trying to help. If you could get the antibodies to work –'

'The antibodies are useless.' His voice had a bitter edge to it. 'The tests failed, and even if they worked, they'd be considered too risky. She died for nothing.'

Chel understood only too well what it felt like to be cut off from everything you knew. But she'd had a reprieve – thanks to him. She didn't know how to give him the second chance he'd given her. So she just took his hand.

They sat in silence for nearly a minute before she broached the other subject on her mind. 'So I guess . . . nothing on the satellites?'

'I'm not exactly in the loop anymore,' Stanton said. 'I thought maybe you would have heard something from CDC. But I guess not. What's happening on your end?'

'We're close to deciphering the end of the codex. There could still be some kind of a locator in the final sections, though we're facing a few significant challenges.'

'Let me help.'

'With what?'

'With your work.'

'Do you have a PhD in linguistics I don't know about?'

'I'm serious,' Stanton said. 'Our processes aren't so different. Diagnose the problem, look for comparables, and then search for solutions from there. Besides, maybe an outside perspective could be useful.'

Chel studied him. How odd it was that three days after he had held her future in his hands, his career had suffered a similar fate, and now he'd come to her for help. What did she really know about this guy, anyway? Gabe Stanton was clearly whip smart, extremely hardworking, a little too fierce sometimes. Chel didn't know much else. They hadn't exactly had the chance to unwind over a glass of wine. Maybe if she looked closer, she wouldn't like what she saw.

Then again, he'd been the one to let in the crack of daylight keeping her life's work alive – at a moment when she'd given him every reason not to. So if Stanton wanted to help, Chel wasn't going to stop him now. She'd just have to make sure that the CDC didn't find out when they eventually reached out to her again.

'Okay, fresh eyes, then.' She leaned in closer to him. 'The scribe's referring to a collapse of his city. Or at least to his fear of its collapse. There are harbingers in the central plaza, in the palace, everywhere. But there's nothing worse to him than the worship of this new god, Akabalam. It's a god we've never seen before, a god of praying mantises. As if this god has just been created at this particular historical moment.'

'Was it unusual for the Maya to create . . . new gods?' Stanton asked.

'There are dozens in the pantheon. And new gods were invented all the time. When Paktul first hears of this one, he wants to learn about him and to worship him. But in this final part of the manuscript, it's as if he has found a reason to be mortally afraid of him.'

'What do you mean, mortally afraid?'

'He uses all the superlatives of the Mayan language to describe his fear – including words that suggest he's more afraid of this new god than of dying. One thing we've been able to translate says: *This was something much more terrifying, which no one ever had to teach me to fear.*'

Stanton walked to the railing overlooking the Getty's sycamore-lined stream, processing. 'So maybe we should be looking for a deeply ingrained fear.' He turned back from the railing. 'Think about mice.'

'Mice?'

'One of a mouse's most powerful fears is its fear of snakes. But no one had to teach mice to fear snakes. It's coded into their DNA. We can actually make that fear disappear by altering their genetic structure.'

Chel pictured Stanton's years spent in a lab, years spent not so differently from hers. He thought in ways foreign to her, using a vocabulary that was mostly unfamiliar. Yet his constant return to the underlying scientific processes at work *was* similar to the way she saw language and history.

Stanton continued, 'So the question we have to ask is: What could your scribe's most powerful fear be?'

'Fear of his city collapsing forever?'

'It doesn't sound like that's news to him.'

'Well, I don't think he's talking about snakes.'

'No, I mean, what fears are so powerful for him that they could create this kind of response? It's got to be something more . . . primal. Something innate.'

'You mean like fear of incest,' Chel said.

'Exactly. Could that be it?'

'Incest was prohibited,' she told him. 'And it wouldn't make any sense anyway. What would incest have to do with praying mantises?'

Yet as soon as she said the words, another possibility hit her – an indictment of her people that she'd dismissed her entire career.

From the beginning, Chel had wanted the codex to prove that her people hadn't brought the collapse on themselves.

But what if they had?

27

My fast has lasted forty turns of the sun, sustained only by cornmeal drink and water. No rain has fallen on our milpas or in our forests, and the water stores have receded. Each corner of the city has begun to hoard water and maize and manioc, and it is rumored that men drink their own urine to quench their thirst.

There are whispers that some have already begun to plan their journey north in search of tillable fields, though Jaguar Imix has decreed that to abandon Kanuataba will be punishable by death or worse. There have been eighteen deaths in the poorest corners of Kanuataba in the last twenty suns, many of them children, starved because they are given lowest priority in the distribution of rations.

Our city was once a center for the best goods within ten days' walk. But jade adornments are useless, and artisans no longer flourish. Mother-of-pearl ear flares and varicolored feather mantles have been replaced by tortillas and lime as the greatest desires of the noble women. A mother who cannot feed her children thinks little of gold medallions, no matter how holy.

At yesterday's zenith I was called to the palace.

I left Auxila's daughters in the cave at the noon sun, knowing my spirit animal would watch over them in my absence. Jaguar Imix, his holiness, newly returned from his distant star war, had called me to the palace to reveal to me the meaning of the god Akabalam, so that I might continue to educate the true prince.

When I came within a few hundred paces of the city center, less than a thousand paces from the king's newly ordained burial temple, I could not believe what I saw. Thick black smoke rose above the tops of the towers of the minor temple, our sacred catacomb. And as I turned the corner, I saw the largest gathering of the men and women of Kanuataba I had seen in six hundred suns.

I knew a large gathering was called for this day, but I could not have imagined its size and splendor. There are no words to describe the feeling I had upon seeing Kanuataba alive again then, as it was in the days of my youth, when my father would walk me through the merchant causeways atop his mighty shoulders. There were whispers among the people gathered that Jaguar Imix had brought a miracle, that he would feed the masses with this mighty feast, that there would be enough to sustain us until the harvest.

I watched men carry large offerings of spice and wood and jade toward the south stairs to the palace. Others carried salt and allspice and cilantro, combined with burn-dried chilis to make the seasoning for turkey and deer meat. Even my stomach growled with hunger. There are no deer or turkey or agouti within two days' walk, of that I was certain. Had Jaguar Imix and his mighty army plundered stores of meat during their star war?

The royal dwarf approached me. I will recount his

words to reveal what machinations he was capable of. He spoke:

– If people knew you as I do, scribe, knew that you would never touch those girls, you would lose those concubines you've taken. Your life could be cut short by ten thousand suns and with it the lives of those girls. So I suggest you never displease me again. –

Never have I felt a greater urge to drain the blood from a man's body and rip his heart out. I longed for some commotion in the causeways, loud enough that I might muffle Jacomo's screams. I would tear him into pieces and bury them in unmarked graves.

Before I could raise my hand, a boisterous sound filled the plaza. A line of blue-painted captives, fifteen in number, were dragged into the causeways. Each captive was tied together to a long pole, lashed by both hands and neck to the man in front of him. Several men were stumbling. Many appeared half dead already.

Tattoos on his torso proved one of the prisoners was of high standing, and I have never seen a noble so afraid of sacrifice. He screamed and writhed as the captors of Kanuataba ushered him along, dragging his feet across the dirt, exciting dust everywhere. From the look on the captors' faces, I knew that even they had never seen anything like it. Such indignity! Only a sickness of the mind could have damaged this nobleman's soul so that he would not accept his fate!

I went into the palace, and navigated past the housekeepers, tailors and concubines. The sweat house is on the top floor, a domed room in the tower, a most holy place for divination and communication with the overworld. As with the secret meals and other rituals, it is most often restricted to the king's retinue.

When I arrived in the sweat bath, I found the king alone, an event I cannot remember in a thousand suns. His face was gaunt and looked less holy than I had ever before seen. There was not even a slave or lower-rank wife in the room, ready to satisfy his urges.

The king spoke:

– I have brought you here to see the creation of the great feast, Paktul, so that you may record it in the great books for all posterity. –

I bent down on both knees beside the hot coals, and the heat was unbearable. But to be inside the sweat house was considered a great honor, and I would show no sign of suffering. I spoke:

– Highness, we must record the great feast, yes, but I would ask you again to explain how the gods have blessed us with this feast but have shown us no mercy elsewhere. So that I may record it in the great books with proper care, may I understand why we feast today, when all other days there is famine? –

The king's jaw clenched. His crossed eyes looked beyond me, as if he was trying to control his anger. His grasp on the royal scepter was rigid. When I finished, he did not rise or bellow; he did not call for the guards to take me away. He only looked down at my hand and pointed at my ring, symbol of the great monkey scribes who came before me.

And he spoke again:

– This ring you wear, the monkey-scribe ring, symbol of your station, how do you think it compares to the crown of the gods I wear upon my head? There is nothing I desire more than to be able to share this burden with my people and to explain the compromises I make to ensure the gods are at peace. This burden is not one that can be learned through books but only by those who came before me, my fathers, who once ruled over our terraced city. It is hardly a burden one who wears the monkey-scribe ring can fathom. –

With this, the king rose in his nakedness. I thought he might strike me, but he only instructed me to rise from my knees. He wrapped himself with a loincloth around his waist and commanded me to follow him into the royal kitchen.

It is rumored there is nothing in the world the royal cooks cannot prepare to the king's taste. They will send assistants for a week's walk to secure guava or mombin that grows only in the highest mountains or to trade with tree people for sweet potato that grows only in the shade of a single ceiba in winter.

I followed his holiness, Jaguar Imix, and I saw the great serpentine flow of these men, devoted to their art, working to finish the preparations for the great ceremonial feast. Every man had an assignment. There were those devoted to the preparation of the sauces and garnishes, who added florets of manioc plant to the various mixtures of chili paste, cinnamon, cacao, allspice. The actual cooking was assigned to others, who presided over large open spits in every corner of the room, grilling meats before adding them to the rich stews stirred in enormous vats at the kitchen's center.

We passed through the tremendous heat of the cooking fires, almost as stifling as the sweat house itself. We were headed for the slaughterhouse, I knew. When we arrived at the door, the king flashed a beaming smile of jade at me.

He spoke:

– Low scribe, there can be no greater divination than the one I received twenty moons ago, the commandment from Akabalam, which will change Kanuataba forever and be our salvation. For nearly a year I have taken in this blood, and it is time for my people to share in my great source of strength. According to my royal spies, these rituals have become commonplace in other nations. Not just among the nobles but also among the lower tiers, and they have sustained themselves by them for many moons. –

I followed him into the slaughterhouse.

Blood coated the floor and soaked my sandals. More than two dozen carcasses hung, skinned and decapitated, disemboweled, blood-drained and disjointed. The slaughter men were separating meat from the bone, each leg and arm providing a different cut that went into a pile of thick fillets. The slaughter cooks used blades of chert to prepare the meat for cooking, trying to conserve every precious sliver for the feast. It took me a moment to comprehend what these appendages were.

Men's bodies hung from meat hooks!

The king spoke:

– Akabalam has commanded that we should partake, that, through this meat, we will absorb the power from those souls that inhabited these corpses. I and my closest minions have gained such power from feasts on flesh, having consumed more than twenty men in the three hundred suns past. Now Akabalam has divined that he wishes to concentrate the strength of ten men in every man of our great nation. Mantises consume the heads of their mates to survive; blessed are they, and, like them, we will all consume the flesh of our own kind. –

And as he finished speaking I knew: this was no god ordained for recommitment of piety. This was something much more terrifying, which no one ever had to teach me to fear.

Much has passed in Kanuataba since the last inscription. Sixty suns have been born from the color of rebirth and died into blackness. Akabalam is spread to every corner of the city, on word that the king had sanctioned it at the feast in the great plaza, when Jaguar Imix fed the meat of our enemies' noblemen to his own. With no rain come to feed the milpas, cooking pots are filled with the meat of the dead, not a single part wasted, every scrap pulled off the bones. The sole prohibition dictated by the king was that no man should eat his own son or father, daughter or mother, as the gods had forbidden it. But I have seen child slaves forced to prepare meals without the meat, only to be sacrificed as animals, salted in seasoning baths of their own making.

I have not partaken in Akabalam, nor have I allowed Auxila's daughters. We survive on leaves and roots and small berries alone. One Butterfly and Flamed Plume would have already become food for the masses were they not protected by my station. The orphans of the city were among the first sacrificed, but in my cave they have been saved. They are watched over by my spirit macaw. The girls do not leave, as I have commanded them, for the savages in the streets are many and ruthless, and they would take the life of any child as sustenance.

The king has disappeared into the recesses of the palace for a royal divination, and none but Jacomo the dwarf, the queen, and the prince are permitted to visit him. The council was disbanded. Jaguar Imix proclaimed that no man can hear the call of the overworld but he and that the council was filled with false prophets! Jacomo the dwarf stands on the palace steps every sunrise. He reads the demands of the king and the sacrifices that must be made to please the gods.

By every setting of the sun, the sacrifices have been made; men and women and children, some noble, brought to the top of the altar by the executioners, their hearts extracted and innards cut out before being fed to the masses.

Yet with each sacrifice, there are more doubts in the streets of Kanuataba of Jaguar Imix's power. I have heard dissent among the commoners. The people live in fear that they shall be sacrificed next. They whisper that Jaguar Imix has lost his channel to the gods, that a curse in his mind has confused his thoughts.

And what power has Akabalam given us? No rain has come to the milpas, no reprieve sent from the overworld to nurture the crops that sustain us.

So much is changed, so much horror! Death is all around us, the city in its cold black embrace. More than a thousand are dead by last report, and many more are cursed, awaiting death. I was right to fear as I did. The curse of Akabalam has fallen over many, sucking out their spirits into nothing, leaving them unable to pass into the dream world, where they may commune with their gods.

The numbers of cursed are growing with each turn of the sun, cursed for their trespasses against their fellow man. The streets overflow with violence day and night, as peaceful men turn against one another, unable to invoke the spirits in their dreams, fighting over what few valuables are left in the markets.

Jaguar Imix and his retinue consumed the flesh of men for many moons in good graces of the gods without being cursed. But whatever god protected them before does so no longer. The king is cursed, his nobles are cursed, and Akabalam has swept our land and destroyed everything.

Akabalam has turned men into monsters, just as I have feared. The time of dreams is the time of peaceful reconciliation with the gods, the time of communing with spirit animals, the time of giving ourselves to the gods as we do in death. But those cursed cannot dream, cannot surrender themselves to the celestial gods or be in touch with their wayobs, who watch over them.

*

Here is the account of my final sojourn to the great palace, where the men of the council once adjudicated. By night I came, carrying the bird on my shoulder, for it was too dangerous by the light of day for any pious man to show his face in the city plazas. I came, guided only by the light of the moon.

I came for the prince, Smoke Song, my pupil, whom I planned to take from the palace. That the boy is not cursed reveals Jaguar Imix's own confusion; when he did not give his own son human flesh, he revealed cracks in his belief.

But Smoke Song is not the only child who will carry on the stories and legend of the terraced city. Flamed Plume and One Butterfly waited back in my cave, from which we planned to retreat to the forests of the lake that my father once sought. As I have still not allowed them to, Auxila's girls have eaten no human meat in my care. We will live off the land, where we will be safe from the dreamless and those who follow them into ruin.

I had not been to the palace or seen the king in twenty suns, and there was a strange falseness to all I bore witness to, a strange suspicion that this way of life in the palace and in Kanuataba was over, that appearances could no longer be maintained. The guards themselves were nowhere in sight, and I made my way to the royal quarters unimpeded.

Because the prince was absent from his own room, I took myself to the king's quarters. The prince must have gone to see his father, which terrified me, for I did not believe that the king would let him leave the palace.

I went to the king's chamber and entered it boldly.

Stepping inside, I saw the prince kneeling at his father's bedside. I knew then that Ah Puch had carried the king's spirit into the afterlife, to spend the cycles of time with other kings, as it is ordained. There was no breath from his lips or beat of his heart. As I had taught him, Smoke Song was not touching the corpse, only waving incense sticks all around the body.

Smoke Song looked up at me with tears in his eyes.

Then the voice came from behind us:

– This is the king's chamber, and his alone, and you will not be forgiven your trespass here, lowly scribe. –

I turned to face the dwarf, who stood ten paces behind. His beard had not been cut in many moons.

I spoke:

– You have spilled your lies onto the causeways and beckoned the people of Kanuataba with your tongue, and they shall hear these lies no more. They shall know that the king is dead! –

– You shall tell no one of this, or I shall have it known that you have not taken Auxila's daughters as true concubines, that you have made no copulation with them and can therefore lay no claim to them. I shall take them as my own, and they will blossom and bear my sons! The king's guards will take them by force! –

I struck the dwarf with my walking stick over the crown of his bulbous head, struck him with the end of it adorned with the pointed jade, and let forth the blood inside him. He fell to the floor, screaming out and calling for the prince's help.

Smoke Song did not move.

The dwarf flew at me and clenched his jaw around my leg. The pain seared through me like fire. I gouged out his eyeball with the point of my jade knife, and he let go. I drove the jade point into his belly with all my strength, and his spirit was extinguished.

Then I turned to the prince:

– You must leave me here now. You must take Flamed Plume and One Butterfly and leave the city. –

When the prince heard this, he spoke to me with new power:

– As supreme ajaw of the city, I command you to come with us, Paktul. I will make you the daykeeper wherever we go. This I command you as king! –

But I knew that what remained of the royal guards would come after me, bound by duty to avenge the dwarf. They would have a thirst for my blood, and I did not wish to endanger the children's lives. I told the prince:

– That you would honor me and make me your daykeeper, Smoke Song, is prize enough for me, prize enough for entry into the sacred world of scribes above. But you must abandon me here, that you may be protected by Itzamnaaj, holy god. –

He spoke:

– Holy teacher, the renouncers are come. I hear their screams! As your new king, I command you to follow me. –

I told the prince:

– Then let me lead you in the direction of my family

whom I have lost, King, in the direction of all those that came before me. –

Holy Itzamnaaj, may I lead them in the direction of salvation in the recesses of the great forests, where my ancestors once lived and shall live forevermore. Where we may worship the true gods and bring forth a new people to usher in the turn of the next great cycle. Flamed Plume will become wife to Smoke Song, and the union shall bless a new beginning, shall generate a new race of men, a new cycle of time. I can only dream of the generations Smoke Song will father with Flamed Plume and her sister, men who will lead their people with decency. And the people of Kanuataba will live on.

12.19.19.17.16

December 17, 2012

28

Chel stood alone in the lobby of the Getty Research building, watching the afternoon sun shine into the glass oculus in the courtyard outside. On the summer solstice, at high noon, the sun would be directly aligned with the oculus, a design mirroring some of the astrology-based architecture of the ancients. This was the bastion of Maya scholarship she'd convinced the Getty board they had to have – that to ignore the most sophisticated civilization in the New World was an historical crime.

It turned out the crime was perpetrated by the Maya themselves.

For centuries, the conquistadores had accused the indigenous people of cannibalism, as evidence of their own moral superiority; missionaries explained burning ancient Maya texts by invoking it; Spanish kings used it to claim land. This blood libel hadn't stopped during the conquest – even in *La Revolución* of Chel's childhood, false claims surfaced again to justify subjugation of the modern Maya.

She was about to hand the enemies of her people the proof they'd sought. The Aztecs had dominated Mexico for three centuries in the post-classic, made art and architecture and revolutionized trade patterns across Mesoamerica. But if you asked most people what they knew about the Aztecs, cannibalism and human sacrifice were the only answers you'd get. Now the same would be true for the Maya; all of Chel's ancestors' accomplishments would disappear into the shadow of this discovery. They'd be nothing more than the people who worshipped praying mantises for eating the heads of their mates. They'd be the people who sacrificed children and ate their remains.

'It's been going on for hundreds of thousands of years.'

Stanton had followed her to the lobby. He'd stayed at the museum with them overnight while she, Victor and Rolando reconstructed the final portion of the codex. Chel was grateful he had; even after everything they'd discovered, his presence here was somehow a comfort.

'There's evidence of cannibalism in every civilization,' he said. 'On the island of Papua New Guinea, in North America, the Caribbean, Japan, central Africa, from the time all our ancestors lived there. Pockets of genetic markers in human DNA all over the world suggest that, early on, all our ancestors ate human corpses.'

Chel looked back into the oculus. The stacks of the library were just visible below, thousands of rare volumes, sketches and photographs from around the world. Each one with its own complicated history.

'Have you heard of Atapuerca?' Stanton asked.

'In Spain?'

'A site there is where they discovered the oldest prehuman remains in Europe,' he told her. 'Gran Dolina. They found skeletons of children who'd been eaten. The conquistadores' ancestors were doing it long before yours were. To be desperate enough to do unthinkable things to feed your family is to be human. Since the beginning of history, people have done what they had to do to survive.'

Half an hour later, as dusk gathered, Stanton sat with Chel, Rolando and Victor, perched on the stools scattered around the lab where they'd been working virtually nonstop. He tried to take in the words the king had spoken to the scribe:

I and my closest minions have gained such power from feasts on flesh, having consumed more than twenty men in the three hundred suns past. Now Akabalam has divined that he wishes to concentrate the strength of ten men in every man of our great nation.

Stanton pictured the ancient kitchen in which they stood. It was eerily reminiscent of the slaughterhouses and rendering facilities he had been investigating for a decade. The line between cannibalism and the disease was clear: mad cow happened because farmers fed their cows the brains of other cows; VFI happened because a desperate king fed prion-infected human brains to his people.

'It really could've survived that long in the tomb?' Rolando asked.

'Prions could survive millennia,' Stanton explained. 'And it could have been lying in wait inside that tomb. That place was a time bomb.' That Volcy had set off, no doubt. He'd gone into a tomb, stirred up the dust, and then touched his eyes.

Victor said, 'Paktul suggests that only those who ate human meat became sick. Presumably you don't think Volcy was a cannibal, so how did VFI become airborne?'

'A prion is prone to mutation,' Stanton told them. 'It was born to change. A thousand years concentrated in that tomb, it became something else, something even more potent.'

He scanned the page for another passage.

Jaguar Imix and his retinue consumed the flesh of men for many moons in good graces of the gods without being cursed. But whatever god protected them before does so no longer.

They now understood the genesis of the disease, but even Stanton didn't know exactly how to use the information. Were there answers in the tomb itself? Two days ago, armed with this, he would've tried to convince CDC to authorize a wide search for Kanuataba. He'd called Davies – now back working at the Prion Center – and told him what they'd found. But there were no experiments the team could run using this information. Stanton thought about emailing Cavanagh, but even if she could get past her anger with him, they still didn't have an exact location to send the team. The Guatemalans would *still* deny that VFI had come from within their borders, so an official team probably wouldn't be let in regardless.

And according to the news reports, CDC had things closer to home to worry about: people were slipping out of LA by land, air and sea, and the quarantine wouldn't hold much longer. Finding the original source would hardly be Atlanta's top priority. Words written a thousand years ago would not convince them.

'If Paktul and the three children founded Kiaqix,' Rolando said, 'I don't understand why the myth said it was an Original Trio. There are four of them.'

'The oral history isn't sacrosanct,' Chel said. 'There are so many different versions, and they get passed down across so many generations, it's not hard to imagine them losing a person in the translation.'

Stanton was only half listening now. Something about the sections he'd just been reading stuck in his mind, and he studied them again. In each passage, the king was proud of how long he and his men had been eating human flesh and the power it had given them. Three hundred suns. For almost a year before the king fed his commoners human meat, he and his men engaged in cannibalism, and they'd clearly eaten brains. So why hadn't they gotten sick? Had the brains they'd eaten been completely free of prion?

Stanton pointed this out to the team. 'Within a month of when the human meat is introduced into the food supply for everyone else,' he said, 'it makes everyone – including the king and his men – sick.'

'What happened?' Rolando asked.

'Something changed.'

'Like what?' Chel asked.

'The ancients believed bad things happened when the gods weren't honored,' Rolando said, invoking Paktul's claim that whatever once protected the king did no longer. 'Many *indígenas* would still tell you disease is a result of the gods' anger.'

'Well, I would tell you disease is the result of mutated proteins,' Stanton said. 'And I don't believe in scientific coincidences. The king and his men must have eaten a lot more brains in that year than the commoners could have in a couple of weeks, right? The disease suddenly became destructive, and there had to be a reason.'

'You think it got stronger,' Chel said.

Stanton considered. 'Or what if their defense mechanisms got weaker?'

'What do you mean?'

'Think of an AIDS patient,' he said. 'HIV weakens the immune system and makes it much easier to get sick.'

Victor glanced at his watch. There was something detached about him. Stanton had to wonder where else the man's mind could be at a time like this.

'So you think something lowered the defenses of the king and his men?' Rolando asked. 'Their immune systems got messed up?'

'Or maybe it was the exact opposite,' Stanton said, connections forming. 'They're in the middle of a societal collapse, right? They were destroying all of their resources, burning down the last of their trees, and running out of everything from food to spices to paper to medicine. Maybe something was artificially raising their defense mechanisms before, and then it stopped.'

'Like a vaccine?' asked Chel.

'More like how quinine prevents malaria, or vitamin C prevents scurvy,' Stanton said. 'Something holding the disease back without them even knowing. The king says they consumed the flesh of men for almost a year without being cursed. And Paktul thinks it's because they stopped making offerings to the gods. But what if they actually lost or stopped consuming whatever was protecting them?'

'Where would they have been exposed to this . . . prevention?' Victor asked, returning to the conversation.

'It could've been something they were eating or drinking. Something plant-based, probably. Quinine was protecting people from malaria long before they knew what it was. Penicillium fungi in soil were probably preventing all kinds of bacterial infections before anyone knew about antibiotics.'

They reexamined every word of the translation, scrutinizing each reference to plants, trees, foods or drinks – anything the Maya consumed before the widespread cannibalism began. Corn breakfast mixtures, alcohol, chocolate, tortillas, peppers, limes, spices. They searched for every reference to anything used medicinally. Anything that could have been protecting them.

'We need samples of all of these to test,' Stanton said. 'The exact species the ancient people used to eat.'

'Where would we get that?' asked Rolando. 'Even if you could find them in the forest, how would we know it was the same species?'

'Archaeologists have extracted residues from pottery,' Chel interjected. 'They've found trace evidence of dozens of different plant species on a single bowl.'

'Inside tombs?' Stanton asked.

Victor stood up and walked toward the door to the lab. 'Excuse me,' he said. 'I'm going to the washroom.'

'Use the one in my office,' Chel suggested.

He left without a word, seeming not to have heard her. He was acting strangely. A sad possibility suddenly occurred to Stanton; he would have to check the old professor's eyes for signs of VFI.

Chel said, 'We have to go down there.'

'Where exactly?' Rolando asked.

'The opposite direction of Lake Izabal,' she said. 'From Kiaqix.'

Paktul wrote that he would lead the children in the direction of his ancestors, and elsewhere in the codex, he'd written that his father hailed from *a great lake beside the ocean*. Lake Izabal in east Guatemala was the only one fitting that description anywhere in the vicinity.

'If he led them toward Izabal,' Chel said, 'and they ended up at Kiaqix, we have to assume the lost city's less than three days' walk in the opposite direction.'

'Izabal is enormous,' Rolando said. 'Hundreds of square miles. The range of that trajectory could be huge.'

'It has to be somewhere in there,' Stanton said.

The lab door opened again. It was Victor. He wasn't alone.

29

In the seconds that followed, Chel came to a series of terrible realizations. First, that one of the men with Victor was his friend from the Museum of Jurassic Technology, who'd once advised the *ladino* military. Then, that the two men trailing Colton Shetter – dressed identically to him, in white shirts, black pants, and boots – were dragging a rolling metal warehouse cart between them.

So when Rolando asked, 'What's going on, Victor?' Chel already knew.

They were here to take the codex from her.

Victor had let these people in. He had picked up the phone, called security down the hill, and gotten them waved by.

Chel circled to the front of the light tables, putting herself between the men and the codex. Through her jeans, the cold edges of the metal table pressed into the backs of her legs.

Taking a step into the room, Shetter turned to Victor. 'I assume those plates behind her are what we've come for.'

Victor nodded.

'Who the fuck are these people?' Rolando demanded. He and Stanton were still behind Chel on the other side of the boards.

'Dr Manu,' Shetter said, 'we will appreciate your and

your colleagues' cooperation. Mark and David have to pack up the plates. I know how fragile they are, so we want to be as careful as possible. I need you to go back and stand with your team.' Reaching into his waistband, Shetter pulled out a gun, then casually held it at his side. It was so small that it looked like a toy.

'What are you doing?' Victor asked him.

'Making sure we get what we came for,' Shetter said. 'I'm sorry, Daykeeper, but I can tell it's necessary.'

Chel glanced at the intercom panel. There were fifteen feet between where she stood and that wall, but to get there she'd have to make it past Shetter's men. They started to walk toward her, pulling the warehouse cart behind them like little boys with a sled. She stayed where she was.

She would die here before she would move.

'Why are you doing this, Victor?' Stanton asked from behind her. 'What the hell is going on?'

Victor ignored him. When he finally spoke, it was only to his protégée. 'Listen to me, Chel. You can come with us. We're going to the land of the ancients. To your true home. But we must have the book. All we can do now is run, Chel.'

She felt tears streaming down her cheeks. 'You're gonna have to kill me, Victor.'

She was wiping her tears on her sleeve when Rolando made his move. She didn't see him dart across the room toward the intercom. She only heard the noise that brought him down before he got there.

And the silence after.

Chel ran to him. It seemed to take forever to cross the room. No one tried to stop her.

She didn't see the blood until she was holding his head in her lap. His hand clutched his belly. Chel covered it with her own.

Shetter's gun was still pointed in their direction. The look on his face belied the steadiness of his arm. Even he seemed surprised by what he'd done.

'I'm a doctor,' Stanton said, starting to move. 'Let me help him!'

'Stay where you are,' Shetter commanded.

'Take what you want and go,' Stanton said. 'But let me help him.' He started to inch over, and, when Shetter didn't stop him, he moved faster. Shetter kept the gun trained on the three of them.

Chel pressed down on Rolando's wound. The blood continued to gush. She whispered to him. Trying to keep him conscious.

Victor stood frozen behind Shetter. Silent.

'Get the plates,' Shetter commanded his men.

It took them less than a minute to load up the codex plates and get them out of the room. The two silent men left first, then Shetter.

He turned at the door. 'Coming, Daykeeper?' He was confident enough in the answer that he didn't stay to find out.

Victor stood there, watching Stanton hold pressure on Rolando's wound with one hand and deliver chest compressions with the other.

Chel held Rolando's head in her lap. She'd streaked

blood from his wound into his hair, and she tried not to stare at the pool spreading beneath them.

'Chel . . .' Victor finally said. 'I didn't know he had a gun. I'm so sorry. I –'

'You did this, Victor. *You* did this. Get out!'

He turned to leave the room. At the doorway he stopped to whisper back to her, *'In Lak'ech.'* Then he was gone.

A minute later, from her place on the floor with Rolando, Chel saw a flash of the truck's headlights playing against the lab windows as it vanished into the night.

She knew she would never see Victor or the codex again. And those would be the last words he ever spoke to her.

I am you, and you are me.

30

Through clouds of ash from the wildfires in the Santa Monica Mountains, a trio of F-15s in formation roared, leaving contrails in the gray night sky.

Two hours after Victor quietly escorted Shetter and his men past Getty security, Chel stared out the car window in silence. The Pacific Coast Highway looked like a run-down used-car lot – hundreds of vehicles wrecked or out of gas and abandoned, barely allowing a path through.

There'd been nothing she or Stanton could do to save Rolando. They were all covered in blood by the time Stanton had given up trying to revive him. Chel cradled Rolando's head for nearly twenty minutes, saying a Qu'iche prayer for safe delivery to the overworld into his ear.

She and Stanton still hadn't spoken a word about what had happened. But they both knew what they had to do.

Stanton pulled his Audi off the highway toward Santa Monica State Beach. The sand was empty. Only a single vehicle sat in the parking lot: he'd called Davies and arranged to meet him here.

Stanton was surprised when he saw another man step out of the car with his partner. 'What's up, Doc?' Monster said.

‘I was worried about you, man,’ Stanton said. ‘Where’d you go?’

‘Cops kicked us out of the Show, so the little Electric Lady and I found ourselves a hideout in the tunnel beneath the Santa Monica Pier. You have no idea how useful a woman who can make her own light is down there.’

If Chel was surprised to encounter Venice’s finest example of a human freak, she didn’t show it. She remained silent, her mind still back at the Getty.

‘How’d you two find each other?’ Stanton asked as they started unloading equipment from Davies’s vehicle.

‘I knocked on your door in Venice,’ Monster said. ‘No one answered, so I let myself in. Brother, your place looks like one fucked-up science experiment, all those mice in there. When you didn’t come back, thought I’d call over to your lab and see if you were all right.’

‘Good thing it was me who picked up the phone,’ Davies said, ‘and not one of Cavanagh’s lackeys. She’s monitoring everything we do at the Prion Center. I couldn’t get a glass slide from there without getting caught. Much less a microscope.’

Stanton looked at Monster. ‘So you got all this from my place?’

‘Electra helped me. She’s still there taking care of those mice.’

‘You two should stay there for now. Until it’s safe.’

‘Don’t know when that’ll be. But we’ll take you up on the offer.’

‘You really think you can find these ruins without the book?’ Davies asked.

'We have the digital copy, the translation, and a map,' Chel said. They were the first words she'd spoken.

'I'd tell you you've gone mad, but you already know that,' Davies told Stanton.

'You got a better idea?' Stanton asked. 'Radio says they crossed the five-thousand mark in New York.'

They transferred the biohazard suits, testing tools, a battery-powered microscope and other equipment needed for a mobile lab into Stanton's Audi. Finally Davies pulled the last bag from the trunk. 'Twenty-three thousand in cash,' he said. 'Everyone in the lab got whatever they could. And this.' He opened the bag wider, revealing the gun from Stanton's safe at the bottom.

'Thank you,' Stanton told the men. 'Both of you.'

'How you gonna get out, Doc?' Monster asked. 'They just sent in another fifty thousand troops to patrol the border. They've got men at every mile, and you'll never find a private plane or a chopper now.'

Stanton glanced out over the Pacific.

The campus of Pepperdine University came into view at the stretch of coastline just south of Kanan Beach. Stanton took a hard left onto a long dirt road and followed it until there was nowhere else to go. It took half a dozen trips by foot up and down the rocky embankment to get all the gear onto the beach. Then they waited. This was one of the most uneven sea terrains in Malibu, making it dangerous for anyone sailing at night, unless they knew every outcropping. And they could only assume the coast guard was still patrolling parts of it.

Finally they saw the beam of a flashlight a few hundred yards out. Minutes later Nina approached the shore in a small dinghy. Her hair was wild, and salt caked her skin.

'You made it,' Stanton said as she beached the boat.

They hugged in the darkness and Nina said, 'Lucky for you, I've been hiding from harbormasters my whole life.'

Even under the circumstances, it was strange for Stanton to be in the company of both these women. 'Chel, this is Nina.'

But the two of them seemed immediately at ease around each other. 'Thank you for this,' Chel said.

Nina smiled. 'Couldn't pass up the chance to have my ex-husband be forever in my debt.'

They loaded the equipment onto the dinghy and headed off to *Plan A*, anchored about two hundred yards out. As they climbed onto the big boat, Stanton heard a comforting chuff. He bent down and hugged Dogma's soft, wet coat close to his chest.

Their destination was Ensenada, Mexico, two hundred forty miles south. Nina had contacted the captain of a larger boat, who'd agreed to meet them in a secluded part of the resort town. From there they'd travel past the Baja peninsula, where they'd have a better chance of chartering a plane to Guatemala. The McGray had a top speed of forty-two knots, which put the trip to Ensenada at about eight hours with refueling.

In the bight that took them to the North Pacific Gyre, Stanton searched the horizon for the coast guard. On her way in, Nina had deciphered the patrol pattern through the bay and navigated several miles out for the safest passage. The only chatter on the radio was from a few others trying to get away, speaking in code.

Out on the ocean, Nina and Stanton alternated at the wheel, with Nina taking on the more difficult stretches. Chel stayed below, sleeping or staring off in silence.

Just before sunrise, they ran into an offshoot of the Great Pacific Garbage Patch, and the hull of the boat gathered tiny fragments of discarded plastic at the bottom, causing it to drag and bump wildly. Only a captain as good as Nina could have gotten them through it, and as Stanton watched her steer them into calmer waters, he marveled at the skills she had honed over so many years at sea.

Comfortable as she clearly was, things had to have been really weird for her all alone out here for the last week. It was one thing to escape from the world, another thing entirely to imagine there might not be a world left to return to.

'You all right?' he asked her once they were past the gyre.

Nina held the wheel, glancing over at him. 'Just thinking.'

'About what?'

'We were married for three years,' she said. 'So we spent about a thousand nights together, minus the third of them you spent in the lab. And the fifteen or so you spent out on the couch when you pissed me off.'

'Practically a rounding error.'

'Well, I was thinking,' she continued, ignoring him. 'We sleep eight hours every night. But during the week we spent only a few hours a day together, right? So we've spent more time together asleep than we ever have awake.'

'I guess so.'

They listened to the gentle rhythms of the ocean. Nina shifted the wheel, changing their course slightly. Stanton sensed something still lingering in the look on her face. 'What?'

She nodded down at the hold, where Chel was. 'You know it's pretty strange to see you look at someone else that way,' she whispered.

'You haven't seen us exchange a dozen words.'

'Don't need to,' Nina said. 'I know better than anyone what it looks like when you want something.'

Stanton shrugged it off. 'I just met her.'

As Stanton finished the words, Chel emerged; it was the first time she'd come on deck in hours. She moved slowly, pulling herself up by the railing. The strangeness of Stanton and Nina's conversation lingered, and Chel seemed to sense a slight shift in the emotional weather.

'Everything okay?' she asked.

'You have to eat something,' Nina said, changing the subject. 'There's a year's worth of junk food down there.'

'I will. Thank you.' She turned to Stanton. 'We should go over the maps and the trajectories together soon. I started projecting the different paths from Lake Izabal and identifying possible places where the city might plausibly have stood, based on what we know.'

'Of course,' he said. 'I'll be right down.'

'I need to make a call first,' Chel said. 'Can I use the satellite phone?'

Stanton handed it to her, and she went back down below.

Nina whispered, 'That woman just lost her friend, she was screwed by her mentor, and people took that book from her. If I'd been through what she has, it'd take me years to even think straight again. But she's down there working. I've only known one other person in the world who could do that. So don't be so damn rational. Get to it, for God's sake.'

The digital display on the phone told Chel it was just after eight a.m. on December 18. Three days to the end of the Long Count cycle. Three days until Victor and all the rest of them realized they'd murdered Rolando over a fucking calendar.

She would never be able to understand what her mentor had done or forgive herself for letting him back into her life. She'd played every detail over in her head – from the moment she'd showed up at the MJT until Victor left the lab – searching for answers. Trying to find some clue she missed about what he was really capable of.

Slowly, Chel dialed the number she knew best. The cell towers were overwhelmed, but this time, after three rings, she got an answer.

Her mother's voice came through static. 'Chel?'

'Mom, can you hear me?'

'Where are you? Can you come to the church?'

'Are you okay?' Chel asked. 'Are you safe?'

'We're safe. But I'll be better when you come.'

'Listen, Mom, I can't talk long. But I wanted to tell you that I'm not in Los Angeles anymore.'

'Where are you going?' Ha'ana asked.

'Kiaqix. From there, we're going to find the lost city.'

When Ha'ana spoke, her voice sounded resigned. 'I never wanted you to take the risks I did, Chel.'

'What do you mean, Mom? . . . Mom?'

The phone cut out before Ha'ana could respond. Chel tried to get service again, but they'd run through a patch of cloud cover, and she didn't want to use too much battery. Besides, what else was there to say? Ha'ana was talking again about the risks she'd taken to get them out of Kiaqix. But Chel knew the real courage would have been in *staying* there.

Stanton descended the stairs. He sensed that she needed distraction. 'You want to tell me what we should expect in Kiaqix?'

Chel said, 'Trees hundreds of feet high, with pink flowers and green moss that looks like tinsel. More animals per square mile than the best safari in Africa. Not to mention the sweetest honey you've ever tasted.'

'Sounds like Shangri-La.'

Stanton reached out and took her hand. She was surprised but happy when he leaned in and kissed her softly on the lips. He tasted like salt. Like ocean air.

Chel never took her eyes off his. But once they pulled back, she reached down and picked up one of the maps. 'Shall we get to work?'

Bahía Todos Santos was the Pacific inlet that led into Ensenada; *Plan A* made it there just before noon. Nina steered them toward a thirty-six-foot Hatteras fishing boat floating five miles offshore. Stanton had insisted they couldn't risk getting any closer, because Mexican authorities were on the lookout for American vessels trying to escape the epidemic.

They hitched up and Nina made introductions. The captain of the other boat, Dominguez, was stocky, and wrinkled from all his time in the sun. Years earlier, Nina had profiled him for a magazine because he was known along the Gold Coast for his ability to find mackerel in the most difficult stretches of ocean. He spoke little English but welcomed the Americans onto his boat with a tight smile.

Once all the gear was transferred and they'd paid him the agreed-upon four thousand dollars in cash, they were ready to go.

Chel called to Nina from Dominguez's boat. 'Thank you. Again.'

'Good luck,' Nina said. She nodded at Stanton, tears welling. 'Take care of him.'

Stanton jumped back onto *Plan A*. A brisk wind blew hard as he rubbed Dogma's head, then stood and embraced Nina.

'Guess it's a waste of time to tell you not to do anything stupid,' she said.

'Too late for that. I hope you know . . .'

Nina cut him off. 'Just get your ass home, all right?'

The trip through the Mexican portion of the California Current passed in a blur, and just after daybreak the following morning, they rounded the Baja peninsula and headed east across the gulf. With their native captain, they had no problem getting past the few coastal patrols near Cabo, and finally they made landfall at Mazatlán. The aroma of fried dough from the mestizo street carts filled the air. Life seemed to be going on as usual here, and if anyone was particularly concerned about VFI, they didn't show it.

After docking, Dominguez paid off a harbormaster, then told the man they needed a van or SUV. Half an hour later, they had an old silver jeep for twenty-five hundred dollars. With the gear transferred, Dominguez waved goodbye.

At Mazatlán International, men with machine guns manned the entrance. People inside eyed Stanton and Chel warily. This was a major hub, and unlike at the port, the sight of Stanton's gringo face clearly unnerved some of the travelers here. At the private air terminal, he and Chel got the bad news: all charter planes were booked, ferrying Mexico's wealthy farther from the epidemic. Complicating matters, they needed a plane large enough to carry the jeep they'd just procured.

After half an hour of fruitless efforts, Chel overheard two diminutive, twenty-something Maya men having a conversation in Ch'orti', a branch of Mayan spoken in southern Guatemala and northern Honduras. Chel didn't speak the modern dialect, but it was a close descendant of ancient Mayan, and from the content of the conversation, it sounded like the guy doing most of the talking was some kind of freight pilot.

'*Wachïnim ri' koj b'e pa kulew ri qatët qamam*,' she told the man, whom even Chel towered over. '*Chakuyu' chäb'ana jun toq'ob' chäqe. Chi ri maja' käk'is uwi' wa' wach'olq'ij.*'

We go to the land of the ancients now. Please, you must help us. Before we reach the end of the calendar.

Ancient Mayan could be spoken with Chel's fluency by fewer than a dozen people in the world – all scholars – and the pilot, who introduced himself as Uranam, had probably never heard anyone speaking it outside the few words his own daykeeper knew. But he understood exactly what she was saying.

'How do you know the ancient tongue?' he asked, staring as if she were a ghost.

'I am descended of a royal scribe,' Chel said, her voice commanding. 'And he has told me in a dream that if we do not reach El Petén, the fourth race of man will be wiped from the earth.'

Several phone calls later, their new friend had procured a decommissioned US Navy plane in from Guadalajara to take them south.

Two days after leaving LA, they were headed into the jungle.

12.19.19.17.18
December 19, 2012

31

The Maya highlands are anchored north to south by a spine of volcanoes that have been active for millions of years. Early highlanders worshipped the volcanoes, but their powerful eruptions, which could swallow an entire tribe at once, eventually drove the Maya south to the Land of the Trees – as they called it in Qu'iche – *Guatemala*.

Four hours into the flight, with the C-2 Greyhound flying at less than two thousand feet, Stanton and Chel looked down at the green canopy that gave the country its name. Uranam, the pilot, was using a radar system to search for the proper coordinates, but from the window all they could see were forested hills in all directions. The colors of the foliage darkened as they circled the perimeter of the area, and Chel worried they might not find Kiaqix before nightfall.

If her assumptions were correct, Kanuataba had to be somewhere between sixty and a hundred miles from her village, at a bearing of 230 to 235 degrees southwest. Volcy had found the city in three days' walk, so the total range couldn't be greater than about three hundred square miles. They'd scour every inch.

'Are we expecting to see macaws?' Stanton called above the roar of the engine.

'Only in the migration season,' she told him, adjusting

her eye shield. 'The village is a point on the migratory path, and in the fall there are thousands, but by now they've moved on.' She continued her search for the cypress-covered hills that would signal they were near the village landing strip. Before they could find Kanuataba, they had to find Kiaqix.

'Hold on!' Uranam yelled out.

Every time they made the transition from the mountains to the valleys and back again, the plane bucked up and down, and just then the port-side wing caught a current and was kicked upward, jostling the entire aircraft. For a minute it felt as if the plane might snap in two.

When it righted itself, Chel saw the ground below. They flew over alternating patches of thick forest and cleared farmlands, where North Americans' appetite for corn and beef had stripped the earth.

A minute later, she saw the massive cypress-covered mountain abutting the valley. Here, fifty generations of her ancestors had lived, worshipped and raised families. She pointed Stanton toward the valley her father had given his life for. *Beya Kiaqix.*

'There.'

The rainy season had made the earth soft, but there were half a dozen mahogany and cedar trunks and large branches blown over in the path of Kiaqix's landing strip. The plane's wheels barely cleared them. Final slivers of daylight were leaving the forest, making the landing even more treacherous. It looked as if no one had landed here in months.

On her last trip to Kiaqix, hundreds of villagers came to the airstrip to herald the return of Alvar Manu's daughter, the great scholar. There'd been a dozen round-faced children holding incense and candles. Now she had to remind herself that today no one knew they were coming.

The plane rolled to a stop.

Uranam hurriedly jumped out and threw open the cargo doors at the back. The crushing heat of the jungle poured in immediately.

They put the biohazard suits, tents, prion samples, metal cages, test tubes, and other glass into the jeep, lowered the lift, and Stanton drove into the mud. When they were ready to make the five-mile drive to Kiaqix proper, Chel rolled down the window to let in some air.

'You'll be here?' she confirmed with Uranam. 'We'll be back in twenty-four hours.'

Fear crawled across the pilot's face. 'No,' he said, backing toward the plane. 'I'm not staying.'

'He agreed to stay,' Stanton said after Chel translated. 'He has to.'

'I don't know what this is about,' Uranam said. 'But I don't want to find out.'

He pointed above the forest. Chel turned to see thick wisps of smoke trailing into the sky, almost as if there was a factory deep in the jungle.

'They're just clearing for next year's harvest,' Chel explained, first to Uranam, then to Stanton. 'That's all it is.'

Uranam looked like a man with his mind made up as he climbed back into the cockpit. 'No. This is something else,' he said, eyes fixed on the smoke. 'From the gods.'

Within a minute, he was firing up the engine.

After the plane took off into the night, Stanton tried to reassure Chel. When they found what they'd come for, he insisted, he would find a way to get someone to pick them up.

But Chel knew it would be impossible to get another plane back in here anytime soon, and she was afraid that, if the weather turned, they might not be able to get out for weeks. Then she turned to look again at the black trails of smoke, and fear gripped her throat. Whatever superstitions drove the pilot away, he was right about one thing: No one would be burning fields this late in the rainy season.

So they started down the road to Kiaqix with no idea of how they'd ever get back. The jeep had a full tank of gas, but Chel knew there had to be a hundred miles at least between them and the nearest Esso station. And, in this part of the Petén, roads were mostly just lines on the map, as hillside erosion and mudslides rendered them impassable for much of the year.

The plan was to stay for the night in Kiaqix and set out again at dawn into the jungle in the opposite direction of Lake Izabal, recreating the path that the Original Trio had taken here but in reverse. The five-mile path from the airstrip was so rutted that Stanton could barely get the jeep out of first gear. A light rain fell. Though they drove over cleared land, the sounds of the jungle were always near: the shrill calls of the keel-billed toucans, the monkeys making their wolflike cries.

Even as they drove through the darkness, Stanton tried to make out what little plant life he could identify around them for any sign of whatever might have protected the king and his men from the disease. On the way down he'd studied the flora that grew in this tropical forest, and he recognized a few trees by their shapes in the headlights: Spanish cedars with their coupled leaflets that looked like outstretched arms, vanilla vines that climbed up the small, thin trunks of copal.

'Where do we stay tonight?' Stanton asked, wiping the blinding sweat from his forehead. He had never been this far south, and he couldn't believe the wall of heat that greeted them when they landed.

The heat wasn't new to Chel, but with this much humidity, even she felt like she was seeing the world underwater. 'Maybe with my mother's cousin Doromi. Or with one of my father's sisters. Anyone will let us stay with them. They know me.'

Neither of them dared mention the fact that there wasn't any telling what they'd actually find in Kiaqix. But not even those dark fears could keep Chel from feeling some of the excitement she always did when she made this drive. Kiaqix was as vivid in her memory as the streets of LA. The long causeways, the aroma-filled market, rows of thatch, wood and concrete houses, like the one she was born in. Then there were the modern stone buildings built recently: the stained-glass church, the expansive meeting hall, the multi-room school.

The medical facility on the road in, for which Chel had helped raise the money, would be their first stop. The twenty-bed mini-hospital was built at the edge of Kiaqix a decade ago. Once a month, a doctor flew in to administer vaccinations and antibiotics. Otherwise it was run by the elder women of the village and a shaman who dispensed traditional remedies.

The road bisected a patch of mahogany trees. Some spots between them were covered with unripened stalks of maize. Though it was drizzling now, there had been a terrible drought in the Petén. Even where tree stumps were too large to uproot, the villagers had planted around them. They were clearly desperate for fertile land.

Soon the medical facility came into view. The villagers called it *ja akjun,* Qu'iche for *doctor's house.* To Stanton, it looked more like a Mediterranean church than a hospital. Wooden columns buttressed a white roof, and an outdoor spiral staircase led to the second floor – an architectural touch that could be found only in a place where it never got cold.

The last time Chel arrived here, nurses had swarmed her, eager to show how the modern and traditional remedies were brought together under one roof to treat machete injuries, complicated births, and the myriad other ills that were part of life in Kiaqix. Now there wasn't a person to be seen. The red door to the hospital stood open, and the only sounds were of the jungle giving over to night – trees whispering in the wind and those eerie cries of the spider monkeys.

'You ready?' Stanton asked her. He squeezed her hand and they got out of the car. He stopped to pull two flashlights out of their supply bag and, as casually as if pocketing car keys, tucked his Smith & Wesson into his waistband.

Once they both had on eye shields, he led them toward the open door.

Something felt wrong right away. The entrance was pitch-black. Stanton scanned the room with his flashlight. It was the clinical bay. Curtain rods separated one examining area from the other. Splintered wooden chairs marked where patients usually waited. There was no life here, and it didn't feel like there had been for a long time.

'In ri' ali Chel,' Chel called out as they stepped inside the darkened room, her voice echoing. *'Umyal ri al Alvar Manu.'*

I am Chel, daughter of Alvar Manu.

No response.

Rounding the corner into the examination area, their flashlights caught paper strewn across the floor. Then chairs, turned over, soaking in puddles of antiseptic that had been spilled on the ground. A ceramic container was shattered, and shards were mixed with soaked cotton balls and long Q-tips. Flies the size of quarters buzzed around them. The space reeked of ammonia and what smelled like excrement.

Stanton reached into his pocket and pulled out two pairs of latex gloves. 'Don't touch anything with your bare hands.'

As she struggled to maneuver her sweaty hands into the gloves, Chel called out loudly again in Qu'iche that she was the daughter of Alvar Manu and that she had come to help. Her own voice sounded weak to her, but it echoed in the empty room.

Continuing through the building, her worry grew. These rooms were not just abandoned – they had been vandalized. Beds lay on their sides and the stuffing had been ripped out. There was glass everywhere. Stanton opened the cabinets and rummaged through the drawers, looking for the medical supplies: someone had taken most of them.

At the far end of the hallway, Chel pushed open the doors to the small chapel. She scanned her Maglite across the front and saw that the large wooden cross had been pulled from above the pulpit and smashed into pieces. The beautiful stained-glass window was in shards on the ground, and ripped pages from Bibles and copies of the *Popol Vuh* were strewn over the pews and into the aisles.

Then she saw a familiar symbol, and all Chel's remaining hope vanished.

Chel heard Stanton come into the chapel behind her. 'Even the *indígenas* believe it now,' she whispered. 'Maybe it's true.'

He said nothing, but Chel felt his hand squeezing her shoulder. When she reached up to take it and her glove made contact, she noticed the hand was bare.

She whipped around. 'Who are you?'

The stranger didn't answer. He was tall. He wore a hooded sweatshirt with a rust-colored stain splashed across it. And he wasn't Maya.

'Qué está haciendo aquí?' she said in Spanish.

How or why a *ladino* was here now, Chel didn't know. Her mother's words of warning echoed in her ears. Her heart pounded as she backed away. *'Estoy aquí con un médico. Gabe! Gabe!'* She screamed, but her voice felt so weak. She couldn't breathe.

The *ladino* lunged at her and pulled her down. He ripped off her eye shield and jammed his hand over her mouth. She tried to scream again, but she couldn't. Chel pawed at his face, but he bore down, wrapping his other hand around her throat. She knew what could be on his hands and squeezed her eyes shut as tightly as she could. Only it was no use: she'd be dead long before she was sick.

I am Chel Manu, daughter of Alvar. Kill me like you killed my father.

That was her last thought before the gun went off.

32

Stanton's hands shook as he turned the key in the ignition and started the jeep. He'd killed a man. The gun he'd used was on his lap, ready to be used again. There had to be others infected out there in the darkness ahead. But it seemed better to start moving again than to stay here.

Chel slumped in the passenger seat next to him, numb. It would be some time before they would know if her attacker had managed to infect her before Stanton killed him. Even the rapid blood assay wouldn't tell them anything for a few more hours.

Tiny clouds of mosquitoes swarmed the headlights as they drove down the road leading on to the village proper. But as they made their way closer, Stanton could see in the high beams what must've been the source of the black smoke they'd seen at the landing strip. It was a smoldering building about the size of the medical facility. The walls had collapsed; limestone had shattered. There was no roof.

'That's the school,' Chel said, all emotion gone from her voice.

They kept going. The remains of single-room houses cropped up on both sides. Four or six stood in clusters every several hundred feet, each with its single door and no windows. Adobe-covered wooden walls had been knocked down; palm fronds that once covered roofs, pulled off. In the middle of the road were dozens of hammocks that looked as if they had been dragged from one of the houses and abandoned. Red and yellow and green and purple cloths were cast aside and covered in mud, and the jeep's tires ran unsteadily over the graveyard of color.

Part of Stanton wanted to drive the car out of town and stay the night in a field. They were done looking for others; now they were trying to avoid them. But he also thought the jeep might draw more attention to them than they'd elicit if they hid it and sheltered themselves in one of the abandoned buildings.

He pointed at one house they drove by that still appeared untouched. 'Do you know the people who live there?'

Chel didn't seem to hear him. She was somewhere else entirely.

Stanton decided it looked as good a place as any. He parked the jeep and led Chel toward the house, holding the gun with his free hand. He knocked at the door, and, when there was no answer, he kicked it open.

The first things his flashlight caught were two bodies in a hammock. A young woman and a toddler. It looked as if they'd been dead for at least a week.

Stanton tried to stop Chel from getting any closer, but she was already in the doorway, staring at the bodies.

The sound of her voice surprised him. 'We need to bury them. I need incense.' She obviously wasn't thinking clearly.

'We can't stay in here,' he told her.

He grabbed her hand again, and they kept going. In the

next dwelling, there were no corpses, just clothing strewn on the ground, a broken hoe and ceramic bowls. Stanton cleared everything out.

'You think it's safe?' Chel managed.

He had no proof, but it was the best they had. 'We need to keep our eye shields on.'

They collapsed against a wall, huddling together, exhausted. Stanton pulled granola bars from the supply pack and forced Chel to swallow several bites. Finally he turned off the flashlight, hoping she might be able to sleep. He would try to stay awake, on guard.

'Do you know why we burn incense for the dead?' she whispered.

'Why?'

'When a soul is taken, it needs the incense smoke in order to pass from the middleworld to the underworld. Everyone here is stuck between worlds.'

Over the last couple of days, Stanton had heard her talk quite a lot about her people's traditions, but not this way. He wanted to reassure her but didn't know how; only the faithful had the right words for times like these. Instead, he turned to what he knew. She was still convinced that something had protected the king and his men from VFI before the outbreak of disease in Kanuataba. Tomorrow they would find it. 'We have the map and the coordinates for Lake Izabal,' he told Chel, 'and as soon as it's light, we'll start searching.'

She nestled her head in the crook of his arm. Stanton felt the weight of her on him and the touch of her skin on his.

'Maybe Victor was right,' she said. 'Maybe all we can do now is run.'

Stanton woke with a start and pulled out the gun. Something was trampling wet leaves just on the other side of the wall. Chel was already crouched by the back wall, listening. There was a high-pitched noise, something squeaking in the rain.

Chel made out a voice speaking in Qu'iche. 'Let the evil winds out, Hunab Ku.'

'What's going on?' Stanton asked.

'My name is Chel Manu,' she called back in Qu'iche. 'I am from Kiaqix. My father was Alvar. I have a doctor here. He can help if you are sick.'

A tiny old woman with hair to her waist appeared in the doorway. She wore thick eyeglasses over her wide nose.

Stanton lowered the gun. Thunder groaned in the distance, and the woman stepped toward them, looking like she might tip over.

'Are evil winds in this house?' she called out in Qu'iche.

'We are not sick. We are here to find where the sickness has come from. I'm Chel Manu, daughter of Alvar. Are you sick?'

'You came by the sky?' the woman asked.

'Yes. Are your people sick?' Chel repeated.

'I am not cursed.'

Chel glanced at Stanton, who pointed at his own eyes. Her glasses must have saved her. The same thing that might have saved both of their lives back in LA a week ago.

'When did you come here?' the woman asked.

Chel told her they'd arrived in Kiaqix about five hours ago.

'Ask her if there's anyone else alive in the village,' said Stanton.

'Fifteen or twenty are in the houses still standing,' the woman replied. 'Mostly on the outskirts. There are more hiding in the jungle, waiting for the evil winds to blow away.'

'When did this begin?' Chel asked the old woman.

'Twenty suns ago. You are really Chel Manu?'

'Yes.'

'What was your mother's name?'

'My mother is Ha'ana,' Chel said. 'You know her?'

'Of course,' she said. 'I am Yanala. You and I met many years ago.'

'Yanala Nenam?' Chel said. 'Daughter of Muram the great weaver.'

'Yes.'

'Is there anyone from my family who is alive?'

'One of your aunts is among the few survivors,' Yanala said. 'Initia the elder. She might have come and found you herself, but she does not walk easily. Come.'

They trailed the old woman down a series of side roads and across milpas. When they turned in to a clearing toward a set of houses nestled on a hillock, Chel was struck by her one and only childhood memory of this place. For a moment, she was a little girl again, bouncing on her father's shoulders as he carried her down the causeway.

But now there was no one trading cornmeal, no music coming from the houses. There was only silence.

They approached the entrance to a small log-built house with a strong thatch roof, still intact. The woman led them into a room stuffed with aging wooden furniture, hammocks and an indoor clothesline. Tortillas were cooking on top of a hearth with large stones, filling the room with the smell of corn.

Yanala disappeared into a back area of the house. A minute later a door swung open, and an even older woman emerged. She had long silver hair braided into a crown above her head, and she wore a purple and green *huipil* draped with a dozen strands of colored beads. Chel recognized Initia immediately.

Without a word, the woman walked slowly toward them, leaning on the furniture. 'Chel?'

'Yes, Aunt,' she said in Qu'iche. 'And I've brought a doctor from America.'

Initia stepped into the light, and her eyes became visible. Both her irises were covered in a milky white film. Cataracts, Chel realized. They'd probably saved her from VFI.

'I can't believe you are here, child.'

'You're not sick, Aunt?' Chel asked as thcy embraced. 'You can sleep?'

'Much as one can at my age,' Initia said. She motioned for them to sit around a small wooden table. 'It has been so long since you have come, and here you are, of all times. How is this possible?'

Initia listened in disbelief as Chel described the events in LA, from Volcy's arrival on.

'You've been in the causeways, you've seen the village center, so surely you understand what the evil winds have brought to us too,' Initia said when Chel had finished.

'Ask her who was the first person here to get sick,' Stanton said.

'Malcin Hanoma,' Initia said after Chel translated.

'Who is that?' Chel asked.

'Volcy had no blood brothers, so Malcin Hanoma, son of Malam and Chela'a, was his planting partner. They went off in search of these treasures from the lost city together. Volcy never returned, but Malcin did. He was injured, and with him he brought the curse upon us, the wrath of the ancestors.'

'How quickly did it spread?'

'Malcin's family was the first to be taken. Their children became sleepless, as did the entire family who shared a home with him. Punishment came from the gods, and within only days the winds spread faster and faster.'

Chel closed her eyes, envisioning the destruction that followed. How quickly had her people turned on one another? How long had it taken for the people of Kiaqix to devolve? To tear down the church, burn the school, and loot the hospital?

'So many terrible things have happened here, Aunt.'

Initia pushed herself up and motioned for them to follow her out a back entrance. 'But not only terrible things. Come.'

*

They trailed her to a dwelling directly behind the house, the door of which was covered with stacks of palm leaves. Together they pulled away the fronds and created an opening.

'Do not let the winds in,' Initia called behind her.

Chel stared in disbelief as they stepped inside. Swaddled in colored hammocks draped from the ceiling, were at least a dozen babies. Some were crying softly. Others lay still with their eyes open, silent. Some slept, their tiny chests rising and falling.

Yanala attended to several at a time; Initia joined her, coddling a little girl who wouldn't stop crying while spooning liquid corn into another's mouth. Initia placed a baby boy in Stanton's arms, then handed a little girl to Chel. The girl was small, with patches of hair across the crown of her head, a wide nose, and dark-brown eyes that darted around the room, never quite catching Chel in her sights.

'A baby must be shown closeness with its mother, sleep in the hammock with her, and take from her breast when it's hungry,' Initia said. 'They have grown disconnected because they have been denied their mothers.'

'Where did you find them, Aunt?'

'I knew which houses recently had births, for everyone comes together to celebrate a new life. Yanala and I went in search of survivors. Some were hidden beneath palm fronds, and others were left in the open.'

Chel glanced at Stanton. 'How long will they be immune?'

'Six months or so,' he said, cradling the boy. 'Until their optic nerves mature.'

'That is Sama,' Yanala said as Chel rocked her little girl back and forth.

The name was somehow familiar. 'Sama?'

'Daughter of Volcy and Janotha.'

'She's their daughter? Volcy's daughter?'

'The only one of the family to survive.'

Astonished, Chel looked at the child. Her eyes were open and wet. This was the daughter Volcy had desperately longed to see as he lay dying in a strange land.

'Do you see what this is, child?' Initia asked.

'What do you mean?'

'The end of the Long Count cycle is but one rise and fall of the sun from now,' Initia said. 'And when it comes, we will witness the end of all we've known. Perhaps we already have. But our youngest survived by the grace of Itzamnaaj, most merciful, and they will be our future. It is said in the *Popol Vuh* that, with each cycle's end, a new breed of men inherits the earth. These children are the fifth race.'

12.19.19.17.19
December 20, 2012

33

Just after midnight, Chel cradled Sama in her arms and watched as Initia pressed dough onto the hearthstone in the main house. In the other dwelling, Stanton checked the babies one by one to make sure none showed early symptoms. When Yanala came to get Sama for her exam, Chel found herself surrendering the baby reluctantly.

When they were alone again, Chel told Initia about their arrival. 'A *ladino* attacked me, and I think he was infected. My mother warned me that they could be here, and I didn't believe her. But she was right.'

'No, that man came here to help, Chel.'

'What?'

'A *ladino* church group got word that people here were sick, and they came to bring food and supplies,' Initia explained. 'Even a doctor. These *ladinos* wanted to help us. There is no one to blame. Not the *ladinos* or the *indígenas* who were cursed. When a man can't commune with the gods in sleep, he loses himself, no matter who he once was. It would happen to any of us. I am sorry this man was driven to attack you by the curse. But I know his intentions for coming here were good.'

Chel thought of Rolando, and she was struck by another wave of sadness.

'I do not blame you or your mother for feeling this way

about the *ladinos*,' said Initia. 'She suffered so much at their hands, and it is impossible to forget these things.'

Chel pictured her mother's disapproving face. 'She's been trying to forget everything else about Kiaqix for a long time,' she told Initia. 'She didn't want me to come back. And she certainly doesn't believe we'll ever find the lost city. She's convinced my father's cousin Chiam never found it, and she doesn't believe it exists.'

Initia sighed. 'I have not thought of Chiam in many years now.'

Chel wondered what, of her childhood, Initia did remember. 'Did you hear Chiam read my father's letters to the village?'

'Your father's letters?'

'The letters he wrote when he was in prison,' Chel reminded her.

'Of course,' Initia said. 'Yes. I listened to them being read.'

Chel heard a hesitation in her aunt's voice. 'What is it?'

'Nothing,' Initia said. 'I am old and I do not remember so well.'

'You remember fine,' Chel said, putting a hand on her arm. 'What is it?'

'I'm sure there is a reason,' Initia said, almost to herself.

'A reason for what?'

'It has sustained you,' Initia said. 'The story of your father's letters sustained you. This is what she wanted.'

'The letters aren't just a story,' Chel said. 'There are records of them. I've spoken to others who heard them, who said they stirred the people to action and inspired them to fight.'

'Yes, that is what the letters did, child.'

'Then what are you saying?'

Her aunt clasped her hands together as if in penitence. 'I do not know the reasons your mother has not told you this before, child. Ha'ana is a wise woman, *Ati't par Nim*, the cunning gray fox, her spirit animal. But you have a right to know.'

'I don't understand,' said Chel.

'Your father was a wonderful man, a loving man,' Initia said. 'He was dedicated to you and to your mother and to his family, and he wanted to protect them. But his *wayob* was the tapir, who, like the horse, is strong, not clever. He was a simple man, without the words to put into those letters.'

'My father went to prison for leading the people.' Chel tried not to sound condescending. 'When he was imprisoned, he wrote those letters in secret and was killed for them. My mother told me everything that happened to him. Everything he did to fight for Kiaqix.'

'But now ask yourself who told you these stories,' said Initia.

'You're saying someone else wrote those letters and my mother wanted me to believe that he did?'

'Not just you,' Initia said. 'Everyone believed your father wrote them. But my husband was his brother, child. He knew the truth.'

'So who wrote them?' Chel asked. 'Someone with him in prison?'

Sticks crackled beneath the hearthstones. 'From the time your mother was a young girl, she was never afraid,' Initia said. 'Not of the landowners or the army. She would walk up to them in the market when she was only ten years old and spit on their shoes. She rejected their calls to modernize us, to change our ways. She helped stop the *ladinos* when they wanted to change what was taught in our schools, when they wanted our children to learn their history.'

Chel froze. 'My mother?'

'By the time Ha'ana was twenty,' Initia continued, 'she was sneaking into the meetings of the elders. When the army hanged a young man from the balcony of the town hall, many became afraid. But your mother tried to convince the men to fight in case the army or guerrillas returned. She said we must arm ourselves. But no one listened to a woman. When your father went to prison, that's when the letters began.'

Chel looked around at the stone hearth, the hammocks, the small wooden table and chairs on the sascab floor, the *huipils* hanging to dry. This was a place where Maya women had done their work for a thousand years. Not on the battlefield.

'Why would she lie?' Chel asked.

'Ha'ana understood her people,' Initia said. 'She could rally the women, but no man would listen to a woman about the ways of war. To rouse the men to action, Ha'ana needed the voice of a man. When your father was imprisoned, it was the most terrifying thing that ever happened to her but also a chance to be heard.'

'But when he died, she left here. She left all of you behind and never came back. How could the person who wrote those letters leave?'

'It was not easy, child. She worried someone would discover what she'd done and come after her – and you. The only way to protect you was to leave everything here.'

'Why didn't she tell me?'

Initia put a hand on Chel's back. 'They killed your father because of the letters, even though he didn't write them. After he was murdered, your mother felt so much guilt. Despite the good her letters had done, she blamed herself for his death.'

Chel was in shock. She had punished her mother for her apathy, for abandoning the place she came from, and Ha'ana had never corrected her. She stayed silent, knowing how hard she had fought and how much she had lost for her people.

'Your mother is the gray fox,' Initia said. '*Ati't par Nim* is always cunning.'

Chel had always thought *Ati't par Nim* seemed wrong for Ha'ana. Now she knew better. The ancients believed that the power of the *wayob* was ubiquitous; they believed in its interchangeability with the human form, its dominion over life, its promise of a person's potential. The fox made people believe what it needed them to.

Suddenly Chel thought of something. She darted over to one of the supply bags, digging through until she found her codex translation.

'Is everything all right, child?' Initia asked.

Chel had assumed Paktul led the children from Kanuataba into the jungle, to a place in the forest where his ancestors had once lived. Yet throughout the codex, the scribe conflated his human form with his animal form – his spirit animal. And Chel and her team had been unable to reconcile why the oral history spoke of an Original Trio who'd escaped the Lost City rather than a foursome composed of Paktul, Smoke Song, and the two girls.

But what if Paktul the *man* hadn't made it out with them?

When Stanton returned to the main house, Chel had energy in her voice that he hadn't heard since they'd sat in the Getty plaza together. 'I think we've been looking for the wrong thing. Lake Izabal doesn't have anything to do with where the trio went.'

'What do you mean?'

'Paktul isn't writing about his human ancestors. It's right here in the translation. He uses the word *I* interchangeably with his spirit animal. He goes back and forth using *I* to refer to his human form and his *wayob*. But we know he was keeping an actual macaw with him in the cave, because he refers to other people who can see it. He shows it to the prince and Auxila's daughters, and he writes about the bird rejoining its flock.'

I told the prince my spirit animal had stopped in Kanuataba on the great path of migration every macaw makes with its flock, Paktul wrote. *I told him that in weeks we would continue our journey in search of the land that our ancestor birds have returned to every harvest season for thousands of years.*

'When he says he'll lead them in the direction of his ancestors,' Chel said, 'I thought that meant his *human* family. But what if he never went anywhere? What if he was killed by the guards, as he predicted, or he stayed behind to make sure the children could escape?'

'Who led the children to Kiaqix?' Stanton asked. 'You think they followed a bird?'

'The prince would've been trained to track game a hundred miles. And the macaw would instinctively have returned to its flock. Kiaqix means the *Valley of the Scarlet Macaw*. It's right along the migration path. The oral history says that the Original Trio considered it a good omen when they saw so many macaws in the trees here. What if they were following one of them because they believed it was the *spirit* of Paktul?'

Chel pulled out the latitude map. On it she'd drawn a line representing the macaws' known migratory path. 'During migration seasons, the macaws fly from the southwest to here,' she continued, 'and the patterns are highly consistent. We can find the exact trajectory and follow it.'

For most of Stanton's adult life, the possibility that three children followed a bird a hundred miles would have sounded insane. Now he didn't know what to believe, but however improbable it was, all he could do was trust Chel's instincts. If they had to track a migration pattern into the jungle, then that's what they'd do.

'Are you sure this is the exact path?' Stanton asked.

Chel reached down into the supply bag and pulled out the satellite phone. 'I found three different sites online, all giving the same coordinates. You can see for yourself.'

She handed Stanton the phone, but when he tried to power it up again, the screen remained blank. It had been dying for hours, and the last bit of juice was gone. Cutting them off from the world entirely.

'It doesn't matter,' Chel told him, pointing back at the map. She seemed almost manic. 'We have what we need.'

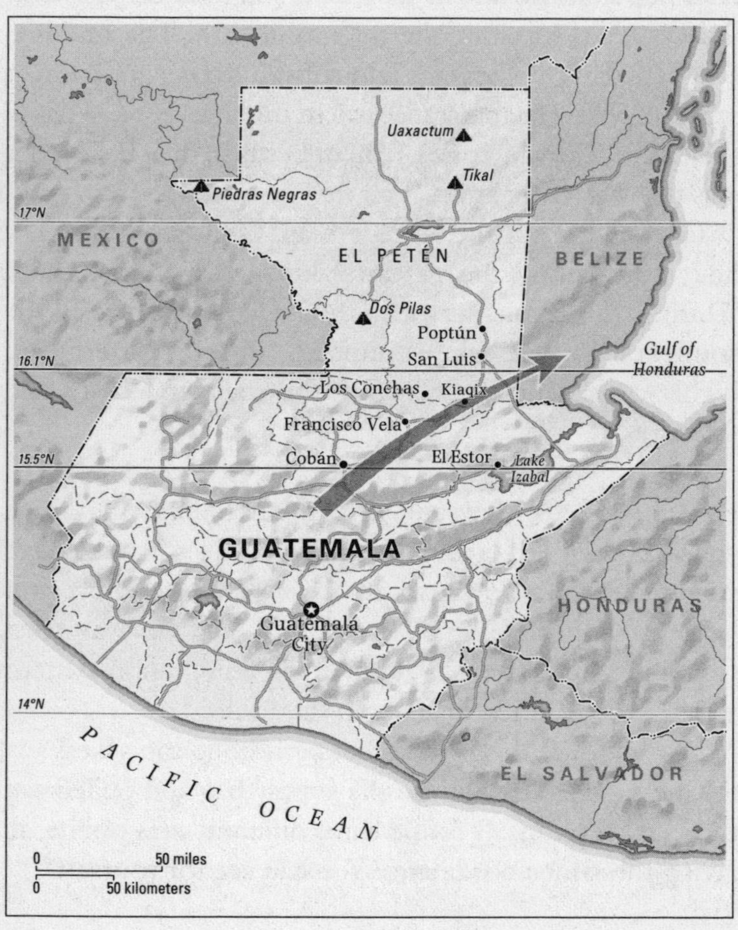

Then Stanton saw something in her eyes that stopped him cold.

'Look at me for a second,' he said.

Chel was confused. 'I am looking at you.'

He pulled out his penlight and shone it in her eyes, studying the blacks of them as he swept the light away. They should have constricted in the light and dilated in darkness.

When Stanton took the light away, nothing changed.

'Am I sick?' Chel asked. Voice trembling.

Stanton turned, quickly kneeling down to the supply bag to get a thermometer to measure her temperature. Then he stayed there for a moment, collecting himself. He didn't want her seeing the fear in his eyes. She needed strength. She needed to believe they would find the lost city, her only hope now. He couldn't let her see his doubts.

34

They left Kiaqix at first light. Soon the sun was cooking the Petén, and the light breeze coming through the open windows of the jeep gave Chel little relief. She could almost feel the VFI inside her. She glanced over at Stanton in the driver's seat. He'd barely looked at her as they'd packed the medical supplies back into the jeep, along with the food Initia had given them. He just said over and over again that, with the disease as concentrated as it was here, the assay was as likely to render a false positive – from contamination – as to be accurate. He was unwilling to accept the results of a test he'd designed himself.

Chel couldn't read his body language very well, but she understood him enough by now to know he would blame himself for the fact that she was sick, for being a second too late. She wanted to make him understand it wasn't his fault – that she would have died there on the floor of the chapel if it weren't for him. But she couldn't find the right words.

She turned her attention ahead again. The macaw's path ran 232.5 degrees southwest. Stanton had set them on a course through the jungle, across alternating patches of overused farmland and uncleared forest. Chel knew that they were looking for flat, elevated places, where the ancient cities like Kanuataba would have been built. Two hours in, the terrain was becoming more rugged. For the most part, there were no roads here at all, and they knew they'd eventually have to go on foot.

The jeep rocked back and forth, kicking up mud. It was almost impossible to see through the windows. Chel's world was getting louder and brighter and stranger: the noises of the car grated, and the howls and screeches of the jungle frightened her in a way they never had before.

She had no idea how long they'd been driving when Stanton stopped the jeep again. 'If the bearing's right,' he said, 'we have to keep going this way.' Ahead was a thicker jungle than any they'd seen, and dozens of felled trees blocked their path. It was the end of the line for the jeep.

'Let's go,' Chel said, trying to show strength. 'I can walk.'

He bent down over the odometer. 'We're sixty-two miles from Kiaqix. If they traveled three days to get there, it can't be much farther, right?'

Chel nodded silently.

'How're you feeling?' he asked. 'If you can't make it, I'll go in alone and come back as soon as I find it.'

'People have hunted around here for centuries,' Chel managed. 'Only two people have found the ruins. You'll never find them alone.'

Stanton carried all the gear on his back – tools for scraping residues from the bowls they hoped to find in Jaguar Imix's tomb, a microscope, slides, and other essentials for spot testing. He walked ahead, clearing shrubs and branches with a machete he'd taken from Initia's house.

They navigated choppy mudbanks and held on to the rough bark of towering trees to help them remain upright. Chel's feet began to blister and her head pounded. She felt like there were a million tiny things crawling all over her body.

After nearly an hour, Stanton stopped. They had just climbed their way to the very top of a rocky embankment, giving them a view of several miles. He held the compass in the air. 'The migration path leads into that valley. It must be there.'

Two small mountains lay ahead, each several miles wide. Between them was a large valley of unbroken tropical rain forest.

'It can't be there,' Chel said. Exhaustion bore down on her fast. 'The ancients wouldn't have built between mountains. It . . . made them vulnerable on both sides.'

The look on Stanton's face told her that, in her condition, he didn't know what to believe. 'Where do you want to go, then?' he asked.

'Higher,' she told him. She pointed at the larger of the two mountains. 'To look for temples above the trees.'

The tree trunks at the foot of the mountain were thin and blackened, charred toothpicks stuck into the ground. There'd been a fire, most likely started by lightning. In storm season, small lightning fires were common; the ancients believed they were a sign from the overworld that a patch of land needed time to rejuvenate.

At the edge of the lightning forest, they reached a more verdant part of the slope. Then, from the corner of her eye, Chel saw a cluster of vanilla vines in the distance, about halfway up the mountain. She turned toward the strange but oddly familiar pattern. Vanilla was common throughout Guatemala; it wrapped itself tightly around tree trunks and climbed up to reach the top of the canopy for rain and light. The vines could grow hundreds of feet high.

But these vines stretched only about fifteen feet into the air, as if the tree had been cut off and stripped of its branches. Chel called out for Stanton to wait, but he didn't hear her. She let him keep going and turned off course. The fifty-plus yards up the slope were interminable, each of her steps more difficult than the last, but she was drawn to the thin, elongated leaves. The dense tangle of vines was looser than it should have been on a tree – a clue that whatever lay beneath was covered with something other than wood bark.

To the untrained eye it would've been impossible to discern, but hundreds of Maya stones had been discovered in the jungle beneath vines like these. Chel's hands shook – with anticipation or sickness – and she barely had the strength to rip the strands away. But finally she could see down to the core. It was a massive boulder, at least eight feet tall, cut into the shape of an elongated headstone.

'Where'd you go?' Stanton had found his way back to her. He bent down to peer over her shoulder. 'What is that?'

'A stela,' Chel said. 'The ancients called them tree stones. They used them to record important dates, names of kings and events.'

These stelae sometimes appeared near cities, she explained, but were also built by smaller villages as homages to the gods. The only thing she knew for certain about this one was that no one had seen its surface for a very long time. Age and weather had cracked off one of the corners.

Chel tried to breathe steadily while Stanton cleared away the rest of the vines, revealing a surface covered in eroded etchings and inscriptions. There was a rendering of the maize god in the middle of the stone, while renderings of Itzamnaaj, the supreme Maya deity, adorned the edges.

Then Chel saw three familiar glyphs.

'What does it say?' Stanton asked.

She motioned to the first carving. '*Naqaj xol* is Ch'olan for very near. And this one – *u'qajibal q'ij* – means we are directly west of it.'

He pointed to the last glyph. 'What about this?'

'*Akabalam.*'

Felled trees and underbrush covered every inch of the slope, and each step was an exhausting challenge for Chel. Up and down they traversed the steep incline, searching for a passable path. They stopped every fifty yards so she could rest. The air was unbearably hot and wet, and with each breath she felt like she couldn't make it any farther. But with Stanton's help she pressed forward, pushing on through another stretch of forest.

Strangely, the pitch of the mountainside flattened out as they headed farther west, giving Chel's legs a short break and allowing her to continue on. After two miles, it no longer felt like a mountain at all. They were still high above sea level, about halfway up to the peak, but the western face had eased into a massive plateau, flat as any plain. Kanuataba meant the terraced city, but nowhere in Paktul's story had he written about agricultural terracing. Maybe instead, Chel thought, the city got its name from this ledge that a river cut into the mountain millions of years ago – a natural terrace that eluded discovery after her ancestors abandoned it.

Minutes later, they found more reason to hope.

Hundreds of ceiba trees, sacred to the Maya, stood in the distance. The trunks had thorns, and the branches were covered with grasses and moss, phosphorescent green.

Kanuataba was once home to the most majestic collection of ceiba trees, the great path to the underworld, in all of the highlands. The ceiba once grew denser than anywhere in the world, blessed by the gods, their trunks nearly touching. Now there are fewer than a dozen still standing in all of Kanuataba!

They continued through the dense area of holy trees that had now returned to the jungle. The ceibas stretched to the heavens, reaching toward the overworld, and Chel could see outlines of gods' faces in the leaves: Ahau Chamahez, god of medicine; Ah Peku, god of thunder; Kinich Ahau, god of the sun, all beckoning her forward.

'Are you okay?'

Stanton was paces ahead, calling back at her. Could he see what she now saw in the leaf patterns above them? Could he hear the call of the gods as she did?

Chel blinked, attempting to see ahead with clear eyes. Trying to form the words to answer him. She stepped toward him, and a break in the ceibas caught her eye. Between the trunks was a sliver of stone.

'There,' she whispered.

They walked a quarter mile to the base of an ancient pyramid and stood together in stunned silence. Mist bathed the structure's top reaches. Trees and shrubs and flowers sprouted in all directions, obscuring every corner. More trees had grown up the stairs, to the top; one façade was so dense with flora, it could have been mistaken for a natural slope. Only at the summit could they see limestone, where three adjacent openings were formed by columns in the shape of elongated birds.

'Incredible,' Stanton said. 'This is it?'

Chel nodded. Broken shards of stones transformed in her mind into angular steps. Slaves and corvée laborers appeared, carrying boulders on their backs. At the base, she saw tattoo artists and piercers, spice-makers trading for chert. The dull and decrepit limestone was, for Chel, now painted with a rainbow of color: yellows and pinks and purples and greens.

The birthplace of her people, in all its glory.

35

They continued across the mountaintop, moving slowly, searching for other signs of the lost city through the overgrowth. The stela and small pyramid were signposts that they had reached the outer limits of the metropolis, but they still had to find the city's center.

Stanton carefully led them over shrubs and massive tree roots extending in all directions, hacking away with his machete in one hand, and gripping Chel's with the other. He tried to keep track of what plants he was cutting through – pink orchids and liana and strangler vines and others – in case they turned out to be relevant.

He also listened closely as they walked. Wolves, foxes, even jaguars could be in the area. Stanton had been on safari once after medical school, and that was about as close to dangerous animals as he ever wanted to get. He was very glad that he could hear only birds and bats in the distance.

They passed stelae and small one-level limestone buildings wrapped from base to top in foliage and small trees. Chel pointed out areas where servants to the nobles likely lived on the edge of the city, and what was once a small ball court where the ancients practiced their strange hybrid of volleyball and basketball. Stanton could easily have missed these overgrown landmarks.

He was trying to keep his eyes on her as much as possible. She seemed stable, but it was hard to know to what extent her symptoms could be exacerbated or accelerated by an arduous hike through the jungle in hundred-ten-degree heat. She would have been better off back in Kiaqix under Initia's care. But he knew she was right that he never would have found the city without her.

Now they had to zero in on the king's entombment temple, the last structure built in Kanuataba before its collapse. Paktul had described the construction as a haphazard project, rushed to completion and built with inadequate resources. Excavating a temple would ordinarily require serious equipment, but Volcy and his partner had been able to do it with pickaxes. So it was likely shoddily built or left unfinished.

The foundation will be laid in twenty days, less than a thousand paces from the palace. The viewing tower shall be built to face the highest point of the procession of the sun and will create a great holy triangle with the palace and the twin pyramid of red.

'To the ancients, a holy triangle was a right triangle,' Chel explained. 'They were considered mystical.' There were many examples of the Maya using 3-4-5 right triangles in the layouts of their cities, construction of individual buildings, and even religious practices. The most notable use of them in urban planning was at Tikal, where a series of integral right triangles was centered on the southern acropolis. 'Jaguar Imix wanted his tomb in a triangle with one of the temples and the palace. The twin temples should be easiest to find first.'

'So we're looking for the *red* temple?' Stanton asked.

'It won't actually be red. Red is the symbol of east.'

'So we're looking for the one that is farther east?'

'The one that *faces* east into the plaza.'

The closer one got to a central acropolis, Chel told him, the larger the structures became, so she knew they were getting warmer. Stanton's arms were exhausted from cutting through brush. The machete felt like its weight had multiplied, and its blade had dulled. Even small branches took too much effort to clear. Sweat poured into his eyes.

Then, twenty minutes later, they came upon a colonnade of pillars. They had been nearly covered with moss, and birds' nests sat atop at least half, but they were still standing, taller than the stela, twelve of them in a square. Whatever original patio joined them had been buried beneath the underbrush long ago, but immediately Chel knew: they were exactly as Chiam had described them.

Her uncle made it here after all.

'Then we have to be close, don't we?' Stanton asked.

'This was a meeting place for upper classes,' Chel explained. 'It wouldn't have been far from the palace.'

'Do we keep going in the same direction?'

But she wasn't listening. Stanton followed her gaze. Ahead of them, the sun's last rays poked through the leaf canopy and struck white stone. Chel let go of his gloved hand and set off almost blithely, paying little attention to the countless obstacles in her path.

'Wait!' Stanton called out. But she didn't respond.

He hurried after her. Before he could catch up, something flew into his mask, nearly knocking him over. Stanton swatted at it uselessly with his flashlight, until it flapped off behind him. He watched it go – a bat, beginning its nightly hunt. When he turned back toward Chel, the last light of day was gone. The stone that had caught her eye only a moment before had disappeared into the darkness.

It wasn't until he'd closed the gap between them that he finally saw what she'd found. She was standing at the base of what had once been stairs, long crumbled away after a thousand years. Stanton's eyes traced the sloping overgrowth that climbed upward from the ground. It was a temple that dwarfed everything else.

'Don't take off like that again,' he said. 'I'm not gonna lose you out here.'

Chel didn't look at him. 'This is one of them,' she said. 'It has to be.'

'The twin temples?'

She nodded, but seconds later she was on the move again.

Chel stepped up to a sprawling limestone substructure. It was built lower than any temple would be, and the walls were half standing, but she recognized it as soon as she saw it and started climbing. Her cotton pants and long-sleeved shirt were wet and heavy. Her hair scratched the back of her neck. But she continued up the overgrown stairs, hopping from one small ledge to the next until she reached the first of six enormous platforms.

'What are you doing?' she heard from below.

She waved Stanton off, concentrating. Chel pictured thirteen men seated in a circle in front of her, their heads covered with animal headdresses, all clapping in agreement with the man who was speaking. All except one – Paktul.

Stanton took her hand as he reached the top.

'This is the royal palace,' she whispered.

Stanton gazed out over the series of raised platforms. 'So this is where . . .'

'They cooked,' Chel said without emotion. He'd expected her to be shaken by standing in the place where her ancestors had prepared human flesh. But Chel's expression was fixed and focused as she looked out into the darkness once again.

'According to Paktul, the palace is the second point on the triangle,' she said. 'So if it's a three-four-five right triangle, then the distance between –'

Suddenly Chel felt dizzy. Her legs were weak.

'Are you okay?'

'I'm fine,' she lied. 'Then the distance from the palace to the twin temple is the first side of the triangle.' She pointed west. 'They never would've built a burial temple in the central plaza, so it has to be that way.'

'Do you need to rest more before we go?'

'Once we find the tomb.'

Stanton helped her down from the palace. They trudged on through the underbrush by flashlight, pushing in the direction the right triangle led them. Stanton continued to whack through brush with the machete, but still refused to let go of Chel with his other hand, even when fighting through the most difficult bits. She was so overheated she felt she might vomit, but she forced it down and kept going.

It was Stanton who spotted it first. From afar it looked like a small mountain, overgrown with small shrubs. It had a square base, maybe fifty feet on each side, and it rose into a four-sided pyramid three stories high. They were fifty yards off from the entrance, but even with all the overgrowth Chel could see that this building was unfinished. The slabs of limestone hiding under the dirt and trees weren't properly cut, and they weren't properly fitted.

'Is it the king's tomb?' Stanton asked.

Chel circled the massive pyramid in search of an inscription. She found none, but when she reached the northwest corner of the temple, something gleamed in the beam of Stanton's flashlight.

Something metal, left on the ground.

Volcy's pickax.

36

'The air down there alone could infect a hundred people. You need to put it on.'

Stanton held out the biohazard suit.

So much sweat already poured off Chel, she couldn't imagine ever feeling cool again. 'I'm already infected. You said heat would only make it worse.'

'The higher concentration you're exposed to, the quicker it can act. The sooner . . .'

She didn't make him finish the sentence.

He helped her into the suit. Chel had no idea how she'd get herself into the tomb with it on; it was as bulky as it was hot. She'd been in plenty of tombs before, and she'd never been claustrophobic. But the idea of descending into the catacomb with this thing on – she imagined it would feel like being buried alive.

With her helmet on, the noise of the world was muted. Looking out through the glass, her entire surroundings – the jungle canopy, Paktul's city, Stanton and his gear – seemed so far away.

'Are you ready?' he asked.

Stanton helped her press awkwardly through the opening in the stone they'd found next to the abandoned pickax. Then he squeezed inside after her and reached over her shoulder to light the path in front of them with the flashlight.

Chel watched her breath cloud the helmet glass as she shimmied forward on her knees. Tracks of what must have been mold had formed along the stones here countless years ago. Even through her suit, the mossy surface felt alien. She knew the scent of bat guano hung in the air, but all she could smell inside her mask was the slightly antiseptic odor of the suit's purification mechanism.

Finally the narrow passage opened up into a larger space. The ceiling was about five feet high. Chel had to lean down a little; Stanton had to crouch. She shone her light at the far wall, marveling at the etchings of sacrificial victims in ornate animal headdresses and of snake-headed creatures with the bodies of men. Chel reached out and touched them, wiping away a thick film of dust with her glove. She had no doubt the drawings were made by Paktul's contemporaries. Each line took hours to carve, and the price of a single mistake would have been death.

On the far end of the platform, stairs led farther down. The temple had clearly been designed as a series of stacked rooms, with four or five staircases on one side, which ultimately led to the lowest level, below ground. There, Chel suspected, they would find several smaller ritual rooms and a larger one where the king was buried – as at the temples of El Mirador.

They kept descending. Each staircase was narrower than the last, and in the biohazard suits they had to turn sideways to squeeze between the walls. The air would get colder as they went down, Chel knew, and she would have given anything for a breath of it, but the suit made everything feel stale and recycled.

Finally they could go no farther. Chel pointed her flashlight ahead into a hallway with cut-out doors on both sides. They were now fifteen or twenty feet underground, and even at midday there would have been no natural light this far below. But the ceilings were higher here; even Stanton could almost stand upright.

'This way,' Chel said, leading him down the hallway. She shone her light into two empty rooms before she found what she was looking for.

In the middle of the most distant chamber stood a limestone sarcophagus.

The final resting place of King Jaguar Imix.

'Is this it?' Though he was right behind her, Stanton's voice came to Chel through a tiny muffled speaker in her ear.

Chel's body was exhausted, but her mind was still hungry to take it all in. One look at the floor told her the tomb had been looted. Still, there was much that Volcy had left behind: carved flints and rusted necklaces, shell pendants, serpentine statues.

And skeletons.

On the floor surrounding the sarcophagus were fourteen or fifteen ancient skeletons, splayed in ritual fashion, all dusted with maroon-colored cinnabar. They had probably died of the same disease that was killing her now, feeling the same way she did: hot, tired and terrified by the knowledge that they would never dream again.

'Who are the others?' Stanton asked.

'The ancients believed that the death of a king stole just one of his thirty-nine souls,' Chel said, 'and that the other thirty-eight lived on or went to the overworld. The *ajaw* needed other souls to sacrifice to the gods during his journey to ensure safe passage.' She pointed at the six smallest skeletons. 'Including children.'

Stanton bent down. 'See the full formation of the ends of the hips of this one? That's a very small adult.'

The dwarf, Jacomo, buried with his king.

A sudden whine in the darkness startled Chel. She turned in time to see an explosion of bats surging toward them.

'Get down!' Stanton called. 'They'll tear the suits!'

The flurry of flying creatures made Chel momentarily lose her bearings. She reached out for the wall, but her hands found nothing and she tumbled to the floor. Above her, Stanton flailed his arms, shooing the bats into the hallway.

Their high-pitched screams faded.

Chel wondered if she had the strength to get back up. The suit mummified her arms and legs. Her muscles ached. She lay there, face-to-face with the skeletons, and felt overwhelmed. Then, just as she was about to close her eyes, she caught sight of something metal hidden in the dust near her. It was a large jade ring with a glyph carved into it.

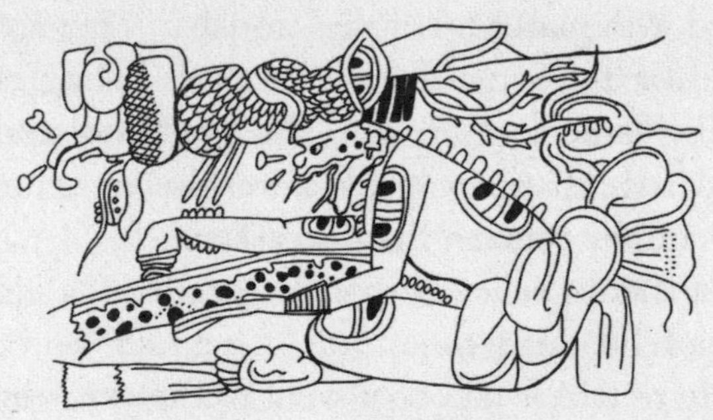

The monkey-man scribe.

The prince had escaped, and Auxila's daughters too, all of them following Paktul's spirit animal – the scarlet macaw – in the direction of Kiaqix. But Paktul, the man, had not escaped. He must have been killed by Jaguar Imix's guards, who had then buried him, his ring, and his book with his king.

She looked at the skulls, wondering which was Paktul's. Somewhere, among these remains, lay the father of her people. They'd never know exactly where, but Chel was content to be in the scribe's presence. To know they'd found him.

Stanton got her to her feet, but Chel couldn't walk on her own. He helped her shuffle over to the king's sarcophagus. Even in her state, Chel saw that the limestone slab was etched with ornate designs from end to end, masterful workmanship lavished on a single stone. She knew that Volcy hadn't gotten inside it either: the heavy lid was still in place, and he never would have taken the time to replace it. He'd probably found the book quickly and known it was all he needed.

'Can you lift it?' she asked Stanton.

Stanton took hold of the stone slab, jockeying it back and forth, one corner at a time. Finally it crashed to the ground, the noise reverberating through the chamber.

Then Chel leaned against the wall again and watched him lift out the bones and artifacts. A jade head mask with pearl eyes and quartz fangs. A long spear with a sharp jade point. Carved jade plaques.

But there were no bowls. No water carriers. No

containers for chocolate or maize. No vessels of any kind. Just jewelry, head masks, and weapons.

All priceless. But useless.

Chel had been confident that they'd find ceramics, that the king would be buried with them, and that they'd find within them the residue of whatever the ancients had been eating. 'I don't know what to say, Gabe. I thought –'

She stopped when she realized Stanton wasn't even looking at her. He simply walked to where the smaller skeletons lay and wrenched the dwarf's skull from his body, which gave easily. 'What are you doing?' she asked.

Stanton pointed. 'The *teeth*.'

'What do you mean?'

'We might be able to extract what they were eating. From the teeth. Food grains can survive forever. Even if they exhausted their supplies, grains they ate a long time before they died could still be here.'

Stanton rapidly gathered other skulls and began to prepare them. For a moment Chel watched him from the wall she leaned on, then she closed her eyes. Everything was somehow still bright. Even in the darkness. And the air inside her helmet was cooking her brain.

'If you need to leave me . . .' she started to say, but she was already thinking only of Paktul, whose ring she'd put on her gloved finger, and then of her mother and how wrong she'd been about her. So she didn't hear Stanton's next words as he went about his work.

'I'm never leaving you.'

*

First Stanton removed all the visible calculi and took scrapings from each portion of the teeth using an X-Acto knife. He did each section three times before putting the scrapings onto microscope slides. This was difficult work under the best conditions; using only a single flashlight in darkness, it was nearly impossible. But, with painstaking care, he slowly did it.

Using a reference text, he compared what he saw on these slides to known plant species. He matched a variety by the uniquc shapes of their starches: maize; beans; avocado; breadnut; papaya; peppers; cacao. Hundreds of deposits sat on the teeth, but it seemed unlikely that any of these common foods had protected the nobles against VFI.

Then, under the dim luminescence of the battery-powered microscope, Stanton saw something unexpected. A starch he needed no textbook to recognize.

Stanton couldn't believe he was seeing the remnants of beech trees here. Beech generally grew in true mountainous climates, like central Mexico. He would never have expected to find it in the jungles of Guatemala, and neither would any botanist he knew. Which meant that this could be an unknown species, native to this small corner of the world.

Beech was the active ingredient in pentosan, which had once seemed like the most promising drug for slowing the spread of prions. But there had never been a safe way to get pentosan into the brain, and no species of beech could cross that crucial blood–brain barrier. So they hadn't tried it on VFI.

But something didn't make sense to Stanton now. Beech

fruit was edible, although its taste was famously bitter. Yet to win immunity from prion disease, the whole city would have to have eaten it, week after week, in quantity.

He crossed over to Chel and gently tapped her on the shoulder. 'I have to ask you a question,' he whispered. 'Did the Maya chew tree bark?'

He knew she was awake, but Chel's eyes were closed. He'd pushed her to continue through the heat of the jungle, to march farther than she thought she could. He had given her hope. And, with hope, she had led him here. But now she was dying.

'In Lak'ech' was all she said.

Stanton hurried back to the slides. He'd remembered something from the codex that talked about the dwarf chewing and spitting something, and he would bet everything on this one instinct: it had been beech bark, and it had been their cure. A new species of the familiar tree had evolved in this jungle, capable of sneaking past the blood–brain barrier. And eating it protected the ancient Maya, up until the day they'd consumed it all.

Stanton had to believe that somewhere outside this temple, the native population of beech trees could have regrown after the collapse, just as the ceiba trees had. Unless the Maya had razed an entire jungle – something even modern man could rarely do – it was impossible to have killed them all. Nature outlasted everything. The only problem was that he couldn't find those trees unless he had some way of recognizing them.

In the jungle night, leaves would be impossible to see. The only way to tell trees apart would be by their bark.

Instinct told Stanton that these Guatemalan trees would share the trait that set all beeches apart: their perfectly smooth, silver-gray bark.

When he emerged from the tunnel, Stanton's flashlight was faltering. He'd been using it for hours. To conserve it, he decided to gather branches from a nearby tree and light them into a torch.

By the entrance to the tomb he saw pines and oaks, but nothing with that smooth gray bark of a beech. Back around the twin temples, smaller plants grew in every crevice, and Stanton gathered a thicker bundle of limbs to use as a second torch when the first one sputtered out. The jungle had gone quieter. Only a symphony of crickets played in the night, so it took Stanton by surprise when two deer sprinted across his path as he bent for kindling.

The torch lit, he pressed on. Feeling the odds against him growing, he forced his way deeper into the forest, where the trees thickened, their trunks like airliner fuselages stuck in the ground. In the darkness, Stanton couldn't begin to estimate their height. It was hard to even stay on a straight path, and he found himself going in circles, seeing the same landmarks again and again.

When he approached the reverse side of the king's entombment pyramid, frustration turned to despair.

He had no idea how he'd ended up where he started. Then another torch failed, and everything went black again. Stanton pawed the ground for branches. His glove touched something sharp and, lighting another match, he looked to see what it was. On the jungle floor, no bigger than the end of his thumb, was a brown lump covered with tiny spines.

A beechnut.

He held the nut high in the air, as if to reverse its path to the ground. Here, so close to the king's tomb, was the smooth-barked tree it had fallen from. Its trunk rose higher than Stanton's match could throw light.

And, to his astonishment, it wasn't the only one.

A dozen stood in a line. Their branches extended toward the face of the pyramid as if they were reaching out to touch it.

Chel floated in and out of the darkness, bobbing like a bird in a brisk wind at the top of the sky. In those moments when she could still see the light, her tongue felt like sandpaper, and the heat made her whole body painful. The disease crawled like a spider through her thoughts. But in those moments when the light disappeared and the darkness came, she sank gratefully into an ocean of memories.

The ancient father of her village – Paktul, spirit founder of Kiaqix – lay beside her here, and whatever came next, she felt safe in his presence. If she had to follow him, if she had to join Rolando and her father, then perhaps she would see that place the ancestors always talked about. The place of the gods.

When he stepped back into the tomb, Stanton saw that Chel was in the same spot he had left her, slumped against the wall with a glazed look in her eyes. Then he saw she'd ripped off her biohelmet. The heat must have been driving her crazy, and now she was breathing in air that would almost certainly make things worse. Stanton considered trying to get her back in the suit, but he knew the damage had been done.

Her only hope lay elsewhere.

Using what remained of the flashlight's power, he began to prepare the injection by crushing leaves, bark, wood, and fruit into tiny particles and combining them with a suspension of saline and dissolving enzymes. Finally he drew a syringe of the fluid and pushed the needle into a vein in Chel's arm. She barely stirred at the prick.

'You're going to come out of this,' he told her. 'Stay with me.'

He glanced down at his watch, establishing a baseline against which to time the first signs of reaction. It was 11:15 p.m.

There was only one way for Stanton to know if the drug had crossed the brain–blood barrier: a spinal tap that analyzed Chel's cerebrospinal fluid. If beech was now in that fluid, it had gone from the heart to the brain and crossed over the barrier into the fluid that surrounded it.

After twenty minutes, he inserted a needle into the space between Chel's vertebrae, drawing the fluid into another syringe. Stanton had known men to scream during spinal taps. Chel, in her condition, barely made a sound.

Stanton dropped spinal fluid onto six slides and waited for them to fix. Then he closed his eyes and whispered a single word into the darkness. '*Please.*'

Placing the first slide under the microscope, Stanton

considered all sides of it. Then he scanned the next slide, and the third.

After studying the sixth, he leaned back in despair.

There were no beech molecules on any of the slides. This species, like every other one Stanton had ever tried, like all the ones they'd used to make pentosan, could not pass the barrier into the brain.

A wave of hopelessness crested inside him. He might have quit right then and just wallowed in the darkness if he hadn't heard Chel making noises on the other side of the tomb.

He ran to her. Her legs were kicking wildly.

She was having a seizure.

Not only had the drug failed; the conditions in the tomb – the heat, the concentration of prion – had accelerated the disease's progress. If her fever climbed any higher, it could kill her. 'Stay with me,' he whispered to her. 'Stay *with me*.'

Stanton felt around for the extra shirt in the supply bag, ripped it into rags, and soaked them in the dregs of their water bottles. But before he could even apply the compresses, he felt Chel's forehead getting cooler. He knew that her body was giving up. He brushed his fingers along the skin of her neck, just under her jaw, and found a thready pulse.

Her seizure slowly subsided, and, for the first time in a long time, Stanton prayed. To what, he didn't know. But the god he'd worshipped his entire adult life – science – had failed him. Soon he'd be walking out of this jungle, having failed the thousands, and eventually millions, who would die from VFI. So he prayed for them. He prayed for Davies, Cavanagh and the rest of CDC. He prayed for Nina. But mostly he prayed for Chel, whose life was no longer in his hands. If she died – when she died – all he would have left would be the knowledge that he hadn't done enough.

Stanton glanced at his watch. 11:46 p.m.

Across the chamber, the ancient skulls seemed to taunt him with the secret they were keeping. Stanton wouldn't let Chel spend eternity in a staring contest with them. He would take her out of here. He would –

It was then that he had the horrible realization that he would have to bury Chel in the jungle. He thought back to something she'd said the night before, when they were slumped against another wall, on the outskirts of Kiaqix.

When a soul is taken, it needs the incense smoke in order to pass from the middleworld to the underworld. Everyone here is stuck between worlds.

How would he burn incense for her? What could he use?

Then it occurred to Stanton that Paktul had written about incense too.

When I set the macaw down and kissed the wretched limestone, the aroma had changed, and I could no longer taste it on the back of my tongue as I once had.

What if the smell and taste of the incense in the air changed for a reason? Paktul knew the king's usual incense combination. If the taste was gone from the back of his tongue, maybe it was because it was no longer *bitter* . . .

Stanton stood up and scooped Chel into his arms.

He had to get her outside.

Carrying her from the king's chamber, he bore her weight back down the hallway, then hoisted her over his shoulder and began up the first set of stairs. As difficult as it had been to get down the stairs alone, they seemed even steeper and narrower than before.

But minutes later they reached the top and tasted the night air. There was a small clearing about ten feet from the north face of the pyramid, with enough room to make a small fire – most likely where Volcy and his partner had pitched their tent.

Stanton laid Chel down in a small crook between tree roots and sprinted to the reverse side of the pyramid. He frantically gathered more beech, circled back around, and dumped the branches in a pile in front of Chel. A minute later he was lighting the kindling, and soon flames danced up into the sky. The acrid smell of the smoke filled the air.

Stanton sat close to the fire with Chel's head in his lap. He placed his hands on her head and opened her eyelids as wide as he could. He forced his own eyes open too, even as the smoke made them begin to tear. If VFI got into the brain through the retina, then maybe the treatment for it had to as well.

For five silent minutes, as the flames grew, Stanton held Chel in the jungle night, looking for a sign. Any sign at all. He brushed the hair from her face to check her pulse. He didn't even notice his wristwatch – he was concentrating on Chel's heartbeat – but the second hand clicked off the last two ticks of the fourth world.

It was midnight.

12-21.

Epilogue

13.0.0.9.3

For millions around the world, it *was* the end of life as they knew it. As long as anyone alive could remember, the arrow of progress had pointed in the direction of technological innovation, urbanization, and connectivity. In the years leading up to 2012 – for the first time in human history – the majority of humans lived in cities, and it had been projected that by 2050 that proportion would rise to more than two-thirds.

The end of the Long Count cycle changed all that. Some of the largest metropolises in the world had been overrun by Thane's disease, and there was no way to know if they would ever be completely safe again. Because there was still nothing that could destroy the protein, new contaminated places had to be quarantined every day as they were discovered. In malls, restaurants, schools, offices, and public transportation from America to Asia, the hazmat vehicles and cleanup crews became something to live with – or escape from.

Within weeks, this contamination prompted a mass exodus from many of the world's largest urban centers. Some economic data suggested that a quarter of the populations of New York, San Francisco, Cape Town,

London, Atlanta and Shanghai might leave within a three-year period. Transplants went to smaller cities, to the reaches of suburban sprawl, to the countryside, where self-sustaining agrarian communities popped up.

LA was in a category by itself. Thane's disease touched every Southland citizen. It was impossible for many to imagine staying, even if it were safe.

The most famous doctor in the world hadn't returned either. Along with the international team of scientists now under his command, Stanton was living in a tent that the Guatemalan Health Service had erected in the ruins at Kanuataba. The day after walking out of the jungle with the samples he'd taken in the tomb, and driving the jeep two hours to a working phone, Stanton returned with the Guatemalan Health Department. He hadn't left the jungle since.

From trees surrounding the king's tomb, Stanton and his medical team had synthesized an infusion that could reverse Thane's disease if taken within three days of infection. The ancient citizens of Kanuataba had overused beech to the verge of extinction. But when they abandoned the city, the trees had returned in full force.

The question of why they were concentrated right around the tomb remained. Species sometimes evolved together, even those working in direct opposition to one another. Microbes got stronger in reaction to antibiotics. Over hundreds of generations, mice became better at eluding their predators, and snakes became better at hunting their prey. Some scientists argued that the prion and the trees had been co-evolving for centuries, making each other stronger and stronger through mutation, until Volcy opened the tomb. The term the broadcast journalists favored was *an evolutionary arms race.*

The Believers, of course, called it fate.

After successfully convincing the scientific community what VFI should really be called, Stanton had stopped trying to give any of the rest of what had happened a name.

On a particularly grueling day in late June, he gave instructions in broken Spanish to his team of mostly Guatemalan doctors and headed for the residential tent. Rain soaked his clothing, and mud weighed down his boots as he trudged forward into the shadow of the twin temples and Jaguar Imix's palace. Jungle living was hard, and he missed the ocean, but he was getting used to the heat and humidity, and drinking a cold beer at the end of a long workday in the ruins felt good.

Stanton made his way into the living area of the tent, put on dry clothes, cracked a Cerveza Sol, pulled out his laptop, and logged on to the satellite Internet service. He quickly skimmed hundreds of emails. There was an update from Monster: until the Freak Show was reopened, the menagerie of two-headed animals he and the Electric Lady had rounded up from all corners of the Walk were living with them in Stanton's condo.

Continuing to sift through emails, Stanton found the latest from Nina – a picture of Dogma on *Plan A*, somewhere in the Gulf of Mexico. She too was inundated with interview requests, whenever she came to shore. She just laughed and said she had better things to do than lionize her former husband. She sent a picture every week from wherever she and the dog went.

'Are you on the computer *again*? Haven't you heard? Technology's dead. Timewave Zero and all that.'

Stanton turned toward the sound of the mellifluous English accent. Alan Davies was removing his safari jacket. He laid it carefully across a chair, treating the garment as if it were the one Stanley had worn when he found Livingston. His white shirt underneath was soaked with sweat, his hair frizzed. The Englishman hadn't taken well to the humidity, something he reminded Stanton of daily.

'Can't believe you're drinking that pathetic substitute for a beer,' Davies said, settling into a chair. 'What I wouldn't do for a pint of Adnams Broadside.'

'London's just a fifty-hour drive through the jungle and four planes away.'

'You wouldn't survive a day out here without me.'

As Davies opened a bottle of wine and poured himself a glass, Stanton dashed off a quick response to Nina, then glanced at the wires and the news sites. Every day now – six months out – the same stories about the disease were recycled, with only tiny details changed, and there was rarely anything of interest. But when he got to the *Los Angeles Times* website, something stopped him cold. 'Holy shit.'

'What?' Davies said.

Stanton hit PRINT on the computer screen, stood up, and grabbed the article off the tray. 'Did you see this?'

Davies scanned it. 'Does she know?'

*

The Guatemalans had bulldozed a path back to the major roads so they could ship supplies in and out by truck. In a health department Land Rover, Stanton reached the entrance, which was manned by the security detail now watching the entire perimeter of Kanuataba. Once they let him by, he found himself in the middle of the circus that the surrounding area had become.

Hundreds of people were camped out in tents, trucks and motor homes just beyond the border. Early on they'd been able to keep the location of Kanuataba a secret, but now dozens of news trucks were parked along the side of the road, and helicopters circled constantly, taking aerial shots of the city and broadcasting them all over the world. It wasn't only journalists who'd come down here; the area had become a kind of religious outpost in the post-2012 age. Even though the Believers couldn't get inside the ruins, Kanuataba was slowly becoming their Mecca.

Stanton passed the sea of tents where men, women, and children of all colors and ages and nationalities now lived, bound by their strange, heterogeneous faith. That the world hadn't been completely destroyed hadn't hurt their cause at all.

Indeed, the events leading up to 12-21 and the discovery of the cure here had ignited a fervor for all things Maya. More than a third of people in the Americas said they believed that a prion outbreak happening at the time of the calendar turn wasn't coincidence. In LA, thousands attended *Fraternidad* meetings, and vegetarianism, Ludditism and 'spiritual Mayanism' gathered more and more followers, especially in the communities to which city-dwellers had fled. They argued that prions – from VFI to mad cow – were the ultimate result of manipulating life in ways that nature never intended.

Two hours later, Stanton made it to Kiaqix. So much of the village had been destroyed, and, along with its connection to the outbreak and patient zero, that meant very few gawkers were inclined to make the trek. A dedicated group of NGOs and villagers who'd escaped the plague were rebuilding here, with the help of foreign donations flowing in from around the world. But, as with everything in the jungle, it was a slow and painstaking process.

Like the hospitals in Los Angeles, the old medical clinic had been leveled, by a team sent from the States, and a new temporary one constructed in its place. Stanton parked the Land Rover and headed inside, waving at now familiar faces. Some were members of *Fraternidad* who'd volunteered to come down and help rebuild. In all there were almost four hundred people living in the village now, and everyone had taken on a role in the reconstruction.

In the pediatric area in back of the clinic, Stanton found Initia tending to the babies orphaned by the outbreak. Most were in hammocks, and a few others were in tiny cribs constructed out of small pieces of wood and thatch.

'Jasmächá, Initia,' Stanton said.

'Hello, Gabe,' she replied.

Stanton quickly checked the babies' eyes. Even the youngest were now six months, which meant their optic nerves would be fully developed soon, and he was vigilantly watching them for any signs of Thane's disease.

'Welcome back, Doctor.'

Stanton turned. Ha'ana Manu stood in the entryway, carrying the eight-month-old they had named Rolando, who was screaming in her arms.

'Are you ever going to call me Gabe?'

'You went to medical school for four years to be called Gabe?'

Chel crouched beneath the A-frame of a new structure in the eastern housing group with four other *Fraternidad* members, preparing to lift another tree trunk upright. Before she could start counting, she heard a whimper.

'Hold on,' she told them. She hurried over to the small bassinet hidden in the shade beneath a nearby cedar tree. Volcy's daughter, Sama, now almost seven months, lay inside with her eyes wide open and alert.

'Chel, look what I found.'

She turned back to see her mother standing with Gabe.

For weeks, Ha'ana had continued to deny she'd written the prison letters or that she'd ever been a revolutionary. Even now she clung to the story that she and Chel's father had written the letters together. Still, Chel considered it a victory when she'd convinced Ha'ana to come down to Kiaqix with her for the first time in more than thirty years. Ha'ana claimed she had every intention of returning to America soon and complained about not having TV or a proper stove. But Chel knew her mother would stay as long as she did.

Stanton walked over and kissed Chel. They'd been finding excuses to visit once or twice a week since January, and it hadn't been long before they started talking about their future. They'd been cleared of wrong-doing by their respective institutions, and had both been invited to keynote at symposiums all over the world and offered faculty positions at various universities.

The fact that they'd gone to Guatemala on their own and found the cure for Thane's disease had shaken up the CDC; Director Kanuth had resigned his post. Cavanagh was the heir apparent, but rumors circulated that the president intended to offer it to Stanton. He wouldn't accept, and Chel knew she was a big part of why. She wasn't leaving here anytime soon, and if they did eventually return to the States, it would be together.

Stanton reached into the bassinet to offer Sama a finger, and the little girl lit up. Chel almost never let her out of her sight. She and Stanton had spent many nights in her wood-and-thatch house, feeding the baby bits of tortilla beside the hearth, until she fell asleep, after which they'd taken full advantage of their privacy.

'Thought you weren't back till next week,' Chel said. 'Is everything okay?'

Stanton pulled the printout from his pocket and gave it to her.

2012 Group Breaks Silence
Saturday, June 22, 2013, 9:52 a.m.

FBI sources have verified that a letter received two days ago by the *Los Angeles Times* was sent from the southern highlands of Guatemala. It was most likely written by a member of the cultlike 2012 group once led by Colton

Shetter, who has now been confirmed dead by the Guatemalan police.

According to the four-page letter, Shetter was tried by and excommunicated from the group he founded for his murder of researcher Rolando Chacon at the December 2012 raid at the Getty Museum. It is alleged that, following his trial, Shetter attempted to maintain his power using force and was killed in a fight with other members of the group. Using details given in the letter, Guatemalan authorities discovered Shetter's body buried near Lake Izabal, one of the largest lakes in Guatemala. In what appears to have been a kind of ritual sacrifice, reminiscent of the ancient Maya themselves, Shetter's heart and all his other organs had been cut out of his body.

The now infamous 2012 group's whereabouts remain unknown, but the letter suggests it is now being led by Dr Victor Granning. It indicates Granning plans to return the 'Cannibalism Codex' to the Guatemalan village of Kiaqix, situated very close to the discovered ruins at Kanuataba, where experts believe the book was written. Granning believes that the exhibition of the codex close to its point of origin will bring much-needed support to the local *indígenas* affected by Thane's disease, by invigorating tourism in the area.

The letter also states that Dr Granning has made an important new discovery in the codex and that he therefore wants the book displayed for the 'millions of new Believers to see.' The former UCLA professor and controversial icon, still sought by authorities for his role in the raid, claims to have found a mistake in the previously calculated date of the end of the ancient Long Count cycle. He now believes the correct date for the end of the thirteenth cycle of the calendar is November 28, 2020.

Chel stopped reading. Somewhere in the far reaches of this jungle, Victor was trying to make amends. Even in his absence, he'd become a kind of mythical figure among the Believers. Many on the new fringe considered his anti-city, anti-technology writings prophetic.

'He's giving the codex back to you,' Stanton said.

There were no easy answers for what had happened – certainly not for how the legacy of her people had ended up in Chel's hands. Whatever recalculations Victor might have made, who was to say some version of his 2012 predictions hadn't already come true, and they were now living in the world he'd dreamed?

Sama giggled, and Chel stared into her little girl's eyes.

It didn't really matter anymore.

Chel was surrounded by the people she loved. And she was home.

She handed the article to her mother. Ha'ana took a quick glance and crumpled it up. 'Come to Grandma, child,' she said, picking up Sama from the bassinet. 'We have more important things to worry about, don't we?'

Author's Note

When I first encountered prions (pronounced 'preeons') in medical school, I became fascinated by these tiny proteins that had baffled scientists for fifty years. They served no apparent function in the brain, violated the central dogma of molecular biology stating that reproduction could only happen through the transfer of DNA or RNA, and caused incurable diseases, including mad cow.

As I read everything I could about prions, I learned that more than 150 people had died as a result of consuming infected beef during the mad cow epidemic, and that some scientists believe many more Britons have been exposed and millions more may still get sick. In my reading, I soon came upon another disease prions caused: fatal familial insomnia (FFI). While the disease primarily affects families in Italy and Germany, several new 'sporadic' cases are discovered every year in other parts of the world, including Central America.

After learning that 'kuru', the first known cluster of prion disease, was found in the South Fore people of Papua New Guinea, and was transmitted through the practice of ritual cannibalism, the idea for 12-21 took shape.

The story of how the date 12-21-12 became so important in the eyes of millions of people, and assumed the place it has in the cultural consciousness, is still a mystery to me. Beginning in the mid-1970s, new-age writers speculated that the end of the Maya Long Count would represent a major day for human civilization, ushering in a global shift in consciousness. Through 'visionaries' like José Argüelles and Terence McKenna, 12-21-12 was linked to astrology, environmental causes, new-age mysticism, spiritual 'synchronization', and growing skepticism about the role of technology in human lives.

But this belief in the importance of the ancient calendar turn took some very strange forms as it spread. Some adherents began to associate it with doomsday theories, claiming that 12-21 would lead to astronomical alignments, collisions with other planets and stars, and reversal of the earth's magnetic poles. In recent years, groups of believers have left their homes and built vast compounds – in the jungles of Mexico, in the mountains of the Himalayas – in which to try to survive the apocalypse they believe is coming.

Still, I have found no evidence that the ancient Maya themselves believed the turn of the thirteenth cycle was any different from their other important calendar turns, all of which they feared and revered. The Long Count is actually a base-twenty calendar, and continues on for another 2,700 years. The original mention of the importance of the end of the thirteenth cycle, which the inscription written at Tortuguero, Mexico, reinforces, comes from the *Popol Vuh*. There it is written that the last Long Count ended at the completion of its thirteenth cycle, and this has led some to believe that the current one will as well.

Despite the widespread popularization of the word, even among scholars, the abandonment of water-deprived cities in the lowlands at the end of the first millennium was likely not a civilization-wide Maya 'collapse'. Over a period of several centuries, at the end of the classic era, cities that had once flourished were slowly abandoned for smaller villages and more fertile ground.

Still, since the nineteenth century, when explorers rediscovered abandoned ruins buried deep in the overgrown jungles of Honduras and Guatemala, theories have circulated about what led the Maya to leave their incredible metropolises, never to return. Pollen samples from the Copán Valley and El Petén, locations of some of the largest ancient settlements, indicate that they were almost completely devoid of human life by the middle of the thirteenth century, after centuries of obsolescence.

Most Mayanists now agree that overpopulation, drought and destructive farming practices leading to deforestation were major contributors to the dwindling population. Other possibilities are more hotly contested. Recently, scholars like Jared Diamond have argued that on-going violence between the Maya cities was a major factor, and pointed out that fighting reached a peak in the period leading up to the end of the classic.

Evidence for cannibalism among the Maya is controversial and limited. But at the ruins of late classic Tikal,

Mayanist Peter Harrison discovered a cooking pit beneath an ancient house that contained human bones with charring and tooth marks. It seems likely that if cannibalism did take place in the lowlands, it was not a significant cultural practice, but rather happened only in times of desperation, when other food supplies were exhausted.

There is no evidence that the Maya suffered from a transmissible prion disease.

New Maya ruins are regularly discovered near indigenous villages: in the 1980s, the ruins of a massive city were discovered at Oxpemul, Mexico, less than fifty miles from a highly populated area. More recently, archaeologists discovered a site at Holtun, Guatemala, where more than a hundred classic Maya buildings were buried in a jungle that had been traversed for centuries.

One of the greatest concentrations of scarlet macaws in Central America migrates from eastern Guatemala to the Red Bank, in the Stann Creek district of Belize. It was along this path that I invented Chel's village of Kiaqix, as well as Paktul's great, lost city, Kanuataba.

Acknowledgments

Without Ian Caldwell, I would never have become a writer. For thirty years, he has inspired me with his creativity, imagination and fraternity. He helped me conceive of 12-21, and gave endlessly of his time and genius on every draft.

Jennifer Joel is the glue and tape and safety pins that hold my kludge of a professional life together. There is no better agent in the business, no more sympathetic ear in difficult times, and no more loyal friend.

A decade ago, Susan Kamil at the Dial Press gave me something like the opposite of VFI, pulling me into a dream that I still haven't woken up from. Her dedication is unparalleled, and every author should be lucky enough to be tortured by her red pen. No one spent more time laboring over every aspect of 12-21 than Noah Eaker – he'll likely give me notes on these acknowledgments after the fact. His brilliant editorial guidance and sense of humor were tremendous assets, despite his believing that because I live in Los Angeles I wouldn't know 'Something is rotten in the state of Denmark' came from *Hamlet*.

Many thanks go, too, to Dana Isaacson, who gave invaluable creative advice and pushed me to focus on the 2012 phenomenon, and to the other professionals who made the book possible: Daisy Meyrick, Jonny Geller,

Clay Ezell, Sam Nicholson, Katie Sigelman, Niki Castle, Karen Fink, Theresa Zoro, Erika Greber, Hannah Elnan, Evan Camfield, Kevin Snow, Will Staehle and Paolo Pepe.

Researching this book, I had the opportunity to consult with giants in the fields of Mayanism and medicine, and without their counsel, this book wouldn't have been possible: Peter Harrison, Brad Schaefer, Robert Sharer, Mark Van Stone, Andy Barnett and T. J. Kelleher.

I am awed by and incredibly grateful to my father, Jim Thomason, who suffered through so many drafts of this book, gave me insightful feedback and support, and has been a light in the darkness for so many over the last eighteen months. My stepmother, Lan Thomason, is a study in survival, and her immigrant story was an inspiration as I wrote. My stepfather, Ron Feldman, has more fortitude than anyone I know, and I will always be grateful for the unwavering dedication he has shown to my mother. Thank you as well to the rest of my family – Hyacinth and Lois Rubin, Bob, Dianne and the Michigan Thomasons, the Katzs, Hoangs, Dangs, Blounts, Nassers, Fishers, and the amazing Cavanaghs.

More than any project I've been involved with, this one took a village. Some of the friends below read so many drafts that they can probably complain about it in fluent Mayan. Others helped me in immeasurable ways: Sam Shaw, Michael Olson, Samuel Baum, Laura Dave, Scott Brown, Nick Simonds, Josh Singer, Jose Llana, Jordanna Brodsky, Joanna and Ken and Phyllis Sletten, Amy Cooper, Mark Lafferty, Andrew Paquin, John and Irina Lester, Sabah Ashraf, Katy Heiden, Adam Hootnick, the Checchi family, David and Bob Kanuth, Jac Woods, Dahvi Waller, Derek Jones, the Bakals, Nancy Lainer, Ines Kuperschmidt, all the collective Kiskers, Sarah Shetter, Joe and Susan Geraci, Jon and Sharon Stein, Claudia Garzel, Nat and Maureen Pastor, Lila Byock, Wil Pinkney, Erik Rose, Dana Settle, Kate McLean, Joe Cohen, Jamie Mandelbaum, David Hoang, Larry Wasserman and Maria Wich-Vila, Sam and Amanda Brown, Olivier and Radhika Delfosse, and Jillian Fitzgerald, whose art appears throughout the novel.

Lastly I would like to thank Michael Fisher – reader, old friend, the best brother-in-law I could hope for – who gave me no choice but to sit down and actually write the book by making a bet that ended up rendering me temporarily unable to walk.

He just wanted a decent book to read …

Not too much to ask, is it? It was in 1935 when Allen Lane, Managing Director of Bodley Head Publishers, stood on a platform at Exeter railway station looking for something good to read on his journey back to London. His choice was limited to popular magazines and poor-quality paperbacks – the same choice faced every day by the vast majority of readers, few of whom could afford hardbacks. Lane's disappointment and subsequent anger at the range of books generally available led him to found a company – and change the world.

'We believed in the existence in this country of a vast reading public for intelligent books at a low price, and staked everything on it'
Sir Allen Lane, 1902–1970, founder of Penguin Books

The quality paperback had arrived – and not just in bookshops. Lane was adamant that his Penguins should appear in chain stores and tobacconists, and should cost no more than a packet of cigarettes.

Reading habits (and cigarette prices) have changed since 1935, but Penguin still believes in publishing the best books for everybody to enjoy. We still believe that good design costs no more than bad design, and we still believe that quality books published passionately and responsibly make the world a better place.

So wherever you see the little bird – whether it's on a piece of prize-winning literary fiction or a celebrity autobiography, political tour de force or historical masterpiece, a serial-killer thriller, reference book, world classic or a piece of pure escapism – you can bet that it represents the very best that the genre has to offer.

Whatever you like to read – trust Penguin.

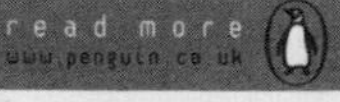